Falling for Your Dark Shades

Jamie Nicole

To the ones who kept chasing after far-off dreams, even when you were scared, had self-doubt, and just needed a hand to hold through the storm. This one's for you. Don't ever stop chasing the one thing you love, even if you're still putting broken pieces back together. And to the ones who are still healing from unspoken things and don't think you'll ever be enough. Remember, you are enough, and you're worth every bit of love.

Contents

Author's Note

While this story is filled with soft moments, warmth, and a lot of love and tenderness, there are also some heavier and sensitive topics that may be triggering. These include: mentions of a previous abusive relationship, alcoholism, anxiety, brief physical violence, and open door romance with explicit sexual content. This book is intended only for adults (18+). I hope Violet and Sam's journey together brings you a little peace and healing of your own.

Sam and Violet's Playlist

Iris - The Goo Goo Dolls
Let Love In - The Goo Goo Dolls
Try - Pink
Stolen - Dashboard Confessional
I Wanna Be Yours - Arctic Monkeys
Paper Heart - Dayseeker
Starving To Be Empty - Dayseeker
Crying While You're Dancing - Dayseeker
Ordinary - Alex Warren
Lover, Please Stay - Nothing But Thieves
Sailor Song - Gigi Perez
Say Yes To Heaven - Lana Del Rey
Favorite Place - All Time Low
Emergency Contact - Pierce the Veil
About A Girl - The Summer Set
Black Butterflies and Deja Vu - The Maine
"Slut!" - Taylor Swift
Snow On The Beach - Taylor Swift

This Love - Taylor Swift

This Is Me Trying - Taylor Swift

Hearts on Fire - ILLENIUM, Dabin & Lights

Fire Meet Gasoline - Sia

Criminal - State Champs

Rosemary - Deftones

Cherry Waves - Deftones

Time After Time - Quietdrive

Yours - Russell Dickerson

Ghosts - The Dangerous Summer

Wait - Knuckle Puck

Hurricane - I Prevail

Infra-Red - Three Days Grace

Left Behind - The Plot In You

Zombie - YUNGBLUD

CHAPTER ONE

SAM

My tired eyes stare hazily into the bright screen as my fingers curl deep into the edge of the granite countertop. The texts start to thread together mindlessly as Lois sends yet another message to my phone.

Lois: The girls, Sam. Let me speak with them.

The bubbles come and go in sync. I imagine her nimble fingers typing out the perfect manipulative response to say next, but I won't respond. I don't want to talk to her, and I sure as hell don't want to add fuel to the fire. But also, my girls don't *want* to speak to their mother. Maybe it's because she left them in a hot car at the mall and forgot about them. Maybe it's from all the times she'd storm in with a bottle of wine at one in the morning. Maybe it's the fact that she threw her medications into the trash and said she was done. Or maybe it's the fact that she looked me right in the eye and told me she couldn't stand the sight of me anymore.

It still hurts. *All* of it still hurts. It's just a permanent bruise at this point.

Groaning, I sigh as I reminisce on the past, wishing I could've done something more, but there was nothing else I could've done. I was there, being the best, supportive husband I could be. I tried. I really fucking tried every single day to be what she needed, to encourage her to go to the doctor, continued to *love* her, but it wasn't enough. I was *never* enough, and maybe one of these days I'll stop blaming myself for not doing more.

In the end, it was just a tragic romance bound to happen, and it broke like shattered glass. It was hopeless, just like this thread of text messages.

Quickly closing out of the texts, I switch my focus on the numerous emails about the restock of items the club has coming in this morning, the arbitrary new disco lights that we don't need, and old emails from my divorce and personal lawyer, David Carter.

A throbbing pain makes its way down the back of my skull, and my head starts to pound relentlessly. The heels of my hands dig deep into the sockets of my eyes, and a gut-wrenching groan leaves my throat.

How can one woman keep ruining my life when we've been done for a decade? The divorce was finalized, written in crisp black ink, and mailed to the lawyer's office. I've had the girls for that long under my wing. They are *my* children, *my* responsibility, and I've spent a hell of a time trying to raise two girls all by myself.

Kelsey is now nineteen, off to college at the University of California, studying to be a structural engineer. Kayla, my fifteen year old, is into playing soccer and wants to become a vet. I still don't know how I managed to move halfway across the country from Oklahoma to California, but I needed to get out—*had* to get out. It was what was best for me and my daughters.

Another low vibration comes from my phone on the counter, but I ignore it. Stretching my back, I push off the countertop and rake a hand sluggishly through my tousled hair as I let out a heavy sigh. It's not even eight o'clock yet, and I'm already dreading the long night I have ahead at the club. Plus, I'll be there this morning, so technically it's a double shift because I just have too much to get done for the weekend. I might be home for lunch, but then it's right back to the club for me.

Just when another email whooshes through my inbox, Kayla taps me on the shoulder as she crunches on a crispy piece of raisin bread. "Dad, you okay? You look a little tired," she says with concern glowing in her bright hazel eyes.

I form a tight-lipped smile and give her a casual answer. "Yeah, just a lot of work stuff I need to get done today. I'm sorry, hun. I'm gonna have to skip dinner tonight. Can I give you some money for pizza? Promise I'll make it up to you."

Kayla shakes her long brunette ponytail as she takes another bite from the almost burnt toast. "I'm going over to Nicole's house, remember? We have our girls' sleepover tonight after practice. You got me that pink boa and rockstar sunglasses for it." She giggles, taking another slow bite from the warm bread.

"Ahh, that's right. I'm sorry, I totally forgot." I sigh as I slick back my dark hair that's threaded with a couple of silvery gray locks. Turning thirty-nine has done me no favors besides killing my back and putting some premature grays in my scruff.

She takes a close look at me and threads her eyebrows together, locking her arms tightly across her white T-shirt that's embroidered with her school's soccer logo. She looks like she wants to say something, but she just flips her long ponytail behind her shoulders and turns back to the faucet to snatch a fresh glass of water instead.

Grabbing my phone up and pushing it deep into the front pocket of my jeans, I knock twice on the granite before giving her a smile. "I'll put your soccer bag in the truck. Meet you out there in five, kiddo."

"Sir, yes sir." She salutes, flashing me a white smile. I turn the corner of the kitchen and snatch up the pink soccer bag that sits in the middle of the hall, right next to the wooden staircase.

Chuckling all the way out to the shiny black Chevy that sits parked in the driveway, I can't help but smile. I'm not allowed to have favorites, but I have to say that my youngest daughter brings me joy no one else could remotely come close to. She's funny, wicked smart, and her love of sports is one thing we've bonded over since the day I took her to her first Sooners softball game when she was just five years old. Call it father-daughter bonding, but she's my favorite girl in the world. I don't think anyone could ever change that, not even a new romantic partner.

Five minutes later, Kayla is buckled in and spinning her soccer ball on the tip of her finger while she hums along to some pop song I definitely don't know. I occasionally laugh at her high-pitched ramblings, but my mind starts being pulled undecidedly back to problems I'd much rather forget about.

The movement of my phone buzzes through the black cup holder and lights up with Lois's name displayed right in the center of the screen. I internally groan, letting the call go to voicemail. *When will she ever fucking give it a rest?*

I scrape a heavy hand slowly down my clipped scruff and groan, letting my glossed-over eyes focus on the numerous cars on the main road instead of the repetitive nuisance that plagues the inside of my phone.

As if on cue, Kayla sets her ball on top of her soccer bag and leans carefully over the center console. She must've seen the texts and missed calls, because her sing-song voice dies the moment my mood shifted from joyful to somber.

I can feel her hazel eyes hovering over me like she's assessing to make sure it's okay to speak. Once she knows it's safe, she takes a deep breath and lets the words she's been trying to hold back for a while fall from her lips. "Dad, why does Mom keep calling you?"

I flick my eyes quickly her way and avert them back to the road when I see a speck of shine in the back of her eyes. It's still a sore subject, but won't it always be? She was five years old when the divorce happened. She went through hell in that house with the inconceivable screaming and bickering coming from her mother.

She was too young to remember it all, but most of the time I was the one picking her up off the floor while Lois had a meltdown, leaving without any notice to her friend Jenny's house. I was always the one who had to clean up her messes as the girls cried that their mother left them without so much as a goodbye kiss or an explanation. The awful memories still make me sick to my stomach to this day.

Clenching my white knuckles against the cool leather steering wheel helps me take a slow, deep breath before answering. "She... she's asking to speak with you and Kelsey," I state quietly as the low hum of the radio whisks around the inside of the truck.

"Oh," is all she can muster out, tipping her head back against the top of the seat. She blows out a held-in breath and stares into the void of traffic that lays ahead on the busy San Diego road. I mistakenly look over and see the trembling of her lips and eyes that gloss over with held-back tears.

Fuck. I hate seeing my little girl like this—all bottled up and teary-eyed over a woman who couldn't do the one goddamn job that she promised she'd do. She was supposed to be their mother, not push them away and break them down, leaving me to pick up all the shattered pieces.

Kelsey doesn't give much thought to Lois, but Kayla does. Even if she keeps it really well hidden, I know deep down she still hurts over what all went down. She so desperately wants a mother who'll be there for her, but all she has is me and Bryson—my older brother.

I always promised I'd be there for her, but it seems some days I'm just so busy with work that I miss out on soccer games and school events. I need to do better. I *have* to do better. But I'm trying. Goddamn it, do I try my best. It's not easy being a single father, but I'll always be there for my baby girl.

"Has she tried calling you?" I ask, knowing the exact answer before she replies.

"More than a dozen times, but I don't want to talk to her. You'd think she'd get the picture already," she grumbles under her breath.

It breaks my heart that she has this inner battle she's choosing to face on her own, but she has to know I'm right here whenever she needs me.

Carefully, I crane my head to the right and look at her, assessing the slight slouch and crossed arms she has while she puts on a brave face. When I'm stopped at a red light, I reach a hand cautiously over and place it on her shoulder, giving her a gentle squeeze. "Hey," I breathe, "you know you can always talk to me about this, right? You don't have to ever say a word to her again if you don't want to. We can get her number blocked, I can tell her to back off, or I can—"

"Dad," she stops me mid-sentence, and motions for me to step on the gas. I was too tied up in the reckless havoc of my ex-wife trying to get in contact with my daughter to notice the green light ahead. "It wouldn't be worth it. She'll never get it. I'll just block her number, I guess." She sighs dramatically, letting her head fall right back against the cool leather of the seat.

She won't. She might talk about blinking her out of existence, but she'll still hold on to hope that one day her mother will come back around and change. Lois will never change, though. She would've long ago if she wanted to. No. She'll just keep torturing me and my daughters till the day we die.

Kayla turns the music up louder, obviously done with the useless conversation. I hate seeing her like this—like she's miserable and tucked away in her mind every time Lois tries to reach out. I've had just about enough of that. I'm about to block her number, too. Put her on the blacklist of my entire family's contact list.

But will I really? No. At least not today...

The rest of the drive is silent, except for the buzz of the radio carrying tunes through the cabin of the truck. My head is about to split open from the vibrating phone that sits inside the cup holder, because I already know it's someone I have no intention to talk to.

When the truck comes to a halt, I look over and give a half-smile to Kayla, letting my knuckles brush against her shoulder encouragingly. "Don't let this bother you, sweetheart. You just have a good day at school, and show them who's boss at practice."

She gives me a big grin, and her eyes finally meet her bright smile. "Thanks, Dad. You remember my game is in the morning, right?"

"Ten o'clock sharp." I nod, thankful I tacked a sticky note to the refrigerator door this week. "I'll pick you up before the game."

"See you around nine." She smiles as she closes the passenger door.

Rolling the window down, I shout, "Bye, Kayla! Remember, give them hell on that field in practice. You'll knock 'em dead tomorrow!" She shoots me a thumbs-up and goes sprinting across the lush green grass in front of the high school, her pink soccer bag dragging against the ground.

I sit and watch her until she disappears through the front doors, along with a blur of other students behind her, then I pull out of the parking lot. When I hit the road again, I sigh, letting my fingers drag through my hair. I try to be the best father I can, but the amount of games and practices I've missed lately is unforgivable. I know she says she understands when work matters come up, but I know her better than that. I need to do better, for her. Because she matters more to me than my business. So tomorrow, I'm all hers for the first half of the day. This is a game I won't be missing.

My girls *are* my world, and I try so goddamn hard to be the best father I can be. With no mother in the picture, I just have to do my best. They deserve that. They deserve a *good* father. And that's what I'll be, if that's the last thing I do.

Club Inferno—the biggest building in the middle of Gaslamp District of downtown San Diego. A sleek nightclub that brings hundreds upon hundreds of young patrons out on the weekends. Some weeknights are even packed, surprisingly. It's a nice getaway from the busy streets of California, a gentle reminder that I no longer belong to Shawnee, Oklahoma. A small town that held me back from escaping Lois's reins.

This is my new home. *This* is where I belong now. And although I miss having my own pool-building business, I still get to do some of that on the side. But now, I own a club, and it's as freeing as jumping off the highest cliff in California and falling into the cool ocean bliss that now surrounds me.

I'm not *hers* anymore. No more controlling, manipulative words that can poison me or my daughters anymore.

Pulling the double doors open, I drag my feet through the entrance, careful not to scuff up the newly polished black marble floors. The crystal chandeliers are sparkling above my head, casting shadows across the lit-up neon signs all along the walls. The club is doused in dark reds and midnight black shades, painting a perfect picture of an inferno-type vibe.

I guess that's exactly the image I wanted, and why I decided to name this place Club Inferno. I wanted something dark, seductive; where couples or newly-single clubgoers could feel like they were escaping into something magical. Make them forget all their worries for just one night.

At least, that's what this place is for me. Somewhere to escape and be free. *I'm free.*

"Sammy!" Bryson shouts over the back of the bar. "Running late again?" he teases.

When I turn my head and see him slumped against the sleek bar top, one hand shining the side of a glass and the other running through his blond locks, I shake my head. That nickname will stick with him till he's in his grave. "Well, good morning to you, too. You know I had to run Kayla to school. I told you."

He rolls his eyes. "Yeah, yeah. I'm just messing with you, Sammy."

My tongue darts out, licking my bottom lip as I lace my fingers through my hair. "You're never gonna drop that nickname, are you?"

"Never." He smiles.

Shaking my head, I make my way to the bar and take a seat on a leather stool, grabbing a checklist of things I need to get done before we open tonight. Fridays are always one of the busier nights, so we have a lot of work to get done.

"Did Chelsea come by with the beer order yet? I think we needed more Budweiser and Corona." Just as I finish my sentence, the front doors open with a bang, and in comes the exact order I've been waiting all week for.

"Speak of the devil." Bryson smirks, his bright hazel eyes twinkling with mischief as Chelsea walks in.

Chelsea's long blonde ponytail hangs down her back, swishing from side to side as she takes long strides into the room. Her eager blue eyes find mine, and I try my best not to stare at her curvy hips in her tight blue jeans. I'm not like my brother who's gawking from the sidelines, probably drooling with anticipation.

"Hey, Sam. I got your order out front. Mind if someone opens the side doors for me so I can roll in the drinks?" Her voice is chipper and excited, and I can see her longing gaze staring at me.

I give her a tight-lipped smile and nod. "Sure thing, Chelsea. I'll have one of the boys in the back open it. Josh should be back there."

She flicks her ponytail over her right shoulder, twisting the strands around a finger, cheeks hot and blushing as she bats her long eyelashes at me. It's not a secret that she has a thing for me, but I just can't get myself to take the bait. She's beautiful and all, but I can't mix business with pleasure.

I give her a friendly nod and send her off, breaking her flirtatious stare.

She smiles one last time my way and gives me a little wave, but her blue eyes scream something other than friendly. More like seductive. "Guess I'll see you next week for your next delivery. Or maybe sooner. We'll see." She saunters off and nods to Bryson before exiting out the front doors. "Bye, Bryson."

When she's outside and away from earshot, Bryson clears his throat and leans both hands against the bar top, a wicked smirk curling his lips.

"What?" I growl, already knowing what he'll say.

"She wants you bad, man." He smiles.

I huff out in frustration and flick the notebook back his way. "Will you shut up?" I snap.

He shrugs his shoulders and acts all taken aback. "Well it's true. She's always so flirty and eager to see you. Why don't you just ask her out already?"

I grit my teeth together and clench my jaw. "'Cause maybe I don't want to."

His hazel eyes grow wide and his jaw drops open. "Oh, that's a fucking lie. Sammy, that girl is hot! And she's sweet, and those big lips. And did you see the way her–"

"Bryson," I warn with a harsh tone. "Quit it."

"When's the last time you went out, huh? Or the last time you got laid?" he asks with a raised brow.

I flinch and roll my tight shoulders back, almost ready to make a bolt from the room, away from my overbearing brother. "None of your business," I growl.

He chuckles out and grabs another glass, taking his time wiping the edges down as his gaze falls back on mine. "It's probably been, what? More than four years, yeah?"

He's not wrong. It has been that long. Actually, more like over five years now. But I'm doing fine on my own.

I shrug, annoyed by this topic of conversation. "Give or take, yeah."

He sets down the glass and gives me a long look. His eyes a little more sincere and clear now. "Look, if I wasn't with Serena, I might've asked her out myself. But Sammy, she's *so* into you. Why don't you just give it a go? At least take her home for a night."

Letting the idea simmer through my mind, I decide that's not what I want—even if it's tempting. She's beautiful and all, but *she's* not what I want. And I'm not about to ruin the chance of losing her business. She's too valuable to this club. Sure, there could be other opportunities in the area, but she's one of the best. Never brings me an order late. Always arrives on time, with no missing merchandise.

Besides, if she's what I wanted, then I would've known it by now. But no. I'm better off single. I've got bigger fish to fry than trying to get laid. I already had my fair share of one-night stands after me and Lois got a divorce, which only lasted a brief couple of weeks. And really, my fair share was *one* time, not more than that. With my girls so young, I couldn't risk the chance of them seeing me with any other woman. And frankly, I still don't want them seeing me with a woman, period. Kayla's not ready. *I'm* not ready. Maybe one day I will be, but today is not that day.

I just need to focus on myself. It'd take a miracle to change my mind. Gorgeous California women can wait. My club and my girls are the only things that matter. At least, for now. Who knows what can happen in this fast-paced city overnight. I guess anything could.

Chapter Two

Violet

The clicking sounds from my laptop seem to mix in with the whispering voices and soft pattering of feet as people come and go through the main sliding doors. San Diego Central Library—the biggest and most exquisite library in this part of the West Coast—is where everyone seems to be on this warm Friday afternoon.

The cascading windows send rays of sunshine through that make little star reflections on the polished floors. It seems like this place is as magical as the day I started working as a librarian here. I got the dream job like I always wanted. Who would've guessed this would be my second home, apart from my cozy apartment that sits right by the ocean?

Everything seems perfect, but my life is far from perfect. Just call it a disaster instead.

As I go through the motions of checking next week's meetings, a reminder for my therapy appointment pops up with a little chime. I quickly exit out of the notice and sigh as I plop back into the office chair. Jenna, my therapist, will probably be so thrilled with my progress. Obvious sarcasm drips through my mind at the thought.

What progress? There is no progress, or that's what I keep telling myself. I'm a sinking ship, and she might as well just set me free to drown.

Rolling my eyes in annoyance, I push back the laptop mouse, finding any distraction to not think about that appointment. I pull my iPhone out from my pocket and start thumbing through social media, reading the latest gossip and drama. Not that I really care, it's just a slow day at the library. I giggle when I see Skylar posting yet another breakup update, wondering just who will be her boyfriend in less than a week. I never really understood how it could be so fun jumping from relationship to relationship. What's wrong with being single for a while?

Although, I'm the last person who should be talking. When's the last time I went on a date or accepted a guy's phone call? A couple years, more than that? No, I guess it was when me and...

I freeze at the thought of *him*. I can't even speak his name without my skin growing cold and clammy. But that's what therapy's for, right? To break out of that bad habit. But trauma is a tough habit to break. Sometimes people never escape. Maybe I'll never escape...

The vibrating motion of a text knocks me out of my spiraling thoughts. I look down to see a group text from Brianna and Taylor.

Brianna: Hey, babe! Don't you dare say you're staying in tonight, because we are going out!

I internally groan at the mere thought of doing anything other than sitting on my velvet sectional and watching one of my favorite romantic comedies, along with having a book tucked in my lap. But then Taylor chimes in and whisks me away from the hopes of a quiet evening in.

Taylor: There's a club called Club Inferno that's been all over social media lately. I've been dying to go! It's right in the middle of Gaslamp District. The perfect place to find a new hottie. ;)

I sigh as I type, knowing this is a battle I won't even come close to winning.

Violet: But I had plans with my TV and couch, and I just bought this new book that I've been dying to read.

Taylor: Nu-uh, you are not pulling that shit. We're going, and that's final!

Violet: But...

Brianna: No, absolutely not. You ARE going out, no backing down. Now go home and find your hottest dress, and we'll be over at 9:45 PM!

I groan and throw my head against the back of the chair, completely oblivious of the piles of people coming in and out of the sliding doors, quickly scattering as they search for books. There's no way out of this, and I damn well know it.

So much for my lonely, relaxing night in. Of course my best friends wouldn't leave me alone. They never do, but what can I say? I'm more than glad to have them in my crazy life. They make me a little more sane.

Violet: Okay. See you guys soon :)

A deep sigh rolls off my lips as I pull at my loose curls. I close my eyes, breathe in a calm breath, and exhale to release all the tension in my shoulders. I shouldn't be nervous, but when's the last time they dragged me out to a club? I can't even remember. What on Earth am I going to wear to a club?

CHAPTER THREE

VIOLET

The Friday night fresh air sweeps through my cracked bedroom window, reminding me that instead of sitting down with some warm tea and a book on the couch, I'm currently standing in a dress that's too tight, with heels so high I think I'll fall over at any second. The snug black dress clings to my body like a suction cup, and the slit in the side of my left thigh is almost showing too much skin. *Almost.*

I spent the last hour sitting at my glowing vanity, curling my hair into perfect waves. My smokey eyeshadow and black eyeliner make my dark blue eyes pop, and the deep red lipstick that sits matted against my lips makes my eyes that much brighter.

This isn't my usual. I like to stay in after a long week at the library—not go clubbing till two in the morning. I'm not an extrovert like all my friends are; they just want me to have a little fun. I guess that's the perk of having outgoing friends. They keep me sane when my mind is far from it.

I wish I could be more outgoing, adventurous, and flirtatious like my best friends. Brianna is a successful fashion editor at Vogue who spends a ton of time at fashion shows in San Francisco. She's quirky and fun to be around, while Taylor's always busy with her personal assistant jobs, working for important business women and telling me all her crazy stories. And me? I'm just a quiet librarian who minds my business. I still don't know why they love me so much. I'm not as fun as them.

I take one more look at myself in the mirror and sigh heavily. This will be good for me. Much better than sulking on my couch all night. I need to socialize, to get back into the dating field, but that honestly just sounds like a bad idea.

Dating in general sucks. It's like no man knows how to properly treat a woman nowadays. And my last boyfriend? Well, he's the entire reason I'm scared of falling again. He started so sweet, but then there was that dark side that didn't come until later. A darkness that nearly ended me...

Before the sick feeling of dread takes me under, a loud knock at my apartment door pulls me free. Giddy laughter sounds on the other side of the door, signaling that my best friends have arrived. When I open the door, Brianna and Taylor lose it when they see what I'm wearing.

"Oh my God, look at you!" Brianna screams as Taylor twirls me around to get a better look at the little black dress that grazes the tops of my thighs. Brianna's light brown eyes ogle me from head to toe, her blonde curls bouncing with every move she makes. "You're such a babe! And that dress? God, it makes your ass look so good. And that slit?! You are definitely going to get laid tonight," she shrieks as she pulls me in for a quick hug.

"Bri, stop!" I laugh, shaking my head. "I am not getting laid tonight. Absolutely not happening," I cringe, rolling my eyes for emphasis.

"Oh, please. All the men are going to be looking at you tonight, you little slut!" Taylor smirks, her green eyes sparkling like emeralds as she stares at my short dress. Her pinned up red hair sits perfectly in a messy bun atop her head, her white heels digging into the wooden floor as she circles me like a starving hawk.

"No, guys. Really, I don't need to try to find someone tonight. I'm only going out because you're forcing me to," I complain with a huff.

"Sure, babe. That vibrator that sits in your nightstand isn't gonna get you anywhere fast. You *need* to get laid properly. So, we're going to find you a man tonight if it's the last thing we do," Brianna promises with a beam of her bright smile.

"Whatever, let's just go," I whine as they pull me out of the comfort of my small apartment and whisk me out the door, shoving me inside the white Cadillac that sits idle on the corner of the curb.

I slump in the front passenger seat as soon as Brianna drives off, entering the busy traffic of San Diego while the city lights flash brightly outside the window. I sigh and lean on the edge of the door as Lady Gaga's "Poker Face" blasts through the speakers. Taylor and Brianna sing along loudly, but I sit mute with my arms crossed over my chest.

"Oh, cheer up, babe! You're supposed to be having fun tonight, not brooding in the corner like a pent-up prisoner." Brianna laughs, leaning over to hit my arm lightly.

"I'd be in a better mood if I was curled up on my couch with a good book," I groan as I stifle out another sigh.

Taylor leans into the divide of the front seats and takes a good look at me, her fiery red hair almost blinding me. "Don't be such a buzzkill. You *will* have fun tonight whether you like it or not! This club is to die for. I know it just opened last year, but seriously, it's the hottest club in San Diego," she says excitedly with a big grin stretched across her contoured face.

"What's the name of this club again?" I ask with furrowed eyebrows.

"Club Inferno," Taylor says with a smirk. "Inferno is right. It's hot as fuck in there, and the men who go are super sexy," she swoons as she sits back against her leather seat.

"Club Inferno, huh? Wonder how the owner came up with a name like that," I ponder curiously, focusing my sights on the busy sidewalks that are littered with dressed up couples and groups who look like they're about to head to the club, as well.

"I don't know. Maybe you can ask the owner yourself." Brianna smirks in the front seat.

"Who's the owner?" I ask, trying not to sound too intrigued.

"I don't know. I didn't look, but I hear rumors that he's ridiculously hot. Like, I'm talking about an eleven out of ten, hot." She smirks as she pulls into a parking spot a few feet from the lit-up club.

"Sounds like someone I wouldn't be interested in. He already sounds arrogant and like all the other men I've dated," I spit out, a snarl hanging on my lips.

"Oh, just shut up and have some fun tonight, please. You're killing my vibes," she says, rolling her eyes while she puts the car in park.

"Sorry, sorry. I'll try to have fun." I sigh as I step out of the car onto the hard concrete, pulling my dress down so it doesn't ride up and expose too much skin.

"Good, now let's go!" Brianna and Taylor scream together. I just laugh and follow them to the front of the club, stopping at the metallic double doors as we get our IDs checked.

I know I'm being dramatic and uptight. They just caught me on a bad day. But really, the bad days seem to blur together most weeks. I haven't been myself lately. Not since the terrible accident. Not since I left my ex. Not since he...

The bouncer hands me my ID back and makes me forget where my mind was going. *Don't go there. Don't do it. Not tonight. Just have fun.*

When I slip through the door, I audibly gasp in awe at what lies ahead. The inside is absolutely gigantic. The club sits two stories high, with a shimmering disco ball hanging in the middle of the crowded dance floor. The walls are pitch black with glowing red signs all around. One that sits behind the bar is also amber red and says *Sinners Welcome*. The bar has a large mirror splayed across the wall with bottles of beer and liquor stacked high against it. The bar top has a sleek, dark wooden hue to it, and the bar stools are made of black leather material. There's dark booths all around that are marked off for VIP lounges, private parties, or reservations made prior. Crystal chandeliers hang from the ceiling as they make shiny patterns on the dark marble floors. An open lounge area sits in the opposite corner of the bar where leather couches and small glass tables are scattered around. I look away when I see a cozy couple making out in a corner of one of the couches and try not to roll my eyes.

Because I secretly wish that was me.

When I turn toward the dance floor, I see the glow of fluorescent blue and red flashing lights mix in with the glittering disco ball as the DJ spins some tracks on a large platform against the wall. The dance floor is crowded—at least two-hundred people stand grinding up on each other as Rhianna blasts through the speakers. Two small stages with poles attached to the center sit in the back corners of the room for anyone to use at their leisure.

Next to the bar sits two long, dark hallways with various rooms attached down the shadowed corners of the corridors. A spiral staircase sits close to the far hallway on the left and leads up to the second floor. From here, I can't see what all is upstairs, but it looks like another bar is hidden up there, and maybe some pool tables. This club isn't anything like I expected it to be. I thought it'd be small and maybe less crowded. Boy, was I wrong.

"Don't you just love it here?!" Taylor asks excitedly, twirling around in her short emerald strapless dress.

"It's a lot bigger than I imagined it to be," I shout against the beat of the music. Taylor pulls on my arm, right in the direction of the dance floor. I groan in annoyance. "Tay, we just got here. Can't we sit down?" I whine as Brianna throws me into the middle of the raging crowd.

"Not until after a couple of dances." Taylor smiles, pushing her back against a tall man in a suit who grinds up against his blonde girlfriend. I groan but go along with them, trying not to focus on the clash of glasses and strong alcohol.

The dance floor is sticky with sweat, bodies splayed left and right while the disco ball spins in slow circles, creating a mirage of sparkles over the crowd. I try to relax, unwinding my tight shoulders as my black dress rides up my thighs. It's one night. I can have fun for one night. What the hell is wrong with me?

Bri knocks me lightly against the shoulder and slides up behind me. "Loosen up, hun. The night's just getting started. You'll be just fine," Brianna beams, grabbing a few Jell-O shots from the bartender who makes her away across the busy dance floor. "Drink up!" she yells, handing me a container of red liquid.

I hesitate a beat, letting my eyes roam over the slosh of red liquid. And I know I shouldn't take it, because it reminds me of drowning. Reminds me of murky green eyes. But with another push from Brianna, I give in.

"Fine," I groan, popping the shot into my mouth and instantly tasting cherry and vodka mixed together. It slides down my throat easily, and I put the empty vial on the bartender's tray. Taylor and Brianna both cheer after I take the shot, and start grinding up against each other as the music switches over to a Beyoncé track.

Deciding to just give in to the hum of my body, I let the upbeat rhythm carry me through the waves of the crowd, giving in to the toxicity of losing myself for a night. This is exactly what I need, a wakeup call that'll pull me out of this maddening spell that I now call normalcy.

There's nothing normal about giving in to the sick delusions of what a traumatic mind feeds the body, so maybe this will make it all just stop. Maybe now my own head won't keep spouting off memories from the past. I'll never go back there. Not unless *he* pulls me back. Someone I don't want to remember. Someone I push deep, deep down until his face is contorted and blurred away.

Someday I won't keep remembering the past. Someday I'll be free.

Chapter Four

Sam

The club is absolutely swarming with customers tonight. Men dressed in expensive suits wearing too much cologne, and women wearing tight-fitting skirts float through the crowded room. The stench of rich liquor and temptation wafts through the air, filling my nostrils with satisfaction that this club is a knockout.

I've always been proud of my accomplishments; all my businesses turned into something that ultimately made me happy. And even though owning a pool company with my ex-wife didn't work out, this one did. This one is mine. She can't take this away from me. This is now my safe haven.

Without giving another thought to her, I let my gaze wander over the distorted faces in the crowd, watching bodies grind against each other. Some couples are hooked at the waist, their arms tangled around each other's neck, mouths panting into the other's. Looking away from the heated couples, my eyes slide to the left, focusing on a lit-up area where I can clearly make out some faces.

A group of women are bunched together in a packed-in circle, each one feeling the beat of the fast-paced music. One a redhead, the other with big blonde curls, but the other one is hidden behind the blonde. I adjust my slicked back hair, pushing a lock back into place. And just before I turn back toward the staircase, I freeze.

The woman who was just hidden is now in view, and I suck in a breath when my eyes fall to hers. It's like the room stops moving, the music fading in the background, and all I can seem to hear is the blood rushing through my ears. My heartbeat picks up speed, and I feel as if I'm running a marathon.

Her long brunette hair falls in spiraled waves down her shoulders, a hint of blonde highlights glowing under the shine of the disco ball. Each glittering pass of the dim lights seems to make her ocean-kissed skin glow brighter. She's lean and toned, her black dress barely skimming the edge of her bare thighs. And when she tilts her head back and lets her carefree smile beam around the room, it nearly knocks me to my knees.

When she looks up for the briefest moment, I swear she catches my eye. Even from the faraway vantage point of the second floor, I see how clear and blue her eyes are. Almost as blue as the sea. Just when I think she sees me, her eyes fall right back to her friends.

My mouth is as dry as a desert, my lungs aching for much needed oxygen. I've never seen beautiful eyes quite like that. Eyes that make me want to hover closer, that make me want to drown in the depths of those crystal diamonds.

Forgetting everything I said earlier, I put all my morals aside. I have to get her name, need to slide the back of my hand against her smooth skin, *need* to hear how melodic her voice must sound. I don't know what's got my mind all wrapped in knots, but it has been since the moment I saw her in my club.

She looks like an angel under the shimmering lights, and I think that's what I'd call her, if I ever got the chance to. I don't believe in love at first sight, but there's just *something* about her that pulls my heartstrings in her direction.

And just like a man on a mission, my mission is now to have her.

Chapter Five

Violet

The vibrations of the music make me a little dizzy, and after a few songs, I just want to sit back and grab a cold drink. "Hey, let's take a breather, okay? I'm dying for some water." Fanning myself, Taylor and Bri agree and follow after me.

Despite how crowded it is, it doesn't take me long to find an empty section with a leather couch. It's set right under some dim lights with a glass table and a drink menu on top. I slide into the seat, sinking into the cool leather as I scan the menu, searching for something I can stand to drink. But before I can find what I'm looking for, Brianna calls over a bartender and orders a round of Long Island ice teas for the table.

"Bri," I say sternly, pinching my brows together to let her know I wasn't planning on drinking much tonight.

"Chill." She laughs, tossing her blonde curls behind her shoulder. "Just enjoy this, okay? You promised you'd try."

Grinding my teeth back and forth, I surrender and agree to calm down. I just don't like the idea of too much alcohol in my system. It's not that I'm against it all, but after my past, it's sometimes hard to keep down…

By the time the bartender comes back with a round of drinks, I'm feeling a little less uptight. So I casually take a few sips and pretend I'm on my couch, in my living room, away from the roar of thunderous crowds, definitely *not* thinking of my ex.

"So, spot any cute guys in the crowd?" Taylor winks, curling her pink lips into a playful smile, her green eyes narrowed like a cat.

"Wasn't looking," I say with a clipped tone, taking the clear straw and stirring it mindlessly in the swirling alcohol.

"What about that one, huh? He's kinda cute." She points to a tall man with spiky blond hair and sharp blue eyes, nudging me when he passes by the table.

I scrunch my nose up and shake my head. "No. Not that one. Maybe you can go talk to him. Seems like your type." I laugh as she eyes him up and down, biting her bottom lip as she thinks about what I just said. She'll end up getting his number by the end of the night, I'm sure of it.

Taking another slow sip of my drink, I set it down and watch the condensation drip down the side, taking my attention away from the rush of the busy nightclub. Is it midnight yet? Maybe they'll let me go home then.

Shaking me out of my thoughts, Brianna slaps me on the shoulder, grabbing my attention just as I'm about to slap her back. She's smirking at me, her eyes flicking back and forth from the bar and then back to me. "Bri, what? I know that look. That's a scheming face you always make when you're up to no good."

A wide grin tugs at her red lips, and then her brown mischievous eyes are on me. "You see that man at the bar? The one on the left with the white collared button-up shirt?" She points him out inconspicuously and giggles loudly in my ear.

"Bri, what on Earth are you–" I go silent when my eyes fix on the man she's talking about, and I almost choke on my own saliva.

He sits on the furthest barstool near the bar, with a glass of what looks to be whiskey resting against his palm. I slowly drag my eyes over him, taking in the way his sleeves are rolled up to his elbows, exposing thick veins that spider all the way down his arms, ending in massive hands. But that's not all that catches my attention—intricate black ink covers his right arm, forming a half sleeve across his tan skin. I don't know why, but my breath catches in my chest the more I assess him.

His large biceps bulge against the cotton material each time he flexes and moves to grab his cold glass of alcohol. His dark blue jeans press against muscular thighs, and a fancy black Rolex watch sits latched against his right wrist. He has sandy-brown hair, streaked with faint gray lines that are slicked back into what would probably be loose and slightly tousled without the mousse in his hair. Dark, clipped scruff shadows his sculpted, sharp jawline. And for the moment, I can't seem to stop staring.

My gaze moves over his graying locks again slowly, analyzing the splotches of silver in his scruff, the dark mustache above his full lips. He doesn't seem to be that old, but he's definitely older than my twenty-eight-year-old self. A single strand of hair falls against his forehead, curling ever so slightly until he's pushing it back into place. I almost wonder what it'd be like to run my fingers through his hair, or maybe drag my nails against his salt-and-pepper scruff...

I jolt out of my daydream, his brown eyes meeting mine. He takes a slow sip of his drink without breaking eye contact, even as the cool liquid runs deep down his throat. Pulling my eyes away from his stifling stare, I look back at Brianna with wide eyes. "What about him?" I ask in a shaky breath, my head a little foggy from how gorgeous he is.

"He hasn't stopped looking at you since we sat down." She giggles, pulling on her crimson skirt while she nudges me a little harder this time. I wish she'd just stop.

"He's not looking at me," I try to deny. "He's looking at you and Taylor." But when my eyes flick back up to his for just a second, I feel the heat of his gaze on me. And this time, I'm *burning*.

"I don't think so, honey," Taylor snides back. "He's looking straight at *you*."

Hesitantly looking back up through my long eyelashes, I gulp dry air when I find his dark eyes smothering me—a small smirk appearing on his mouth, contorting into something that dares me to challenge his gaze. I suck in a deep breath and look away, grabbing the edge of my drink as I try to swallow some of my nerves down.

He's just a man, and he probably isn't even remotely interested in anything I have to say. But why is he still staring at me with such a heated gaze? I think I just caught fire.

"You're going to go talk to him." Brianna smiles deviously, narrowing her eyes as she smirks over at me.

"*What?*" I choke out, the strong liquid flowing down my windpipes uncomfortably. It's like I just swallowed glass, the feeling leaving my throat burning. "No. No way. I can't."

"Yes, you can," Taylor encourages. "He's incredibly hot. Like come on. He's clearly older, probably has a lot of money, dresses nicely, and I see no wedding band on his finger." She smirks, her green eyes darkening as she stands up and pulls me along for the ride.

Fear eats me alive, and I suddenly can't breathe. The air is too thick for my lungs. "No, Tay. Please. I can't. I'm not—"

She cuts me off, and Brianna joins in, pulling me toward the bar, but my heels stay planted to the spot I'm in. "You're not what?" Brianna challenges. "Look at you. You're hot and single. Don't waste it by being boring. Go talk to him," she encourages as she drags me closer to the glossy bar top.

"No, guys. Come on. I'm too... I can't..."

Brianna stops me from saying anything else, silencing me with the press of her palm against my chest. "Look, you're going to talk to him, and he's going to buy you a drink, and then me and Tay are going back to the dance floor. And you're going to go up there and flirt with him and twirl your hair and get his number," she says sternly.

The closer I get to the edge of the bar, the faster my breathing gets. I feel like I'm going to faint right on the spot. "But I… he's too… I can't…" I stutter out in a fit of nerves, but she won't listen to anything I'm saying. Neither of them will.

"Go on, babe. You can do it." Brianna gives me a push to the edge of the bar, only a few barstools away from the man with the pretty brown eyes.

"Have fun," Taylor whispers in my ear with a laugh as she drags Brianna the opposite way, disappearing through the sea of people on the dance floor.

My heart is thundering in my chest, the sinking feeling bubbling up inside me feeling a lot like fear. They left me all alone, mere inches from a man who has my blood rushing like a raging river in my ear. I don't even remember the last time I talked to a guy, nonetheless a man as hot as him.

I take a seat in an empty barstool, letting the leather creep along the back of my thighs, cooling the fire that's igniting my insides. I'm going to kill them when we get back to the car. Grabbing on to a single menu, I start to scan the drinks nonchalantly, hoping my wide eyes don't give me away. I'm so nervous, and the alcohol buzzing through my body isn't helping my nerves at all. It's only heightening them.

As I flip the menu over, I don't look up. Maybe I'm just scared that if I do, I'll lock eyes with those smoldering brown irises. Was he smoldering? And am I sweating? I'm suddenly aware of every single thing I'm doing wrong. Am I slouched? Do my eyes look bloodshot? Is my red lipstick smeared? Does my hair look okay? Am I still in one piece?

Suddenly, my rambling thoughts are silenced, and all I can hear is the sweet sound of a deep voice. "Is this seat taken?" When I look up, all I see are dark pools of honey.

Fuck.

"Umm, no," I answer shyly, holding my breath as I tuck a loose curl behind my ear. He tracks the movement like he's committing it to memory, making me lose my train of thought.

"Mind if I sit?" he asks with a raised brow. I nod and then he pushes back the empty barstool next to me, lightly brushing his leg against mine, prompting a chill to run down my spine at the contact.

The menu is now bent due to my overabundance of nerves. Brianna and Taylor are going to pay for making me suffer through this.

He takes the menu from my hands, flattening it until the creases are no more. A slight chuckle leaves his lips, and then he smiles my way. "Can I buy you a drink?" He looks me over slowly, and my eyes widen when his gaze flicks to my bare thighs, making heat flood in places it shouldn't.

"Umm, sure," I respond meekly, letting him slide the drink menu to the side, all attention on me now.

He gives me another once-over, his eyes mischievous as he assesses me slowly. "So, what's your drink of choice?"

I blink up at him, surprise lighting in my eyes, but then I do something that shocks me. I muster up an ounce of courage and fire back a question without warning. A question that comes out a lot like flirting. "What do you think my drink of choice is?" I bat my eyelashes, lean against my elbow, and *fucking* smile.

What the fuck is wrong with me? I don't do this. *Ever.* But he looks so good. I can't seem to resist.

He chuckles at the question and drags his big brown eyes over me slowly. I can see the calculations and assumptions he's making swirl and tick like a clock in his brain. He'll never guess right. He's just like any other guy. They always get it wrong.

His eyes flick back up to my face as a gentle smile spreads over his mouth, forming a dimple that presses deep into his left cheek.

Fuck. He's so pretty.

"Hmm, let me think," he starts slowly, his words slipping like melted butter off his tongue. "You don't seem like the type to drink hard liquor." He gives me another flick of his dark eyes, and a jolt of electricity seems to crackle deep in my spine.

The longer I listen to him, the more I hear a bit of an accent. Southern, maybe. Like he came from somewhere else that's far, far away from California, but I can't place where.

"Fireball? Definitely not," he retorts. "Tequila? Can't see it. But hmm, let me guess..." He takes another good look at me and stares deep into my wide eyes. Those warm brown eyes seem to sear right through me as I try not to melt into them.

God, those eyes. Those fucking doe eyes.

He continues on with his mission to find exactly what I like. "Rum? Maybe. Vodka? Most likely. Whiskey? Maybe a whiskey girl. But you..." He leans in closer, and I can smell the expensive cologne dripping off his skin. It smells like sandalwood and the salty spray of the ocean. It makes me a bit dizzy, if I'm being honest with myself.

Leaning just a smidge closer, I can practically taste the whiskey that encompasses his lips. Can almost feel how good his mouth would taste with his tongue gliding against mine...

I focus on deep breaths as he rests his large hand on the surface of the counter, barely brushing the tips of his fingers against mine as goose bumps start to crawl slowly up my arm. He laughs lightly, finally forming a final guess with a slight Southern drawl dripping off his tongue. "Malibu Tonic? I'm guessing you're a fruity cocktail kind of girl. Maybe even as sweet as one."

My mouth falls open because he just guessed right. Wait—did he just call me sweet?

"How did you know that's one of my favorite drinks?" I ask with a wide-eyed stare.

"Just an assumption, sweetheart. I'm pretty good at reading people. Especially ones as pretty as yourself." He smirks, turning toward the bar to call over one of the bartenders.

Sweetheart? Pretty? Oh God, I'm in trouble.

As soon as a pretty blonde bartender comes over, he wastes no time giving the drink orders. "One Malibu Tonic and one Jack Daniel's Tennessee Whiskey on the rocks."

"You've got it," she beams brightly over the sleek bar top.

"Thanks, Hailey." He smiles as he watches her waltz off to start the drinks.

I frown as a lack of confidence washes through me. He knows her name, probably even flirted with her before I came over. And what is this uncomfortable, itchy feeling that's glossing over me? It's not jealousy, but it's *something*. Something I can't quite put my finger on.

I don't know this man, and I don't even care that he's buying me a drink, but obviously that's a lie. I *do* care, even though I shouldn't. I don't date, and there's a clear reason I don't anymore. But that's a dark place I don't want to go to tonight, or ever again.

He notices the shift in my mood as I sit up straighter and clench my jaw into place, focusing on not losing myself for the night.

"You alright there? You look a little tense," he says, hovering his thick fingers closer to my hand as I pull away from him.

"I'm fine," I bite back a little too harshly.

He doesn't respond, only nods. He knows something is off, but he doesn't press.

After a couple minutes of awkward silence, the bartender comes back over to drop off the drinks. I can't help but notice the flashy nametag on the front of her black low-cut tank top. The name *Hailey* is scrawled in sparkly cursive letters, and then I feel shame instantly cover my face.

Stupid. You're so stupid.

I take a sip of the fruity liquid and let it slide down the back of my throat, along with the bitterness and possible jealousy that was there just seconds ago. I don't even know his name, and I'm already acting like this? Jesus. I'm in way over my head.

I *don't* get jealous, but what was that? What is *this*?

He takes a swig of his amber-colored drink and swallows, a gentle smile returning to his handsome face. "So, you come here often?" he asks, trying to break the ice.

I shake my head. "No, this is actually my first time here."

"Thought so." He chuckles under his breath.

I tilt my head and thread my eyebrows together. "Oh? You come here a lot or something?"

"Something like that, yeah." He smiles, a smug look crossing his features like he knows something I don't.

I can't help but notice the way his thick fingers flex around the crystal glass, or the way the dark ink glides across his tanned skin. If I wasn't looking close enough, I would've missed the thin lines of ink that form into a detailed, shaded pocket watch against his forearm, or even the crashing ocean waves that seem to swallow the watch hands.

Before I can ask about his tattoo, he places a large hand over the ink and clears his throat, making my eyes snap back up to his. "Think I would've remembered a pretty face like yours."

He brings the clear glass to the tip of his lips and throws his head back, letting the whiskey envelop his taste buds. I just stare incredulously at him, trying to form coherent thoughts when all I can repeat in my mind is what he just said to me.

He thinks I'm pretty. Did he just say that out loud?

When he sets the glass back down on the shiny surface of the bar top, he lets his eyes trail back to mine. I can see questions brimming in those glossy brown eyes. He's searching for something. "So, how are you liking the club? Up to your standards?"

The way his dark eyebrows raise and the way his eyes seem to dive deeper into mine makes me stutter. *He's just a guy. Snap out of it.*

When I realize just where I am and what I'm doing, I turn the tables and try my best to push his interest away. I don't need a distraction. I don't need *him.*

Crossing my arms over my chest, I give him a quick shrug and act like I'd rather be anywhere else. "Honestly? It's okay, I guess. It's a little loud for my taste, but it's decent." I watch him raise a brow as I take another sip from my fruity concoction.

"Oh? Just decent? Tell me more of your thoughts." He puts an elbow on the bar top and leans his knuckles against his cheek, waiting for me to continue.

I must've just struck a nerve because now he's really intrigued.

I shake my head, letting my curls fall down my back. "Nah. You don't want to hear my thoughts. They're... Well, they're..." The blaring music from the dance floor makes me lose my train of thought, and my words seem to fail me. So much for a witty comeback.

"Enlighten me." He smirks with a husky breath, his eyes fixed intently on me while he stirs his drink. My insides seem to turn to liquid while just watching him swirl the alcohol around. He should probably stop, or maybe I should just leave. But that won't get rid of the butterflies that seem to be fluttering in my core.

Who even is this man?

I gulp at the sharp eyesight of his dreamy brown eyes, my knees knocking against the smooth counter walls anxiously. "Well, there's no food here for starters. I'd kill for some chicken strips right now," I groan, salivating at the thought of food, even if my stomach is twisted in knots.

He laughs at my response. "Sweetheart, this is a fancy nightclub. This ain't some cheap bar with finger foods."

I snap back at him. "Well, it'd be a hell of a lot better if this club did have some."

His eyebrows raise in defense, and he presses a large palm my way to halt me right there. "Alright, calm down, tiger. Gonna start seeing claws in a second if you don't simmer down." He laughs as I sigh in response. "What else?" he asks with a longing stare.

"What else, what?" I question, swirling the straw in my drink mindlessly as my eyes fix back on him.

"What else would you change about the club?" His gaze doesn't drop from mine, and his right palm rakes down his scruff slowly, like he's completely invested in what I have to say.

Why does he care? It's not like he runs the place. And as a matter of fact, when was the last time a guy ever listened to me?

Relaxing my tight shoulders, I sigh and let my eyes flick to the neon signs that are hung all around the back walls. "The signs are all red. It'd look better if there were also pink ones. Gives some nice contrast without being overbearing."

He drags his thumb over his bottom lip, eyebrows knit and eyes assessing me like I just said something he could use. "Nice contrast, huh?"

I shrug and take another sip from my drink. "I mean, I think so."

After another few seconds of silently looking me over, he smiles. "Wouldn't be the worst idea. Anything else?"

"Why do you care? I'm just rambling."

He shakes his head and sighs. "I might be closer to the owner of this place than you know. Might give him some good ideas." He smirks, and all I can do is roll my eyes because there goes that perfect *fucking* dimple again.

Can this man get any more gorgeous?

Dragging my tongue across my bottom teeth, I narrow my eyes and challenge him. He gives me a wicked stare right back, threatening me to go ahead and spill it. So, I do.

I lean forward, so close that I practically skim over his broad chest and inhale the scent of his fresh cologne. "Okay then, you asked for it." He just gives me a smug smirk and lets me continue. "The alcohol menu could use some more options. There's too many beers. Make it more cocktail and mixed drinks friendly. And the VIP booths? Maybe save some for walk-in guests."

He stares on, continuing to listen to what I have to say. "The DJ? He needs to mix up the tunes. These songs get old pretty quick. Put some throwbacks in there, play some upbeat rock songs. Maybe open up some private rooms for the guests who want to chill in a quieter area where they can think. It's fucking loud in here." I cross one leg over my knee and give him a devious smirk, proud of myself because I just let him have it.

A low whistle comes from his lips, and he leans back and gives me a once-over, a small chuckle coming from deep within his broad chest. "You're a little firecracker, aren't you?"

I shrug nonchalantly and fake a smile. "It's just what I'd do differently. Not that my opinion matters."

"Sure it does, sweetheart. I'll be sure to give the owner the rundown when I see him next." He winks at me, giving another deep chuckle that tells me he *definitely* knows something that I don't. I wish he'd stop that. I'm not trying to rein him in, but maybe I already am.

A weird flutter runs through my stomach, so I chase it down with another sip of alcohol, letting the burn fill the void of holding on to a feeling I don't want. But still, I can't shake the feeling of wanting this conversation to continue. I don't want to leave yet. Not necessarily. Maybe a few more minutes wouldn't hurt.

He takes another long look at me, and I can't stop myself from staring into the pits of his deep brown eyes. I almost missed the slight sparkle of some lighter flecks in his eyes that almost glow like yellow tiger eyes.

And just as he's about to ask me something, his phone buzzes loudly in his pocket, interrupting whatever he was about to ask me. One glance down at his phone and his face drops. "Excuse me," he apologizes, standing up to go take the call. But before he can turn the corner, he looks back and smiles brightly at me, and then he says loudly, "Just stay there. I'll be right back. Sorry, sweetheart."

I watch him disappear around the corner, and I can't help but to think how I wish he was still sitting next to me. I still smell his scent lingering in the air, heavier than any expensive alcohol or sweat that encases the club. It makes me feel a little uneasy.

Shit. Maybe I do kind of like this guy. Maybe I can just forget my promise to myself and try to get to know him. But then again, I don't think I ever want another man in my life again. Because he might break me, too...

Slowly stirring the last remnants of the fruity liquid in my glass, I find myself wondering when he'll be back. I still smell him on my skin, and he didn't even touch me besides that one single graze...

Another minute goes by, and just when I think he's back, I see red hair flit through my vision. Brianna is suddenly grabbing my wrist and dragging me toward the front double doors.

"Bri? What the hell?" I ask with a hiss, trying my best to pull out of her hold, but she's too strong. "I'm not ready to—"

"Nathan's here. You know, the guy she had a one night stand with? The one who won't leave her alone now?" Taylor yells over the boom of the music.

"Can't you just avoid him? We've barely been here over an hour," I whine.

They both look at me with speculation in their wide eyes, but Brianna brushes it off. "I think you had too much to drink. Let's go." She clamps down on my skin until I'm being forced through the doors. And as I take one last glance back, I see brown eyes searching for me over by the bar.

A knot forms in my stomach as I'm dragged out against my will, but I just let it go because they're not listening to me now. The only sounds I hear are high-pitched bickering and remorse filling the air.

When I'm buckled in and the car is lurching into the busy city street, I glance back and see the faint glow of red disappearing from my view, Club Inferno now only a faint memory of what could've been.

As the sounds of pop music and distilled voices fill the air, I whisper out into the moonlit sky, letting the cool breeze calm my pounding heart, "I didn't even get his name..."

Chapter Six

Sam

The high-pitched whistle pulls me from my thoughts as my attention filters back to Kayla's soccer game. Coach Oliver drops the whistle and yells for one of the girls to run, which leads to more chanting from the other parents surrounding the field.

Even after I stayed up past two in the morning to close down the club, I promised Kayla I'd be here to cheer her on. So here I am, ten o'clock sharp, a black coffee in my hand as I rub the sleep from my eyes.

I didn't get a wink of sleep last night because I was thinking about *her*. The one with ocean-blue eyes. The woman who walked into my club and started a fire in my lungs. But I didn't even get her name. She disappeared before I had the chance to ask. Maybe if I wouldn't have answered that fucking call in the first place, then maybe I wouldn't have let her slip through my fingers. I might've got her name or at least gave her my number.

God, I wish I could've at least got her name. Now, she may as well be lost to sea, because San Diego is a big city. The chances of running into her again are slim to none.

The sounds of scuffling and cheering pull me back to the present, and I almost miss Kayla kicking the soccer ball into the net. And just like that, she makes her first goal of the day.

I just about drop my coffee when I push off from my lawn chair and scream her way. "Go, Kayla! That's my girl!" She turns my way and gives me a huge grin, her cheeks bright red from the exertion of the game. I always knew she was a little soccer star. Always has been since she was in first grade. She might even take the sport to college, get a scholarship, and go play professionally. There's nothing she can't do.

A whip of brunette hair flashes in my peripheral vision, and my heart automatically skips a beat thinking it's her—the woman from the club. But when I turn my head in the direction of the chestnut-colored hair, my face falls. It's not her.

Audibly groaning to myself, I smooth a hand down my clipped scruff and rake my fingers along my jawline, letting all my pent-up energy subside. No matter how many brunettes and pairs of blue eyes I see around the crowd, I keep thinking it's her.

Jesus. I should get a grip on myself. She's not here, and she's not going to be. Whatever I felt back at the club was just a fluke, nothing more. Besides, the last thing I need to be doing is bringing home a new woman to Kayla. She's not ready for that—maybe she never will be. Maybe *I* won't ever be ready for that again.

But why can't I get her out of my head then?

Minutes go by, which turns into nearly two hours, and then the game's almost over.

Another high-pitched whistle, and my head is back in the game, getting lost in cheering on number twenty-two, my baby girl. "Behind you!" I warn. Kayla surprisingly hears me and turns her head right when another player from the other team tries to swipe the ball from her, but my little girl is faster.

Kayla pushes ahead and steers toward the goal. There's only seconds left on the clock, and this can be the shot that makes her team win. After a slight stumble and a hard kick, the black and white ball goes soaring. And just as the coach calls it, in goes the ball.

They won! "Yes, attagirl!" I clap, standing and giving her my biggest grin. She flashes one right back at me, and runs over as soon as she high fives the other teammates.

"Did you see that, Dad? Did you see me?" She screams in glee as she runs up to me. I grab her and tug her into my arms, giving her the biggest bear hug she's ever received.

"I did. You knocked them dead just like I knew you would." When I let go, she giggles and swipes her ashy-brown ponytail over her shoulder, grabbing for the blue Gatorade she requested for the game.

"I'm gonna be team captain in no time," she beams, her pearly whites shining under the sunlight.

"I have no doubt about that, kiddo."

When she turns around, she finds Nicole's mom celebrating the team's win, her arms curled tight around Nicole's back while her messy blonde curls get tangled up with her mom's. Kayla's smile drops, and I see that faint longing in her now sad hazel eyes.

I let a sigh escape my lips as I watch her just stare at her friend while her mother smooths her hair out and tells her how good she did in the game. I try to nudge Kayla, but she's lost in the fog.

I know that look. Fuck, do I know it. It's exactly the face I made all those times Lois would miss every single one of my daughters' dance recitals, gymnastics meets, even Kayla's preschool Christmas show. She never once showed up for either of my girls, not even if they begged her.

Kayla doesn't really talk about it, but I know how much it bothers her. I know how sad and heartbroken she is to not have that motherly support in her life. It wrecks me to see her so hurt. I just wish she'd take all her frustrations out on me instead of keeping them bottled up. But I'm no better. I do the same. Keeping all that pain and hurt sealed tightly inside my chest under lock and key has been my normal. Maybe I shouldn't do that anymore.

Wet tears pool in Kayla's eyes, and every part of me is trying to hold my own in. I want to wrap her up in a big hug, tell her everything's going to be alright. But that's just not the case. I may show up for her, but that doesn't change the fact that her mother doesn't. She never even tried.

It shouldn't still feel this raw, so open like a fresh wound, but it does. Because every time I see that hurt and disappointment in Kayla's eyes, I remember every single moment Lois disappointed me. But what's even worse is seeing my best girl silently grieve not having a mother. She wants one, and she deserves the best. Always. But I can't give her that. No matter how hard I try, I can't change the fact that her mother doesn't care about her or Kelsey. Not really...

Kelsey may hide it better, but Kayla could never. She's just a teenager who never truly got to heal from the trauma she endured as a child. She may not remember it all, but I do. How I grabbed the girls and left as fast as I could once the divorce papers were signed. How they kicked and screamed the entire way because they didn't understand what was happening. How I felt completely defeated driving hundreds of miles to start a new life that I wasn't completely ready for. In the end, it's what was best for all of us.

But I tried. Fuck, I tried so goddamn hard to keep our little family together, but she made it impossible. She never wanted them or me. She only wanted someone to control. But she can't do that anymore. She might try, but she'll lose every time.

And if Lois ever tries to hurt my girls again, she'll have more than me to deal with.

I shake my head of those negative thoughts and glance over at Kayla, watching her kick the ball of her cleat into the green grass while her head is down, eyes away from Nicole and her mother.

Slowly moving over to her, I give her a light squeeze on the shoulder and nudge her arm. "Hey. You okay, kiddo?"

She peeks up and fakes a smile, her eyes still a little red from the building tears. "Yeah, I'm fine," she lies while she wipes away a tear that almost escapes.

"Hey." I sneak in front of her and put both hands on her shoulders, dropping down where she's eye level with me. And through her hazy eyes, I see a faint smile. "I'm so proud of you, honey. You led the game. You scored that final goal. You played amazing. You should be proud of yourself, too. I know how hard you've been working in practice lately. It paid off."

She tugs on a small grin and gives me those big hazel eyes I always love seeing. "Really?"

"Really. You were the best one out there."

"You're just saying that because you have to." She rolls her eyes and shoves me playfully in the chest. I pretend like she almost knocked me over, which makes her giggle even more.

God, I love hearing my little girl laugh. That's the only sound that I ever want to hear. No tears, no hurt, just joyous laughter. "No, I really mean it. You were amazing."

She throws herself into me and wraps her arms around my back, squeezing me with all her might. "Thanks for coming to watch me play, Dad. It means a lot."

I squeeze her once more and then let her go. "You're welcome, baby. I wouldn't miss it for the world."

When she gathers her belongings up and follows me to the truck, I put her pink soccer bag in the back and climb in the front, waiting for her to close the door and buckle her seat belt around her body. "So, I was thinking. You wanna go for some ice cream and go to the arcade for a couple hours?"

Her bright eyes widen in glee. "Really? But I thought you worked today?"

Adjusting the rear-view mirror, I look back over to her and shake my head. "Nah. I don't work till later tonight. I'm all yours this afternoon."

"Yes, yes, yes!" she chants. I can't help but to chuckle at her excitement.

"So, what do you say, kiddo?"

"Duh, let's go!"

I breathe out a laugh and start the engine, letting it rev to life while I back out of the parking lot. There's a lot of things I love in life, but spending time with my little girl is one of my favorites.

When I'm five minutes out on the road, Kayla calls my name. "Dad?"

"Yeah?"

She twirls her hair around her index finger while her other hand wraps around the blue Gatorade bottle. "I may be fifteen, but I really love when you take me on father-daughter dates."

My smile widens as I turn onto a busy street, my eyes flicking over to her for a second. "You're never gonna be too old for those, kiddo. We'll keep doing them as long as you let me."

"Pinky swear?"

"Pinky swear." I nod, holding out my pinky to her. She wraps hers around mine. This was always our way of keeping promises to each other, and I don't plan on ever stopping.

She may not have a mother, but she'll always have me. That I can promise.

CHAPTER SEVEN

VIOLET

S unlight filters through the private library room while my foot taps impatiently in tune with the sound of Jenna's voice. I canceled my in-office visit a few days ago. Maybe because I feel more comfortable behind a screen and inside a library; it brings me ease.

My co-workers don't mind that I use it during lunches or meetings. As long as no guests have it booked, I'm free to use it as I please. So I do. And besides, there's plenty of other rooms. This one just happens to be my favorite because I have a perfect view of the fountain that sits in the middle of the outside courtyard. The one with roses and lilies all sprawled around a vibrant garden.

Jenna's voice brings me back to the present, and I start to run through the endless list of sayings she's bound to repeat.

Keep focused. Try to stay positive. Have you given those new anxiety meds a try? Go out, have fun. Keep moving forward. That's what she always says. And even if some days she's right, I still know what's best for myself. At least, I think. She'd state otherwise.

"Violet, are you listening?" Jenna asks through the flat laptop screen, her jade green eyes prowling like the Cheshire Cat's.

I snap myself back to reality and sit up straight, pushing back a fallen piece of hair from my face. "Mhm," I answer in a daze. *What was she just telling me?*

"Okay. Why don't you repeat what I just said then?"

Shit.

I pick at the end of one of my nails, biting my bottom lip and look absentmindedly at the pink keyboard. She got me. Paying attention is not something I've ever been that great at. But it seems like the last couple of years have been the worst when it comes to that sort of thing.

She sighs, obviously disappointed in me. I look up with pitiful eyes, hoping she'll let this time slide, but she only asks the inevitable next. "Are you still having nightmares?"

My thumb sinks into the side of the oak table, and it feels like tiny needles are jabbing deep into my palms as my teeth clamp together. Sweat coats my skin, and the room is suddenly ice cold. "I—Umm, no. Not really." Lie. That was a big, fat lie, and she knows it, too.

Her almond-shaped eyes thin out, and I know she'd like to inject some common sense into me. I shouldn't lie to her, but I really don't want her worrying or trying to get me to try a new sleeping pill. The last one didn't work. And it's not that I haven't been sleeping, just sometimes the nightmares keep me up till dawn. "Not really isn't an answer, Violet." I can hear the disappointment slip off her tongue; it sounds like static to my ears.

Leaning forward and stretching my sore arms, I give her an apologetic smile. "No, Jenna. I'm fine. My sleep has been okay. Besides, I don't really have them anymore. The nightmares..." Another lie. Maybe I just want her off my back for a bit. Melatonin or not, nothing helps. The nightmares are there to stay. Maybe for the rest of my life.

She taps a black ink pen on the edge of her white marble table, probably deciding what to do. Call me out on my lies or just pretend like my problems don't exist. But they exist alright. They nag me like a pesky mosquito that just won't die. "Well, try to do your meditations before bed like we talked about. And try to relax. Maybe go out. Meet someone new."

Meet someone new. Yeah. Like the gorgeous six-foot-tall man who disappeared from my grasp. I was so close. So fucking close to getting his name. But maybe it wasn't meant to be. Maybe I'm not meant for anyone. Not after what happened with Jason. Not after he...

"Sure," I respond absentmindedly, my head now swimming with flashbacks of silver and bottles strewn around my feet.

"I'll see you next week. Have a nice day, Violet." The video call clicks to an end, and I'm left with a black screen and a void of silence.

Just when I'm about to get lost in a sea of memories, the door to the room is shoved open, which makes me jump from my chair.

"Vi, catch!" Brianna slings a bag of chips at my head, and I catch it just as she slams the door shut.

"Bri, what the hell? You can't just go around slamming doors in the library." I giggle as she pulls up a rolling chair next to me. Taylor follows on her heels and takes a seat across from us.

"She clearly thinks she can." Taylor laughs while handing me a packaged grilled cheese sandwich.

"What can't she do?" I tease, pulling the wrapped sandwich my way and unfolding the edges.

"There's nothing I can't do," Brianna sing-songs, flipping her blonde curls while she sips on her mango smoothie.

"Yeah, except maybe get Violet Mr. Hottie's number," Taylor chimes. Brianna almost chokes as she waves her arms sporadically.

"Okay, okay. That was not my fault entirely," she tries to interject, but I wave her off.

"Bri, you pulled me out of there before I could even get the words out," I whine pathetically. Maybe I could've halted her, but I was just too late once we got in the car.

Sliding down in my chair with a huff, Brianna tries apologizing again. "Look. I'm really sorry. I take full responsibility because I know he was so into you." Her words push a button deep in my gut, and I feel the regret twist like a knife against my spine.

"It's fine. He probably wasn't that interested. I just—"

"Oh, no. You must've not seen how absolutely smitten he was with you! The man couldn't stop staring. And did you see the fucking smirk on his face when you went over to him? He wanted you so bad," Taylor swoons, her red locks bouncing against her shoulders as she tells me again how much he was into me.

Shaking my head, I pick a piece of my sandwich apart and laugh. "You two kill me."

Taylor and Brianna smirk at each other, their big eyes plotting something I can't get out of. And then they look at me, big toothy smiles while they lean my way.

Oh, boy. What are they scheming this time?

Brianna grabs the edge of my chair and spins me around until I'm looking straight into her mischievous brown eyes. "We're going out again tomorrow night."

"Yeah, we were going to go to the movies tomorrow, right?" I look between the two of them, but they only cackle in response. "Bri, you mean going out to get popcorn and snacks, right?" I press.

She shakes her head and smirks, her blonde curls bouncing like all her pent-up energy. "Not this time. We're going back to Club Inferno."

I scoot the edge of my chair back and press a palm out, trying to stop them from coming closer. "No, that's *not* what we said we are doing tomorrow."

Taylor swings around and grabs the edge of my chair, making it impossible to back away any further. "Too bad. We're repaying the favor and trying to fix it."

"Fix what? Nothing's broken," I retort.

"Uh-huh. You've been moody all week, and we know why," Brianna presses. "You didn't get your hottie's number or his name, so we're taking you back until you see him again."

My heart starts thumping wildly just thinking about the chance of seeing those dark brown eyes again, smelling his fresh scent, feeling the flames from his tanned skin heat my body.

Fuck. I *do* want to see him again. How did that small interaction with him get caged in my brain? *He's just a guy.* But is he, really?

"What if he's not there?" I whisper out vaguely, trying to hide my disappointment.

"Oh, I have a feeling he'll be there." Brianna winks a sparkly eye at me and grabs at her smoothie while Taylor eats her sandwich with a shit-eating grin. Brianna is hardly ever wrong, so I'm betting on her being right this time.

I throw the unopened bag of chips her way and laugh when it goes toppling over the table. "You better be right, Bri."

She lifts an eyebrow and curls her pink lips my way. "Don't worry, babe. You'll see him again. And this time, you're going to get more than just his digits. Maybe even his tongue." She flicks her tongue out, and I almost choke on a sip of lemonade.

My hand goes flying over to her, and Taylor snorts when I smack Brianna across the shoulder. "You two are too much," I giggle.

"But you love us!" Taylor shouts across the table.

"Yeah, I really do." I smile, thankful that they exist to keep me sane in this crazy world. I don't really know where I'd be without them by my side.

A smidge of anxiety flutters through my stomach as I think about the possibility of seeing Mr. Brown Eyes again. Brown eyes. I kind of like that nickname.

Okay, brown eyes. Please be there tomorrow. Please, please, *please.*

CHAPTER EIGHT

SAM

"Nick called off at the last second. Did Julie come in to cover?" I ask, frazzled as I close the door behind me to my office.

"Julie's already here. She's upstairs, running the bar," Bryson confirms as he paces alongside me in the dimly lit hallway.

"Perfect," I mutter as I thumb through my phone, checking emails to make sure the bonus checks went out on time. As a gift for the club doing so well, I wanted to do something nice for my employees. A little extra money before the holidays ring in is never a bad move. Even though it's only the end of August, it's never too early.

"Oh, some new guy called on the phone earlier. Said he wanted to set up a meeting with you? Apparently, he said he'd love to discuss the possibility of a new DJ gig at the club." Bryson eyes me suspiciously like I did something behind his back, but honestly, I just forgot to tell him I was looking to mix up the sounds of the club.

I stop in front of a decorative hanging mirror, turning toward him before we make our way into the public's eye of the club. "I may have reached out to him a few days ago."

Bryson narrows his eyes. "What's wrong with the one we have?"

Oh, nothing. Just a blue-eyed beauty whose name I don't even know basically told me the music was lame. And did I reach out the very next day to a DJ whose music might be more suited to her likes? Yes, yes I did, and for purposes I don't quite understand.

Am I just wishing she'll magically show up if I change one thing about the club, or am I being completely delusional in thinking I'll ever see her again?

I sigh and slide my fingers through my brown locks. "Nothing. I just thought maybe we could change it up a bit. I'm not getting rid of Dustin, I just thought maybe it'd be good to branch out a bit. Maybe play some more alternative and rock mixes some nights. Might bring in new guests." Guests like the brunette who got away.

He rakes a heavy hand over his jawline, letting the wires in his brain cross for a minute before he nods in agreement. "You know what? That's brilliant, actually. When'd you think of doing that?"

Shrugging my shoulders, I start to trail my way to the end of the hall where a crowd of guests linger by the steep staircase. "Let's just say someone might have inspired me."

"Fascinating." Bryson gives me another curious glance before he heads up the staircase that has fairy lights twisted around the railing. "I'm gonna go see how the bar's managing. I'll catch up with you later, Sammy. Are you planning on working on payroll later?"

"Yeah, later tonight. Right now I need to go check on some things by the front." I give him a small wave before I push through the thick waves of guests, flashing them a big smile, making sure everything is running smoothly.

A pair of women with hot pink mini dresses and caked on makeup bat their long eyelashes at me, peeling on seductive smiles to try to get my attention, but I keep walking. Bryson would've had a field day if he got his eyes on that. He'd probably be giving me a hard time about it the rest of the night. But the only woman who could make me look twice is the blue-eyed beauty. She could write me an entire thesis on things she hates about this club, and I'd *still* ask her to come back.

Hell, I could change a thousand things about my club, but I'd only do it if it'd bring her back. *Please, come back.*

Even though I don't know her, I *want* to know her. That firecracker personality of hers is contagious. She may be shy, but she's definitely got some bite to her, and I like that.

I push her out of my thoughts and trek along till I'm close to the front of the bar. Ripples of sparkles and the haze of red lights catch my eye, right before I just about trip over a sleazy-looking gentleman's Prada dress shoe. "Sorry about that," I apologize while he ignores me entirely. Instead, he's focused on the young woman draped in gold on his arm.

Fighting the sea of people, I finally see the faint glow of the *Sinner's Welcome* sign hanging above the middle of the bar, but before I can stop myself, I go crashing into someone, our chests colliding with a thump. My reflexes kick in and my arms reach out, catching them from falling to the ground.

Jesus, I'm a real walking hazard tonight. When did this place get so packed?

"I'm so sorry. I wasn't watching where I was walking," I apologize quickly while my hands brace around her arms.

"Sorry, it was my fault. I wasn't looking, either," she spills out hurriedly.

Wait. That voice. That soft lilt and hint of shyness. My heart stops. *It can't be.*

When my eyes adjust and reality sinks in, my mouth drops open. The woman standing, nonetheless in my arms, is *her.* The blue-eyed goddess who took the breath from my lungs the second I saw her. "It's you," I whisper out, my fingers still latched on to her soft skin.

She falters and steps back, right out of my reach as my hands drop to my sides. "You," she repeats, her dark blue eyes shining like sapphires under the soft lighting of the club.

God, she's beautiful.

Am I imagining her? Surely I must be. But she's here, solid and real in front of me.

My eyes slide down her silky navy-colored dress, admiring how the color accentuates the striking ocean-blue color of her irises. Her spiral curls fall over the spaghetti straps, and the sun-kissed highlights at the ends of her brunette hair make her look like sunlight. There's a long slit on the side of her sleek dress that ends near the top of her thigh, and it takes every single particle of me to not reach out and wrap my hand around her back.

"I didn't expect to see you again," I say honestly, suddenly speechless because she just knocked the breath out of me, literally.

"My uh, my friends invited me to come back out. I didn't think you'd be here, either," she says timidly as she brushes a stray lock behind her ear. I track the movements like I'm memorizing the way she moves. My thumb involuntarily flexes against my dark denim jeans, wishing I could touch her hair instead.

I look around for a second and spot flashy red hair and blonde curls over by one of the tables, and then I turn my focus back to her. "You ran away last weekend. Didn't even give me a chance to catch your name." I smirk playfully, but that only causes her to shy away more.

She looks briefly down at the polished marble floor and then back up at me nervously. "I didn't mean to," she says slowly. "And besides, you got a phone call."

That's right. The phone call. The one that made me miss the opportunity to ask her for her name.

"Right... but why didn't you stay?" Her ruby red lips part open, but then she clamps them shut before anything escapes from her pretty mouth. Shit. Did it sound like I was blaming her for leaving when I was the one that walked off? Licking my bottom lip in frustration, I act fast. "Sorry, I'm not putting the blame on you. I just wondered where you ran off to."

Idiot.

She shakes her loose curls and gives me an apologetic smile. "No, you're fine. My friend had a crisis and pulled me away. I didn't necessarily want to go." Her pure blue eyes and quaint apology tugs at my heartstrings, and I can't for the life of myself look away. So instead, I ask her for a second chance.

"Well in that case, care to join me for another drink?" I tilt my head in the direction of the lit-up bar, hinting at two open barstools that have our names written all over them.

She looks back over her shoulder in the direction of her friends, hesitating for a second like she might say no. But instead, she turns my way and smiles. "Lead the way."

Brushing my hand against the small of her back, I steer her in the direction of the bar, careful not to step on her elegant silver heels that shine like gemstones under the glow of the red lights. Her brunette waves sway gently as she walks, and I get the faint whiff of vanilla and lavender that seems to drip down onto my black button-up shirt. I have a feeling that scent will be burned into my nostrils by the end of the night, maybe even lingering into tomorrow.

When we're all situated on the leather stools, I get Hailey's attention and watch her bounce happily over to me. "Hey, guys. What can I get you?"

I look once at the pretty blue-eyed woman next to me and let my smirk say the rest. "A Malibu Tonic and my usual."

Hailey winks my way and smiles. "Of course. Be back in a jiffy."

When I look back at the beauty, she shakes her head in disbelief. "You remembered my drink order?"

I shrug nonchalantly and scoot just a smidge closer to her. "Of course I did. Who could forget that?" She stares at me like she didn't hear me quite right, but then she just relaxes her shoulders and leans against the dark wood of the bar top.

"I mean, a lot of people can't remember names. But you didn't even know me, and yet you remembered that little detail about a drink," she says unbelievably.

"I remember a lot of things. Like how you picked apart the red signs and the DJ, or how you so sweetly said how bad the menu was." I give her a teasing smirk and watch her cheeks grow bright.

She's fucking adorable all embarrassed. Maybe I could paint her dark shades of red...

"You remember all that?" she asks with wide blue eyes. The poor thing looks mortified.

"Mhm." I chuckle. "Speaking of names. Didn't quite catch yours, angel." I knew the name would taste right the moment I first thought of it; she looks like one.

Her glossy red lips part open, and she just stares at me all wide-eyed and surprised. Maybe she liked the name, too? "Violet," she finally replies. Her name is like music to my ears.

Violet. Beautiful name for a beautiful girl.

"Violet. That's a pretty name." She blushes once again which makes me smile wider. "I'm Sam."

"Sam..." she hesitates. "Nice to meet you."

"Trust me, the pleasure is all mine, sweetheart." I hold out my hand, waiting for her to take it. It takes her a moment to take my hand, but when her fingers lock around mine, they fit like they were made for me to hold. I barely notice when Hailey drops off our drinks. I'm too captivated by the angel sitting right in front of me.

When her hand drops from mine, I still feel the imprint of her dainty fingers, and it burns like fire.

"Is Sam short for Samuel, maybe Samson?" she wonders out loud.

"Just Sam," I press, giving her an easy smile.

She hums and takes a sip of her fruity drink while I take one from mine, letting the taste of the smooth whiskey run down the back of my throat. As much as I love a cold drink, I think I like sitting beside her even more.

I take the quiet opportunity to give her a once-over, slowly examining her body language. Her knees are locked together, back straight as a board, and her fingers are latched in a vice around her beverage. She seems a little nervous or maybe uncomfortable. The last thing I want is for her to be uncomfortable or somewhere she doesn't want to be, so I intervene.

My knee slightly knocks against hers, and it grabs her attention. Her blue eyes drift up to mine, and there I go again being drawn in like a moth to a flame. "This isn't your scene, I'm guessing."

She sighs and shakes her head defeatedly, making a loose curl fall over her shoulder. "How'd you guess?"

"Wasn't hard to notice." I chuckle softly. Before her eyes fall from mine, I ask, "What is your scene then?"

She swirls the thin straw in her drink, speculating the question. When she stops the slow movements of her wrist, she responds, "I like more quiet environments, honestly. Like bookstores or coffee shops. There's nothing like strolling through the bookstore downtown with an iced latte in my hand, smelling the fresh pages of printed books."

Her blue eyes light up like she's talking about something she loves, and her glowing smile tugs deep inside my chest. Books. I like bookstores, too.

"Books, huh? What's your favorite?" I inquire, tilting my head to study her eager expression. She stalls a second, questioning if she should really answer. But I hope she answers.

Let me inside your mind, pretty girl.

Without further thought, she answers, *"Pride and Prejudice,* if we're talking about the classics." My eyes widen because what are the chances she'd say one of my favorites, too?

"We are all fools in love," I quote perfectly, making my words drawl out like sweet poetry.

She chokes on a sip of her drink and gawks at me. "You know about Jane Austen?" Her eyes are big blue orbs, and I can't help but to capture a visual image of them, planning to burn them in the back of my brain.

I nod in reply. "Mhm. Read a lot of her books."

"No way!" She audibly gasps and shakes her head like she's not hearing me right, but she is. "What other classics have you read?"

"Too many to count, but to name a few, Charles Dickens, Herman Melville, F. Scott Fitzgerald." I could go on, and honestly, I want to, but the bodies of people behind us make it a little too noisy to get caught up in talks of books.

"You've read *The Great Gatsby?*" she questions while she fiddles with the edge of her straw.

I shrug my shoulders and laugh. "Hasn't everyone?"

"Not exactly..." She eyes me suspiciously while I watch the condensation drip down her glass, her glossy lips wrapping around the straw as she takes a generous sip. She makes sure her stare doesn't waver from mine for even a second, and I can't help but to focus on how her lipstick leaves a mark on the tip of the straw. I nervously gulp at the image.

"What?" I chuckle, letting the edge of my knee fall against hers. She doesn't flinch away. "Don't act too surprised. Some men like to read the classics, too." She shakes her curls and lets out a carefree laugh.

God, I love the sound of her laugh. It's so light and relaxed and melodic. Maybe I can capture that on tape one day.

I swallow air in my lungs, realizing what I just thought. When's the last time a woman has made me want to do that? Maybe never.

"You're... different, Sam," she says serenely, carefully watching me out of the corner of her perfect eyes.

Different, huh? I can work with that.

"A good different, I hope." I chuckle as I lean the side of my knee into hers. Just a gentle touch that says *give me a chance.*

"The verdict's still out," she beams, making my heart stop with how breathtaking her smile is.

I want to dig deeper, keep searching for more answers about her. Like where she came from, what she does for a living, where she's been hiding all this time. So I reach, hoping I'll find what I'm seeking. What *am* I seeking? Is it her? "What do you do for a living?" I ask curiously.

"Why don't you guess?" She leans her elbow against the smooth surface, her other hand still tracing faint lines against the condensation that's dripping down her clear glass. There's a slight smirk that's forming over her full lips.

Oh, so she likes games? I can play right back. Just throw me the ball. I could spin circles around her all night long.

"Is that a challenge?" I arch an eyebrow and give her a devilish smirk right back, signaling that it's game on.

"Maybe." She smiles playfully, batting her long, dark eyelashes my way.

"Let me think for a second." Sliding a palm down the side of my clipped scruff, I give her a nice once-over, grinding the gears in my head to make the best assumption. I don't miss the way her breathing increases as she stares at me, waiting for my guess. "Quiet, a little shy, likes books, drinks coffee, would rather be indoors than go out to a noisy club like this."

She scoffs and puffs a breath out. "You're doing so well. Keep going."

I'll gladly accept that invitation.

"Hmm. Let's see..." Quiet, shy, loves to read. Maybe she works in a bakery, or a desk job, or maybe... *Books.* That's it. "Do you work at a bookstore by chance?"

Her eyes light up like Christmas lights, and I know I must've scored a touchdown. "Close, very close. I'm actually a librarian."

I knock on the smooth wood and pull on a huge grin. "Ahh. Of course, that makes perfect sense. Which one do you work at?"

"San Diego Central Library."

Parting my lips into surprise, I say, "Funny. I pass by that building every time I drive to work."

"Oh?" she questions with curious eyes. "Do you ever stop in?"

"Think I might just have to now," I say in a low tone.

She stares in wonder for a moment, letting the pieces of the clock fall into place. Maybe I should drop by sometime. I think I have to now. "And you? What do you do, Sam?"

"Let's just say I'm a businessman," I reply with a curt smile.

"Oh?" she asks. "What kind of business?"

"Wouldn't you like to know." I end the statement with a smirk and watch her mouth drop open, but nothing comes out that's audible. Maybe I don't want to tell her just yet. Maybe I want her to stick around and find out. I don't need to give away that I'm the owner of this club just yet. People always expect things of me when I tell them who I am, and I don't exactly want that from her. Not that she'd do that, but I'm used to people taking advantage. For example, my ex-wife...

I quickly change the subject back to her. "What else do you like?"

She clears her throat and shakes off the waiting stare in her eyes. "Depends what you're asking."

Putting the focus back on her, I gently nudge the back of her hand with mine, letting the heat from my skin lick flames against her. She falters as I take my time lingering my hand there. "What other interests do you like? Besides books."

It's like she wakes up from a dream, blue eyes growing bigger as she sucks in a breath. "Why the interest in me? I'm not..."

Did I just trigger something? Did I do something wrong?

"You're not what?" I ask carefully, preparing to walk over pieces of glass if I have to.

She looks around quickly, flicking her eyes to a group of obscenely loud women by the back wall. She swallows a gulp of air down, and her body goes rigid. "I'm not like the rest of these women here. I'm..." she stutters but quickly composes herself. "I mean, look at me."

"I am looking," I say quietly, my eyes delving deep into those pools of ocean-blue orbs. Her gaze doesn't fall from mine this time. "And that's the point, angel. You're not like the rest of them. You're interesting. You caught my attention, and you're stunning."

She shakes her loose curls in disagreement, but then stops cold, dropping her jaw wide open. "What did you just say?"

"I said you're stunning," I repeat clearly.

Her mouth twitches, and it's like she doesn't quite know what to say. "Oh, no," she responds. "Thank you, but I'm..."

I press a palm softly over her thigh, silencing her from saying another word. "Sweetheart, half the bar is staring at you."

"They are not," she snorts out. "You're bluffing."

Does she really believe she's not eye-catching? Did someone make her think that about herself?

"No, I'm really not," I say firmly, which makes her blue eyes widen in stunned shock.

She whispers over the noise of the club, but she's loud enough for me to hear. "But, Sam. I'm not—"

"Stop," I say nicely, pressing my palm firmer against her deliciously soft skin. She looks at me with big doe eyes, like I just stepped on a nerve. And there's this glossy stare in her eyes, one I can't quite place. What is she thinking right now?

She was so easy-going and relaxed when we first started talking about books, now she's shying away when I throw a compliment at her. She's hot and cold. One minute so sure of herself, the next lacking confidence. Maybe she's just bashful or doesn't take compliments easily, but I see through her like a wall of clear glass. Somebody made her feel like she wasn't enough. That has to be it.

When I catch that unsure glance in her eyes and watch her shyly look down at her silky dress, an idea lights up in my mind. *Make her believe it.* So, I decide right here and now to show her exactly how gorgeous she is.

"Just wait here a second." I slide off my barstool, slipping my hand away from her thigh and retreat away from the bar. As I walk, I can still feel the heat of those blue pools behind me, but I don't turn around. Not until I'm far enough away and out of reach, but still close enough to step in if I need to.

When I turn around, it doesn't take long for a tall man in a pressed suit to slide into my seat. Something snaps in me as I watch him smirk Violet's way, acting like he can just swoop in and steal her. Maybe I want to steal her instead.

I strain my ears, leaning in just enough to make out the obnoxious man's voice.

"Excuse me, miss?" the stranger asks her with a gleam in his murky eyes. He pushes my drink out of the way, and I fucking growl under my breath.

"Yes?" she asks hesitantly, but I don't miss the way her big eyes flick back in my direction, like she's in need of saving. She doesn't need my help. Like I said, *stunning*.

I see the way other men are looking at her. Like she's a piece of meat they can sink their teeth into. She's not fucking food, and they certainly can't play with her. I don't know why I'm suddenly pissed off, but I'm positive none of them can treat her the way I could.

Wait. Do I want her? She's certainly drop dead gorgeous and witty and way too sweet for me. She doesn't need my help to tell her that, but maybe I should. Maybe I just want to get rid of whoever the hell is talking to her right now.

The five-foot-nine-ish man slicks his greasy black hair back and places his meaty hand way too close to her hip. "Sorry to intrude, but I saw you across the way. Do you maybe want to join me in a dance, or can I buy you a drink?"

"Oh, I..." She's caught off guard, I can tell by the way she's pushing away from him and fidgeting with the navy skirt of her sleek dress. She wants out.

That's enough for my liking.

I stalk back over to her and slide in alongside her, placing a hand firmly on her knee. "I've got her taken care of. Thanks for the offer, though. But she won't be needing that drink." I say it nicely, with a forced smile, but there's a slight edge to the way I speak to the man. It's like I'm saying... *mine.*

His eyes just about bulge out of his head, and he quickly gets out of *my* seat. Maybe my scowl scared him off. "Shit. Sorry about that. Didn't realize she was with anyone."

Give me a break. He saw me. He must've seen me with her; he just wanted to take what isn't his. She's not mine, but I suddenly have this possessive compulsion to make her mine, to at least show him she's taken.

When he sees I'm not moving my hand, he gets the message and backs away, another apology slipping from his mouth. I don't move my hand, not until she glances down and stares at it.

I slowly remove it and settle back into my original seat, but I let my knee knock back against hers like it was just a few minutes ago.

"See? Stunning, just like I said," I confirm with an easy smile, suddenly relaxing now that I'm back in her space, breathing her lavender scent. "And as for me, I've had my eyes on you ever since you stepped foot through that door last weekend. You're gorgeous, sweetheart. An angel at best."

She laughs softly, and crimson coats her heated cheeks. "Sam, that's... Thank you. That's sweet. You didn't have to save me, though."

"I think I did, angel." The way she looks at me after I say it makes a lump form in my throat. Those are the softest blue eyes I've ever seen.

Time to test the waters.

"You're not seeing anyone, are you?" I ask hesitantly, like I'm afraid of what her answer might be.

"Me?" She laughs. "No, I'm not seeing anyone."

Knitting my eyebrows together tightly, I respond in a vague tone. "I'm surprised a girl as beautiful and sweet as you isn't taken."

"I'm not—" she starts, but the way I'm physically gritting my teeth stops her from going on with that sentence. She gives another sigh and starts again. "I stay busy and I don't go out much, so..." She shrugs apologetically. "What about you? Are you seeing anyone?"

I scoot to the edge of the barstool, letting the denim slide along the leather until I'm staring directly into her eyes. Close enough to smell the sweet scent that's dripping off the nape of her neck. I can almost taste it. "The only woman I'm seeing right now is the one sitting right in front of me."

Her sapphire eyes form into big marbles, and she sucks in a breath like she just got hit with bright headlights. "I have to..." She tries to get up, but I palace a heavy hand on the top of her thigh, halting her from running.

"Stay. Please," I whisper, begging with all my might. She stays like I ask, but there's something like fear hidden beneath her baby blues. What is she so afraid of?

I suddenly have this heightened need to do something, anything to make her stay. I don't want her to run away again, and I don't want her leaving without knowing she'll come back.

Wait. What am I saying? I don't do this, whatever *this* is. It's not a date. And frankly, I don't date anymore. Or, I haven't in a long time. But there's something so *different* about her. She's not boisterous or loud like most women around here; she's not even fond of attention. Most women who come into my club command it, but her? Violet's not like them. Not even a little bit. I like that. I like *her*.

Fuck. I like her.

Gulping down some of my anxiety, I quickly think of something. Whether this is a bad idea or the most catastrophic, idiotic thing I can manage, I *need* to try. Maybe she'll run away after all, but at least I can say I tried.

I want to... touch her, show her how good I could make her feel. I want her to see she's worth more than she might think. I want her to know she's worth *everything*. She's so bright and vibrant and shy as can be, and I just need to try this one little thing before she disappears from my club forever.

This is an awful idea. A horrendous nightmare that could all come crashing down. But what if it doesn't? What if this actually works?

Can I stand to watch her walk away, or do I risk it all for a chance on an angel who just happened to fly right into the palm of my hand?

Fuck it. I'm all in. Relationship or not, I want *her*.

I trace the edge of my thumb lightly over her smooth skin, dipping lower into the crevice of the inside of her thigh. Not too far up, but close enough to get her attention. Her breath falters, and it makes a smile float across my mouth. "Violet," I say slowly, tracing every syllable with the edge of my thumb, engraving it into her soft skin.

She gasps as I continue my leisure strokes, but I don't dare stop. "What happens if I stay?" she whispers almost mutely.

"Why don't you find out?" I give her my best devious smirk and watch her silently fall apart in the palm of my hand. She's right where I want her to be.

"You make me nervous..." she falters as she lets her hand drop to her thigh, right where I'm tracing perfect circles.

"A good nervous or a bad nervous?" I chuckle, continuing the slow motions over her upper thigh.

Another lungful of air leaves her lips, and I know I've got her sweating now. "Maybe both," she confesses.

Right where I want her, between nervous and turned on. That's *exactly* where she's sitting.

"Not trying to make you nervous." I laugh. "Unless you're into that." I cock a thick brow up and watch her take a large gulp from her glass.

Nervous little thing.

"What do you mean?" she quivers after she takes another generous amount from the coconut-flavored drink.

I stop the lazy movements of my thumb and rest my hand atop her thigh, feeling the heat from her skin sink into mine. "I'm gonna go out on a limb here and ask something that may sound a little strange."

"Try me," she challenges timidly. And God, I want to take her up on that offer right fucking now.

I dart my tongue across the bottom of my lip, and her big, wide eyes track my every single movement. "When's the last time a man took the time to make you feel good?"

"What?" she chokes out. That only makes my smirk widen.

"The question was simple, sweetheart," I state, letting my hand roam higher, just enough to rest beneath her short skirt.

She sucks in a breath, watching as I tempt fate. "Um. I don't know. I... I'm not sure." She seems a bit frazzled at the moment, but I think I know why.

"Do you *want* to feel good?" I drawl out, letting my words fall effortlessly from my lips. She still hasn't taken her eyes off me.

"I... I..." Her words fail her once again. She's too distracted by my wandering hand that's climbing up her creamy thigh.

She feels so fucking good.

"What would you say if I told you I wanted to do that for you?" I pin her with a smoldering stare, my eyes alight with flames that want to burn for her. And there's no missing the heat that's flaring right back into those pools of blue.

Good fucking girl.

"Sam..." she warns with fiery red lips.

"Violet," I taunt, fixing her with a mischievous grin.

"What exactly are you asking?" she voices meekly.

This is it. It's all or nothing. One night. Give me *one* night.

I lean forward, letting my lips linger against the shell of her ear, then I blow softly and whisper, "You wanna follow me to the back hall?"

"For *what?*" She's so flustered, I fucking love it.

Lingering by the side of her face, I push back a strand of brunette hair, and I'm not quite prepared when that wave of lavender hits me. I suddenly want to drown in her scent, soak her up until she's all I can smell.

The longer I stay right here, practically on top of her, the faster my blood rushes through my veins. Forget the pop of champagne, forget the blaring pump of music on the dance floor, forget *everything* in this entire club except *her*. She's the only thing I can feel, hear, and smell now.

She's all I can see.

I chuckle and lean back, letting the back of my hand brush her cheek as I let it drop back to her thigh. Her breath stills with every motion I make. "Jesus, Violet. Isn't it obvious?"

Diamond eyes as wide as the moon stare blankly at me, and I know I've done my job well.

"Let me... indulge your needs," I whisper out, sliding my hand *up, up, up* until I'm hovering in dangerous territory.

There's no air left in her lungs, and the shade of her pretty cheeks is as red as her glistening lipstick. Whatever's going on in that pretty mind of hers is something swirling and spinning uncontrollably. Pretty soon all that pent-up energy is just going to pop like a helium-filled balloon. And when she does, I'm going to be the reason she bursts into flames.

Her shallow breath is shaky and unsteady, and I can see how badly she's trying to say no. But there's a glimmer burning in her eyes, shining like sparkling stars. I see it so clearly now. She secretly wants to say yes, and I hope she will, because I don't want to just make her see stars. I want her to *feel* like she's floating on top of entire galaxies.

The sweet scent of her is incredibly intoxicating, and don't get me started on the deep blue speckles scattered like glitter across her irises. She's a fucking vision, just like striking lightning.

My brain's all staticky and fuzzy, but that doesn't stop the need that's building in the pit of my core. The timer's up, no seconds left. This is it. Right here, right now will be my only chance. So I do what my brain is screaming at me to do. I ask her one more time.

"So, angel. What's it gonna be?"

CHAPTER NINE

VIOLET

"I ... I don't know..." I breathe out, my mind in complete shambles as his whiskey-breath swirls around me like fog.

My ears are ringing like bells, and my skin feels zapped with electricity. The crowded club is stifling, but the weight of his calloused palm that's inching incredibly slow up my thigh makes my skin feel like it's on fire. I can't concentrate on anything but the slow, Southern drawl of Sam's voice.

"Angel..."

He called me angel, asked if I wanted to go back into the hallway with him. That's a bad, bad idea, but why does it sound so enticing?

I'm treading into dangerous waters, but the way his smoldering eyes and devilish smirk tempt me drag me into deep black waves.

I shouldn't trust him or any man standing in this room, but the way Sam's looking at me has me melting into a puddle.

My mind tells me to say no, to run far, far away, but my heart says for me to stay.

Follow him. Take his hand and chase after him.

He leans in closer; the scent of his woodsy cologne making me completely dizzy. And when that deep, gravelly voice slips out, I nearly topple over. "I could make you feel *so* good, angel."

Give in, angel. Angel, angel, angel. That's all I hear. I need some fresh air; I *need* to get a hold of myself.

My fingers lock around the hem of my blue skirt, and my words are mixing like the blur of red lights. "I need a moment. Where's the bathroom?"

He nods his head to the closest hall. "Right down that hallway. First door on your left." His hand still lingers like fire on my skin, like he has no intention of removing it, and his brown eyes look like molten lava now.

Sliding off the barstool and away from his intense stare, I stand tall and feel his hand fall from my skin. I almost wish it was still there. Wasting no time, I bolt for the bathroom, paying no mind to anyone who stands in my way. I have to get out of here, out of the vicinity of *him* before I lose control.

Whatever booming song is playing over the speakers is all washed out. I push myself through an entanglement of bodies, not even apologizing when I dart right past a couple who's heavily making out by the spiral staircase, but I just keep moving.

Keep going, don't look back. I *can't* go back.

As I make a sharp turn into the dark hallway, I take notice of the dimly lit lights hanging like lanterns at the top of the jet-black walls. Ornate mirrors decorate the dark walls, their silver framing reflecting against the clear glass. It almost reminds me of *Phantom of the Opera,* the first time the Phantom takes Christine down to his lair. It's moody and elegant and incredibly jaw-dropping. Almost as captivating as Sam's eyes.

I push him down out of my thoughts and drag my silver heels across the slick marble flooring. As soon as I spot the glowing white cursive letters of the ladies restroom, I push through the door and try to catch my breath, stumbling as I go.

I gasp a sigh of relief when I'm inside, but oh my God, it's just as fancy as it is out there. Right by the door is a plush velvet couch with fairy lights twinkling across the rouge walls. Even the bathroom stalls are highlighted in flashy signs. White marble lines the sinks, and out of the corner of my eye, I spot a bright vanity in another small section across from the stalls.

A group of giddy women brush past me with glasses of champagne and wine in their hands, laughing amongst themselves as they head toward the vanity with a phone camera ready to go. It's suddenly too loud in here again.

I make my way toward the sink and lean my hands on the edge, ready to assess the damage that's been done. My eyes widen when I see how flushed my face is. *Have I looked like that all evening?*

No. Sam did that.

My stomach churns as heat slides over my body, making the beautiful space feel likea stifling sauna. I turn the faucet on and splash cold water on my face, praying that'll make the heat stop. But it doesn't. I'm still burning from the inside.

His sultry words slip back into my mind, and I'm suddenly a puddle once again. *I could make you feel good, angel. I could indulge your needs.*

The need to soothe the ache between my thighs is excruciating, and it's really hard not to focus on how much I *do* want Sam to fix that urge.

Let Sam take care of you, my conscious whispers.

No. I don't do this. I don't hook up with men, period. Not even ones with dark brown eyes and a Southern drawl that could put me on my back. I don't *want this*. But a part of me wants to push down all my fears and take a chance on him. Even the parts of me that are scared to death to get involved with any man ever again.

Taking a paper towel and patting my face dry, I start to pace back and forth, letting the click of my heels echo around the room, hoping this will be enough to dissipate the need that's making my blood rush like a raging river through my ears.

Five laps around the bathroom didn't do anything but stimulate my hunger for something *other* than food. This is useless. I just need to go home. It'd be so easy to slip out the front door and catch an Uber, pretend like I never came back here in the first place. I could just forget Sam and his stupid brown eyes. But I *can't.* He's burned like charcoal in the back of my mind now.

Another wave of desire hits me so hard I have to grab for the sink before I fall to my knees. I clamp my thighs together and squeeze my eyes shut, but that only starts the heated images in my mind—Sam kneeling in front of me, lifting one of my legs over his broad shoulder, sliding his calloused palm up my inner thigh, his tongue working slow circles between my legs...

I grit my teeth together in pain and stare at my flushed reflection in the wide mirror. My eyes are giant blue saucers, and I have a desperate desire to do something about this ache between my legs.

Let me take care of you, angel. His sultry voice floats through the abyss of my mind, and I can't ignore this deep desire any longer. I either have to get out of this club right now, or I need to let Sam fix the mess he started.

Pushing myself back from the sink with a huff, I strut over to the door and pause just as my hand lingers over the black handle. I close my eyes for a second and think really hard about what I want, letting the cogs spin out of control in my head. When I open my eyes, I take a deep breath and pull the open door, regretting my choice already.

My answer is Sam.

Barging straight out into the hallway, I stop cold when I see a tall, handsome figure leaning up against the wall with his arms crossed over his broad chest. When I stare into his glowing brown eyes that look like they could swallow me whole, I yelp under my breath.

It's Sam.

A drawn-out smirk slowly conjures over his plush mouth, making me want to retreat right back to the bathroom and away from his tempting brown eyes. "You decide what you want, angel?"

"I think so…" I whisper across the hallway, pretty sure I just made the walls themselves shiver.

He pushes himself off the wall and takes a step forward, just as I take one back. "There's two choices I see. You can either choose to stay, or you can leave. It's up to you; I'm not the one who gets to decide."

Blood rushes in my ears, curving my judgement for the worst. "What if I choose to leave?"

His face falls slightly, disappointment swirling through his eyes. His throat bobs when he says, "Then I'll just have to live with that."

I bite my lower lip nervously to ease the stupid question I'm about to ask. "What happens if I stay?" I whisper quietly.

His brown eyes flare with flames of hope, and the smirk that had fallen just seconds ago is curved right back on his pretty mouth. There's a hunger building in his eyes, one that might just eat me alive. "Well, if that's the case, then I have something in store that might just feed your appetite."

Gulping on nothing but fear and heightened need, I slowly take another step back out of his reach, but he follows my lead and takes a step closer to me. It's a game of tag, and he has every intention of catching me.

"I need your answer, Violet." He stalks toward me like a wolf on the prowl. Like he's ready to sink his teeth into my flesh, swallow me whole. He'd surely rip me apart like the Big Bad Wolf. He'd make me his Little Red Riding Hood, drape my red cloak around his broad shoulders while he feeds my desires. Need pulses through my core, a need I've never felt quite like this. Like I could just give in to the pleasure. I almost hope he'll devour me with that smirking mouth and those haunting brown eyes. Teeth and all.

Get yourself together, Violet. I don't do *this,* so why is my body begging him to?

"I… I…" Another step closer and then another, he pursues me like a cat chasing a mouse. I keep backing up down the dark hallway, scraping my heels along the slippery floor, watching as he hunts me with smoldering eyes.

"Speak up now, angel. Can't hear you over your erratic breathing." He smirks as he paces on, one step closer to catching me. My lungs ache with the need for oxygen, but all the air is sucked out the moment my back collides against the end of the wall. There's nowhere left to hide. I'm trapped.

One more step and he's caging me in, making my eyes blow wide. His large arms circle me, big hands skimming the sides of my hips. The musk of him is *everywhere*. Late summer nights, saltwater, smooth mahogany encasing the air. He smells like everything I desire.

"Sam," I pant out, grabbing the front of his button-up to get some leverage before my knees give out. Lust blisters through my body, sliding down my spine as heat resides between my thighs.

I shouldn't do this. Shouldn't listen to what my body is screaming for me to do. But the thought of him touching me is overbearing.

"Yes?" he asks breathily as his hand trails slowly up my thigh, teasing the end of my dress as he starts to climb higher. He stops before he goes further, clearly waiting for permission.

"Sam, I..." What's wrong with me? I can't even speak, too distracted by his calloused fingers tracing light circles over my heated skin.

"Cat got your tongue, angel?" he teases, his slow circles tantalizing and driving me completely wild. He leans in and brushes his lips over the shell of my ear, gently blowing as he whispers, "I can feel how badly you want this, Violet. The way your body responds to me." He slides his other hand over the small of my back and brings me closer to his body, making me gasp. "You're practically burning for me."

And he's not lying. I'm on fire for him.

The lilt of his silky voice places me in a dreamlike trance. His calloused fingers dancing across my skin make me tingle all over. He presses his leg between mine and starts slowly spreading them, making my breath come out in waves of need. "Sam..." I whisper, but he doesn't stop. He has no intention to.

"You know, there's a million ways to seduce a lady, angel. I could teach you so many things. Make you feel things you've never felt." He drifts his lips over the nape of my neck, causing me to audibly breathe out a moan of need.

"*Oh*?" I ask audibly, my own voice betraying me as I give in to his coaxing.

Run, leave. But I have no intention of leaving now. Not until Sam touches me. Fighting this need is like quicksand. All-consuming. Deadly. *Smothering.* I can't do anything but let it take me down.

My eyes close briefly as his warm palm skates over my skin, hovering *up, up, up* until he's right *there.* Teasing his hand against my inner thigh, he comes painfully close to gliding over my lace. "Is this what you want? You want this?" Taking his sweet time, he barely brushes over my clothed sex, teasing me in all the best possible ways.

I can't control myself anymore. I moan, telling him exactly how much I want this. "Mhm."

Touch me. Make me burn. Light me up like the stars that twinkle in the night sky.

"Say it, angel. Wanna hear you say it," he whispers, his lips tickling along the shell of my ear. Softly blowing against my skin, his warm breath makes me break.

"Yes, *yes*," I pant out. "Want you to show me."

"Say please," he teases, working slow circles against the top of my clit, making me stifle out a whine.

He presses harder, drawing pleasure from deep in my core. It makes me drag him closer, and I'm practically biting at the folded collar of his shirt. "Please, Sam. *Please*," I beg like a woman starved of pleasure.

"Good girl," he praises. My eyes blow wide at the meaning of the words.

Good girl. The praise, the low timbre of his voice, the jaw-dropping size of his hands.

This man's going to kill me.

As his hand starts to raise the bottom of my dress impossibly slow, the sudden realization hits that we could be seen. Anyone could walk back here and see what we're doing. We could get caught, kicked out, or even worse, banned.

I grab his wrist sharply and stop his movements momentarily, my voice shuddering with fear. "What if someone sees us? They'd..." My words are silenced by his hot breath blowing down the length of my neck.

"I promise you, no one's gonna see. It's too dark, and we're out of view. No one can stop what's happening, angel."

Angel. His voice sounds like a string quartet, full of bass and baritone, so gruff and heavy that I could get lost inside the music all night long. I fear he might be my new favorite song.

Flicking my eyes back and forth each way nervously over his shoulder, my body starts to relax when I only see darkness shrouded in the back of the hall. No one's down here. It's just me and Sam. I press the small of my back against the wall and let Sam take the lead again.

He chuckles as he leans in, removing my hand from his wrist as he continues his slow journey up my thighs. "See, no one's gonna know. It's just you and me, pretty girl. Just us, causing a little trouble." His lips clamp down teasingly on my neck, causing me to groan loudly into his ear.

"Sam..." I mewl as he swipes his thumb across my clothed folds, making my back arch for more.

Yes, yes. Give me more, Sam. I want more.

As if he can read my thoughts, he pushes the ruined lace to the side, exposing me completely to the cool air of the club. I shouldn't be doing this—letting an impossibly handsome man ruin me in the back of a club, but I don't care anymore. I've never felt desire so pent-up like this before. I *want* him to touch me. *Now.*

I suck in a breath when his digit swipes over me, collecting slick from my center. He doesn't even give me a moment to react until he's drawing painfully slow ministrations around my puffy clit. The room crackles and fizzles, and for a moment, I'm lost in a sea of bliss.

"Jesus Christ. You're so fucking wet, and I've barely touched you," he groans like he's enjoying this as much as I am.

"I—*Oh*." I get lost in the haze as he glides two fingers through my drenched folds, hooking them at just the right angle to hit that sweet, spongy spot that makes me see stars.

"Ahh. There it is. Right *here*," he purrs in my ear as he goes knuckles deep into my wetness, building the twinkling stars around my vision like I'm seeing fucking heaven. His thumb works tantalizing circles on my clit, drawing me to the pleasure point where I'm about to break.

"Fuck," I moan out as I grab the front of his cotton shirt, groaning into the nape of his neck, letting his soft scruff glide across my cheek as I hold on for dear life.

"That's right, angel. Let me hear you. Tell me how good I'm making you feel," he growls, driving my need to come right this very second.

"So—soooo. *Oh*. Good," I moan as my walls tighten around his thick fingers, sucking him in as I begin to break.

"That's a good fucking girl," he bites out as he works me through the first wave, his thumb drawing tight circles on my mound as I spill white-hot heat all over him.

It's like nothing I've experienced before. My ears ring, my spine singes with heat, pleasure courses through every single particle in my body. I feel like I'm floating. Dizzy and dazed. And my legs shake like they'll give out any minute.

Just as I'm about to topple over, he catches me and holds me up through the extreme wave of pleasure. "Whoa, easy there. Feel a little lightheaded?" He chuckles, one of his arms encircling my back to hold me against his strong chest.

"I'm okay," I choke out hoarsely. He smiles my way and slowly drags his fingers from my dripping hole. I mourn the loss of his thick fingers. It's like they were made just for me.

Quit thinking like that. This is a one-time thing. No more. But I want more. God, I want so much more.

A heated smirk slides over his plush mouth. His dark brown eyes are now blown out and completely black, making him look like the handsome devil he is. He slowly lifts his index and middle finger to his mouth, and what he does next has me losing my fucking mind.

Deliciously slow, he pops his digits into his mouth, seductively licking and cleaning the slick from his fingers. I gulp down saliva and stare wide-eyed at his gesture. If I was turned on before, I'm a fucking inferno now.

"God, you taste so fucking sweet, angel," he groans as he shifts his leg between my thighs, bending it just slightly as he cages his strong arms around me once again. I clearly smell the aroma of sweat, longing, and whiskey encompassing his tongue. It makes me breathless. Makes me wonder if he tastes as good as he smells. Makes me want to let him slip his tongue into my...

Oh, God. *Stop.* But I can't. My mind is spinning out of control.

His rough palms drag me out of spiraling thoughts, breaking me free of my blurry mind. "Now, angel. Gonna need you to do something for me." He lowers me down on his thigh, right in the middle of his pristine jeans. My slick covers the dark denim, and he fucking growls when he sees what a mess I'm making.

My brows knit together in question as one of his hands dips down to the small of my back. "What is it?" I whisper out. His hot breath blows across my face, making me stifle a moan in the back of my throat.

God, the things I would do to have his mouth on my neck again, sinking into my flesh until he brings me to my knees.

Lowering me down as far as I can go, he grabs my hips and brings my chest flush to his. His heart's beating as fast as mine. Just like galloping hooves colliding on sand, a stampede that's about to begin. He glares wickedly down at me with lust-blown eyes and a smirk that makes me weak in the knees. "I want you to ride me," he says, his voice gravelly and hot against my sweat-coated face.

I stare at him wildly, gawking at his words. "You want me to... ride you?" I vaguely ask.

He chuckles in amusement. "On my thigh. Want you to cover my jeans and make them all wet, gorgeous. Don't be shy now," he coaxes melodically, dragging my hips forward until I'm resting right smack in the middle of his muscular thigh.

"Oh," I breathe out as he slowly grinds my clit into the denim of his jeans, showing me exactly what he wants me to do. He lets his grip loosen around me, letting me set the pace at my own leisure.

I take a deep breath and drown out the noise of the club, only focusing on his ragged breath and my own staggered panting. Closing my eyes, I let myself go, digging deep into the erotic pleasure and ecstasy that's overtaken me like a drug. My clit drags against his rough material, making me lose myself all over to the intoxication of how good he feels against me. When he pulls me closer against him, my pussy catches against a wrinkle in his jeans, causing me to groan against the weight of him, digging my painted nails into the black material of his shirt.

There's nothing even remotely close for how incredibly mind-blowing this sensation is. It's like a splash of the most dangerous and tempting beverage I could ever down in one go. A shot of whiskey mixed with a sprinkle of Sam. Call it drunk on him—his touch, the deep timbre of his Southern drawl, the smirk he coats on filthy words.

He's my drug of choice for just this one night. Tonight, I'll drown in him.

Feeling the building pressure low in my fluttering stomach, another moan leaves my open lips. "There ya go. That's a good girl. Ride me just like that. You're doing so fucking good," he praises low in my ear, his tongue lapping against the most sensitive area on my neck, right by my collarbone.

"Sam," I whine, a desperate plea leaving my mouth as he drinks me down like his favorite brand of whiskey.

"That's it, angel. Take what you need." His soft lips kiss up my neck, trailing fire along with his wicked tongue.

Rubbing my puffy clit on the curve of his muscular thigh, I grind hard into him, hitting that certain sensitive spot again and again as I rut back and forth into him. Gripping the edge of his cotton shirt isn't enough, so I tug harder as my orgasm starts to build like a euphoric symphony. I swear I'm about to rip it clear off his tanned skin.

"Feels—*so good*," I choke out, words failing me once again. My breathing is ragged and shallow as he presses his tongue against the shell of my ear while he whispers dirty incantations, putting a spell clear over my body.

"Yeah? You like that, don't you? Dirty fucking girl." His low, gravelly voice feeding me praises as more slick runs down his jean-clad thigh.

I'm making a mess, but clearly, he gives no fucks. Neither do I. I want to paint his thigh, to make him as addicted to this as I am. I want him to remember how much he can make me come from just the low bravado of his deep voice. That alone will be my undoing until I forget his name.

I never want to forget his name, and I'm afraid I never will.

"Attagirl," he growls as one of his hands gently massages my lower back, his other resting firmly on my thigh as I take pleasure from him again and again.

I moan at the eager praise he's giving freely. This is so hot. *He's* so hot. And he's *so* good with his dreamy words. He could sweet talk me into the early hours of the morning if he wanted to. Just like this. Me on his lap, his thick fingers massaging me, telling me what a good girl I am.

He picks up on the pleasurable moans I'm breathing for him, chanting them like a prayer repeatedly just for him. "You like that, huh? Like being told how good of a girl you're being?" He smirks again, dragging his lips over my jaw as he leaks his entire scent all over me. I want to taste it, drink it down till I'm gone off him. Suffocate on his intoxicating scent as it spirals me into a pit of warmth.

"Yes, *yes*," I whine as he presses his thigh deeper into my center, feeding the waves of pleasure that keep knocking me off my feet.

Almost there. Almost, almost. So fucking close to breaking for him.

"Come on, angel," he coaxes seductively into my ear. "Be a good girl and come for me. Wanna see you coat my thigh with your sweet cum. *Stain me,*" he growls like a predator about to take his prey down in one gulp. Lowering his hands to my ass, he squeezes and rocks me forward, pressing the bulk of his thigh into the most sensitive spot of my clit, making me ride out the pleasure of my building point that's about to explode.

Dropping his soft lips against my neck, he sucks right above my collarbone. Right where it makes me lose control. I feel his smirk grow as a low groan reverberates from his mouth, taking his time to bite down, feeding his own desires with the chase of combined pleasure. He's getting off as much as I am, which is hot as hell and nothing like I've ever felt in my entire twenty-eight years on this Earth.

The blaring music and chanting crowd disappears from the hidden corridor of the hall, becoming muddled and distorted as I focus on what's right in front of me—the strong arms that grip and clench me down on his thigh, the dark eyes that envelop me like a thick blanket as I slide deeper and deeper into a dreamlike state. I can't hear anything, can't *feel* anything other than my ragged moans, Sam's labored breathing, the feel of his smooth denim against my throbbing bundle of nerves, the calloused fingers that tease me relentlessly, the hot breath that blows down my neck as he crowds my space.

It's just me and Sam; nothing else matters. Nothing else but this. Whatever *this* may be.

Jarring forward, I catch the edge of my clit on a wrinkle as it tugs, screaming at me to let go. *Let go, let go.* I can feel the white-hot heat take hold of my body, can feel it slowly, sensually sliding down my center as my insides flutter and clench around nothing. I'm about to come, about to release my heat all over him. And he knows. *He knows.*

"Don't be shy, angel. Let me have it. Come for *me,*" he growls dominantly, wrapping his big hands tightly around my waist as he pushes me down deep against the denim covering his thigh, pressing my throbbing bundle of nerves at just the right spot as I feel myself let go.

I flex my fingers into the collar of his shirt and squish my face into the crook of his neck as I come hard, feeling myself spill while I tense up over his leg. Unable to control myself, I throw an arm around the back of his neck and lace my fingers through his slicked back dark locks, holding on for dear life as I moan his name embarrassingly loud into the shell of his ear.

Hearing my breath hitch, he hums in approval. "That's it, sweetheart. Say my name. Just like that. What a good girl you are," he praises as he flexes his thick fingers around my thighs, rocking me gently to ease the orgasm, making sure to get every single ounce of release out of my dripping pussy.

I take a minute to come back down to Earth. Back to where I don't hear the endless ringing in my ears. Back to where I don't see the bright lights covering my vision anymore. He slowly lets his hands loosen around my waist, gently leaning me back against the jet-black wall as he slides me off his thigh. My breath hitches when he slides the ruined lace back into place, covering my overstimulated pussy. I wince as he brushes up against my sensitive clit and let him pull the edge of my navy-blue dress back over my shaking thighs.

He takes a careful step back, lets his heavy eyes rake over my body, assessing that I'm still in one piece. My legs wobble underneath me, and his hands are right back on my hips, steadying me just like his pools of caramel eyes seems to do for me. "You okay?" he asks once I'm back on steady legs, concerned eyes making me lose my breath all over again.

"Yeah. I'm... I'm good," I breathe out quietly, still trying to recover from two intense orgasms.

He takes a beat to look at me, mouth partly open and big brown eyes just staring like he's looking at an angel. But that's right, *I'm* an angel. *His* angel. At least that's what he keeps calling me. I'm starting to like the nickname, starting to get used to the idea that he could just keep chanting it like a prayer.

He's dangerous, tempting, a bad habit I could get used to. Not to mention, he's laced in trouble, bred to be a complete menace. But I just can't seem to find the will to care now. I want more, *need* more. I *want* more of him.

It's like he hears my exact thoughts. Maybe he wants more of me, too. He lifts my chin and brushes his calloused thumb against my puffy bottom lip, his dangerous brown eyes trailing down to the crimson color. He looks like he wants to sink his mouth down on them. Holding my breath, I shake the image of his whiskey lips on mine. I'm not ready for that, might not ever be truly ready for that again. So I let the enticing thoughts slip from my mind, making it float far, far away from my imagination.

He drops his thumb from my glittery bottom lip and trails it along the side of my jawline, like he's mapping out the lines of my face for his memory. "Your friends are probably looking for you," he murmurs in a low voice, disappointment coated in his words.

Oh, shit. Brianna and Taylor. I completely forgot about them. They've probably been trying to find me for more than half an hour. Not that I've noticed. I've been too busy having multiple orgasms with the hottest man in San Diego.

I swallow the longing to see him again and nod. "Yeah... I'm sure they are."

Lingering his softening gaze at me, a gentle smile tugs on his lips. One that's filled with hope and maybe a little yearning. I can't lie. It tugs at my heartstrings a little to see the lighter flecks of brown glisten in his pretty eyes. Eyes that just might haunt me when I leave this club tonight.

He brushes the back of his knuckles over my cheek, a gentle caress that'll linger like permanent ink. Something painful tugs in my chest, but I kick the feeling down.

Don't go there, Violet, I warn myself. But again, against my best judgement, I set my subconscious aside for the night.

Slowly fishing a shiny card out of his back pocket, he takes my hand and slides it into my palm, gently closing my fingers over it as he retrieves his warm, calloused fingers from mine. He hesitates a beat before taking a step back, then he gives me a heart-clenching grin and pulls me in yet again with those syrupy brown eyes. They seem to take my breath away.

Giving me one more once-over, he steps forward until his lips are caressing my ear, making my breath catch. "Come back to me, angel," he whispers softly into my ear, his melodic voice floating through my body, making my knees weak and my head a little dizzy.

When he steps back out of bounds, his calloused fingers dance down my arm, creating goose bumps all across my skin. Before he lets his arm drop, he catches my hand and brings it to his lips, leaving me with a parting kiss that has me swooning as his big brown eyes serenade me. His lips are warm, pillowy, featherlike, and oddly, I feel loss when they leave the back of my hand. He pins me with one more soft smile, then he turns on his heel and walks away from me, his pace slow and steady as he leaves the vicinity of my space.

Pressing my back against the wall to hold myself up, I stare at his broad shoulders, mapping out how many steps it takes him to disappear into the sea of people that seem miles away from where I'm standing. Leaning my head back, I play on repeat what just took place over the last hour or longer. Tracking time with Sam is like trying to count the cracks in the floor—impossible and not attainable. I could get lost in this club with him again, spend a little time exploring him, maybe...

Cursing under my breath, I whisper, "What did you get yourself into, Violet?" He's going to be stuck in my head like a song on repeat. A song I can't stop playing. Like a scratched record in a player, his name will be etched in my mind for all of time.

Opening my eyes, I let a sigh escape my lips. Almost forgetting the card in my palm, I cautiously uncurl my fingers and run them along the edge of the glossy red business card. As I turn it over and read the cursive letters, I freeze. I read it once, twice, three times, but it just makes my eyes widen more and more each time. Reading it once more, I make sure my eyes aren't deceiving me in this dim lightning. Digesting the words slipping off the card, I choke on the sudden realization that my eyes are not playing tricks on me. The shiny black letters printed on the card come back the same each time I read it over.

Club Inferno
Sam Brooks
Owner

I'm completely breathless as my eyes glaze over his phone number printed in tiny numbers under his full name.

Holy shit. Sam *owns* this club? And does he have a brother?

Oh no. No, no, no, no. This is bad, *so* bad. I'm in so much fucking trouble. I just... Oh my God. The *owner* of the club just got me off in *his* club. *This* is how I find out he owns the biggest fucking club in downtown San Diego?

Taking a deep breath, I rest my head back against the cold wall and try to get a hold of myself as I rethink everything that went down tonight. The drinks, the conversation about books, the relentless flirting, the fucking part where he made me come twice in a row!

I close my eyes tightly and try to swallow down my orgasmic highs from minutes ago, concentrating on nice, deep breaths. When I slowly open my eyes back to the dimly lit hallway, I try to come to terms with myself, but I just *can't.*

I've never had a man make me feel so bold and sexy before in my life. And the way he was all about what made me feel good? Well, it was exhilarating, to say the least. When has a man been like that with me before? Never.

Flexing my fingers into tight fists, I pull myself together and push myself off the wall, fighting every single particle in me that wants to come back. I need to breathe, need to push the thought of Sam Brooks and his fucking brown eyes out of my system. But once I slip into a sea of strangers out in the open crowd, my heart suddenly aches for him to take my hand and lead me to safety. The safety of his strong arms and big brown eyes...

Fuck. He's going to be the bane of my existence, isn't he?

CHAPTER TEN

VIOLET

"Y ou did *what* with the OWNER?!" Brianna screeches from the top of her lungs in the front seat, making me cover my ears from the high-pitched squeal that threatens to blow my eardrums out.

"Bri, oh my God. Take it down a notch, will you?" I bite out harshly.

"Wait, wait, wait," Taylor halts me, slapping me on the back of the shoulder while she shrieks in my ear. "You're telling me that *you* went to the back of the hall with the owner of the club and fucking rode his thigh?!"

Rolling my eyes into the back of my head, I groan and lean against the passenger window. I already regret letting them in on my dirty little secret. "I... Yes. That's what happened," I answer truthfully.

"Violet Skye Emery!" Taylor screams over the thrum of the stereo.

Ugh. I hate it when she uses my full name.

"What!" I throw my over-the-shoulder Coach bag to the floor with a thud and press my heel firmly into the rubber mat under my feet.

"Don't *what* us!" Brianna laughs. "I have a right to be excited. You let that sexy brown-eyed man make you come on his thigh. Now *that* is worth talking about." She curls her sparkly pink lips up into a smug grin and flips her tight blonde curls over her bare shoulder, her mini neon green dress almost bursting at the seams.

"And don't forget how he finger-fucked you!" Taylor chimes in from the back.

I groan and cover my eyes, deeply regretting this entire night. "I knew I shouldn't have said anything." I shake my head in annoyance and let my eyes watch the bursts of light coming from the busy city streets. Instead of listening to Brianna, I drift off and try to count every Porsche I see drift by us.

"This is so exciting! Vi, I'm so proud of you!" Taylor beams from the middle of the seat, her big red hair tied in a messy bun with dark ruby lipstick to match.

Turning my head back in the direction toward my friends, I sigh. "It's not like I won a medal or anything." No. I just had the sudden urge to give in to Sam's deep drawl and his stupid brown eyes.

What even gave me the impression that it was remotely okay to slip away with him in the first place? And why do I crave more?

Taylor takes me away from my undecided thoughts. "Are you going to see him again?"

I think hard about that, conjuring up a hundred different reasons why I shouldn't. But I can't ignore that nagging little voice clawing on the inside of my ear, telling me that I do want to see him again. But again, I can think of more than enough reasons to say no.

"I... I'm not sure," I whisper, hesitating with every word. It was just a one-time thing. It meant nothing. Absolutely nothing. At least that's what I keep telling myself.

"Come on, babe," Brianna whines out. "You have to! Don't you want to see him again?"

Want to? Yes. Will I? I don't think so.

Taylor snickers my way and winks a sparkly eyelid at me. "Maybe next time make him put his cock in your—"

"Taylor!" I gasp, my jaw dropping as I shove her back into her white leather seat.

"What?!" She snorts out a laugh and kicks the back of her five-inch heels into the bottom of my seat.

Ouch.

"Can we just stop talking about it now?" I fold my arms over my chest and pout my bottom lip out, praying to the high heavens that I get back home in under fifteen minutes so I can put this conversation to rest.

"Not a chance." Brianna smirks, inhaling on the end of her dark blue vape that has swirls of black sparkles encircling the deadly contraption. She blows out a puff of smoke my way and lets the fake cherry flavor evaporate up through my airways.

I hack up a cough and fan away the smoke, rolling down the window to get some air in the now stuffy car. "Ugh. Give me that." I glare and snatch the vape away from her in a hurry, making sure it's out of her grasp, I tuck it under the back of my leg to drive home a point.

"Hey, I was using that!" She claws for her precious vape with a row of sharp, glittery red nails, but I bat her hand away.

"Nu-uh," I tsk. "Don't you know smoking's bad for you?"

She gives me the petty middle finger and steps on the gas pedal just as she's about to miss the yellow light. "Yeah. Well, a few puffs isn't going to hurt anything. Gee, what's got your panties in a twist, you grump?"

"Hmm. I wonder. What do you think?" I give them both my best annoyed glare. My lips in a tight line, eyebrows knit, and narrowed eyes that could kill.

Brianna rolls her eyes and pulls a smile on her lips while she coasts along Fifth Avenue. "How was it, really?"

I pause the music with the pad of my thumb and sigh, letting the turn of the tires reel my mind back to Club Inferno. "It was..." Trailing off, my head goes fuzzy as I think about those big meaty hands all over me.

"Well, go on. Be honest." Taylor giggles from the back of the car, waiting for me to speak up.

Finally, I give in to the question and answer honestly. I've got nothing to lose. "It was—incredible. His fingers. They were so... *big*. And the way he stretched me. It—" I stop myself from going on, but they both just look at me with wide eyes and open mouths. *Great.* "What?" I ask with a little bite to my voice.

"You're definitely seeing him again." Brianna giggles like a high school girl talking to her crush for the first time. They really need to tone it down. I'm not in the mood for this.

"I don't know, guys." My voice drops an octave as I lean back into the leather seat, letting the cold material distract me from what I'm trying very hard not to think about. *Sam.*

"You should see how red your cheeks are. You fucking like him!" Taylor shouts in accusation as she points out the color of my cheeks. I groan and bat her hand away.

But that's it. That's what I'm afraid of... liking him.

"I don't like him," I try to counter, but the shakiness of my voice gives me away.

"Liar," Brianna taunts. "You little slut," she teases.

Great, now I'm a liar and a slut. Perfect.

"I'm not seeing him again," I press, setting my jaw into a grimace as I watch the fog from the ocean cover the townhouses in the near distance.

"The hell you aren't!" Brianna yells into my ear, causing a painful static to rumble down my eardrum. "Babe, he gave you *two* orgasms and asked for nothing in return. Guys don't do that, like, ever. Don't let him pass you up."

I turn her response over in my head, questioning the truth of her words. But the more I think about it, the more I realize she's right. Guys *don't* do that. But he did. *Sam* did.

"Go see him again." Taylor smiles while pressing lightly against my shoulder. "He asked you to come back."

Come back to me, angel. I still hear that low, breathy sentence that made goose bumps glide down my skin. Still feel his breath, hot and shaky down the base of my neck. I scratch at the back of my neck to make that little itch stop, but it doesn't. Instead, the printed business card inside the palm of my free hand is burning a hole through my skin, lighting flames to fuel the desire to pull out my phone and send him a text.

No. I'm putting a stop to this right fucking now.

"But I don't do *this*!" I wave my hands dramatically and kick my heel into the floorboard, sighing heavily as I collapse back into the passenger seat.

"Do what, exactly?" Taylor asks over the rumble of the engine.

"Whatever I just did…" I whisper out quietly.

What *did* I just do?

"Just think about it. You've got his number. Maybe you should just give it a couple days and call him. You know he wants you to." Brianna gives me an encouraging smile, but I let it pass me by.

I stare out into the black night sky, faint stars twinkling overhead, the salty ocean breeze permeating through the fresh air outside. Closing my eyes tightly, I try to clear my mind, but Sam's right back in my line of sight. Big brown eyes and all.

Ugh. What mess did I just get myself into?

Chapter Eleven

Sam

The lit-up laptop screen flickers in front of me, my vision going in and out as my mind blurs the numbers together. My index finger taps on the Enter key sluggishly, which makes me backtrack to hit Delete. Again. It goes on like that for minutes. Fuck, maybe an hour. I don't know anymore. Running payroll shouldn't be this challenging, but my mind is mush at the moment.

I sigh and drag my palm across my mouth, instantly regretting it when the lush scent of *her* trickles through my nostrils. I smell her *everywhere*. Sugary vanilla perfume sticking to my cotton shirt, the lilac scent of her spiral curls peppering all down my scruff, and the delicious pheromones of her arousal still coating my fingers. Her scent is fucking intoxicating.

My left hand drops to my thigh slowly, fingers tracking over the wet denim that's now stained with her slick. Fuck. Now I'm thinking back to how I had my digits buried deep inside her, how I made her moan my name like a sweet siren's song, how she rode my thigh until my vision was nearly black.

Pressing pause on the erratic thoughts, I reel back the reins and control myself before I lose all my self-control. Groaning, I fall back into the leather of my office chair, pushing all thoughts aside of the blue-eyed beauty I had caged against my body.

Before I exit entirely out of the payroll I've spent way too long on, a deep voice clears in front of me. "Having trouble there?"

I jump so high I almost knock the hot cup of coffee and laptop clear off the side of the mahogany table. "Jesus, Bryson! You scared the shit out of me. How long have you been standing there?"

He chuckles and pushes himself off the edge of the doorway, making his way over to the side of my chair. "Long enough to see you can't hit a simple button." With one scan of his hazel eyes over the open sheet, he slides the mouse from under my hand and pushes process on the screen. "There. Payroll's all done now."

Giving him a weighted sigh, I say, "What would I do without you?"

He props himself up on the side of the dark stained mahogany table. "I don't know. Not a whole lot it seems." Pining me with a mischievous smirk, he asks, "So, care to tell me what's got you all distracted?" He says the last word with a little seduction in his voice, making my eyes roll to the back of my head with annoyance.

I put on a stony expression and lie straight through my teeth. "I'm not distracted." The click of his tongue tells me I've been caught red handed.

"That why you've been mindlessly staring at numbers on the screen, deleting shit, and having to go back to fix it?" He pushes the sleek black mouse clear out of my reach and folds the laptop closed so I have to look him in the eye. He's not going to give up till I tell him. Shit.

Groaning, I press the heel of my palms into the side of my temples and push the wheels of my chair back. "Give me a break, Bryson. I'm tired, and it's one o'clock in the morning."

He gives me a husky laugh and shakes his head in disbelief. "Who was the girl?"

My heart pauses in my chest as I try to push down thoughts of Violet's ocean-blue eyes, but it doesn't work.

"I don't know what you're talking about," I murmur, hoping he'll drop the subject entirely. But I know my brother, and he doesn't stop till he gets exactly what he wants. He's stubborn and driven like that, just like my father.

He shoves me hard in the shoulder and scoffs. "Don't play with me, brother. I saw you at the bar with her. Fuck, man. I haven't seen you smile like that since… Since…" His voice trails off, and he doesn't pay any mind to finish that sentence.

Lois. That's who he meant to say. Back when I thought I was marrying the love of my life…

I drop my head and sigh, all thoughts of Lois disappearing when Violet's name leaves my lips. "Her name's Violet."

Bryson crinkles his bright eyes and smiles. "Violet, huh? Pretty name. Didn't know you had a thing for brunettes." He waggles his thick eyebrows and shoots me a wink.

Letting a laugh go, I exhale and stare across the room at a blank spot on the shiny black walls, just below where AC/DC's *Back in Black* framed album hangs. "Well, guess I didn't, either."

He nudges my knee with the bottom of his polished shoe and flashes me another smirk. "Where'd you two disappear to?"

"Nowhere," I say firmly while I catch his ankle and push him away from my space. He's already invaded far too much of it tonight. He wasn't even supposed to know about Violet.

"Bullshit," he spouts off, calling me out on my failed attempt of steering him away. "You practically sprinted after her down the hall. I saw!"

Goddamn it.

Throwing my hands up in defeat, I give up. "Fine. You caught me. Happy?"

He gives me a wicked grin and nods. "Very, because I have a good idea what you were doing." The heat in the light green of his eyes is malicious and filled with trouble.

"I…" Trying to drive him away from *that* subject, I come up with nothing but my own dry mouth that's parched from words.

"Look at you, all tongue tied," he smiles. "Good for you, Sammy. I'm happy for you. I hope she treats you better than Lois did." There it is. The name that drives a stake further into my heart, spreading splinters and cuts all up and down the entirety of my chest.

My jaw locks into place as I push the hurt down. "Don't mix the two together, Bryson. Violet is *not* her," I grit out through clenched teeth.

"No, she sure as hell ain't." He shoves his hands into the pockets of his black slacks and gazes through now serious hazel eyes. "You gonna see her again?"

I pick apart his words, repeating them over a second time as I contemplate what I'll say. Of course I want to see her again. I can't get her sparkling blue eyes or her scent out of my mind. It's as if she's cast a spell over me with her soft, lilty voice. A voice that sounds angelic.

I muddle out another sigh and slick a hand back through my locks. "I gave her my card. Said to call if she needed anything."

His eyebrows shoot up at that. "Ah, hell. She's got you wrapped around her pretty little finger, doesn't she?"

I slap his knee away from my leg and frown, warning him to quit. "Will you just stop? It was a one-time thing."

But do I really want it to be a one-time thing? No, I fucking don't. But he doesn't need to know that.

"Oh?" He purses his lips and taps the end of the table with his nails. "Is that why you gave her your card?"

"I..." Drawing out a blank, I card a hand through my hair and kick the side of my sturdy desk, knocking over a cup of black ink pens while I'm at it. Perfect.

Bryson stares at me a minute with prying eyes, his fingers tapping impatiently on his thigh, jaw ticking up before he decides to strike again. "What are you doing here, Sammy?"

What am I doing? Hell if I know. I wasn't supposed to drag her down the end of the hall. Wasn't supposed to crowd her body and cage her in while I made her moan into my ear. There's just something about her that drew me to her like a moth to a flame, and I didn't want that flame to die before I got a hold of her.

"Shit. I don't know, Bryson," I groan, dragging my hand slowly over the entirety of my face.

"That's alright. You'll figure it out. I'm just happy you're starting to get back out there. You know, since you keep turning down Chelsea and all." He winks my way, teasing me about the blonde, but I don't bite.

"For the last time, I'm not into her like that," I spit, slitting my eyes as I send a glare his way. He apparently does not get the hint.

"Oh, but the brunette's got your attention?"

I shake my head, frustration clear in my tone. "Just cut me some slack, please? Jesus."

Jumping off the edge of my office table, he slaps me on the back and makes his way slowly over to the wide double doors that are coated in black paint. "I'm just giving you a hard time. What are big brothers for, right?"

"Right." I scratch a hand over my scruff and blow out a breath exaggeratedly, throwing him a smile for good measure.

Before he walks out, he turns back toward me and says with a grin, "One more thing." I fight to not roll my eyes. "What are you planning to do if she calls?"

I clasp a heavy hand around the leather armrest, mentally tossing back and forth what I will do. Would I stir the pot, have her come back for more, take her out?

No. I'm not dating. I *don't* date. But maybe I should. Maybe I *want* to take her out. Or maybe I just want to make her orgasm with my fingers again.

Fuck.

"I'll cross that bridge if it happens," I say with clenched teeth.

"*When* it happens," he corrects. With another chuckle, he smiles. "Night, Sammy. Try not to dream about Violet too much. And maybe let me do payroll next time." Then he's walking out, letting the door close gently behind him. His words seem to echo around the dimly lit space.

Try not to dream of Violet too much.

Well, it's too late for that. She's already stuck in my brain on repeat.

After I get back home from a long shift at the club, I throw the truck keys on the kitchen island and make my way up the creaky stairs, careful not to be too loud so I don't wake Kayla. Family photos of me, Kayla, and Kelsey line the cream-colored walls. Some include Bryson, my mom and dad, even one of my grandparents. None of them include Lois. Not a single damn one.

She never made an effort to be a part of my family after the wedding; that's why she's a ghost in all the photos. Nonexistent. A mere phantom in the vicinity of my life. Pain shoots through my chest from the thought of her, but I keep climbing, pushing her far out of reach of my thoughts.

When I get to the top, I slide around the corner and peek into the first door on the right. The one that's ajar just enough for me to see into. Leaning my head in, I see Kayla's long chestnut locks thrown over her silky pink pillow with her fuzzy white blanket tucked underneath her chin. Fluorescent stars sparkle across the ceiling as her galaxy night light spins in a slow circle. And just when I think I've woken her, she blows a deep breath out and tosses in her sleep, but she stills again right after.

I stand there a minute in the archway of her door, wishing I could keep her this age forever. But in the blink of an eye, she'll be getting her permit, then her license, driving off to college, following her dream to be a veterinarian, saving as many animals as she can. And then it'll just be me in this big, empty house. Alone. My heart clenches at the thought.

I wish I could freeze time, maybe go back to when I got to take my girls to Disneyland for the first time when we moved here. I'll never forget that day or their cheery, bright faces with wide-eyed stares. That will probably go down as my most favorite memory with them. At least, for now. We still have so many memories to make.

Being a father was always something I wanted; it was more like a dream. I just never thought I'd have to do it alone. I didn't sign up for that, but that's what I got. Unfortunately, till death do us part and the promise to raise our children together fell through the cracks with Lois. But wallowing over something that was broken long ago is no use. I did my part, and there's not a second I regret having my beautiful daughters.

Gently closing the door, I whisper out, "Night, kiddo."

Turning on my heel, I tiptoe two doors down and sneak into my room, letting my body collapse into the navy bedspread. As I fall onto my back and pull my phone from my pocket, I see one missed text chime on the screen. My heart pounds at the thought of Violet texting, but my hopes are suddenly crushed when I see it's only Lois.

I sigh out and rake a hand roughly through my hair, throwing my phone over so I can't see her name burning into the whites of my eyes. The woman has no ounce of personal space or respect. Does she not get it? I just want her to leave me alone.

For the love of God, just give me peace. That's all I want. To be able to live without her breathing down my neck every couple of days. Funny how someone can still ruin your life from thousands of miles away after ten years. She just doesn't stop.

Rolling onto my side, I close my eyes and turn the negative thoughts off, pausing the ache in my chest that still burns every time she tries to snake her way back into my life. She needs to learn to let go, just like I do. The girls don't want her. *I* don't want her. What doesn't she get about that?

But then again, it was never about wanting me. She never really wanted me, just like she didn't want my girls. So why do I still feel so heartbroken over the whole situation? Maybe one day I won't be. Maybe someday, someone will love me like I loved Lois once upon a time.

CHAPTER TWELVE

VIOLET

My mind is in shambles the next day at work. All thoughts muddled and disorganized. Forget concentration. The only thing I'm actually remotely fixated on right now is the memory of those smoldering brown eyes. And maybe the way his thick fingers worked inside me, curling up impossibly deep to hit that sweet spot that made me see stars.

Yep. And there I go. Again. Back to thinking of that incredible night at Club Inferno with the hottest club owner who exists in California. Not that I go to clubs often. I don't. At least, not in the last few years. Clubs usually trigger me, but oddly enough I find myself wanting to go back.

I mindlessly turn the flashy card over in my palm. Memorizing his phone number, etching his name into the depths of my mind, reading the letters over and over until the silhouette of his towering body is burned into the back of my brain.

As I continue to twirl the card on my thigh, I think of those lust-blown eyes, that ragged panting noise he made as he blew against the shell of my ear, the way those big digits felt curled up inside me, the way he called me a good girl and told me how well I was taking him.

The lewd images in my mind make warmth pool between my thighs; beads of sweat coat my forehead. My throat is tight from the way I'm trying to push down a held-in breath.

Get it together. You're at work.

Slipping the business card back inside the front pocket of my light blue jeans before I get myself in trouble, I try to focus on something else. Anything at all that'll distract me from pulling out my phone and typing his digits into my contacts. Paperwork, reorganizing shelves, cataloging, wondering how big his...

Stop. Don't do it.

I fall against the back of the leather chair with a huff and tap impatiently on the edge of the white matte desk, watching one of my co-workers take a stack of books back to where they belong in the library. Instead of answering emails or working on my outreach program for the nearby public schools, I'm basically useless. No matter how hard I try, I can't get Sam Brooks out of my head or his fucking devilish smirk. I'm royally fucked.

After another few minutes of toying with my bottom lip and trying to keep the heat from rising in my cheeks, I feel his business card burn me through the thin fabric, coaxing me to take the plunge and jump. I run my thumb across the smooth edge, playing with fire the longer it stays in my grasp. Will I get away scot-free, or will it scald me just like his warm skin branded me?

Clicking the laptop screen to life, I decide I *do* want to play with fire. They always said curiosity killed the cat. Might as well take my curiosity all the way then. Not like I haven't already sealed my fate.

When I open up a browser, I quickly type in Club Inferno and hold my breath as I press the search button. It doesn't take long until I click the first link and watch shades of dark crimson paint the screen. My eyes scan the page, sweeping across five-star reviews of how successful the club has been in the past year.

Has it really been open an entire year without me knowing? The most successful nightclub in San Diego and I had no idea? But again, I've been a hermit, always turning down Bri and Taylor's offers to go out. This year is the first time I've actually ventured out and tried to actually have fun. And look what happened. I met *him*.

I stop all movements of the mouse the moment those dark brown eyes appear on the screen. There he is. Slicked back sandy locks pushed back to perfection, a tailored black suit that molds like clay around his broad muscles, that same devilish smirk curling across his plush lips. He looks so fucking good. As good as the night I met him.

I flick to another picture and another and another until my eyes cross. One of Sam standing next to a tall man with blond hair. The next one he's behind the bar, smirking up at the camera. Another one is with his big hands wrapped around the back of a black chair, looking all enticing and sexy. Every single picture looks better than the previous. How's that even possible? How can a man be *this* good looking? And how is he making butterflies flit through the bottom of my stomach like I can't even control myself? He's just a man. A man who's had his fingers curled inside me. A man who's called me a good girl. A man who makes me want *more*.

More of his fingers, more of his praise, just more of *him*. I don't exactly know what that means, but God do I want to find out. And that in itself fucking terrifies me.

I keep digging through every link I can find, sweat coating my skin every time his smoldering eyes lock with mine. It's like I'm back in that dark hallway all over again—my thighs burning from the flooding heat in my core, my throat dry as his warm breath dances across my neck, his thick fingers dragging over my skin as he whispers filthy words meant just for me.

I'm so lost in the haze of that night and the heat rushing between my thighs that I completely miss Janet calling my name. "Violet!" she hisses. I gasp and snap the laptop closed, covering my tracks from being caught red handed.

I look up wide-eyed and spacey as I take in her thick glasses and beady gray eyes that are narrowed into thin slits. Gulping, I brush off a bead of sweat on my forehead. "Yes?" My voice comes out like a squeak.

"Please tell me you finished that catalog of the fantasy section." Her thin finger taps impatiently against the back of the book that's pressed against her chest, and her short dark bob with silver strands curls against the side of her ears.

Giving her an impish smile, I shake my head. "Not quite."

She shakes her head in disappointment and frowns, making me feel a little smaller in the desk chair I'm glued to. "What's gotten into you this week? You seem a little distracted."

Distracted? You can say that again. With work? Not so much. But she doesn't need to know I'm practically drooling over a handsome nightclub owner who has magical fingers.

"Just a little tired," I lie.

"Mhm." She turns her nose up and pushes her glasses up to get a better look at me. "Well, make yourself useful and come help me with this stack of books. Since you can't seem to finish one simple, little task."

Rolling my eyes, I push the seat back and stand up, quick to grab some of the overflowing books in the black cart she's been wheeling around all day. I get to work stacking while she scoffs and bumps my shoulder unapologetically.

I have to laugh because she's always so grumpy; in a grandmotherly sort of way who disapproves of whatever ridiculous trend the kids have going on nowadays. Most days she gets on my case and irritates the crap out of me, but some days I just smile and throw a joke or two her way. It's oddly comforting working with her. Even though she tells me all the time I need to be sharper and more focused, she has her moments where she'll give me a gentle smile and act like I'm her favorite co-worker. Sometimes she'll even bake me chocolate chip cookies if I ask nicely.

Besides, she was there when I could hardly pick myself up from the floor. And for that, I'm eternally grateful.

Getting to work on stacking books on the labeled mahogany shelves, I leave my thoughts of dark brown eyes and painted black walls back at my laptop. For now, I need to focus on anything but Sam fucking Brooks and his experienced fingers that I desperately want inside me again.

"Take a deep breath. Listen. Focus. Relax." Jenna's collected words float through my ears, sending me into a relaxed state as I lie flat on the leather coach.

Drawing in a deep breath, I slowly release it and let my mind take me deeper into the abyss of the past. Hypnosis is a technique Jenna's been trying with me to get me to heal from my past anxiety and PTSD. Or at least try my best to come face to face with it. It's been a struggle, I'll just say that. Absolutely nothing makes me want to relive that scene ever again. But it's always there stirring in the back of my nightmares, haunting me till it drags me back down again.

"Slowly let your mind wander back to that cold, rainy night. Back to the living room where it all started," she says, her voice a little further away now. "I want you to envision a glass bottle. Focus on the size, how it feels against your palm, how solid it is."

Flexing my fingers into the sides of my thighs, I draw in a shaky breath and focus on the tick of the metronome, letting the pendulum pull me into a deeper trance. The room is blanketed in darkness, only the crack of thunder and the single cylindrical beer bottle sits ahead of me while I stand there wide-eyed and afraid. Sweat beads along my forehead, and my breathing becomes shallow the moment my fingers reach out and grasp the thick, cold base of the glass.

"Breathe, Violet. Just breathe. It can't hurt you. It's not real," she says in a direct tone, adamant that I listen to her. But I'm not listening. I can't when it's right there, taunting me with its sharp glass and sloshing liquid.

I hold the object in my hand loosely behind my closed lids, pretending it's not a poisonous snake that'll sink its venomous fangs into my wrist like that faded scar that prickles and stings my skin every time I think about that horrible night that happened a few years ago. It's not real. *This* is not real; it's only an illusion.

"It *feels* real," I grit out through bared teeth, my palms pressing deeper into the leather of the couch until I'm pretty sure I might rip holes right through the fabric at any moment.

Darkness swirls around me; my stomach churns as the bottle pulsates in my hand, terror lighting my skin ablaze the longer I stay under this thick fog of an illusion.

You're okay, Violet, I think to myself. *He's not here. He can't hurt you anymore. He's locked up tight.*

Pain flares in my wrist, tethering my fate to the half-empty bottle of alcohol that shakes in my hold. I'm about to drop it, about to watch the glass crack and shatter like I did so many months ago. But before I lose control and watch it cut my skin apart, Jenna's voice fills the room.

"Picture the glass as another object. Something that brings you peace. Maybe your favorite scent, another memory that makes you feel safe, a blooming flower."

The lavender scent of her office surrounds me, sticking to my clothes like I'm in an open wildflower field. Just like the lavender shampoo I always use in my hair. The slow ticks of the pendulum whoosh through my ears as the glass becomes wobbly against my palm. She must sense my growing panic because my breathing escalates as the bottle tips to the edge of my palm. One more step till it's crashing on the ground and shattering into a million pieces that'll surely cut me open once more.

"Focus, Violet. You are in control. *You* are the glass. Don't let it take you down," she warns in a faraway place.

Don't let it take you down. Be the glass. But I'm not glass. I'm the window that's just been shattered and fractured. One that can't be replaced.

One more gasp and it's falling from my hand uncontrollably, my fingers shaking from the weight of holding it for that long. How did I balance it so long? Just as I squeeze my eyes shut and wait for the sound of breaking glass, I hear light movement and the room seems to stop spinning. Cringing, I fear the worst is yet to come, but it doesn't. No clatter or crashing glass. No spilled liquid splattering down my legs. There's just... silence.

When I look up, my eyes go wide. I see the bottle perfectly balanced in a big, calloused palm. Black ink swirls up tanned skin. My heart stops when I glance up in a hurry and meet a pair of warm brown eyes. Eyes I recognize from the dark hallway lit with dim lights.

Sam.

He's only there a flicker of a second, enough for me to take in his gentle eyes and warm smile, and then I'm tossed from the hypnotic session and jumping up from the couch, my eyes blown wide and my breathing ragged, still in a daze from what I just saw.

Did I... No. I didn't mean to think about him. Not really. He appeared out of nowhere. I was caving in, getting ready to meet the inevitable, and then he just stopped it. He stopped it from shattering...

"Violet, are you okay?" Jenna asks with concern etched in her voice, but she sounds so far away because my brain is trying to piece together what just happened.

Sam. He... saved me.

"Y—yeah. I'm fine," I rasp out, shaking my long brunette waves from my face.

"You broke out of the trance. You've never done that before on your own." Jenna stops the pendulum from swinging and places her other hand on the white marble table, her golden bracelet glinting from under the glow of her Mac laptop.

"No, I guess I haven't…" I say in a daze as I stare off into the corner where hanging vines tumble out of the clay pot in the center of the window.

This room always seemed so bright to me. Whitewashed walls, a big glass window on the left side of her office, the smooth marble desk, the numerous abstract pictures that could make you think twice about what the artist was trying to portray in the rainbow colors. And let's not forget the array of plants she has strewn around her big office. Sometimes it gets too much, but today I don't seem to care much because now all I can think about is Sam.

Sam… The one who caught the bottle. The one who stepped in when I didn't have the strength to hang on. But *why* did he show up in the picture? I wasn't thinking about him. I wasn't… I don't even know now.

The brain's a mystery, but this is just strange. Why would he just appear like that?

"What were you thinking about?" she asks with a quirk in her dark brow, her cat-like green eyes big and curious.

"I… I was just…" My words are mismatched, and my mind's a blur.

Do I tell her about Sam? No, I shouldn't. She doesn't need to…

"Violet?"

My mouth parts open, eyes still wide from the surprise of seeing him during the deep dive into my subconscious. Those big brown eyes gazing at me, staring deep inside my mind like he knew how afraid I truly was. "I…"

"Yes?" She lifts her eyebrows and nudges me on with the slight tilt of her head, waiting for me to answer.

There's a moment of silence, a tick in my mind that screams to set his name free. *Sam, Sam, Sam.* He's all I can think, and I'm about to spill my secrets in front of Jenna.

"I met someone." There it is. I did it. I spilled.

Her dark green eyes grow wide, and her thin red lips flip into a huge smile. "You met someone?"

"Y—yes," I stammer out, my fingers digging into my thighs while I huff out another sigh.

Fuck. Now she's going to drill me with questions. Questions I don't know how to answer.

"Violet, I'm so proud of you! Wait. Where did you meet him, and what's his name?" Her green eyes light up behind her lit-up laptop, her hands clasped together on top of the marble. She's so intrigued and excited.

I fidget against the leather couch and cross my arms across my chest, trying to shield myself from telling the truth. "Brianna and Taylor kinda dragged me out to a club, and I met him there. His name's Sam, but he's uhh—he's the owner of Club Inferno."

Her jaw drops and then a small smirk reaches her lips. "That's... wow. That's so..."

"Unlike me?" I laugh. "Yeah, I know."

She leans forward in her pristine office chair and taps her manicured nails against the marble, itching for more information. "Did you go on a date with him?"

Shaking my head slowly, I bite my lower lip with nerves. "No. Not exactly..."

"Not exactly?" She cocks a brow and gives me this *tell me the truth* look.

"We... uhh." The back of my neck is beaded in sweat, and my nails dig into my flesh. Here goes nothing. "I kinda hooked up with him..."

Her hand falls flat on the desk, causing the slap to echo around the room. Her eyes are gigantic like a full moon. Did I just stun her? "Oh. *Oh!* I see. Violet, that's..."

"Terrible?" I scrunch my nose and wait for the inevitable.

"No, no." She stops me with the wave of her hand. "I wasn't going to say that. I was going to say that's a big step for you. You haven't seen anyone else since—"

Since Jason, but she knows better than to use that name around me. At least, she tries not to trigger me with it. We're working on it. One step at a time.

"No. He's the first guy since then," I confirm with my eyes locked on the wooden floor.

"A step toward healing." She smiles. "Are you going to see him again?"

I knot my fingers together and shrug. "I don't know…"

"You don't know?" she asks, her voice coming off soft and kind.

I… don't know.

"No. It's a bad idea," I answer hurriedly, brushing off any thought of going back to see him, even if I'm dying to see those warm brown eyes again.

"What's so bad about it?"

"I…" I'm tongue tied and silenced again.

What's so bad? The thought of getting involved with a guy makes me want to puke. I can't even comprehend trying to date someone, let alone have sex with *him*. But I basically did. And I can't lie, I wanted to explore more of that. More of *him*.

Fuck. What's wrong with me?

"I think this could be good for you. Something healing. A new experience. Maybe even… happiness?"

Happiness. When's the last time I was happy? Was there a time with… Jason? I can't remember. I would've remembered, so why can't I think of the last time I was happy? Maybe I never was.

"I don't know, Jenna," I whisper out defeatedly, my body tense from whatever this conversation is.

"Just think about it, okay? Don't throw it away, even if you're scared. I know you are, but this could be a chance to get you out of your comfort zone again, to just be *you* again." She gives me an encouraging smile which makes me feel a little lighter. "Promise me you'll think about it?"

I nod, agreeing that I'll try. "Okay."

She smiles in approval and checks her watch, eyes widening when she sees we went a couple minutes over. "Okay, Violet. Great session today. I'll see you next week?"

Pushing myself off the leather couch and making my way toward the closed door, I nod. "Yeah, I'll see you then." Before I reach the door, she stops me.

"Oh, Violet?"

Turning back her way, I ask. "Hm?"

"Sleep on it tonight, will you? Don't let the opportunity pass you by."

Nodding in understanding, I give her a tight-lipped smile and slip out the door. "Promise I'll think about it. Bye, Jenna." Before I give her another moment to ask me anything else about Sam, I sprint out of the office and avoid any more questions.

When I'm back in the safety of my car, I groan and let my back hit the soft seat, letting my eyes close for just a second. What have I just done? Name-dropping Sam was *not* on my to-do list today. But neither was seeing him show up in my head in the middle of my hypnosis session...

Was this a sign? *Should* I go back to his club? What would that mean exactly? Do I want to go back? Of course I do. Fuck. I *want* to see him again. Whether that's to talk about books or have him sweep me back into his hallway so he can cage me against the wall and whisper dirty things into the shell of my ear.

My thighs clench just thinking about it.

Oh, fine! I sigh out heavily and push a lock of brunette hair behind my ear, turning the key in the ignition and deciding my fate. "Fuck it. I'm going back, and that's final."

Jenna was right. This had to be a sign, and I want to find out what exactly it means.

Chapter Thirteen

Sam

"Go on, Kels. Tell me the exciting news you've been dying to share with me all day." I lean against the recliner in the spacious living room, feet kicked up while I watch Kelsey flit around her bright dorm room excitedly.

"Hold on. Just one second. Let me grab it." She flips her long blonde ponytail behind her shoulder and reaches for something under a neatly stacked pile of papers and multi-colored binders. She always was the most organized one in this family.

I wait patiently and glance around the part of her dorm that I can see. Half her wall is covered with a banner of a glistening wave breaking against the sand with a picturesque sunset behind it. A calendar with a multitude of hibiscus flowers hangs next to that with a white board underneath it. Her class schedule is scrawled neatly across the board, along with to-do notes posted at the bottom in bold letters. A replica of the Golden Gate Bridge sits next to her open laptop in the corner of a wooden desk. She always was so impressed with bridges. Didn't matter the shape, color, or design. She's just always been obsessed with them.

My little future structural engineer. She's going to change the world one day.

"Found it!" she shouts, scrambling with a paper as she hides it behind her back. When she turns toward the camera, she holds one palm out. "Okay, you ready to be amazed, Dad?"

I chuckle in amusement. "Show me what you got there, kiddo."

Her bright smile is ecstatic when she unfolds the paper and holds it up to the camera, waving it back and forth excitedly while she jumps up and down. "I did it! My first big research assignment on infrastructures. My professor gave me an A!"

I jolt up straight and smack my knee in celebration. "That's my girl! See, I told you you'd pass with no problem."

"You were right. You're always right." She sets the paper down on the desk by her pink keyboard and grabs her phone while doing a quick spin in her rolling office chair—the velvet rose gold one I bought her right before she went back for sophomore year.

"Kels, you're already killing it. That and then your first calculus test you passed with flying colors? There's no stopping you. You're gonna get straight A's again, aren't you?"

She giggles and bats her baby blues my way, giving her long hair another flip for added dramatics. "You know me so well, Dad. And you know I'll try my best."

And she will. She's always been a genius—never once coming home with B's or C's. She's a perfectionist, and she's smart as hell. Both my girls are. God. How'd I get so lucky? I may be partial, but my daughters are literally angels. Smart, polite, good-natured, kind, and all-around amazing. After growing up with their mother, I didn't know how they'd turn out. But I guess I got them out just in time. They're literal godsends.

"You're gonna go far, Kels. Before I know it, you'll be graduating and designing bridges like no one's ever seen before." I stare in awe through the phone, smiling like an idiot as I imagine her life successes. I wish time would slow down a little.

She scoffs and shakes her blonde mane out. "Only the finest ones. But first, I have to go to grad school, then we can start talking about business moves."

Shaking my head in amazement, I scratch a hand down my clipped scruff and sigh. I'm not ready for her to grow up just yet. "Stop growing so fast, will you? Where'd my little girl go?"

A small smile curls over her pink lips, and it looks like she tries to brush a flyaway out of her face, but really she's just getting teary-eyed. "I'm still your little girl, Dad."

I choke down a sob and try to not get too emotional, but it's hard when I'm looking at a put-together nineteen year old who just won't stop getting more beautiful by the day. "Yeah. You'll always be my little girl." I smile. "I miss you, Kels."

"I've been gone for only a few weeks now, and we talk all the time!" She erupts into a fit of giggles which makes me bark out a laugh.

"I know. I know. I just miss you is all. Kayla does, too."

She hugs her off-the-shoulder sweatshirt close to her body and gives me a genuine smile. "I miss you guys, too." Before I can say anything, she changes the subject before I go getting all foggy-eyed again. "How's the club going? You and Uncle Bryson keeping busy?"

Letting a long sigh out, I lean back into the recliner and card a hand through my tousled hair. "You have no idea," I say. "It's been packed every single weekend lately. Which is good, but your poor old man needs a break."

She chuckles on the screen and looks up all bright-eyed with rosy cheeks. "You're far from old, Dad. And good! I'm glad it's been going so well. I'm happy for you. You deserve good things."

You deserve good things. Man, my daughter is about to make me cry.

"Thanks, kiddo. Means a lot." I smile.

Jesus. The older she gets, the more she looks like her mother. She's the exact spitting image. Tall, bright blue eyes, warm blonde highlights, high cheekbones, a beauty that could snag anyone's attention. And that scares me a little, makes me worry about the college boys. But she's smart; she knows how to handle herself. It's not like I haven't given her 'the talk' multiple times. Even if she did try to push me out of her room every time I tried. I chuckle at the memory.

Being a single father of two girls is not for the faint of heart, but I wouldn't trade them for the world. They *are* my entire world, and there's nothing I love more than them.

A few high-pitched squeals come from the end of the phone, and I'm betting those are Kelsey's friends. "Hey, Dad. I gotta go. Me and some of the girls are going down to the beach for a bonfire, and we need to get ready."

"Alright, Kels," I reply with a fatherly nod. "You make smart decisions now, you hear?"

She rolls her eyes and gives me a big toothy grin. "I'm always smart."

"Yeah, you are," I say quietly. She always has been. Always the responsible one in her group of friends. Thank God for that.

When she waves to the camera and tells me bye, I do the same and end the call, watching the screen fade to black. Then, I quickly check my text messages. Just one new one from Bryson and another from one of the bartenders asking for a night off this Friday. No texts from a new number I'm wishing would pop up on the screen. One from the pretty, blue-eyed woman that I'm dying to hear from.

Will she call eventually, leave a voice message with that sweet angel voice of hers? Scoffing, I groan. Who am I kidding? I may never see her again. But God, I wish I could. Out of all the women I've met in California, why'd she have to be the one who made my breath catch?

Stretching my arms overhead, I get comfortable and start to doze off against the warm seat, forgetting about the angel who belongs to San Diego. That is until I hear the back door bang open and sniffling coming from the hallway.

"Kayla?" I ask concerned as I turn around and see her hazel eyes red and teary.

Oh fuck, who hurt my little girl?

She swipes her purple sleeve along the bottom of her eyes, wiping away a falling tear while her phone hangs from her left hand. It's lit up, and I can vaguely see a text message thread, but I can't make out who it's from.

"What's wrong, sweetie?" I ask calmly, pushing myself off the recliner in a hurry, but careful to approach her. When she flicks her red-rimmed eyes my way with her bottom lip jutted out, I'm ready to knock someone's teeth out.

"I... I got..." She quivers her lips, blinking another tear down the side of her face as her hands shake beside her. She can't even finish her sentence without another sob being strangled from her throat.

"Kayla?" I say with desperation in my voice, holding my hands out steadily in front of me so I can try to calm her down, but she jolts out of my reach before I can snag the phone. I try again, more gently this time. "Hey, you gotta tell me what's wrong, kiddo."

Her teary eyes go soft, but when she looks back down at her phone, she loses it. "Why..." She backs up to the wooden staircase and pins me with the most heartbreaking stare. "Why couldn't you have married someone normal!" And then she's running up the steps, tears splashing across her cheeks until she's out of sight and slamming her bedroom door shut with a bang.

My heart stops right there on the spot. *No. Lois wouldn't.* But she would. And she just fucking made my little girl cry.

I rake a hand down my face excruciatingly slowly, cursing under my breath as I take in what just happened. Lois was messing with Kayla again, and I'm not going to stand for it this time. I will not continue to let her torture me or my girls anymore. Period.

There's no stopping me. I race up the staircase, skipping steps so I can get to Kayla's room faster. I can hear her quiet sobs from the hallway, and it makes my stomach churn just listening to her sulk. This isn't supposed to happen. This isn't *supposed* to keep happening, but it does, and I'm about to do something about it real fucking fast.

Gently clamping my hand over the doorknob, I carefully twist my wrist and watch the door fall open. Tiptoeing inside her room, I make my way over to her bed where she's thrown herself face first over her pink silk sheets. "Kayla?" She stirs against the fluffy pillow and slowly sits up, her face tinted red with tears smeared over the sheets. It makes my eyes fog up. "Talk to me, kiddo. What happened?"

Her fingers play with the ends of her purple cardigan, eyes blinking back tears as she looks down. "Mom's being Mom." Her voice comes out muffled and sniffly.

I drag my palm over my mouth and sigh, sitting on the balls of my feet as I crouch down to her level, just so she'll look at me through her cloudy eyes. "I'm sorry, baby. I'm so sorry." And I mean that with all my heart. I never want my girls to hurt, *especially* from the woman who failed them. "Can I see?" I hold my palm out, hoping she'll finally hand over the phone.

"Yeah," she whispers out. Handing me her iPhone, she shows me the text thread. When I grab a hold of it and scan over the words, my temper snaps.

Mom: What makes you think you're so special avoiding my calls and my texts? Newsflash, you're not. You're lucky to have me. You think you can just move halfway across the country with your father and ignore me? After everything I've done for you? You're acting like a brat.

My knuckles crack in my free hand; my teeth clench together like a drawbridge slamming shut. A brat? Who the fuck does she think she is calling *my* daughter a brat? I'm furious. No, I actually think my lungs are burning from rage. Lois just messed up for the very last time. I've had it with this woman.

Pushing myself off the floor and handing Kayla her phone back, I stride toward the door with clenched fists. "Dad, don't!" she yells with a warning tone, but it's too late. Lois took it too far.

"I'll be right back, Kayla. I just have to do this one thing."

Storming down the staircase with a blurry mind, I don't even make it to the garage before I'm grabbing my phone out of the pocket of my jeans and dialing her number with rage flowing through my veins. I can't think, can't focus clearly, not until she's picking up the line on her end.

"Ahh, Sam. I was expecting your call," she sing-songs in an all too fake voice, delighted that she started a big, fat mess.

"You have no goddamn right, Lois!" I'm done playing nice today. If she wants a war, then so fucking be it.

"What are you talking about?" I can hear the smirk in her sly words, and it just makes me tick more.

"You know what I'm talking about!" I growl. "This is what you do to get my attention? By being fucking mean to my daughter!"

She waits a beat before answering, then she throws a show in the background. "Well, if that's the only way to get through to her."

The side of my foot goes flying into the side of the truck tire, and I instantly regret it after pain flares in my toes. Shooting my hand out, I brace myself and take a deep breath. "Lois," I grit out sternly, "that is *not* how to get through to anyone, and you know that."

The nerve she has. I swear to God, if she says one more nasty thing about Kayla, I'll blow a fuse.

"That's how I get to you," she retorts, and I can already see the flashy smile she must be wearing with honor.

My face falls and so do my legs. Sliding slowly to the ground, I let the anger wash out of me, and in its place comes a deep wave of guilt and hurt. She wanted me to lash out, wanted me to react how I did just so she could cause more drama in my life.

Rule number one: never, ever raise your voice or argue back with a narcissist.

I knew that. I fucking *knew* that, and I still lashed out.

Goddamn it.

I'm not into arguments, never been one to just go beast mode and sink my claws into someone, *especially* Lois. Being calm, patient, and caring is what I do. But this? No. This was an out of the blue moment for me. I was so blinded with rage that Lois would say that to my daughter, I didn't think about the consequences of reacting the way I did.

Closing my eyes and resting the back of my head against the truck, I grab a fistful of tousled locks and blow out a long, drawn-out breath. God knows I need to take a breather to calm the hell down.

"Sam?" Her vindictive tone rings through the speaker, but I can't make myself talk. I just sit there, holding back tears, wishing the pain would just finally stop. But it doesn't.

I lost her more than ten years ago, so why won't the gut-wrenching ache of losing her just leave already? Instead, the pain radiates like poison in my chest every time I think of how it used to be—easy—and then the effects of the toxin spread all over again like poison ivy.

Finally finding my voice, I croak out a throaty response. "What do you want from me, Lois?" And then a splash falls onto my jeans, my eyes suddenly wet with tears.

I'm so tired. Tired of fighting, of defending my position. Of apologizing to my girls for how their mother refused to fight for them when all I did was try my hardest to make sure they made it safely out of a toxic situation.

If I had to count the number of times I spent with Lois in doctor appointments, walking through rehabs, sitting in counseling sessions, and trying to console her, there wouldn't be enough. I was there with her through it all—holding her hand, encouraging her, promising her that I'd make things work. But she chose the alcohol over me. She chose it over our girls. Well, *my* girls. Because the truth is, she never wanted them. She liked the idea at one point, but what happened after that? She wanted them gone, and I just couldn't live like that any longer. My girls didn't deserve that.

She never... Fuck. She never even loved them. Not like a mother should. And that's why I left. For my girls, I left to make their lives better. Because I wanted to give them the entire world. I wanted to show them how unconditionally they were loved. By me, Bryson, my parents. Not her... not Lois. And it fucking kills me to see Kayla so upset over a mother who never wanted her. Kelsey may hide it; she may very well not be as bothered as Kayla, but I know they're both hurting.

It breaks my heart that I couldn't give them a mother who truly loved them. As for me, I wish she never made that promise to me at the altar—to love me till death do us part. She couldn't keep that promise, and I really wish she could've.

There's a crackle on the end of the line, a fizzle coming from the speaker. Like maybe we're being disconnected. But I shortly realize, that's not the case at all. It's just her opening another bottle of wine... The line goes dead, and so does my heart.

Ten minutes go by, maybe twenty until I'm able to lift myself off the ground. It's like an anchor weighs me down, pulling me to the bottom of the ocean floor until I can't reach the surface anymore. But with a little push, a little pull, I make it out alive.

Climbing the stairs is a chore after it feels like I just fought my way out of a deadly jungle. But step by step, I make it up the steps just fine. When I reach Kayla's room, I drag my feet over the plush pink carpet by her bed and then collapse next to her without so much as a sigh.

It's quiet for a few minutes; neither of us has the strength to say anything. That is, until Kayla whispers out, "She's been drinking, hasn't she?"

Carding my fingers roughly through my strands, I nod. My voice is strained as I confirm quietly, "Yes. She's been drinking..."

Another beat of silence swirls around the room. Emotions are high; pain takes hold of every bone in my body. And Kayla—her head tilted down, pouty lips trembling, another teardrop dripping down her cheek. I carefully brush it away, wishing I could just wipe all her pent-up pain away and make it my own.

She leans her head against the side of my arm and looks up at me with her teary hazel eyes, apologies spinning in her flecked irises. "I'm sorry if it seemed like I was blaming you earlier—about you not marrying someone normal. I didn't mean it."

I push a messy strand of light brown hair off her face and flash a reassuring smile down at her. "It's alright, kiddo. You have every right to be upset. And don't for a second think anything of that text or any other mean things she's sent you. None of it's true. None of it at all."

Giving me a curt smile, she still flicks those worried hazel eyes my way. "Are you okay, Dad?"

Am I okay? Absolutely not. But I'll put on a brave face and smile through the pain of knowing we'll never be that perfect, happy family I thought we would be the day that I said yes to Lois at the altar. Because five years later, my entire world started spinning off its axis. The day Lois picked up a bottle of wine.

"No, but thanks for asking. And you? How's my girl doing?" I gently nudge her shoulder, another soft smile flashed just for her.

"Better now that you're here." The smile she sends me makes my heart mush. "But you know what would also make it better?"

"What?"

"A fuzzy cat I could cuddle with when I'm sad," she smiles, hinting at the obvious. She's wanted one for a while, maybe this will finally push me to the breaking point of saying yes. It's hard saying no to her when she's giving me those puppy eyes.

"Maybe soon. I'll think about it," I laugh, shaking my head. "Come here, kiddo." I pull her into a tight hug and squeeze her. "I wish I could've given you the mother you deserved. I tried so hard."

She shakes her head and nuzzles deeper into my chest. "I know you did. But you know what? It's going to be okay because I have you. And you're the best dad I could ever ask for."

Undeniable love floods through my chest, and a tear slips down my own face. "And you're the best daughter, Kayla. I love you, more than life itself."

"And I love you," she ricochets back to me.

"We're gonna be okay," I state. "We just... have to keep moving forward. One day at a time."

And that's what we'll do. One day at a time. We're going to be just fine, without Lois. I have my club, my daughters, my brother, my parents back in Oklahoma who still support my decisions to this day. What more could I ask for? Nothing. They're all I need.

But then, ocean-blue eyes cross my mind. Full lips, long brunette hair with pretty blonde highlights. A smile that makes me dizzy.

Violet.

What if... No. She's not...

Ah, fuck. Why is she still filling visions in my head?

CHAPTER FOURTEEN

VIOLET

The last few days have been nothing but me tossing back and forth the idea of going back to Club Inferno. Back into those crimson red lights where dark brown eyes lurk in the shadows. Eyes that light a fire deep in my core. I've been fighting it—the need that's been thrumming like honeybees in my ears. But the noise got too much and now, I'm standing in front of the lit-up sign of Club Inferno, awaiting my undoing.

Taking a shaky breath, I compose myself as best as I can. I smooth out the sparkly midnight-blue dress that flows down to the middle of my thighs, run my fingers through my spiral curls, and double check that my silver heel straps aren't loose. But all I'm really doing is stalling. I'm a fucking wreck, and that's all my fault. I chose to come back; now I have to play a game with fate.

After a second glance behind me—back toward the filled parking lot—I take a deep breath and accept my choice. *This is it. No turning back.* So I hold my head high and walk through the thick double doors, my smile stapled to my face, my shoulders rolled back when the bouncer at the front hands me my ID back.

This is it. This is my fate and whatever happens, I'll swallow it down with pride and take it like a big girl—a smile and all. This is what I wanted, right? But I'm suddenly nauseous and a little dizzy over this drastic choice. But nevertheless, I straighten my back and push forward, my eyes on the gleaming prize in front of me.

First thing's first. Where is Sam?

As I make my way through the entrance and into the club, the dim shades of red lights make my dress almost glitter. The bar is crowded with people scattered around the bar top, dressed in fancy attire and flashy jewelry. The dance floor on the other side of the club is packed with bodies spinning under the crystal lights of the disco ball. Twinkling fairy lights line the edge of the stairs and the top of the second floor glass interior balcony.

This place is so crowded, and loud, and so not *me*. Why did I even come back?

Oh, right. I'm here to see brown eyes.

Brown eyes. His new nickname. A nickname that *I* gave him.

I click my heels over to the lit-up bar. Various alcohol bottles line the back wall, their colors mixing together and reflecting off the mirror. When I reach the middle of the bar top, some rugged man slams his glass of rum down loudly to the right of me, sloshing liquid over his clenched hand. Flinching, I cringe at the noise and flex my hands into my dark blue dress, trying to calm my racing heart.

I shouldn't have come. This was a horrible idea. Why did I think I could ever come alone?

I should be home, reading a book while the TV flickers in front of me. I shouldn't be *here*—chasing after something that might be out of reach.

Questioning myself is useless, because I know why I came. I came to find Sam. I came to... ask him *why* he showed up during my hypnosis session? That was odd and frankly, it was probably nothing. But I don't just see random shit in my head during those sessions. Maybe that was just a one-time mishap. Maybe...

Before I can keep second-guessing myself, the pretty blonde bartender waves a hand at me and flashes me a smile. "Hey, long time no see," she teases. *She remembers me?* "Can I get a tab started for you?"

"Oh, no. Thanks." I shake my head and cross my arms over my chest. "I'm actually here to see if Sam was around?" Hopefully she doesn't notice my cheeks are heated and my palms are sweaty from just speaking his name.

How does he have such an effect on me?

Her eyes light up knowingly as she nods behind me. "He's actually right behind you."

Before I'm capable of registering his deep voice, he's calling my name. Well, he's calling me by the *nickname* he's picked for me. "Angel."

I look up slowly into the mirrored-wall and gasp when I see a pair of brown eyes reflected back at me. Nerves blast through my body, and when I spin around quickly to see him, I nearly topple over when I see just how handsome he is tonight. A crimson button-up shirt, sleeves rolled up to his elbows, exposing his tanned skin that's corded with veins spiraling down his forearms. His black ink twists around his right arm, the crashing waves blending in with his big muscles. He's got smooth black slacks that mold to his muscular thighs. One of his big hands pushes through the gel that slicks back his dark strands while his other rests in his pocket.

He's so... gorgeous.

His eyes flicker over my body as he rakes a hand slowly through his salt-and-pepper scruff—analyzing my dress, my legs, my *eyes*. I'm nearly out of breath the way he takes in all of me like a fine wine that's being savored.

"You came back." There's almost longing in his voice, like he was counting the seconds down for me to just stroll back into his club.

"I came back," I reply quietly, just loud enough for him to hear over the clattering and clinking of drinks being made behind me.

He looks at me a beat, his eyes flashing with something I can't trace. "Was starting to wonder if I'd ever see you again." He pushes both his hands in the pockets of his slacks, just staring curiously while people shift around me in a blur.

Not knowing what to do with my hands, I slide them down to my sides and play nervously with the slick fabric, suddenly nervous all over from the weight of his stare. I shrug and timidly curl my crimson lips up. "Guess you got your answer."

He chews on his bottom lip, looks at me with curious eyes, and nods his head to the right—toward a corner with black leather booths along a lounge area with neon red signs hanging overhead. "Come on." Leaving the noise of chants from the bar behind, I follow behind him.

He picks an intimate corner that's barren of other guests and slides into a moon-shaped couch, signaling for me to sit with the pat of his hand. Carefully, I slip in beside him, leaving at least half a foot between us. But nevertheless, I can feel the heat permeating off his large body, can smell his strong cologne overpowering the stench of sweat and lust floating around the club. I'm already a mess beside him.

Without giving him a chance to speak, I blurt out, "Why didn't you tell me you were the owner of the club?"

"I don't know," he plays coy while his eyes shimmer with trouble. "Guess I was having too much fun listening to your complaints about my club."

My mouth parts, and I gasp in bewilderment. "You guess you were having too much fun listening to me *rant*?" I repeat loudly.

This man. The nerve.

He nods and taps the edge of his thumb on the top of his thigh. "Yes, fun." He's got a witty tone about him, and he's having way too much fun with this—teasing me.

I feel the tinge of red paint my cheeks, and flurries of excitement swirl inside my chest. I'm both amused and embarrassed, but mostly I just can't believe he'd let me make a fool of myself.

I cross my arms tightly across my chest and fix him with a hard stare, but the twitching on the side of his mouth tells me he's holding back a laugh.

Seriously, what is with him?

"I'm sorry. Did I hear you correctly? You thought me ranting about chicken fingers and the lack of pink lights in your club was funny?"

He shrugs his broad shoulders and tilts his head to the side, the dark brown in his eyes lightening just a little under the tinted red lights. "Just a little. Or entertaining. Enticing…"

My eyes widen as I register the words. Funny, entertaining, *enticing…*

He thinks I'm enticing?

"Now I'm just embarrassed," I say with my crimson red lips in a tight line, my arms still hugged against my chest. If there was ever a moment I felt mortified, it had to be now.

He chuckles under his breath. "Don't be. I thought it was kind of adorable." A slow smile tugs over his plush lips, and my breath is momentarily lost at sea.

He thinks I'm adorable…

Guys don't say things like that to me. That can't be right. He couldn't have meant to say that to me. He couldn't be talking to *me*, but the special, attentive stare he gives me is laced in piqued interest. But again, my mind likes to play games with me. Maybe he is interested…

I narrow my eyes and play right back. "You're bluffing."

He raises a thick brow and sneers my way. "Am I?" I part my lips but nothing comes out—just a puff of air and instant silence. So he asks again, "Does it look like I'm bluffing?"

Rolling my eyes to the back of my head, I laugh. "You're a tease."

The tip of his tongue darts across his bottom lip, and a flash of a smolder glimmers in his dark eyes. "Do you like being teased, angel?"

"I… Um. I…" I gulp, my mouth suddenly dry and bare of any witty remarks. I can't beat that, can't say anything back because he's stolen the oxygen right out of my lungs. Being teased is not something I enjoy, but the way he's staring at me—his eyes fixed on me like I'm a rare gem—makes me feel like I'd ask him to just so I could chase that contagious laugh of his all over his club.

His eyes, his intense stare, the way his body is leaning into mine and creating a cloud of heat is too much. *He's* too much. I can't... do this.

Pushing myself out of the plush seat, I shake my head and take two steps away from him because I can't handle his suave charm any longer.

"Okay, that's it. I'm leaving." I've made up my mind, and I'm not letting him or his electric brown eyes tell me otherwise.

"Wait a minute," he chuckles out. When I turn back around, he's holding an arm out like he wants me to stay. "You just got here."

"Yeah, well—" My voice drops off as a familiar song floats through my ears. But it's different somehow. A mix of somewhat alternative with that deep bass of rock. A sequence of songs blurred together, but one that just happens to be my favorite.

My eyes flick to his, and there's another ghost of a knowing smirk—like he knows *exactly* what he's doing. Like he knows I happen to love this band.

"You changed up the music?" My head tilts to the side in curiosity, but the confusion is still rampant on my face.

"Mhm. Decided to mix it up a little. Hired a new DJ. Asked him if he could blend some new and classic rock songs together." He shrugs as if it's not a big deal at all, but it's a massive deal to me.

I pinch my eyebrows together in confusion and try to get my mind wrapped around this. "Why did you do that?"

He slides his tongue across his teeth and fixes his eyes on me. "Decided to take your advice."

A jolt rushes through my nerve endings. "Why on Earth would you take *my* advice?"

Another shrug of his shoulders, another quick remark. "Because your opinions aren't half bad. And I kinda hoped you'd come back," he says while stretching an arm behind his head, scratching nervously. My spine stiffens as he continues. "Thought maybe you'd give it another chance."

The music that's blasting over the speakers seems to fade from my ears as his words twist around my mind. *I hoped you'd come back. Maybe you'd give it another chance.* But he's not really talking about the club, is he?

No. He's talking about himself. Give *him* another chance.

I take a breath and slide back into the leather seat, my ears ringing and my balance a little off center.

That is why I came, after all. To give him another chance because I *just* couldn't stop thinking about him.

His deep timbre takes me off guard, and I nearly jump from my seat. "Why'd you come back, Violet?" When I turn to face him, my breath catches as I glimpse into those deep brown eyes that are studying me, analyzing my wide-eyed expression.

Words have suddenly failed me.

"I... I..." I stammer, finding it difficult to put together a coherent sentence when he's looking at me like *that.*

He bites his lower lip and shakes his head, leaning his back into the leather as he spreads his muscular thighs further apart. Those big, powerful thighs opened and relaxed my way. I have to fight hard to tear my eyes from the tempting view.

"Don't be shy now," he spurs on. "Think we're well past that now. Don't you?" The devilish smirk that materializes over his lips sends heat between my thighs, and I have to grip the edge of my blue dress before I fall apart. He's referring to the time he had me caged between his big arms, his hot breath blowing down my neck, his fingers deep inside me—stirring dark desires I didn't know existed till I saw his brown eyes staring into mine across the bar.

And just like that, there's that inky feeling sliding its way back into my body. I want him to do that to me again—*now.*

"I want..." My words get cut off by my inconvenient flaw of not being able to ask for what I want. I have trouble with that—with telling someone exactly what I want. I can thank my jackass ex for that. He basically ruined everything that was mine. He ruined my ability to speak freely...

Sam pulls me back to Earth and says my name with a little more insistence. "Violet."

"I, uhh... I..." Grinding my fingers deep into the dark leather, I grit the words through my clenched teeth when I look into his eyes that are fixed right on me. And with the flicker of that deep brown color, I break. "I want you to make me feel good again..." It comes off quiet, but he hears me just fine because he rears back and pins me with those dark eyes of his.

"You want me to make you feel good again?" His eyebrows thread together and his tongue drags slowly over his bottom lip like he's teasing me. But my stupid self gives in, and all I can manage is to follow the trail of his tongue with my eyes.

I wonder what else that tongue is good at doing...

Shying away, I look down and mumble out, "Yes..."

Am I ashamed of how badly I want him to explore me with his hands again? Maybe. Am I delusional into thinking he actually *wants* to give me more? Probably. But the way his pupils expand the tiniest bit tells me otherwise.

He wants to *ravish* me.

"That can be arranged... angel." The last word makes me choke on my own saliva.

Angel. How is that suddenly my new favorite name? It sounds like a choir the way he says it—all bedroom-eyed with a deep drawl.

"What's the catch?" I press my heels firmly into the shiny flooring, standing my ground.

There has to be a catch, right?

He shakes off the question with a simple remark. "There is no catch." And by the sounds of it, I think he's telling the truth, but my unsure mind thinks otherwise.

Grinding my teeth together, I ask for good measure. "What do you get out of this?"

Sam raises a brow and gives me a once-over, making my heart rate skyrocket. "The same thing as you, I suppose. Pleasure and good company."

Pleasure and good company—two things that mix together too well.

I purse my lips together and mull over this—let it simmer till my brain's wracking with questions. Except I can't decipher any of them. I'm a mess, sitting in front of the hottest club owner I've ever seen in my life, my thighs clenched and hands fisted in my short dress. I sure as hell don't know what I'm doing, but whatever it is seems dangerous.

"Is there something I need to sign? A terms of agreement or contract?"

He throws his head back and lets a deep chuckle rumble from his chest, clearly amused by my question. "This isn't a business proposal, Violet."

"Well, I don't know. I was just asking a question," I mumble. "Have you... done this before?" The question comes out hazy, like I'm scared he actually does do this all the time—picking up women at his club and taking them for a spin in the back hallway.

With a quick shake of his head, he whispers, "Never." My breath hitches at that.

"Never?" I ask again, pretending I didn't hear him the first time.

Another shake of his head. "I guess you're just... an exception." My lips part and all breathing ceases.

He thinks I'm an exception?

Oh.

"Me?" I place a hand over my chest while he stares back at me, making the shadows of crowds around me fade away.

He gives me a slow nod, confirming his answer. "Yes, *you.*"

I sit there and think, breathing slowly, tossing choices around my frazzled head. Do I stay or do I go? There's only two choices, but why is it impossible to choose?

Option one: I run as fast as I can back to my car and never look back.

Option two: I stay and let him do what I'm desperately wanting him to—*explore me.*

I can do this. I can make a choice. It shouldn't be that hard, but God, it is.

Mindlessly twirling a loose curl between my fingers, I blow out a breath, stumped. "I don't know…" But then his soft drawl breaks through the noise, and everything seems clear for a second.

"You came back for a reason, angel. You came back looking for something." I tug my eyes back up at him and watch as he eases himself a little closer, where I can smell the fragrant cologne permeating all around me—cedar and palm trees. Yeah, that's it. He smells like the West Coast, like my favorite place.

"I—umm." There I go, losing my train of thought again to this hunk of a man. Flexed biceps and all his glory.

"What is it you're after, Violet?" he whispers, filling my ears with sweet incantations that I don't know how to answer. And those eyes—the coffee-colored brown orbs that float endlessly through my mind—just won't let me think straight.

What do I want? I haven't known how to answer that in a very long time. Maybe Sam can help me find what I'm looking for…

"I… I don't know." My head tilts downward as I let out a ragged sigh, accepting that maybe I'll never know what I truly want.

Before I have time to sulk, Sam's slipping a hand beneath my chin and tugging it upward, till I'm face to face with those stunning eyes.

Yep. There I go again, getting lost in swirls of cinnamon irises again. Is this my new favorite color?

The pad of his thumb traces lightly over my chin, and the calluses he has seem to leave invisible marks on my skin—like stardust trails.

"I think I know why you came back," he answers, his fingers still grazing slowly over my skin, making me burn for him. "You came back to explore your fantasies. Came back to indulge in your needs…" He drops his hand down lower, letting the tips of his fingers graze along my neckline, causing me to groan at the touch.

Oh, God. Please. I almost beg him to keep going.

As if he hears me, a smirk curls across his lips. "So, angel." He slows his strides and lingers across my collarbone, skating laps across my flushed skin. And then, he whispers words that send me over the edge. "Let me... *explore* you." He lets his hand drop to my thigh which sets a chain reaction off in me.

Sam Brooks. The man that you are.

My eyes follow suit, staring at the way he caresses my outer thigh with rapt attention. It makes my breathing unsteady, makes me want to ask him to leave it there, but I don't.

Toying with my bottom lip, I question my own thoughts out loud. "No strings attached?"

He nods once, his eyes steady with mine. "This all stops when you want it to." His calloused fingers ingrain my skin, branding his mark all over me like a fresh tattoo.

I swallow the building lump in my throat and sputter out, "Just a couple questions." He pays close attention to me and nods, so I ask with my head tilted. "I've been checked at my doctor, and I don't have anything. So I was wondering, are you... I mean, have you been tested lately?"

He nods with clear eyes, the curve of his lips turned up on his face. "Yes, do you want to see my papers?" It comes off teasing with a slight chuckle.

Shaking my curls out, I digress. "No, that's okay. I believe you." And oddly, I do believe him, which is weird because I don't trust guys in general. But the way he's holding my stare like a magician is something I can't waver from. There's no trickery in his eyes, no flash of sinister games. So I decide I do believe him. He's telling the truth.

"You sure? I can show you my results."

"Sam, I said it's fine," I chuckle out.

He lifts an eyebrow like he wants to keep pushing the subject, but he falls to a different matter. "And you… are you on birth control?" His voice is steady, eyes still focused straight on me like I'm the only thing that matters in the moment.

"Yes," I murmur quietly, not quite sure what to ask next, but he beats me to it.

Keeping his hand flat on my thigh, he presses light circles into my heated skin with the tip of his thumb, grazing closer to my inner thigh. "How old are you, sweetheart?" My breath hitches because there it is. That vague Southern drawl that sets him apart from any of the locals. I like it—how it sounds like a deep staccato rolling off the tip of his tongue.

"Twenty-eight," I gasp out as he inches a little higher, a little closer to where I'm singing for him. "And you? How old are you?" I need a distraction, something to take my mind away from all the blood circulating in my core.

"Thirty-nine," he answers with a straight face. "That alright with you?" His eyebrows knit together like he's focused, maybe a little worried I'll retreat.

I give him a quick once-over and take in the slight tint of silver in his scruff, the couple of gray strands threaded through his slicked back hair, the way his chest rises a little more as he stares blindingly at me, awaiting an answer.

I've always had a thing for older men, but this one? Sam Brooks? Well, I think he might've been made just for me.

So, I nod my head slowly and flash him a shy smile. "That's… perfect." He sends me a relieved grin and skims his thumb over my thigh again, a touch of warmth in his calloused skin.

And that's that. Both tested, both clear on our ages, both in this for two things. Pleasure and good company, like he said earlier.

No strings attached.

His fingers continue to brush against my thigh, igniting lightning through my bloodstream, making me want to melt right into this spot. The flickering red lights above me and the boom of the music can't coax me away from the way his deep brown eyes are burning into mine, like he wants to swallow me whole. Both of us are in a trance—a trance I can't seem to snap myself out of.

After a beat, he pushes himself up and stands tall, right in front of me, hands sliding down inside his pockets. I already miss the heat of his fingers. He tilts his head curiously and flicks his dark eyes over me, licking his bottom lip while he hones in on me like a wolf. He looks starving, looks like he wants to pounce, and God, I wish he would.

Another few seconds go by, like an hourglass has been set. But before the sand runs out, he pulls his right hand out of his pocket and holds it out for me—palm open, hand outstretched, just waiting for me to take.

"So, angel. What do you say? Wanna spread those wings a little and follow me?" The deep timbre of his voice casts a spell over me, makes my mind a little hazy, and has me ready to say yes in a heartbeat. But that little voice in the back of my mind tries to talk me down.

This is a bad idea, Violet. Don't do it. Don't follow him to the back. But I push those negative thoughts away and instead change my tone. *He'll make you feel so good, Violet. He'll take such good care of you.* And that's all there is to it. The choice is made.

Sam. I choose Sam.

Carefully, slowly, I slide my hand into his and seal my fate. "Show me how to fly," I whisper out of breath. With a sly smirk on his face, he takes my hand in his and leads me to my destiny.

And into the lake of fire I go.

Chapter Fifteen

Violet

The loud bass of the music reverberates down my spine, clashing with my frantic nerves as sweat beads across the back of my neck. I'm well aware that I'm following him into the unknown, but I don't care. I'll follow him into the fiery gates of hell if that means I can have one more taste of how his hands feel skating across my body.

He guides me past sweaty bodies, through the thick fog of lust blowing around the crowded dance floor. I feel my skin prickle with desire when we enter the long, dark hallway to the right. This is it. There's no going back now. I've entered the deepest trenches of Club Inferno with Sam holding the gates wide open for me, and I don't think I want to go back home. Not today, not this very minute, not even for a second.

For tonight, I'll leave all my doubts and fears behind me. I'll forget how reckless I'm being and how scared I actually am. Eerily, Sam's warm hand feels a little like a safe haven in this ominous, dark hallway that's glistening with glitter and flickering lights.

Sam turns his head back to me and smirks, his firm grip on me tightening, the shadows making the dark brown flecks in his eyes look almost black. As black as a panther's fur, eyes that want to pounce and consume me whole. It makes my heart hammer louder in my chest, like an entire group of miners might just axe their way right through my skin.

He makes my blood boil. Makes it pump like spewing lava. Hot, tingling, a force of nature I just can't control. But I'll let him cover me, burn me alive just for tonight.

Tonight, I choose *him*.

When we get to the end of the hall, he leads me to the left—to a massive door I hadn't noticed before. Maybe because I was too busy being pinned against the wall by a tall, smoldering man with the deepest brown eyes I think I've ever seen. The door is painted a deep crimson color with just a touch of shiny finish, and the doorknob is saturated in fine gold. My blood races in my ears when he takes a silver key out of his pocket and turns it in the lock. It opens with a click, and I can't help but gasp when he whispers in a husky breath, "This way, angel."

Leading me in, the door closes behind him with a click—no one else can get in. I suck down air and try to slow my breathing, but the nerves seem to be crushing down on my lungs. What is this I'm feeling? Nervous, excited, absolutely panicked? Yeah, it's all those blended together.

When I look up, my mouth parts up in awe as I take in the massive space. A large leather couch sits in the middle of the room, and a long pool table with red, smooth felt sits in the right-hand corner. The lights glow dim in here against the glistening black walls that are coated in shiny glitter. Black marble floors shimmer under the crystal chandelier above, reflecting its shape across a hanging painting of a moonlit beach front. An electric fireplace crackles a few feet behind the leather couch, creating popping sounds with each crack of the red embers. The feel of the room is homey, warm, and private. I can still hear the occasional clubgoers from the outside of the door, but it's mostly quiet in here. The only thing I can seem to hear is my blood rushing through my eardrums and my heart galloping a hundred miles an hour.

"This room. Is it—"

Sam chuckles, stepping out from behind me and ending a few paces to my left. "It's mostly mine, yeah. I rent it out to parties, but I've got other rooms for that. This room is kind of my go-to place. Somewhere I can come when the noise gets too loud or just to play a round of pool with the boys."

I glance up and peel my eyes over the red velvet of the pool table, imagining him gathered around it, laughing with his friends. I don't really hate the image. "So you're telling me you don't usually bring women back here to ravish them?" I giggle out. He matches my laugh.

"Can't say I've brought any other woman back here but you, angel." When I turn to look at him, his eyes are genuine, and there's not a trace of a lie on his curled lips. "You're the only one." Something about that statement hits me in the gut. *The only one.* But I don't linger on it.

Suddenly remembering why I'm back here, I gulp as the quiet words drift from my lips. "Are you going to put me back on your thigh?"

His eyes focus intently on mine, but there's heat flaring like flames inside. "No, not this time." He smirks a devilish grin my way as he adjusts his rolled-up sleeves at his elbows. And then he takes a step in my direction, and another one and another one, until I'm a hot mess.

My fingers twist into the blue fabric of my dress, my eyes blowing wide as I feel my chest tighten at the thought of being alone with *him.* Sam Brooks. The club owner, the absolute menace who was sent to break into my closed-up boundaries.

He takes another step in my direction until I feel the heat sliding off his massive body. I take a step back and almost slip, gasping breathlessly as I ask, "Where do you want me?"

He stalks toward me, a sly smirk on his face as he starts to back me toward the leather couch. I have no room to go around, no room to say no. My body just moves pliantly at his command as his thick fingers push gently against my hips.

"On the couch, sweetheart. Right. Here." He pushes me gently down into the cool leather, and I land with a soft thud with my back pressed firmly into the black cushion. I squeeze my thighs together and dig my fingers into the edge of the new material.

I'm suddenly extremely nervous. Sweat beads against the back of my neck; my lips tremble as I watch the way he glides over to me. His shirt clings to his big biceps, his slicked back hair throws smoky gray colors under the dim lighting, and his brown eyes glow against the embers of the fireplace as he ends between my legs.

He bends down, running his calloused fingers languidly over the curve of my thighs. My body tenses, fingers digging into the leather of the couch as I try to get a grasp on reality. I'm here in *his* club, on *his* couch, with *his* hands exploring my thighs. My breath hitches when I see a smug smirk ghosting across his lips. His eyes are like lit candles, burning just for me, and I think I like that.

Sam tries his best to part my thighs, but I hold back, afraid to show him what I look like bare. What if he doesn't like what he sees? What if he suddenly changes his mind? What if he tells me to leave? What if I'm not good enough?

What if I'm not what he wants?

Suddenly, I'm overstimulated by all the unknowns, still haunted from my past. Still haunted from *him*. A man I'm no longer in contact with, but he still haunts my dreams, my thoughts, my insides. He's still everywhere. My gaze drops to the black marble floors, fixated on the intricate details of each polished section. Maybe this will help calm me down—counting swirls in the floor while my heart races in my chest.

As if he senses my blinding fears, seeing through all my insecurities, his blown-out eyes ease up, his brows knitting together as he stares up at me with a soft gaze. He cups my chin and lifts my eyes to him, which stills my breath. "Hey," Sam says with a gentle voice, "you nervous?"

I stumble on my words and nod, letting the gut-wrenching feeling slide down my closed-up throat. "Mhm." It's all I can hum out.

His lips curl into a gentle smile while one hand lingers on the top of my thigh, the other grazing softly under my chin. "You don't have to be nervous, sweetheart. Just relax, breathe."

Breathe. I can do that. I *can*, can't I? But the way his lighter brown flecks shine beneath the dim lighting gives me butterflies.

But I give it my best go, taking a deep breath in and letting it out slowly, starting to relax every limb in my body. Slowly, I uncoil my fingers from the leather and gently place my palms on top of the couch, showing Sam I *can* relax.

"There ya go, angel. Just breathe. In and out. Nice and slow." His thumb draws tender circles into my flesh, stroking along my inner thigh, making my breathing a little easier. "You wanna tell me what's got you so nervous?"

I try to look down, but he keeps his hand rested underneath my chin, holding my gaze. Squirming, I try to shuffle my hips against the squeaky leather, but he stills my body with the touch of his large palm on my thigh. My eyes shift to his, and there's no escaping those soft chocolate eyes that seem to stare straight into the depths of my shaking soul.

"I just... I haven't really. I'm not..." Fuck. I can't even think straight, let alone speak without making a fool of myself. Maybe this was a bad idea. Maybe I'm not ready. Maybe...

Sam presses his calloused fingers softly against my jawline, scraping over invisible scars of the past, but he never lets go. "Have you ever had anyone go down on you before?" His words are so *gentle*, not at all condescending, which makes me unclench my jaw just a tad.

Humiliating laughter rings inside my mind as I think about the past. I was never even remotely taken care of in that way. It was all about *him*—my un-kempt ex. He never once thought about making me feel good. It was just all about going down on him or what made him feel good. I was just... there.

I shake off the memories and huff out a breath. "I mean, a couple times, but it wasn't... It wasn't for my pleasure. A couple licks here and there so they could slide in easier." I shrug. "So, no. I guess I really haven't..."

Sam's brows knit together in a tight line; his jaw tics as he looks at me with both softness and something bitter in his eyes. His nostrils flare like he's angry. But why would he be angry? His fingertips leave my chin, and it feels like I just lost a clutch on myself. But then, his hand lands on my other thigh, and he lightly strokes up and down in a straight line.

"Well, that's a real shame. They must be fucking blind to pass up a woman like you. A real *fucking* shame," he spits out, venom on his tongue.

Oh, he's mad.

"But don't worry, angel, because I'm gonna take real good care of you. I'm gonna make you feel *so* good. I can promise you that. Is that what you want?"

I nod eagerly as I take in the words that just left his lips, still stunned by the way he just told me how good he'll make me feel. "Yes, please. Please, Sam." Maybe I'm a little too eager because I'm wrapping my fingers firmly around his wrist like I'm digging my roots straight through his tan skin.

He chuckles lightly and smiles up at me, the dark flecks of his eyes seeming to sparkle under the lights of the private room. "You gonna relax for me?"

"Mhm." I nod quickly, suddenly itching for him to be on me.

"Attagirl." He winks. I nearly choke on my own saliva at the sound of him saying *attagirl*. It's a simple word, but he's telling me what a good girl I'm being, and it sends butterflies flitting through my lower regions.

Attagirl. Fuck. This man is going to kill me.

Sam's fingertips start to graze up and down the tops of my legs, the pad of his thumb dipping down to my inner thigh as he starts to massage the area tenderly. I know what he's doing, know what he's capable of doing as he looks up at me with hungry, dark eyes. He wants to *devour* me, and I sure as hell am not going to tell him no. The hottest man I've ever laid eyes on wants *me*. I'm not going to let that pass me by.

"Need a little liquid courage to relax?" he asks as he cocks one eyebrow up, his head turning to the side as he looks at me with curious eyes.

He pulls over a glass of whiskey on the rocks from the small jewel-embedded table next to the couch and gives it a shake, clinking ice against the clear cup. I must've missed him pouring it when I was awestruck with the room. I should've known. It's his signature flavor.

I shrug and curl a smile. "It wouldn't hurt."

"Alright then, angel. Tip your head back just a little. Gonna give you a taste of my whiskey," he says with a sultry tone.

I do as he says, tipping my head back just an inch as I watch him get up from the corner of my eye. He clenches a palm against the glass of amber whiskey, swirling it around. The ice hits the edge, making a clinking noise that sounds a lot like how my insides feel—all tingly and alive with nerves.

"Tip your head a little more, that's it," he approves as he places a hand under my chin, coaxing my lips open with his calloused thumb. "Keep that pretty mouth open for me, angel. Gonna give you a taste."

Catching my breath is impossible right now because his lips are *so* close. Close enough to sink down on mine.

I watch him tip his own head back, taking a large gulp of his whiskey on the rocks. My eyes grow wide when I see him leaning over me, his thumb pulling my mouth open wider. He lets the alcohol pool out of his mouth like a running faucet, flowing down through my own mouth. The whiskey and the taste of saliva mix together while it slides slowly down the back of my throat. Our lips don't touch, not quite, but I can almost feel how soft they'd be.

"Swallow," he commands as he closes my mouth, still hovering over my body as he watches me down the bitter taste. I feel the burn simmer through my stomach, tasting *him* on the tip of my tongue. His cologne sends me into a hazy fog where all I can see is him as his dark eyes begin to grow pitch black.

"Good girl," he praises. My mouth gawks open as he sinks back down to the floor, situating himself between the center of my legs as he slowly begins to part them.

Sam clicks his tongue when he sees my body sewn to the back of the couch. "Now, angel. I can't reach you all the way back there. Come here." He pulls me to the edge of the leather couch, the palms of his calloused hands latching onto the back of my thighs. And then he's parting them, running his thick fingers nice and slow up the inside of my thighs until he's hiking the bottom of my blue dress up over my hips.

I can't breathe, my voice being held back by the drowned out whines and moans I'm already holding in. I know I'm going to fall apart as soon as his tongue meets my center. He's going to *devour* me, lick me clean till I have nothing left to give. I have this aching feeling he'll work me till I'm spent.

He drags his lips against my skin, sending trails of sweet kisses up the inside of my thighs. I suck in a breath from the tingling sensations he's sending straight through my core. He skims his lips higher, lifting my skirt flush over my thighs, until his warm breath blows gently over my dripping pink lace.

A low whistle leaves his lips. "Look at you, already soaking for me," he purrs, dragging the tip of his curved nose against my clothed folds. I hold in a whine and buck my hips forward, silently begging him to keep going. He chuckles out a response, his dark eyes smoldering as he takes the tip of his thumb and starts slowly caressing me. He gauges my reaction, my wide eyes and panting breath, then he slowly starts to circle my clit through the dripping lace.

"*Sammm*," I whine out, my manicured nails digging into the leather of the couch. This feels so good; *he* feels good.

"*Yeah*? Does it feel good?" he teases, pressing harder against my buzzing bundle of nerves.

I thrust my hips up and groan. "Mhm, need more. Need you to—"

"Shh," he whispers. "I've got you, angel. Just getting ya nice and worked up. Want you dripping for me. Want this pretty pussy messy and sticky so I can drink you down nice and slow," he purrs out with mischief written all over those syrupy brown eyes.

Before I can speak, Sam takes his tongue and runs it slowly over my clothed core, further soaking my ruined lace. I stifle out a moan and buck my hips forward, begging for more. "Sam, please," I beg, my heels digging into the surface of the dark floor, asking once more for his mouth.

God. I've never been one to beg before, but Sam brings it out of me. I'm hungry and salivating for his touch.

"That's what I thought," he teases as his dark eyes shift up toward me. "Now, let's get these off, shall we?" He tugs on the lace and drags it slowly down my legs and over my high heels, bunching up the soaked material as he shoves them deep into the pocket of his slacks. He spreads me wide, my pussy on full display as he sits back on his heels, staring at me while he slides a palm over his clipped scruff, his eyes blown wide. Groaning deep and long, lust swirls in his dark pupils. I can barely breathe as I watch him take me in nice and slow, his eyes alight with fire that I want to dip my fingertips into and play with.

"Goddamn. You're fucking perfect, angel. Look at that pretty pink pussy dripping just for me." Sam smirks, his eyes black pits as he leans in, his meaty hands holding me down while his cool breath blows over my sensitive center.

I squirm beneath Sam, feeling sweat pool underneath my long locks as I watch him become mesmerized with my glistening, sticky core. "Sam," I whimper, barely making a sound because I'm trying so fucking hard to hold myself back from crushing his face against my center.

"Mmm, *yeah*. You're such a messy girl. Think I need to clean you up," he purrs, licking his lower lip with hunger as his thumb lightly traces over my sticky folds.

"Please," I beg, groaning with need. "Your mouth, Sam. I... I need it," I whine.

"Yeah, ya do." He smirks.

The next thing I know, Sam's leaning down and licking a thick, clean stripe all the way from my dripping hole to the top of my glistening mound, his nose dragging deliciously through my curls as he flicks his tongue, groaning as he savors me. I moan loudly, body writhing beneath him as he takes his hands and holds my hips still.

"You taste so fucking sweet, angel. The sweetest pussy in California," he murmurs between licks. "Just hold on. Let me give you what you deserve." He dives back in, his thick fingers spreading my folds as he devours me whole. His warm tongue languidly slides up and down rhythmically, collecting drops of slick as he works me nice and slow. I buck my hips up every time his tongue glides over my tingling mound, feeling the electric zaps of lightning shooting like sparks down my spine when he takes his time and drowns himself in me.

Sam works and works and *works* me over, drawing meticulous circles around my puffy clit while my eyes roll into the back of my skull. I toss my head back in elation, savoring the way he takes me to heaven. I can feel the energy coursing through my body, *feel* that aching desire being met as he feeds on me, his tongue going up and down ravenously until I swear I see stars in my vision. I tangle my fingers into his sandy locks, hearing him groan under my hold as I fight to keep a grip on reality. I'm so close to spilling, so close to elated bliss as my body hums beneath my skin.

"Eyes on me, angel. Wanna see those beautiful blue eyes when you fall apart against my tongue," Sam purrs as he licks another long stripe up the center of my folds.

When I snap my eyes open, they blow wide as I look down at the hungry beast of a man beneath me. He looks completely *wrecked,* black eyes searing into my heated gaze. His scruff is dripping in my glistening arousal while his smooth tongue flicks across my aching bundle of nerves, his large hands holding my thighs down, making sure I can't escape. I'm a panting mess, my high-pitched moans drowning out the blaring music from the other side of the club as I start to break. Another wave of slick hits his tongue, and I'm fighting everything inside to just hold on a few more seconds, but that's asking a lot of myself.

As if Sam sees right through me, he growls, "Don't hold back, angel. I wanna see you, wanna *taste* you. Come on, now. Give it to me." He pulls hard on my aching clit and sucks, firing off every single nerve ending in my body until I can't hold on anymore. I'm gone.

"Sam—*fuck*," I moan as I feel the tingling sensations run flush down my spine, igniting fireworks in my mind that make me completely dizzy and breathless, and then I'm spilling myself all over him. He groans while he laps up every bit of it, growling *good girl* through the pleasurable licks. He keeps me there until there's not a hint of release left between my thighs, eating me up like he's starving for *me*.

When Sam's finished, he looks up through clouded eyes and smirks. "How was that, angel? Did I make you feel good?"

I nod my head up and down slowly, having trouble finding words to say at this exact moment. "You made me feel—so *good*," I pant out breathlessly. "I've never felt anything quite like that before."

Sam chuckles up at me. "Well, that's good because I'm not done with you yet."

"What?" I ask with wide eyes. Not done with me yet?

He shakes his head wickedly. "Oh no, angel. That was one orgasm. You're gonna give me another."

"Another one? But I—"

"I know you have one more in you, sweetheart. Let me get you there. Let me make you lose control." The way he says it sends me into a fog. A nice, blissful haze.

He slides me forward, holding my hip down with one of his hands while his other starts to play with my sensitive clit. "I can make you come in so many ways, angel. This time I'll take you there with my fingers. Know exactly where to get you." He smirks, his blown-out eyes looking directly like black pits of desire—a pit I'll gladly follow him into.

Panting out with a needy whine, I watch him drag his middle and ring fingers down my folds, slipping slowly into my dripping hole. "*Oh,*" I moan as he bends his thick fingers up to reach that spongy, soft spot that makes dampness collect like raindrops on his drenched knuckles.

"*Yeah?* Feel good?" he asks with a smug smirk tugging on that handsome face of his, my release still sticking to the grays that are threaded throughout his scruff. The sight of it makes me drip more for him.

"Mmm, yeah. Feels so—*good*," I manage to murmur out while digging my nails into the shoulder of his crimson shirt.

"That's what I like to hear," he responds, licking his lower lip seductively. He pushes the pad of his thumb against my clit while drawing slow, meticulous circles. His other fingers pump in and out of me in rapt attention, drawing out wet, squelching noises that just seem to turn Sam on more. "Come on, angel. Tell me how good I'm making you feel," he purrs as he continues pulverizing my insides.

"So fucking good. Oh my God, Sam," I whine as he bathes me in pure ecstasy, coating me in desires I didn't even know I had in myself. All I know in this moment is that I want more, *need* more of him.

"Mmm," he growls low, "that's good, angel. Wanna make you come again." His blown-out eyes tear into my whimpering soul, and there's not a damn thing I can do to slip out of his hold now.

"Please, Sam. Feels *so* good. Your fingers, your—*fuck*," I whine as he ruts up inside me, pushing on that sweet, spongy area that makes another wave drip down his huge knuckles.

Jesus. The sight of him knuckles deep inside me and those striking eyes staring up at me could take me to heaven. This man could make me kiss stars, and I think I like it a little too much.

"Come on, messy girl. Spill for me. *Soak* me," he growls as he speeds up his meticulous circles against my throbbing clit, his thrusts tantalizing, tormenting me with how fucking good I feel beneath his touch. The wet noises of his calloused skin rutting up inside me is deliciously sinful, filling me to the brim until I can barely hold back. I'm about to come again, but this time feels different than the last.

"Sam, I'm gonna... gonna..."

"Give it to me," he demands with the bite of his snarl and blown-out black pupils.

One more hit to my spongy walls and he's knocking the orgasm out of me. His thumb stays firm on my clit as I clench around him, my orgasm washing through me like a raging hurricane that destroys whole cities with its powerful riptides. I spill myself effortlessly, experiencing a new sensation that almost overpowers me as it takes me on the ride of my life. My elated moans fill the emptiness of the room as I release hot, damp waves of arousal all over his crimson button-up.

Holy shit. Did he make me... squirt? The glisten of my release tells me he definitely did.

"Oh, *fuck* yeah, angel. That's a good fucking girl," he praises as his fingers slowly massage my insides, working out my mind-blowing orgasm while I fight to keep upright.

The sticky arousal glistens on his salt-and-pepper scruff, slick coating the front of his soft shirt while he's knuckles deep inside my dripping pussy. He looks completely wrecked with his tousled brown hair falling onto his sweaty forehead, eyes still blown wide, his tongue licking his swollen bottom lip seductively while he works me nice and slow with those meticulous fingers of his. He's a work of art, a perfect masterpiece that I don't want to stop looking at.

My breath comes in waves as I watch him start to slowly clean all the slick from my sore, over-sensitive pussy, his strokes languid when he licks all along my inner thighs—cleaning up the mess we both made. When he's finished cleaning me, he wipes his mouth with the back of his hand and smirks up at me with that devilishly handsome grin that's now burned into the back of my brain.

After he pulls the edge of my dress over my thighs, he pushes himself up off the ground with a hefty groan and collapses next to me on the plush couch.

We both sigh, breathing heavily, and then he looks over at me and smiles. His eyes relax into a honey-glazed color that burns holes through my vision. He's so pretty when he smiles, eyes alight with messy locks sticking to his sweaty forehead. He looks fucking wrecked, but he looks so good like that. I almost wonder what he'd look like with me down on my knees, between his legs...

"How was that, angel? Did I meet your expectations?" He smirks, letting his head fall back against the cushion, glowing eyes staring right through me.

I smile, taking a deep breath as my aching muscles relax next to him. "That was the best I think I've ever felt. You were... incredible," I beam as I see a hint of a sparkle in those thick pools of honey. It's almost like he's beaming with sunlight at my response.

"Glad I could make you feel good, angel. You deserve it, and I'll happily get on my knees for you any day." My breath hitches at the response. He'd really get on his knees for me any day? He'd do that for *me*?

Something stirs inside my gut. A wave of emotion about to flood out of my eyes, but I hold it down. No one's ever done that for me. Why would Sam want to? I'm nothing. I'm not... special. So why choose me?

The touch of his warm skin against mine pulls me out of my deep thoughts, knocking me back into the real world that's not my black mind. His calloused fingers slowly trail up and down my thigh, a gentle rhythm that puts me at ease. Suddenly, I feel like I should move, get up from the comfort of this cozy couch. I want to make him feel good too, thank him back for what he did for me. It's only fair. He deserves that—to feel just as good as me.

He's not forcing me or even incentivizing me to, and I like that. I like having a choice. So I'll do this for him because *I* want to.

Slowly, I slide from the couch, ending on my shaky knees as I crawl between his muscular legs. Laying my palms flat on his slacks, I dig my fingertips into the meat of his thighs. If there's one thing I know, it's that I want to taste him just like he tasted me.

"What are you doing down there, hmm?" he asks curiously, one eyebrow raised high as he analyzes me.

Brushing my fingertips higher, my hands now rest on the edge of his leather belt. "What does it look like I'm doing?" I smirk up at him, blinking flirtatiously.

Where the fuck did I get all this courage from?

His eyes darken while he runs his tongue smoothly over his bottom teeth, giving me a crooked half-grin that makes me weak in the knees. Shaking his head, his voice comes out a bit softer. "You don't have to do that, sweetheart."

Shrugging, I shyly smile. "But I want to."

He looks at me a beat, something swirling in his glistening irises that I can't quite place. Affection, infatuation, surprise? Maybe all those things.

"You're not... *them*, Sam. You're *good*. You gave me indescribable pleasure. So let me repay the favor. I *want* to do this. Just... just let me make you feel good, too." I swallow thickly, taking a breath before I go getting all sentimental. But that small smile curling over his plush mouth is making me blush again.

God. He's beautiful.

Nodding, he leans forward, narrowing his darkening eyes as he smirks devilishly my way. He licks his lips hungrily when he gazes into my wide eyes. "Think you can handle it?"

My breath hitches, watching the way he's teasing me, dark eyes alight with mischief written in those flecks of black charcoal. If he thinks he's turning me on again, then he's damn right. I'm already wet and pooling in between my sticky thighs.

I lean forward and undo the buckle of his belt, slowly threading it through the loops. Then I toss it to the floor in a heap and smirk smugly up at him. "Oh, I can handle it," I say happily, accepting the challenge.

Sam cocks a thick brow up and relaxes into the comfy couch, spreading his legs as he nods down to his black slacks. "Alright then, angel. Let's see what you can do with that pretty mouth of yours."

Giggling silently, I leisurely unzip his pants and tug down his slacks, along with his black briefs. When his erect cock springs free, I gawk over how absolutely massive he is. Long, thick, precum leaking over his slit—the swollen, red tip begging to be kissed. He's so fucking big that I can barely form a coherent sentence. He's absolutely sensational.

"What's the matter, angel?" he teases, cocking his head to the side, a sarcastic smile tugging at his lips. "Still think you can handle it?"

I watch him carefully, narrowing my eyes as I smirk up at him. He's challenging me, coaxing me to take a hold of him. Sam doesn't know this yet, but I can't pass up his challenges. They're too enticing. I may be timid and shy most of the time, but this time, I need to show him that I *can* handle him.

Leaning my elbows forward, I inch my hand over his muscular thigh, ghosting over his weeping cock. "Oh, I can handle it. Watch me." I smirk.

Sam lifts his brows like he's trying to crawl inside my scrambled mind until he finds exactly what he's searching for. But somehow, he knows I can handle it. So he leans back into the leather and nods his head in approval. "Go on, then. Handle *it*," he challenges with a smoldering stare my way.

I lick my glossy lips seductively as I reach my hand around his thick girth, slowly spreading the building precum up and down his long shaft as I indulge in the lewd, wet noises my hand makes around him. He groans, shifting his hips forward while he relaxes his back against the leather, indulging in his own ecstasy. Keeping my eyes on him, I lean down and slowly lick up the thick vein on the underside of his cock, languidly taking my time and ending at the tip as I swirl my tongue in slow circles over his swollen head.

"Christ," he groans, his dark pupils turning carnal as he watches me take him in my mouth. Hollowing my cheeks out, I start to bob my head up and down carefully, one hand wrapped around the base of him while I work the bottom of his shaft, my spit mixing in with the precum.

I feel him squirm beneath me, his cock spasming in my mouth as I take him deeper, feeling my drool coat his slick cock. I suck him, tease him with my languid tongue, my hand, my throat. He tastes *so* good—the salty bitterness sliding down the back of my throat as I drink him down like a fresh glass of lemonade on a hot summer day.

Before I choke, I take a breather and pull off him, but I keep my hand wrapped around his thick length to keep his blood pumping. Drool and precum cover him, and he groans with each stroke I give him. He gazes at me with cloudy eyes, looking absolutely fucked as he takes me in. Messy lips, crimson lip gloss smeared over his throbbing cock, a bead of drool connecting from his weeping tip to my lower lip, cheeks flushed pink. He's looking at me like he thinks I'm perfect, like I'm worthy of so much more. It makes my gut twist in knots.

Stop it, Sam. I'm not trying to grow feelings for you. But it might be too late for that. I think I'm already falling with every glance and flick of those gorgeous brown eyes.

"Fuck, angel. Didn't know you were so good with that pretty mouth of yours. Not so shy now, are you?" He chuckles, tracing my bottom lip with the tip of his thumb, catching the strand of drool that connects me to him like an intricate spider web spun around his swollen cock.

"Guess not," I breathe out in a daze. The way he's looking at me seems intimate, even through his big, blown-out eyes. It's like he's fawning over me, the position I'm in—between his knees, hand wrapped around his shaft, drool pooling in my mouth. It's too much, too affectionate. And now, I'm a blushing mess once again.

"Well, go on, angel. Keep going. Being such a good girl. Don't stop on my account." He chuckles, sliding his tongue menacingly over his bottom teeth, ending with a quick wink in my direction.

Crimson fills my cheeks, but I get back to work. I take him back in my mouth, slowly sliding *down, down, down* until I'm nearly choking on him. A muffled, gagging sound slips from my throat, and he tenses underneath me, groaning my name. He takes a hand and wraps it around my waves, holding it out of the way so I can devour him without it flying in my face.

"Attagirl, that's it," he hisses through clenched teeth, my tongue twirling around his tip as I slide up and down his shaft, ending at his balls while I coat them with drool. "Goddamn," he moans, cupping the back of my neck while my hair is wrapped firmly around his hand. When I come back up for air, he rasps out, "Think you can take me deeper?"

My heart speeds up, climbing into my throat while I try to swallow back any hesitation. He's *so* big. It'll be hard, but I'll try. As long as he can guide me, I think I can do it. "Yeah, I can try," I pant out as he smiles warmly down at me.

"Alright, angel. Gonna guide you, okay? Just wrap your hand around my wrist if it gets too much. I don't want to hurt you."

He doesn't want to hurt me... Why does that make me want to burst into tears? All I've ever been is hurt. But Sam doesn't want to hurt me? Oh...

Carefully easing me down, I take him slowly into the back of my throat while he guides me down against him. I hollow my cheeks out and open my throat as he moves me *down, down, down* until my nose is grazing against the coarse, dark hair at the base of him. When I come back up again, gasping for fresh air, he asks if I'm okay. But I just nod up and down until he smirks and pushes my head back down. I eagerly oblige.

Sam picks up his movements, guiding me back and forth on his messy cock as he starts fucking up into the back of my throat. The pacing is swift, erratic, desperate the way he drives my mouth down on him over and over again. I'm so fucking full of him that obscene, squelching noises come out of my throat while I mouth-fuck him again and again and again. I'm drowning in my own saliva, the drool pooling out of my mouth and onto his large length while I gag and choke him down.

I won't lie. I fucking *love* this. Love pleasuring him with my tongue, my throat, my whole entire being. And I won't be mad if this is more than a one-time thing.

I can't hear the thumping music out on the dance floor anymore, can only hear his stifled moans and the throat-fucking noises reverberating across the room. My eyes water, mascara running down my face while his hand tightens and pulls firmly on my hair. My own moans fill the space between the two of us as my hand slips under my dress, the other gripping the end of his crimson shirt.

Circling slowly against my aching clit, I feel pleasure run through my body while he ruts his hips up, choking on another moan. "Look at you, angel. Already soaking again, yeah? Choking on this fat cock made you wet, didn't it?" he teases relentlessly as he lifts my mouth up off him, watching the drool pool down his length.

"Mhm, it did." I nod as the breath leaves my body. His salty taste still lingers in the back of my throat while my hand goes back to slowly working him.

I moan out in pleasure, feeling the precipice of my own orgasm about to wash over me as he watches with wrecked black eyes. "Gonna come again, angel?"

"Ye–*yeah*," I pant, feeling the white-hot sensation starting to take over. Before my muscles collapse underneath me, he places a sturdy hand on my shoulder to keep me from falling over. "Sammmm," I scream out in bliss, letting him work me through my orgasm, talking me through it.

"Oh, fuck yeah. Such a good girl spilling for me again. There ya go, what an angel," he purrs while I fight to keep my eyes open, letting the aftershocks of a third orgasm run through me in just under half an hour. I've never come this many times in a day, let alone years by a man. But Sam? He's a pure menace who keeps me on my toes.

Sam keeps me upright as I lean into his meaty thighs, one hand languidly stroking him up and down as the slick and drool collect in my palm. "Sam," I whimper out in a pathetic plea.

"What do you need, sweetheart? Tell me what you want," he coaxes, his thick fingers gently massaging the back of my tight shoulders.

"Want to... want to finish you off. Want to make you come," I groan out tiredly.

He looks down at me, his gentle eyes gazing through me as a light chuckle sounds from his lips. "You seem pretty tired. You sure you can—"

"Yes," I snap, my eyes heating into his like swirling fire. "Let me finish you off. Gag me, Sam. Fuck my mouth. Please," I beg with big, watery eyes.

He lets a chuckle out, eyes blowing black as he smirks down at me. "Such a dirty girl, aren't ya? Alright. Since you asked so nicely, I'll give you just what you want." He grabs a fistful of my hair, holding me in place as he brings his weeping dick up to my panting mouth and thrusts in, hitting the back of my throat while I gag and swallow him whole. I sit there like the good girl he thinks I am and take it, on my shaking knees, my nails digging into the meat of his thighs.

His thrusts accelerate as he snaps his hips up, his grunts swallowing my name on elated moans. "That's a good fucking girl. *Yeah*. Taking me so well, angel. Shit," he groans, thrusting harder into the back of my throat. I'm almost out of air, but I keep going anyway.

He's so close. I can feel it by the winded breaths and breathy moans, his body coming to life every time his cock kisses the back of my throat. It's like he's everywhere all at once—his salty precum sliding down my hot throat as I feel him about to burst.

"Fuck! I'm not gonna last any longer, angel. I'm gonna... gonna..." He huffs as he tightens his fist through my messy curls. I inhale his musk, the smell of sweat and sex consuming me whole the way he fucks into me nice and hard. Just when I feel like I'm about to run out of breath, he thrusts deep inside my throat, my nose gliding against the base of his wiry hairs. His cock spasms and before I know it, he groans out a gut-wrenching moan. Hot ropes of white cum fill me up, shooting down my throat as I drink down his salty release.

"Christ," he breathes out with a rasp, releasing the last of his cum inside my mouth. I swallow down his large load, reveling in the salty taste of him that now swims inside my gut.

Slowly releasing his grip on my hair, he pushes me back and slides out of my drool-encased mouth. When I finally take a breather, I cough a few times, choking on nothing but my own spit. I watch him through hazy eyes as he tucks his softening cock back into his briefs, sliding his slacks up his hips as he zips himself back up. He reaches down, cups my chin, and takes a good look at the absolute wreck he made me into.

"Look at you." He laughs, gazing into my tear-soaked eyes while his thumb gently grazes against my mouth, wiping away the lip gloss and evidence of my drool. "I really did a number on you, huh?" he teases.

"Looks like it." I smile.

He smiles back, and it's so warm that I have to stop and take a long, deep breath. He's positively radiating right now, and it makes something tug hard in my stomach. "Let's get you cleaned up, yeah?" he asks.

Carefully unbuttoning the red collared shirt, he peels it off and throws the pristine white T-shirt he was wearing underneath over his head. I can't help but gawk at his tanned, glowing skin and the ripped muscles across the expanse of his chest. He's so fucking gorgeous, he almost doesn't look real.

"Come here." He chuckles, taking his soft T-shirt in his hand. He leans forward and runs the cotton material across my messy mouth, under my watery eyes with clumpy mascara sticking to my eyelashes, over my sweat-covered forehead, all while pushing my messy curls back over my shoulders with one soft graze of his fingers. He's so gentle with his large hands, almost delicate the careful way he traces every inch of my face until I'm all cleaned up. I can't help but stare up at him the entire time he takes care of me. I've never experienced this, never known *this*.

Why is he doing this for me? Surely I'm dreaming and I'll wake up with one single pinch to my skin, but even after several blinks, I'm still here and he hasn't left. He didn't leave me to clean up the mess on my own. He did it all for me...

"There you go, all better." He smiles gently, his caramel eyes a lighter brown now as he stares back at me, something warm and admirable in his flecked, starry eyes. It's nothing like I've seen before. It's new, uncharted territory—just like this entire night. "Feel better?"

"Yeah," I say in a daze. My eyelashes bat up at him slowly while I stare at him mesmerized, not even registering I'm still down on my aching knees.

"Good, that's good." He nods slowly, thumb still trailing along my jawline smoothly. It's like I'm in a fog, my mind racing at whatever *this* thing between us is. He's a menace, I'll give him that, but he's so, so... caring.

Sam throws on his silky long-sleeved shirt, but his eyes never leave mine as he moves through the mundane motions of buttoning up each intricate button. His tanned chest leaves my view the moment he clasps the third to last button up, and I almost mourn the loss of his sweaty, glistening chest.

"What are you still doing down there on the floor?" He laughs while he scoots over to the right side of the couch, leaving the left side wide open for me.

"Oh, I don't know. Guess I got stuck." I blush bright red, nervously giggling with a shake of my head. But honestly, I'm just *so* tired, and I can't stop staring at the mess of tousled brown locks and the honey-colored eyes that I want to slip into.

For the moment, I want to run my fingers through that soft, tousled hair. It smells like warm sand with sea salt mixed in. He smells like somewhere I'm meant to be.

"Well, come on now. Let's get you up. Come here." He bends forward and lifts me up from the hard floor, turning me around to where I'm facing away from him. Leaning back into the leather armrest, he parts his legs as he scoops me up into his lap, pulling his strong arms around my waist. One hand gently slides up and down my bare left arm, his calloused fingers trailing smoothly up my skin, the other hand eases my head down into his chest so he can stroke slowly down the back of my hair.

My body is so confused, muscles tensing with every stroke of his fingertips. I shouldn't stiffen up, shouldn't shy away from him because he feels *so* warm, but yet my body doesn't remotely know what's happening. Why is he being so soft and gentle with me? Why isn't he leaving me, telling me to get up so he can kick me out of his club? My mind must be playing tricks on me. This isn't normal. At least not normal for me...

I'm not used to soft. Not used to anything but verbal demands and sharp tugs of my wrist. Why isn't he yelling at me? Why isn't he...

Sam immediately notices my tight, strained muscles and carefully grips my shoulder. "Hey, why are you so tense? You okay?" he asks with knit brows, glancing down at me with concern lathered all over his syrupy eyes. Those super soft eyes make me want to cry. No one's ever looked at me like that...

Gulping down a tear, I shrug and give him my best perplexed look, fluttering my long eyelashes at him. "I don't know. I guess I'm just known to be a little tense," I whisper out, my eyes still staring into those big pools of warmth. Right now I'd like to drown in them, forget exactly why I'm so uptight.

He smiles softly at me, chuckling out as he rubs the back of my neck, his fingers feeling like magic the way they dance over my skin. "*Relax,*" he coaxes. He slides me up a little further on his chest and rests one arm lazily over my hip, the other hand drawing gentle circles into the crease of my upper arm.

Relax. The word slips through me, pulling every tense muscle out of its binds, releasing me slowly from any worries or anxiety that tries to bubble up in my chest. I'm here with Sam; I can relax. I don't have to always go into fight or flight mode after being physical. This is a safe space. *He* is a safe space.

I nuzzle into the middle of his chest, resting my hand on the warm button-up, letting my fingers brush right over his heart. I can feel it beat a million miles an hour, the galloping hooves pumping in his veins. But I also feel my own heart, steadily pacing right along with his. They start to mix together slowly—two hearts colliding as one.

He's just as nervous as I am, it seems.

Thump. Thump. Thump. It's like my beats almost match his. A swift race of only two bodies colliding into the other, both running toward the other until we mesh into one. Two falling stars predestined to fall together. Binary stars.

I nestle my cheek into the silky material of his button-up, my hand slipping under his shirt so I can feel that hot, sticky skin and the flex of his strong muscles. He brings his arm across my back and languidly strokes up and down my spine, calming any tension that's settled across my muscles.

He smells *so* good. Summer pine scents sticking to his sleeves, sweet whiskey collecting on the tip of his tongue, and just a hint of the sandy surf breezing through his tousled locks. I get so lost in the calming scents that I'm just now realizing he's stroking the back of my head, fingers combing slowly through my messy hair of curls as he caresses my lower back with his other hand.

I close my eyes, breathe him in deeply, and relax into his soothing touch, feeling every brush of his calloused fingertips the way he rubs the back of my head and lower back gently. And there I go, getting lost in the warmth of him, wishing I could just stay here all night. But with one more light stroke, my eyes flash open in a panic when I realize what this is.

Aftercare.

Aftercare? Sam is giving me... aftercare? But why? No one has ever done this before. Not like this. Why would he *want* to give me that? I'm not special. I'm not... anything. At least that's what he always told me. My ex. Leaving me chilled and alone on the floor was what he did half the time, only chasing his own pleasure.

Before a tear leaks from my eye, Sam rips me out of my distant nightmare with his deep, gravelly voice blowing gently through my ear. "You okay?" he asks as he trails his index finger up and down my forearm. I wish he'd never stop.

"Oh, mhm," I hum out, nuzzling back into the side of his arm, wrapping myself into a tight cocoon so maybe he won't leave just yet.

Stay. Please, just stay.

He rests his chin gently on the top of my head while he idly lingers a finger on my jawline. "You thirsty?"

Slipping my eyes up to his, I smile. "Yeah, I actually am," I murmur against the warmth of his shirt rubbing gently across my cheek.

"Alright, angel. Let me just go grab some water for you." He shifts his weight carefully, sliding out from underneath me and repositioning me against the soft cushions of the couch, away from the edge. I already miss the warmth of his body and his ocean cologne spinning around me. "You gonna be alright if I'm gone for a few minutes?"

Flicking my eyes up to him, I analyze the question, but don't think too long on it. I nod. "Mhm." I'm used to being alone. I can stand for him to be away for just a few minutes, right?

He shoots me a small smile—one that makes my heart flutter. "Okay, angel. Be right back." But before he goes, he softly caresses my cheek with the back of his hand, leaving trails of fire with me as he walks toward the door. I place my palm right where his hand was, like I'm holding on to that soft touch, tucking it into my pocket so I can feel that warmth on a rainy day.

Feelings I can't describe start to bubble up inside me. Emotions stir in my wide eyes, and I'm suddenly second-guessing what's happening here. He's going to get me water, but that small, timid part of me feels like this should be his exit. He shouldn't come back, shouldn't take care of me anymore than he already has. I feel guilty for being the reason he's in here and not out there greeting guests or shuffling around paperwork in his office.

I'm not an exception. I'm just... me.

Without thinking, I halt him in place just as his large palm grazes the doorknob. "Wait, Sam."

He turns his body around, those warm pools of caramel making me choke back tears once again. "Yeah, sweetheart?"

Sweetheart. There's so much endearment in a nickname like that. I melt a little more each time that name flutters off his tongue just for me.

"Shouldn't you go back to work? I mean, don't you need to go do what you normally do?" I worry my bottom lip between my teeth, my body suddenly freezing from the loss of the furnace that was just holding me seconds ago.

He flashes me a soft smile and lets his eyebrows relax back down. "No. Bryson's got it under control."

"Bryson?" I tilt my head, scrunching my nose up as I ponder who he's talking about, but then I slightly remember seeing the name mentioned on his website.

He stifles out a laugh and leans against the closed door. "My brother, Bryson. He's the co-owner of this club."

My eyes widen in shock. Of course. That's who I must've seen standing next to him in that picture on his website. The one with slicked back blond locks and hazel eyes. Yes, that makes total sense. They look so much alike.

"Oh! I see. You... have a brother?"

He smiles my way and nods. "Mhm. He may only be a year older than me, but he sure as hell gives me a hard time."

"I'm sure he does," I giggle out, imagining what sort of trouble those two got up to when they were younger.

He raps his knuckles on the door twice softly and gazes at me while his hand slides down to the intricate doorknob. "But anyway, I'd rather spend a little more time with the pretty librarian who landed in my lap." My breath hitches at his words, and tingles start to slide down my insides.

Giving me one more smile and a quick, "Be right back," he tugs the door open, allowing the flow of carrying music and echoes to enter the room. He disappears behind it when he closes the door with a click, making the loud music suddenly go silent.

I breathe out a sigh and relax back into the leather, letting my fingers slide against the warm material beneath me. I still smell him, that woodsy summer scent I could get stuck on. It engulfs me, making me churn with need. And then I feel that low tug in my gut when I think of those smoldering dark eyes and that lazy, crooked smile that seems to send my heart into a marathon.

Gulping down fear, I suddenly realize what's happening. I'm getting attached to him... I shouldn't because I don't need another heart shattered into a million pieces. But what if Sam is different? He *is* different. So maybe I need to let my concrete walls down—just enough for him to slip through. Maybe he'd knock all my fears and trauma aside. Maybe, just maybe, he'd be exactly what I've always needed. A rock that'll never let me fall again.

But again, I can't do that. I'm too... fragile. And fragile girls tend to break. But I'm already broken, so what does it matter?

Closing my eyes, I concentrate on the growing ache between my thighs and breathe in his fresh cologne that's left lathered in the leather of the couch. It's soothing, almost like a bedtime lullaby that can hum me to sleep. I'm so close to fading off, drifting into a calm sleep until I hear the rustling noise of a door being jarred open and the sound of party-goers floating through the dimly lit room.

Once I push myself to a sitting position, Sam joins me on the couch, brushing his leg against mine. "Sorry I took so long. Thought you might be hungry, too."

Before I can ask what he means, he brings a basket of crispy chicken fingers in front of me, smiling over at me as he holds them out for me to take. My mouth drops open, and I gawk at him in utter shock.

Chicken? He got me... chicken? He remembered what I said?

Blinking once, twice, three times in appall, I finally reach out and grab the red basket, the side of my hand brushing up against his. "Chicken fingers? I didn't think you had any food here? I thought you said..."

He laughs and places a hand on my thigh softly. "Well, if I remember correctly, some pretty girl just waltzed into my club a couple weeks ago and started complaining about there not being any food. *Specifically* chicken." He narrows his eyes at me playfully and gives me a light squeeze.

Raising his brows with a smirk, he continues his conversation. "She got me thinking maybe I could use a private menu. Something not quite open to the public yet. I thought maybe she'd want to try it out first, ya know?"

My jaw drops in awe, and I'm suddenly speechless for a few timid seconds. But when I build the courage up, I play right back while grabbing a hot chicken tender. "Oh, yeah? Well, maybe she does," I say flirtatiously.

Scooping up a dab of ketchup on the end of the chicken tender, I bring it up to my mouth and take a bite of the delicious goodness, groaning while it slides down my throat. "Holy shit! This is really good, Sam. How did you do it?" I ask with a little bounce in my seat, delighting in the way he's smiling over at me, watching me enjoy the food.

Sam chuckles while grabbing the other half from my hand and taking a generous bite. I don't miss that tiny implication of darkness in his eyes. Flirting, perhaps? "I may have went and bought an air fryer last weekend and a shit ton of chicken."

I shake my head with wide eyes and question, "Why?"

He leans back into the couch and stares at me for a beat before he answers. His eyes glaze into mine while the few gray strands in his scruff catch the dimly lit lighting of the glowing room. It looks like he's contemplating what he wants to say. He slightly shrugs and smiles over at me. "I guess... I kinda hoped you'd come back. So, I went out on a limb just to see what would happen."

I suck in a breath, dropping a piece of chicken into the basket on my lap. Did I just hear that right? He did all that for *me*? I shake my head and run my rampant thoughts together. Sam changed the music for more, cooked me chicken, made me feel pleasure like I've never felt before in my life, even gave me *aftercare.*

Sam is something out of a dream. So charming, handsome, dominant but yet so *soft.* I really need to be careful with him. He's... perfect.

"Oh," I finally gulp, unable to get any other words out.

He just smiles at me, his big brown eyes wading like water into mine. I'm afraid I'm falling hard. No, I'm jumping straight off the cliffside into the rocky waves that'll surely drag me under the blue abyss.

But all my fears can invade my mind later. Right now, I just want to enjoy his company. I want this to last for as long as possible before I slip back into my anxious, restless nights without his touch.

I nod down to his pocket—the one he stuffed my panties into. "Are you going to give me those back, Mr. Club Owner?" I tease lightly, watching the way he smirks over to me with a devilish glint in his dark eyes.

He shakes his head. "I don't think so, angel. Think I'll just keep them. Besides, they look better off you." He winks and then my cheeks flush bright red.

I laugh it off while he keeps his palm grazing against my thigh, eliciting tingles and goose bumps up and down my arms. "You're a menace, Sam Brooks."

"Don't I know it, sweetheart." The low timbre of his deep voice shakes my entire being. I'm afraid I'll get addicted to that enchanting voice of his.

I'm in big trouble, but there's no going back now. It's too late for that. He's already had a taste of me, just like I've had a taste of him—salty, sweet, *delicious*. I want more. *So* much more, I fear.

Chapter Sixteen

Sam

My mind spins vivid images of Violet for the next forty-eight hours on repeat. I just can't seem to get her out of my head. Her silky, smooth skin, the way her ocean-blue eyes look like sunlight, her lilty laugh that makes it hard for me to breathe. And those *lips*.

God. Those crimson lips that stained the base of my cock two nights ago in my club.

I suck in a deep breath, remembering how deep she took me. How *wrecked* she made me feel each time her eager tongue slid up and down the base of my shaft, coating me completely in her saliva. The way she peppered sweet kisses and kitten licks over the entirety of me. I rake a hand slowly over my mouth, my other gripping the leather of the steering wheel so tight that I think I might swerve into the other lane.

Keep it together, Sam. She's just a woman. But she's not just a woman. She's so much more than that. She's... perfect. Sweet as can be, shy with maybe a bit of a mouth on her, smart, funny. And so, *so* fucking beautiful.

She's the one woman who's caught my attention in the entire state of California and held it for more than five whole seconds. But there's that one thing. That one teeny, tiny roadblock. Well, more like two.

One: this is casual, nothing more. And two: I'm not ready to bring another woman into Kayla's life. Kelsey might be fine, but Kayla? I don't want to disappoint her more than I already have. Lois did that—ruined things. What kind of father would I be if I brought home someone I didn't know would last? I don't want to find out. Not yet, at least.

Flicking my right signal on, I turn, casting away the deep ache in my gut that's pulling me back to those pretty blue eyes. Once I turn and move over to the next lane, my phone lights up and vibrates in the pocket of my jeans. When I fish it out, Bryson's name flashes across the screen, so I answer.

"Yeah?"

"Hey, Sammy. Just wanted to double check that I was picking up Kayla from school today, right?" Bryson asks through the other side of the phone.

"That's right. Kayla's gonna freak when she finds out you're taking her to buy new cleats and the pink soccer ball she's been talking about nonstop." I chuckle, thinking back on last night when she pulled up yet another picture and asked me if I thought she'd look good with those shiny cleats at her next game.

His laugh echoes through the phone. "Well, I *am* the best uncle, after all."

"That's what she always says." I shake my head, watching the blur of cars go around me.

Bryson grabs my attention as I zip along 12th Avenue, the towering palm trees lining each side of the street. "Oh, I almost forgot. Benny was at the club Saturday."

Jolting forward, I almost choke on the sip of water that just went down my throat. "He was?" Why am I blanking on missing the professional critic who reviews my club?

Oh, right. Because I was in the back of the club half the night making sure Violet was taken care of. A spark of electricity zaps through the bottom of my spine as I remember just how good she felt in my arms.

Bryson calls my name, making the fog around my head dissipate. "Uhh, yes. And you know what? He was quite pleased with the change of music. Think it impressed him. He might actually rave about it all over his website."

A big smile curls against my mouth because that in itself is a victory. Benny's one of those hard-ass guys who loves to tear down clubs. But this time? I don't think he will. And this is all thanks to Violet. I should thank her for that.

"He talked to you?" I ask, stopping at a red light just ahead.

"Yup. He was looking for you, but you were nowhere to be found. You didn't answer your phone, and you weren't in your office. Hell, where were you, actually? I don't recall seeing you the last half of the night. You take off early or something without saying anything?"

Taking a minute to think, I gulp and try to come up with something that won't sound too ridiculous or fake, but I come up empty-handed. "Umm. No. I was there all night."

"Where? In your *private* room?" he says it like he's using air quotes, which he probably is. But then he pauses when I say nothing.

Shit. Did I just give myself away?

"Wait a damn minute. Were you with... no." It's right on the tip of his tongue, and I know what he's about to say next. I just wish he wouldn't. "You were with that brunette, weren't you?"

Oh, for Christ's sake. Why is he always right?

"N—no," I try to lie, but the stutter in my voice gives me away.

"You were! Holy shit, Sammy. I knew it!"

"Okay, okay. You caught me. Now drop it," I warn, keeping my tightened grip locked around the steering wheel.

"No fucking way! You tell me right now what happened," he yells into the phone, making me wince from the static.

Rolling my eyes, I scoff. "Nothing happened." But it did. *Everything* happened that night.

"Liar," he calls me on my bluff. "You totally nailed her."

My hand flexes against the phone. "Stop it, Bryson."

But he doesn't stop; he keeps fucking going. "You must have it bad. I haven't seen you go after a woman in a long, long time. Was it good?"

"I'm not answering that."

"Yeah, it was. Wasn't it? Lucky guy."

My nostrils flare and my jaw tics in agitation. The last thing I want to have right now is a conversation about Violet with my brother. Because he's relentless when it comes to women in my life, and he's starving to get any information out of me. Mostly because he does want to see me happy, which I get, but he takes it too far sometimes.

"I'm serious, Bryson. Knock it off. We're not... we're..." I can't finish that thought because I don't exactly know what we are. But there's that statement Violet said—*no strings attached*. And I'm *not* looking for a girlfriend or an end of summer fling, but then what is it? Not exactly a hook up or a one-time thing.

It's... *different*. Whatever this is, it's nothing like I've experienced before.

"You're not what? Exclusive? Dating? Seeing each other? Hooking up? Falling in—"

"Don't," I cut him off, putting an end to his ranting questions. I can't do this right now. I can't...

As I near the intersection of the next street, something pulls in my mind, making me swerve into the far left lane. I should still be going straight, past the light. But when I see the top of that big, famous structure around the corner, my mind goes blank. Before I can make a conscious choice, I make a swift turn left onto Park Boulevard—right into the parking lot of the library Violet works at.

"Sammy, you still there?"

I can hear Bryson still spouting out suggestive phrases about me and Violet, but I ignore him, too busy staring at the sliding doors that'll lead me to those big blue eyes.

Putting the truck in park, I take a breath and wave off my brother. "I gotta go. I'll… just text me when you get Kayla."

"This isn't over, you know. When I bring her back home tonight, your ass is telling me *everything* that happened, period." It sounds more like a threat than a promise, but I just brush it off. There's no stopping him, especially when it comes to my love life.

"Fine." I sigh. "Goodbye, Bryson." I end the call before he can say another word. "Damn it," I mutter under my breath, irritated at both him and myself. I wasn't supposed to end up at the library, but I also wasn't supposed to meet *her*. The woman I'm *definitely* falling for.

Turning back is an option. I could put the truck in reverse and speed right out of this parking lot, but the gas is already cut, the keys pushed deep into my pocket, and I have no intentions on backing out now.

Without a second glance, I hop out of the truck and hastily make my way toward the sliding doors, ignoring the handful of students that are parked on benches out front, and walk straight through the entrance.

I should've had a plan, should've had some semblance of restraint. But when I thought of those beautiful eyes and that dazzling smile, I didn't have the heart to make myself stop. My mind's on autopilot, and the only thing that'll make it stop is *her*.

As I waltz through the sliding doors and enter the massive entrance aligned with floor to ceiling windows and hanging pictures of history pieces, I push on through to the main floor of the library. Children's laughter fills the air as I turn a corner where towering bookshelves sit adorned with colorful spines of books. Computers lay scattered around, the busy circulation desk crowded with guests checking out books, and sneakers squeak across the polished floor. It's been a long time since I've been to this library; it's almost overwhelming.

I stop for a second and comb my fingers through my hair, hoping it doesn't look too messy. Pulling against my snug red flannel, I take a moment to assess just what my plan is.

Plan? Wait, I don't actually have a plan. I came here on a whim, hoping I'd find Violet. But I forgot how huge this place is. Wouldn't it be weird to ask a random worker where she is? What if she isn't working today? What if I look like a complete idiot standing here with my hands in my pockets, not even knowing what the hell I'm doing?

But I do know, don't I? I'm here to see *her*. The woman who might be my undoing.

Without another thought, I trudge deeper into the library, quietly glancing around, hoping I'll find just what I'm looking for. Maybe I could just...

I stop in my tracks, sucking in a breath when I find *exactly* what I came here for. There she is, right next to the children's section, kneeling down with an open book in her hands, right at eye level with a little girl with long blonde hair and eyes full of wonder. Violet's reading to her, pointing out something that makes the little girl chirp out a giggle, and Violet just smiles back with big blue eyes.

Something tugs deep in my chest as I watch from a distance, my mouth dropped open as I take the scene in. A part of me wondered if she was good with kids, and this just fills in that answer. She's absolutely radiant today—wearing a light pink sundress, her long brunette waves half up with a white ribbon tied effortlessly in the back, a thin white jacket draped over her arms, a pretty pink blush staining her cheeks, and those same ruby red lips I haven't stopped thinking about. The sunlight seeps through the cracks of the bookcase behind her, making her glow against the warm rays. I have to steady myself because she looks like an angel. She *is* an angel. And she's absolutely breathtaking.

The way she's being with that little girl right now? Well, that just makes me fall harder. A part of me wonders if she'd be like that with Kayla—if she ever got the chance to meet her. And then another thought slips freely from my mind, landing right against my chest. She looks like she'd be a good mother...

Just as I fix a longing stare at her, she looks up and spots me.

Great. I've just been caught staring.

She does a double take and shakes her head, like she thinks she's imagining me. But after a moment, she's handing the book to the little girl and standing straight up, fixing her gaze right on me as she strolls over. My heart feels like a track, and I'm the racehorse that's dying to run over to her.

"Sam?" Violet asks in surprise, her eyes wide with delight. "What are you doing here?"

I shrug nonchalantly and give her an easy smile. "I was in the neighborhood. Thought I'd drop in to pick up a book."

"Oh?' she asks with wonder in her eyes. "What kind of book?"

I lace my fingers nervously through my locks. "I was hoping you could help me find one."

She tugs on a pretty smile—one that makes my heart beat faster—and nods. "I can do that." She crosses her arms over her chest and leans against a wooden bookshelf. "What do you think you're looking for?"

Drawing a blank, I gulp down nerves and shrug again.

God. She makes me so nervous; I can practically feel the sweat building against the collar of my flannel.

"I'm not sure exactly." But when she looks up at me with those stunning blue eyes, I think I found exactly what I'm looking for.

"Well, we're going to have to fix that then," she giggles. Tugging my arm, she leads me through a maze of shelves, down rows and rows of hundreds of books, past magnificent portraits and art pieces that could be in museums.

When she lets go of my arm and looks back with a slight blush to her pink cheeks and a gentle smile tugging at her red lips, I get lost in her eyes, letting the stack of books surrounding me fade away. All I see is her, and I'd spend the entire day chasing after her through a maze of books if only it meant I got to taste her lips just once.

Yes, the thought of kissing those pretty red lips is the only thing I want to be doing at this moment.

She bites her lower lip slowly, letting her eyes roam up and down my frame, her arms crossed like she's analyzing every part of me. Whatever she's doing, I kind of like it, and maybe I want to analyze every part of her too—starting with her beautiful mind.

"You just gonna stand there and stare, or are you going to give me some recommendations?" I smirk her way, asking playfully in hopes she'll play along.

She shakes her head and laughs carefree. "No, I'm just trying to get a good feel of you," she mumbles.

Raising an eyebrow, I smirk. "Think you've already got a pretty good feel of me. Wouldn't you say, angel?"

Her cheeks heat with a tinge of red. "Stop teasing me." She laughs.

"Didn't know I was," I reply with a wink, making her blush all over again. I fucking love it when she does that. She's so pretty when I'm making her fall apart from teasing.

"Well," she says with her head held high, brushing a curl behind her shoulder, "we're never going to get a book picked out at this rate."

"I've got all day," I state matter-of-factly.

She looks at me for a beat, grazing her hand against a crimson spine of a history text, the red blending in with her blushing cheeks. One more flick of her eyes and she's throwing questions around. "So, you read classics. And I'm sure you're into history?" She knits her brows together and pulls out a text on Ancient Rome, skimming the pages before she tucks it back into the bookshelf, reading me like I didn't want that one.

I take a step forward and brush a hand over the textbook she just put up. "Classics, yes. History, sometimes. But yet, not exactly my cup of tea."

She hums and gives me a once-over, turning to the next aisle that's decorated with darker shades of books. Picking up a classic horror, she holds it up for me, reading me so well. "What about horror? You look like you could be into that."

I huff out a laugh and nod. "Getting warmer, angel." Taking the book from her hand, I circle around her and place it back where it came from. "Sometimes a little horror is a good thrill for an evening, especially when it's chilly outside."

Her blue eyes shine like I'm fascinating her, and she seems to be hanging on to every word I speak. "So that means you're into thrillers, right? A little mystery, suspense, murder?"

I lean against the wooden bookshelf and cross my arms comfortably, settling in so I can look at the prettiest librarian I've ever seen. "Can't enjoy my late-night coffee without a little thriller."

Lifting an eyebrow, she ponders, "Sam Brooks takes his coffee late at night?"

"In the morning, the afternoon, whatever chance I get," I confirm.

She looks at me a moment, questions swirling in her blue orbs. "Let me guess, you drink it black?"

"How'd you ever guess?" I laugh, letting my shoulders relax against the smooth books behind me.

She shrugs. "Just a general assumption."

I lift a brow and let my eyes linger across her pretty face. Okay, my turn. "Now let me guess," I start. "You like yours extra sweet, with extra creamer."

She tilts her head to the side, taking a good look at me. "Looks like the mystery is solved."

I chuckle and push off the bookshelf, taking a step closer to her. The smell of lavender fills my senses, clouding my mind for just a second. "What about you? What's been your favorite book lately?"

"Mine?" she asks, surprised. "I thought you wanted a book for yourself?"

I shrug. "I asked you a question."

"This isn't about me." She shakes her head and tries to take a step back, but I follow.

"No? Well, enlighten me." I stare into her curious blue eyes, watching the realization tick into place.

"Do you... you want to read one of my favorite books?" she asks, appalled, like someone just slapped her in the face.

"Mhm." I nod, taking one step closer to her, right into her pretty mist of perfume.

"Why?" she whispers, her wide eyes scanning mine.

I take a chance and brush the back of my knuckles against her arm. She sucks in a deep breath at the touch. "This'll just..." I take a moment to collect my thoughts, "let me inside your mind a bit more."

She gawks up at me, and I watch as her fingers curl into the soft fabric of her dress, trying to figure out why I just asked her that. "Oh," she stutters out, her wide eyes still daunting.

She's so cute when she's nervous.

"What's the last book you read?"

"Oh, you wouldn't like—"

"Try me," I challenge, my eyes darkening and narrowing with the hint of a playful smirk gathering across my mouth.

"Okay then," she smiles, "follow me."

I'm quick to follow on her heels like a cat chasing after its owner. She leads me around a few large bookcases, to the other side of the library, close to the back of the room where books are spread wide and far, encapsulated by an archway that blocks out some of the sunlight, where nobody is currently standing.

When I look up, I chuckle when I see the word *Fantasy* in big, bold letters above the aisle. "Fantasy section, huh? I should've known."

She flips around to look at me, a smile taking over her dark red lips. "Yeah? What gave me away?"

"Isn't that what all the pretty girls are reading nowadays?" I ask with a big grin, watching her eyes melt into swimming pools. A pool I want to drown in.

She shakes off a blush and sucks her bottom lip between her teeth, her gaze averting as her fingers skate over the colorful hardbacks. "You think charm is going to get you far, Brooks?"

I laugh under my breath and nod. "I'd like to think so, angel." She rolls her eyes, but I can see she's fighting off a big smile. But that's okay. I know I just dipped beneath the surface and got under her skin, just enough to raise the red tint in her cheeks.

If making her blush was my job, I'd be rich by the end of the day.

I watch her search through one of the middle shelves, thumbing through books, looking for something that already piques my interest. The way her smooth hand meticulously glides against the pristine spines keeps me watching. "Ah. Here we are," she says happily, snatching a book from the shelf. When she hands it to me, the side of her hand lingers against mine, enough to get my blood running.

Taking the palm of my hand, I drag it over the thick binding, letting my eyes scan the front of the cover that has a dark forest twisted with ominous vines around the edges. "*Incinerate the Darkness*," I read out loud as I flip the book over to see just what I'm getting into.

"One of my new favorites." She smiles over the view of the book, stirring my mind when those beautiful eyes flick up to me.

I smile back and lower the book. "War, romance, magical creatures?"

Her eyes glow a little brighter as she responds. "More than that!" She laughs. "Think of two species who hate each other. War is raging between them, sending turmoil and ruin throughout the forest. That is, until the main female vampire finds Xylas, the werewolf that'll set everything into motion that might stop an entire war."

My brows raise with intrigue. She got me hooked from the very first breath she took. Locking my fingers around the spine of the thick hardback, I tilt my head her way. "You make it all sound so... intriguing."

"Really?"

"Mhm." She could sell me on any book in this library; I don't think I'd ever say no to that melodic voice of hers. "I can't wait to read it."

Her eyes widen in surprise. "Wait—what? You'll really read it?"

I lightly shrug. "Why not? You sold me on it. And besides…" I pause, taking a small step forward. "This'll just let me get to know you better. Your interests, what you like."

A pink blush stains her face while she tries to brush it off with the back of her hand. "I—uh. I'm not all that interesting," she says shyly.

When she tries to pry the book from my hands, I wrap my fingers around her wrist and stop her. "Funny. I think you're the most fascinating thing in this entire library."

She opens her mouth, closes it, and then repeats the motion, clearly speechless from my words. Nothing comes out, but I can see from her big eyes that she can't quite believe what I said.

If someone made her feel uninteresting or boring, I'd tell her every day how unique and captivating she really is.

I take this opportune moment to step forward, just enough to where I have her backed against the bookshelf. Her skin is flushed as soon as I reach out and twist a silky strand of hair around my finger, letting my other hand flex against the pink material of her dress. The room seems a bit smaller in this corner—sunlight dousing her in rays of yellow, her lavender scent swirling around my head, making it hard to breathe the closer I get to her.

Hooking her fingers into my flannel, she steadies herself, her breathing rapid, eyes shining like diamonds right into my soul. My own breathing escalates as I take in this beautiful angel, getting lost in her starry eyes.

"Sam…" she whispers breathlessly as I brush my knuckles across her cheek ever so slowly—reveling each trace, wanting so badly to carve my initials into a locket so I can place it around her neck and claim her as mine.

Mine. That's a fragile word, a scary thought of calling another woman mine. But Violet? I think I'd love nothing more than to call her that—*mine.*

Carefully, I tip her chin up—just enough to see the pretty deep blue irises swirling like galaxies in my vision. She knocks the breath from me. "Has anyone ever told you that you look like sunlight?"

She sucks in a breath and shakes her head. "Sunlight?"

"Mhm," I hum as I push a piece of sun-kissed hair behind her shoulder, lingering my fingers along her collarbone. I can feel how fast her pulse is racing against the tips of my fingers. "Your hair looks like it was kissed by the sun. The way the blonde blends in with the darker brown. And then there's your eyes..."

I stare into her sparkling blues, fixating my gaze on her wide eyes, the way she's starstruck and can't seem to find words. There's so much tension in the air—thick like a fog, but light enough to find my way through. She's trembling beneath me, her fingers twisting deeper into my flannel. She almost looks like she'd kiss me back if I leaned in. Quite frankly, the only thing I am thinking about right now is kissing those red lips of hers. They're probably soft as rose petals.

Leaning my head closer, I get a whiff of her vanilla perfume mixing in with the lavender scent of her hair. I breathe her in like fresh air, like she's my new favorite scent. Floral, mixed with sunshine, and dipped in sugar. There's not enough air left between us because our chests are flush to each other, both our hands twisted in each other's clothes, and all I can see is her.

Kiss her, my subconscious whispers. So that's what I'll do.

Just as I lean down, coasting my lips against her jawline, a book tumbles off the bookshelf and lands between us, startling us apart. Her eyes grow large, and she looks completely frazzled as she dips down to scoop it up into her arms. With one reach, she pushes it back into place on the shelf and turns back to me, still as flustered as before.

"I—um. I should probably get back to work." She looks up at me, her cheeks still flushed but painted in a multitude of shades of bright pink.

Sighing, I run a hand through my hair, trying not to look too disappointed that she has a job to do. "Yeah, I guess you should." I wish she didn't have to so we could get lost together in the sea of books. I wouldn't mind exploring that pretty mind of hers a bit more.

With one more restrained look my way, she nods her head in the direction we came from. "Come on. I'll get you checked out."

Following her to the circulation desk is easy. What's hard for me is keeping my eyes off her. Clearly, I'm not looking anywhere else. It's like she's hypnotized me, cast a spell over me so every time I blink, all I see is her. She makes me forget my problems, pushes me past my boundaries, and almost takes the pain of Lois away. And when she grabs the book from my hands, her eyes make me fall a little more.

She takes her time scanning the barcode, handing me back my library card that's hooked around the black keyring. And when she holds out the thick hardback, she smiles. "The book's due back in three weeks, unless you check it out again. Don't be late."

Don't be late. I wouldn't dare ever be late for her. Not in a million years.

I nod and take it from her, making sure I slide my hand against hers to feel her warmth one last time today. "I wouldn't dream of it, angel." And there she goes, blushing that pretty pink of hers all over her cheeks. I want to capture it with my camera so I can flip it out whenever I'm having a stressful day at the club.

She glances at another guest behind me, then back at me, biting her bottom lip nervously like she's not quite ready to say goodbye. "Well, I hope you enjoy the book, Sam. Really, it's so good."

I chuckle and flash her a smile. "I'm sure I'll love it."

"Keep me updated?" She looks at me with hope filling her eyes, and it tugs on something hard in the pit of my stomach.

"Does that mean you're gonna text me?" I tilt my head and watch nerves float through her.

She shrugs and tugs on a small smile. "I haven't decided yet." But I see it so clearly in her eyes. She wants to.

Playing hard to get, are we? That's alright. I'll have no problem chasing after her. Even if it's through the entire state of California. Once I catch her, she's mine.

I can feel impatience growing on the older woman behind me, so I decide to take my leave. With one more glance her way, I look into her deep blue eyes and give her my best smile. "I'll see you later, angel."

She throws a bashful smile my way and leans her elbow against the desk. "Bye, Sam."

As I make my way out of the busy library, I still feel her eyes on my back like flames, and they're about to burn me alive. My smile stays glued to my face the entire stroll to the car with the thick book tucked under my arm, the other swinging gently against my side. When I unlock the truck and slide into the seat, I rest my head against the leather and sigh as I let Violet run freely through my mind.

This wasn't in my plans for today, but I'm so glad I made that sharp left turn on a whim. If I didn't, then I never would have seen how radiant she looks surrounded by books. It's her niche, I can just tell. She's got this soft glow that surrounds her when she's talking about books. I think it's the prettiest view I've ever seen.

A minute later, just as I start up the engine of the truck, my phone buzzes in my pocket. When I pull it out, an unknown number appears in my view. But once I open the message, I know exactly who it is. *Violet.*

Enjoy your fantasy romance book, Mr. Club Owner. Try not to let the werewolf jump out and bite you later. Might just have to change your club name to Fangs.

I throw my head back in laughter, my lips tugging into a massive grin, so much that my face is hurting. Such a flirty text. "God, this woman," I groan out, quick to respond back to her message.

Sam: If I had fangs, then I'd just have to sink them into you instead.

I end the text with a winking emoji, sending it off with a swish as it goes through, and then I save her number into my contacts. But instead of using Violet, I type in her name as Angel, along with a halo emoji.

Perfect.

And then I sit there for minutes, smiling like an idiot that's falling head over heels. And maybe I am. Maybe I'm falling faster than I realize. And somehow, I think I'm okay with that.

The next afternoon, I'm standing in the sweltering sun while the heat beats down on my tan skin, sweat dripping down the back of my neck. The smell of chlorine sticks to my hair while I fish out some leaves with the pool net. It's oddly relaxing, reminding me of the good days when I owned a pool company. I used to love that—being able to build a pool from scratch, make it into a masterpiece and do it all over again the next week.

But then Lois had to go and mess it all up. Ruin a business I built from the bottom up just to make us go belly up and cut ties with faithful clients. It still stings, still feels like it was just yesterday when I was closing up shop and moving out to the West Coast. Putting it behind me was hard, but also moving on was just as rough.

God, I miss it some days—like today. I miss working with my hands, being able to spend my days in the shining sun, even miss getting my skin all torn up with calluses.

So this is one reason I come over to my neighbor's every couple weeks—to work on their big inground pool. I get to craft with my hands again, get to enjoy something I used to love. Well, *still* love. I still get to have the best of both worlds.

Maybe someday soon I'll build my own in the backyard. Make it into a little sanctuary that's just mine.

Laura and Caleb Baker were the first two people who welcomed me when I moved into The Groves—a quiet suburban neighborhood that seemed perfect for me and the girls. Right outside Gaslamp District in Paradise Hills, but far enough from the busy downtown noise. And now? Those two are my best friends. From helping me find my way around this big city, to helping watch my girls, to being a shoulder to lean on when I was in the trenches with Lois. They were a rock when I felt like my world was spiraling.

I really don't think I would've made it out here without them and my brother. Hell, some days I just scrape by. But for now, I'm pretty happy where I am. I've got everything I need. But still, I feel like there's just *something* missing. Something maybe a certain blue-eyed beauty might fill...

Just as I sweep the blue net across the top of the glittering water, I feel my phone vibrate in my pocket. With one hand steady on the metal pole and the other digging deep in my pocket, I pull the phone free and swipe my thumb to unlock the screen. My eyes immediately light up when I see a text from Violet. The name Angel and the halo emoji with wings just top off the warmth in my chest.

Angel: I expect to have an update on the first five chapters by Friday.

Laughter filters out of my mouth, and I can't help the grin that's curling over my lips. I text back instantly.

Sam: Is that a demand I hear?

I send the text off with a whoosh, but I add a smiley face after. The little bubbles appear, signaling she's typing, then her text comes through a few seconds later.

Angel: What do you think? ;)

Oh, so she wants to flirt. Perfect. I can do flirting. I type out the best response I can muster up.

Sam: Okay, pretty girl. What do I get in return?

The bubbles appear and disappear for about a minute before she sends the text through.

Angel: Whatever you want...

And that right there gets my blood boiling. The sun's stifling rays can't even touch me the way she does. Hot, smoldering like the way her tongue felt gliding up and down me in a steady rhythm that made all breathing cease.

Sam: And if I don't finish?

I send the message, testing the waters.

Angel: Then I'll just have to come find you...

The smile on my face stretches so wide that my cheeks hurt. I don't even realize Laura coming out into the backyard until I hear her call my name from across the pool.

"Who is she?" Laura asks curiously. When I look up, I almost drop my phone into the pool from the intrusion of my flirting with Violet. Stuffing my phone back into the pocket of my swim trunks, I play it off like I have no idea what she's talking about.

"What, who?" I ask coolly, hoping my wide eyes and the blush on my cheeks doesn't give me away. But nonetheless, she reads me like a lit-up highway sign.

"Don't play dumb with me, Brooks. You know better than that." She sends me a snarky smirk across the glassy pool and flips her long auburn hair over her shoulder, narrowing her cat-like green eyes my way. "I'll ask one more time. Who is she?"

Well, shit. I guess there's no hiding Violet from her.

I sigh and relax my shoulders. "Her name's Violet."

"That's a pretty name." Laura raises an eyebrow and slides out a lounge chair. She plops down and crosses one leg over her knee, getting all comfortable while she grabs her glass of iced lemonade. Waving her arm frivolously in the air, she demands, "Well, go on. Tell me where you met her."

I huff out a breath and rake a hand through my sweaty hair, mixing chlorine into my strands. "I actually met her at my club."

Her mouth drops open like she's in shock. "Wait. You're telling me you picked up a woman at your club?"

The net slips from my hand, but I quickly grab it and give it a death grip when I answer. "It wasn't like that. I just..."

"You just what?"

I pause a beat, thinking about the first time I saw Violet from the second floor of my club. All smiles, her hair curled in perfect beach waves, her eyes as deep as the ocean. I couldn't let her go without talking to her just once. "I, umm... I saw her dancing with her friends and thought she was attractive. So I waited for the opportunity to approach her at the bar, and it kinda just went from there."

She shakes her red mane out and takes another long sip, like she's still registering my words. "Okay, wait. You, Sam Brooks, gave a woman your phone number?"

"I gave her my card. There's a difference."

"Mhm," she hums, rolling her eyes exaggeratingly. "Yeah, big difference there. So are you two like... dating?" She says the last word so delicately that I almost miss it.

"Not exactly..." I mutter under my breath, hoping she doesn't catch my words.

She leans to the front of her lounger, pinning me with dark eyes while she sips on her cold drink. "Not *exactly*?"

Oh, fuck. I walked right into that one.

I drag the net slowly through the water, just for a second until I have the courage to clear my throat and look up. She's still staring hard at me, so I break. "We're kind of hooking up, I guess."

And there she goes. She pushes herself straight out of the lounger and chokes on a sip of lemonade. "Wait, wait, wait! Let me get this straight." Taking charge, she starts pacing across the hot cement, her flip flops flopping with every stride she takes. "You're hooking up with a woman who you met at your club, and you're smiling like an idiot while you text her?"

Shrugging, I throw her an innocent smile and nod. "Yeah, guess I am..."

"What's she look like?" she asks, head tilted.

"Long brunette hair, around five foot five, long legs, and her eyes..." I pause a beat and rub at the back of my neck, smiling like an idiot at those deep blues sparkle in my mind. "She's got these big blue eyes. And her smile..." My voice drops off as I get lost in memories of her all over again.

She stops pacing and faces me head-on, her mouth dropped open. "You like her, don't you?"

"I, uhh. I..." My words tumble off the tip of my tongue as my fingers curl against my tan swim trunks, just itching for Laura to stop fishing for answers. But what can I say? No? Lying won't do any good because she sees right through me, and I can't admit out loud that I don't like her because I *do*.

God, I like her so much. It's almost painful to keep in.

"Sam," she says sternly, almost like she's scolding me. "Spit it out."

The grip on the pole tightens until I almost break the end of the net against the dark blue tiles at the bottom of the pool, and then, I crack. "Okay, okay, I like her! You happy now?" I dive out through tightened lips.

"I knew it!" She throws up her arms in glee and yells for her husband. "Caleb, get out here right now!"

Groaning, I drag a palm over my scruff and sigh, letting a chuckle out while Laura dances in a circle. She's been waiting for this day to come; I just didn't know it'd come so soon, or ever.

Caleb sprints through the back sliding door, almost tripping over the rubber mat that's laid out on the back porch. "Fuck," he mutters under his breath as he catches himself, his round reading glasses pushed up the curve of his nose, his black hair unkempt from whatever project he was working on in his office. "Sweetheart, I was just in the middle of prepping for my big case for next week. What's so urgent?"

Laura wraps an arm around his back and leans her head on his broad shoulder, staring over at me with a smile twisted over her pink lips. "Sam's got a crush."

Caleb's light blue eyes widen as he stares at me across the pool, looking like he just got hit by a car. "You mean, Sam likes someone?"

"Mhm." She says it with pride written all over her green eyes, like this is a once in a lifetime experience. But for me, I guess it is.

"Well, I'll be damned," Caleb chuckles out, flashing me a big grin. "I never thought I'd see this day come."

I drawl out a long sigh and shrug an arm up, giving up the fight. "Well, neither did I. I'm just as surprised as the two of you."

Caleb gives Laura a loving stare, his eyes shimmering with affection. She gives him a look that says *I love you* written all over her eyes, then he pulls her in and wraps his arms around her waist, kissing her like they just said *I do* to each other at the altar.

I turn away, not wanting to intrude on an intimate moment that should be private. Maybe I turn my eyes because it stings a little. That was supposed to be me and Lois. Well, it was for a short time when we were first married, but it never quite looked like that. These two—they have chemistry like no one else I've seen. They're perfect for one another.

Caleb's one of the best lawyers in Southern California, and Laura's his stay-at-home wife who keeps busy with her vibrant plants and vegetable garden. Sometimes I see them dancing in the kitchen, getting lost in each other's eyes when they're sitting at the dinner table. Even just holding hands by the pool—they make everything look so damn romantic.

It's not that I'm jealous; I'm far from that. I just wish I had that still. Had someone I could hold hands with. Make them laugh. Tell them how beautiful they are every day. Maybe even show them my secret hideout at the private beach I found the first week I moved in.

And then it hits me like a tidal wave, water spritzing against my face like a salty ocean wave. *Violet*. What if she...

No. This is casual. That's all it is. But is it? It already seems much more than that...

Laura knocks me from my deep thoughts. "What made you change your mind about not seeing anyone?"

"I..." I pause and drag my fingers under my chin, staring straight into the glistening tiles at the bottom of the blue pool, gears spinning in my head. That's easy. Her ocean-blue eyes, her smile that makes me weak in the knees, the pretty blush she tries to hide every time I flirt with her. "She's just so... different," I whisper into the California breeze, letting my words carry off into the wind like a secret.

"Different?" Laura smiles, her voice hopeful that this means something big.

"Yeah..." I quietly murmur to myself, staring off blankly into the depths of the clear water. My voice is in a far off place, just like my mind.

"Shit." Caleb gawks from across the pool. "He's got it bad." And it's true. I do have it bad—like a fever I can't quite sweat off. I've got a crush on a beautiful blue-eyed California woman, and I don't know if I'll be able to stop myself from falling harder the next time I see her.

Laura smiles as she leans against Caleb's chest, her eyes staring at me with a warning in her emerald irises. "Careful there. Might just fall in the deep end." She winks at me, all warning gone from her hopeful eyes.

"Too late," I mutter under my breath. I'm already diving head first, and I don't think I can save myself from drowning.

CHAPTER SEVENTEEN

VIOLET

F riday night is in full swing at my apartment. Taylor's sprawled across one side of the dark purple couch, her neon green nails scratching into the velvet each time she takes a sip of her strawberry wine. Brianna's on the right side of me—her hand stuck in the clear bucket of popcorn, her light brown eyes big as she stares at me while *A Cinderella Story* flickers on the flatscreen behind her.

"Violet!" Brianna squeaks beside me. "He really took you back to his *private* room?" She says it in a hot, heavy voice, her eyebrows arching as she pops another piece of buttery popcorn into her mouth.

"He did." I nod nonchalantly as I take a small sip of wine, letting the sweet taste serenade my tastebuds.

"And he went down on you? Parted your legs on his couch and went to town with his tongue?" Taylor asks excitedly, practically choking on her wine as she pushes herself to a sitting position.

"That's what he did," I say shyly, trying to hide over the clear rim of the wine glass in my hand.

Brianna leans into my tucked legs, taking the pink cotton blanket with her as she gives me a heated stare. "Did he make you come?" she asks with raised eyebrows, like she's an investigator searching to crack the case of every detail that went down that night.

Swallowing another drop of wine, I clear my throat and feel my cheeks turn bright. "Three times," I murmur low.

Taylor spits out a mouthful of wine into her glass, and Brianna nearly falls off the edge of the couch. "No! Three times?!" Brianna shouts at the top of her lungs while I cover my ringing ears.

"Mhm." I nod proudly.

"Three times? Holy shit," Taylor mutters in awe. "Kevin doesn't even make me come three times."

"Well, what else did you two do?" Brianna questions, her eyes wide as she searches mine in wonder.

Gripping my own fuzzy blanket tighter, I flex my fingers into the warm material and bite my lower lip. "I may have gone down on him, too. As in deepthroat..."

Gasps ring around the room, silencing the quiet voices filtering from the television speakers. "You little slut!" Taylor throws a teal sequin pillow my way, and I duck before it hits my head. "Was he big? Tell me he was big."

"Very," I gush, setting down the wine before I spill it all over my clean blanket.

"Jesus, three times..." Brianna murmurs under her breath, her voice stunned like she's frozen over the number. "What else?" she asks enthusiastically, a bright smile taking over her glossy lips.

Dragging my hand nervously over the top of my thigh, I pause for a beat, letting anxious thoughts flood my insides. "Well, it was kind of weird. He, umm... he cuddled with me after. Pulled me tight against his chest and just calmly stroked my back. And it just felt... safe."

When I look up, Brianna and Taylor give each other that knowing look—one only shared between the two of them. Their faces both serious and concerned.

"Babe," Brianna nudges gently as she places a hand on top of my knee, "that's called aftercare. It's normal after you're physical. Or it *should* be."

A pang of uneasiness floods my system, and flashes of the past sting my eyes—me lying on the cold, wet ground, left to pick myself off the floor the minute my ex was through getting off. Pushing the painful memories away, I swallow. "Yeah, I know. It just kind of startled me. I wasn't... expecting that."

Brianna sends an encouraging smile my way and squeezes my knee. "I know, babe. It's a new experience for you, and it's scary. But just know not every guy will be like... well, you know who." She pauses for a second to assess the way I flex my fingers into the blanket, ready for a blow to happen. But none comes, so she continues. "It sounds like Sam is a good guy, and I think he likes you a lot."

"Oh, I don't know," I say skeptically, playing absentmindedly with the fringe on the end of my cozy blanket.

"He totally does," Taylor adds on with a smile.

"Maybe." I look down and twist my fingertips into the ends of my silky pink shorts, laughing quietly about the way he brought chicken into the back of the club for me. "Funny story. He made me chicken strips after we cuddled. I kinda complained there wasn't any food choices on the menu, and I guess he took it to heart."

A shrill gasp comes from my left while Brianna squeezes my legs. "What the hell, that man *does* like you!" Taylor screams across the other half of the sectional. "Chicken? One of your favorite things to eat? That's insane, and you didn't even have to ask!"

Brianna shoves her way into the conversation. "Yes, babe! See. He likes you! God, I'm so glad we pushed you to go talk to him."

I giggle out and shake my head, sliding a little further down into the velvet cushion. Flipping my phone over in my hands repeatedly, I think of those dark, smoldering eyes and that devilish smirk. "I'm glad you guys made me go talk to him. He's... pretty great," I admit out loud.

As colorful images line the flatscreen, Taylor interrupts my silent yearning through a mouthful of popcorn. "Are you going to see him again?"

Sucking my bottom lip between my teeth, I mull over the question. "I was planning on it, yes."

"That's our girl!" Brianna shouts into the void.

Before I can react to my two giggling friends, I feel the vibrations of my phone in my lap. As I pick it up and unlock the bright screen, my eyes light up when I see Sam's name scrolled across the top. He sent me a text message. Eagerly opening it, I can't stop the smile that spreads across my face.

Sam: I may have stayed up past midnight last night because some pretty girl set a clear expectation for me to be done with the first five chapters of a personally recommended book by Friday.

Biting down on my bottom lip, I quickly type out a message and press Send as butterflies flit around my stomach. He called me pretty...

Violet: And did you by chance meet those expectations?

The bubbles dance around the screen for a few seconds, then his message comes through.

Sam: I exceeded them. Made it to twelve. Did I pass with flying colors? :)

Heat blooms in my cheeks, and I can't stop the flirtatious giggle that slips out of my mouth the moment I hit Send.

Violet: Looks like it, Mr. Club Owner. Shall we make it fifteen by Sunday? :)

"What are you giggling about over there, hm?" Taylor asks, making me gasp when she pries the phone from my fingers and starts thumbing through our texts.

"Taylor!" I groan, grabbing for my phone, but she just raises it higher so I can't reach. "Oh my God, Vi. You and Sam have been texting a lot. And look at how flirty the two of you have been!"

"Let me see." Brianna snatches the phone from Taylor's clutch. I try diving for it, but she just shoves me out of the way and breezes through the text messages, her mouth wide open. "Oh, I was right. It *is* him! And holy shit is he *obsessed* with you. Look at him calling you pretty! And wait a second—he showed up at your library and chose a book that *you* love?" Her voice is high-pitched and piercing as she flicks through every single one of our texts.

I lean forward and grab it out of her hand, tossing it on the coffee table out of her reach. "Okay, guys. You had your fun. Happy?" I ask annoyed, rolling my eyes as I try to hide the flush of crimson on my cheeks.

"Umm yeah, babe!" they scream in unison. Brianna smirks up at me with bright brown eyes. "He's totally into you." She tosses a piece of buttery popcorn playfully my way, but I dodge it as it lands beside me.

"But wait," Taylor halts us with a serious tone, one hand up in the air. "Have you kissed him yet?"

A deep, unsettling feeling pulls down my spine, rattling my mind as I shake my head slowly. "Umm. No. Not yet."

"Why not?" Brianna questions, blinking up at me with big eyes.

"I, umm," I choke, knotting a hand through my loose curls, trying to find the words to say. "That's intimate," I whisper out in a quiet tone.

They both just blink at me for a beat until Taylor opens her big mouth. "And sucking his cock isn't?" she bellows, causing me to choke on saliva.

But still, I don't back down from my stance. "That's... different." And it is. Kissing means so much more than any other forms of physical contact. It would mean this is real. I'm not saying that what we have now isn't genuine, but like

I said—no strings attached. I *can't* get attached. But what's this? Having him swim through my mind constantly and the incessant flirting we have going on back and forth with each other?

I don't know what this will be in a few weeks, or months, or however long we keep this up for. But for now, it's just innocent fun. Feelings or no feelings, I *have* to keep myself in check before I lose myself again…

Just then, my phone starts buzzing on the top of the coffee table. Brianna dives for the phone and then stares wide-eyed at me, her mouth dropped in disbelief. She tosses the phone to me and nudges my side. "It's him, he's calling! Answer it!"

My mouth parts in shock, and I jump off the couch, pointing a finger before my friends try to follow me to my room. "Stay here," I say sharply while they sit back down and pout with giggles bursting from their mouths.

Walking swiftly to my room, I shut the door tight and turn the lock. Resting my back on the painted door as I take a deep breath, I slide my finger across the screen to accept the call. With a shaky voice and nerves running down my legs, I answer with a small squeak. "Hello?"

"Angel," he answers in a deep baritone voice that makes my knees buckle. "This a good time to talk?"

I shuffle away from the closed door, ignoring the high-pitched giggles that are ringing around my living room. "Umm, yeah. Right now's perfect."

"Great." I can hear him smiling through the phone.

I gaze at the lit-up neon numbers on the digital clock, seeing that it's nine-thirty at night. Throwing myself on my back into the silky sheets, I tilt my head. "Shouldn't you be working?"

He chuckles through the end of the line. "I mean, I'm at work and in my office. Does that count as working?"

Rolling my eyes, I bite into the flesh of my bottom lip, fighting off a smile. "Well, isn't talking to me distracting you from getting actual work done?"

I can see the crow's feet crinkling his brown eyes through the phone now. "Nah. Think talking to a pretty girl is the perfect distraction." Butterflies assault my stomach, and I can't fight off the giant smile that's growing over my mouth.

"You and that tongue, Brooks," I tease, curling my toes into the silk of my bed.

"Yeah, think I quite like using my tongue on you," he drawls through the phone, making my thighs clench as memories come swimming back of his head between my legs, the flat of his tongue exploring me until I shook with pleasure.

Pushing the aching need away as best as I can, I steer the conversation another way. "Why'd you call?"

"I wanted to talk to you about *Incinerate the Darkness*."

I giggle into the phone, twisting a curl absentmindedly around my index finger. "So you're ahead a few chapters. Tell me, what'd you think of the first meeting? Or, alliance, I guess you should say."

He blows out a breath through the end of the phone. "You know, this book isn't half bad."

"Yeah?" I sit up on my elbows, my eyes big and filled with hope.

"Yeah. The main characters, I like them. Strong, smart, powerful. And the mouth on that vampire? Kind of reminds me of someone," he says with a low chuckle. I can almost see his lips curled into a perfect smirk.

"Oh? Well, I was thinking she reminded me of you, seeing as you have a mouth on you, Sam," I challenge back with my bottom lip curled between my teeth. He lets out a loud laugh that floats through the speaker, making my ears ring from the beautiful noise. God, I really like his laugh.

We stay like that for around thirty minutes—talking about the plot, discussing his theories of what might happen next, bouncing questions back and forth. I almost lose track of time, almost forget my friends are waiting for me in the living room. But a part of me doesn't care because I'd rather talk with him on the phone all night long.

"I never caught your last name," he murmurs through the phone.

"Emery," I reply without a second thought.

"Emery…" he says it like he's assessing every letter, every curve. "What about your middle name?"

"My middle name?" I question, tilting my head to the side.

"Yeah, you know, so I can put your full name in my phone."

I silently laugh at that. He doesn't want my full name to put in his phone. I have a feeling he just wants it so he can speak it anytime he wants, use my full name around me so I'll fall a little more each time he says it.

"Tell me yours first," I challenge.

"Alexander." There's no hesitation whatsoever.

Sam Alexander Brooks…

"Skye," I finally say after fiddling with the edge of my blanket.

"Violet Skye Emery…" He drags the name out like he's memorizing every syllable, engraving the name on his desk with permanent ink. "Beautiful…"

I blink, forgetting where I am, what day it is, because all I can possibly think about is the smooth, measured way he just drew out my name. But I do the same in my mind, repeating his full name a million times over, slipping it deep inside my pocket so I can trace the invisible curves when he's not within reach.

After a minute of composing myself, before I hang up, he stops me before I can say anything. "Look, if you're not busy tomorrow night, do you maybe wanna come hang out for a bit at the club? Say around nine-thirty?"

My stomach does somersaults. "Umm, yeah. I could do nine-thirty." I hide the excitement in my voice as I speak in a composed tone.

I hear a sigh of relief through the phone which makes me silently giggle. "Okay then, angel. Guess I'll see you tomorrow night."

Biting the inside of my cheek, I grin from ear to ear. "Can't wait."

"Well, I guess I'll let you get back to your friends, I can hear them giggling in the background." He chuckles. "I need to go take care of some things out front." There's a pause between his next sentence. "I'm looking forward to seeing you."

Another flip from my stomach, and I'm unwinding. "Me too."

He laughs once more and sighs. "Good night, angel."

Angel. The nickname has my chest clenching.

"Night, Sam." And then I'm ending the call, holding one hand against the side of my head so I don't pass out from lack of oxygen. I still can't believe I talked to him for more than half an hour. And it was so easy, like gliding through a swimming pool.

Clutching my phone to my chest, I walk back into the living room and calmly sit down, holding my huge smile in as best as I can.

"Well?" they ask in unison, leaning forward like I'm the most interesting thing on the planet.

Taking a breath, I exhale and spill. "I'm seeing him tomorrow night at his club."

Brianna and Taylor both belt out shrill shrieks, clapping their hands as they hound me with questions. I just roll my eyes and push Play on the movie again, a big smile on my face while I answer their ridiculous questions.

Butterflies stir inside my stomach as I think of those big brown eyes, anticipating his calloused hands on my skin again.

God, I am so in over my head.

Chapter Eighteen

Violet

Nine-thirty at night, just as Sam asked. Here I am, right inside Club Inferno, awaiting something that almost feels like destiny. I'm standing right by the busy bar, the dance floor disco lights flashing brightly over my silky pink dress, the skirt resting right above my shaky knees. There's a big bow tied in the back, thin straps criss-crossing over my shoulders, and Versace stilettos to complete the revealing outfit. I've never been the one out of my friends to care about dressing up, but for Sam, I'm finding I want to. Maybe it's the way he looks at me, like I'm more than just a nobody. He looks at me like no one else has before, and I'm starting to like the attention coming from him more than I probably should.

The stench of expensive cologne and alcohol surrounds me, the heat of the club sweltering. Intimate conversations and the echo of the blaring music from the dance floor courses through my ears, adrenaline pumping through my veins. I spin in a circle, clicking my heels on the shiny floor as I look from the crowded bar to the sea of dancers, in search of Sam.

Sam. *Where* is Sam? Maybe I could go search for his office. Would he be in there? Or should I text him, let him come find me? Or maybe...

I jump as someone approaches behind me, their towering form casting shadows across the floor which resemble the signs of a man. He clears his throat and makes his presence known. "You looking for Sam?"

Turning abruptly, my loose curls whip behind my shoulders. I blink twice as my eyes peel over the tall, muscular man, my mouth parting as familiarity creeps in. He's got light blond hair half slicked back, but strands of smooth hair fall onto his face. Hazel eyes stare back at me, a smirk that mirrors Sam's. A tight-fitting black suit hugs his broad body, and his handsome, sculpted, clean-shaven face could probably dazzle any of the clubgoers here tonight.

Bryson. He looks so much like his brother, even has the same deep drawl as him.

I shift my weight and tilt my head, assessing him like he is me. "You're Sam's older brother, right?"

"That's right." He smiles, his hazel eyes shining in recognition. "And you must be Violet."

Lowering my gaze for just a second, I fold my arms over my chest and look back up, a hint of a smile on my lips. "You know my name?"

He shrugs, a low chuckle leaving his lips. "I've seen you with my brother the past couple of weeks. Wasn't trying to pry, but I had to with him being my brother and all, you know." He rakes a hand through his blond hair, pushing back a piece from his face. "So naturally, I got him to talk, and he told me your name."

Heat rushes to my cheeks, a tinge of embarrassment twisting around my nerves. Hopefully he didn't say *too* much, like what we're doing together. "Right, since you're his brother." I shake off a laugh, and he must notice how stiff my body is because he quickly changes gears.

Stepping forward, he holds out an open palm. "Apologies. Where are my manners? I didn't formally introduce myself. Let me start over. I'm Bryson. Bryson Brooks, the co-owner of Club Inferno."

I take his strong hand, and he closes his fingers over mine, giving me a friendly handshake. "It's nice to meet you, Bryson. And as you know already, I'm Violet. Violet Emery," I say with a curt smile.

"The pleasure is all mine, darling." Yep. He's got the same Oklahoman charm as Sam. The nickname doesn't go unnoticed.

When he drops his hand, he slides it into the pocket of his pressed black pants, his eyes giving me a quick once-over as he takes in my dress, another smirk forming over his mouth. "My brother treating you good, I reckon? Taking care of you?" There's a hint of an implication coming off those words, like he's digging for more information, but I won't give it to him. I'm sure he's already got a good idea what exactly Sam and I have been up to.

My cheeks flush, and before I can respond, a big hand comes down on Bryson's shoulder, and out steps Sam. His eyes are partly narrowed on Bryson, but they ease up when he meets my gaze, and a wide grin tugs at his lips. "Yeah, Bryson. Taking *real* good care of her, don't you worry." His response makes me blush, and tingles run up and down my spine the moment his eyes drink me in like his favorite brand of whiskey.

"Don't I know it, Sammy," Bryson says with a smug smirk, hitting Sam playfully in the back before he steps to the left. He turns to me and nods, hazel eyes brushing over me once more. "It was lovely to meet you, Violet. I'm glad somebody's finally keeping this one company." He tilts his head to his brother, and I watch Sam's cheeks turn bright red. But he just rakes a hand through his tousled sandy-brown hair, shaking it off like it was nothing.

"Don't you need to go tend to some matters upstairs? You know, the ones *away* from here?" Sam jabs his tongue against the inside of his cheek, arching his eyebrows up as he flicks his gaze to the staircase next to the dark hallway, clearly sending a message that he wants to be left alone.

Bryson gets the message fast. "Right, right," he says with a knowing smile. With one more glance my way, he dips his head in a goodbye. "Hope to see you again soon. You two have fun now." He throws a playful wink my way, then disappears through the thick crowd before him.

When he's finally gone, I turn to see Sam relax his raised shoulders, a sigh drawing off his lips. "So that was your brother?" I ask with a laugh. "He seems nice."

"Mhm. Nice, sure. But he's a flirt and a pain in my ass. His girlfriend really needs to keep him in check." He chuckles, sliding a hand down his jawline while his honey eyes trail over me, a smile reaching his lips. "You look pretty tonight, angel."

I gulp at the compliment, the blush in my cheeks building as I look up shyly at him. "Thank you," I stammer. "And you. Well, you look... *good*." And he does. A clean white button-up hugs his broad shoulders, sleeves rolled to his elbows like usual, black ink swirling around his right forearm. Dark jeans cling to his muscular legs, and his hair is tousled and untamed instead of slicked back and styled. But what I notice most of all is that his chocolate eyes stand out the most. Those gorgeous brown flecks sparkling under the neon lights that send my heart racing.

He drags his tongue over his bottom lip, and I track every movement carefully. Throwing me a smile, he nods to the left. "Come on, this way. I'll show you my office. Need to take care of something real quick."

Pulling me close, he keeps one hand at the small of my back and steers me forward, leading me through a sea of bodies. My breath catches as his sandalwood scent envelopes me, the smell of fresh soap and the warmth of his body making me off center. But like a rock, his arm holds me up as he leads me around the busy dance floor, into a small hallway I haven't noticed before. This one's not as long as the other, only holding three rooms. One centered at the back has two black double doors, the other two adjacent to each other.

Red lights flicker above me, strewn across the tops of the shiny black walls. And just before I can get a word out, he's turning the intricate doorknob that's carved in gold and leading me in. "Welcome to my humble abode."

"Wow, this is your office?" I ask in awe, my eyes widening as I take in the massive space before me. A large mahogany desk sits in the middle of the room with a sleek laptop, empty coffee mug, and pieces of home covering the smooth desk. A glowing red *Club Inferno* sign hangs right next to a cascading window, the black curtains open just enough to see the shine of the city lights trickle through. Wooden shelves line the left side of the room—marketing and business books stacked from row to row. A closed filing cabinet sits next to a detailed model of Gaslamp District, right beside another lit-up sign that spells out *San Diego.*

"All mine." He smiles as he slides his hand out from the curve of my back, walking around the side of his smooth desk. Just when he's about to say something, his phone lights up on his desk, and he groans at the interruption. "Give me a minute, angel. Won't take long." He slides his thumb over the screen and greets whoever's on the other line with a deep businesslike voice, "This is Sam."

Scanning the room, my eyes widen when I turn and see an array of rock albums hung over the entirety of the dark walls. I slowly make my way over, my fingers tracing against each glass frame like it's ancient art that should be admired. The Goo Goo Dolls, AC/DC, Nirvana, The Beatles, and so many other bands fill the space between. But when I see Deftones' album *White Pony*, my body freezes in front of the untouched glass, the pale blue album cast in low lights. My fingers skim over the glass like I can reach in and grab it, brushing lightly over the edge of the frame it's encased in.

Sam never mentioned he had such good taste in music. Music *I* like.

I can feel his eyes hovering over me, even through his quiet conversation on the phone. The heat of his gaze seems to scald me, burn me right to this spot. And through the reflection of the glass, I can see his eyes tracking my every movement, his conversation lost to the brush of my fingers on the frame. When I turn, his fingers are tracing over an open file, but his eyes stay locked on mine in a trance.

"No, I'm listening. Go on," Sam forces out, but I know the truth. He's not listening because he's focused on *me*.

He's looking at me...

After another couple minutes, he's clicking the phone call to an end and setting it down on the sleek desk. Closing the file, he looks back up at me. There it is—the tension in those honey-glazed eyes. I feel it like the heat of summer dripping down my back.

"You never told me you had such good taste in music," I say quietly.

"You never asked." He's stuffing papers into the open file and closing it, his lips curling into a grin as he shuffles toward the filing cabinet. "A Deftones and Goo Goo Dolls fan?" he asks across the room while I trail toward his mahogany desk, sliding my fingers along the end of the smooth surface.

"They're two of my favorites," I say as he opens the top drawer, slipping the file back in its place.

"Looks like we have more than just books in common then," he chuckles through the air.

Sam goes on, talking about his collection of albums at home, but his smooth voice is drowned out the moment I pick up a silver picture frame from his desk, my mouth parting as I take in the image. Two little girls sit on opposite sides of Sam as he crouches on green grass, his arms slung around each of them. One has long, straight blonde hair with bright blue eyes. The other is younger—a purple soccer jersey donned, big hazel eyes, and chestnut hair piled in a high ponytail. And then there's Sam—a little younger, a huge smile splayed across his face, tousled sandy-brown hair, and brown eyes that seem to shine like sunbeams.

Sam. Does he... Is he a dad?

When I lift my eyes, he's gazing at the picture in my hands, walking slowly over to me. I can't really read his expression, it's too vague. Happiness, surprise, a blank stare? "Are they yours?"

He comes to a stop right next to me, brushing against my side as he pries the picture carefully from my hands. "Yeah. They're my girls."

"They're beautiful," I whisper, afraid to move from this spot, hoping I'm not dipping too much into his personal life.

Pride fills his eyes. "Thank you. They're... incredible." He blinks, a little teary as he stares with admiration in his gaze.

Two girls. He has *two*? I bet he's such a good dad.

"What are their names?" I ask, hoping he'll tell me more than just that.

"This one's Kelsey." He points to the blonde first. "She just turned nineteen and is studying structural engineering at the University of California. And this is Kayla," he says proudly, pointing to the brunette. "She's my youngest. Fifteen years old. My little soccer player. She wants to be a veterinarian one day and says she wants to open her own practice for sea turtles." Pride flares in his eyes, a love so deep I can see it practically jumping out of his chest.

My eyes soften and my heart skips a beat. An ache pulls deep inside my chest, creating palpitations that turn into unbearable yearning. He *is* a good father. I can see it in the way he's looking at his girls, all the love in the world spilling from his eyes. And that makes me melt a little, makes me fall just a bit more. I've always had such a soft spot for good dads, but Sam? He has to be the best one.

"You must be so proud, Sam. A structural engineer and a future veterinarian? They must be so smart. And the three of you look so... happy," I gush as I watch him swipe his thumb across the picture, his smile so soft as he gently places it back down on the desk.

"Thanks, angel. And I am extremely proud of them. My girls are my world," he says quietly, a hint of affection written all over his starry eyes.

His girls are his world. I love that confession so much. I like...

God. I like *him*.

I can see it now. He probably takes them to the movies all the time, plays soccer with his youngest, takes them on long road trips, goes on rides with them at Disneyland, feeds them love and affection, telling them all the time how much they mean to him. I see it all like a pretty portrait, every scene playing out in front of me like I'm *right there*. But I stop the yearning that's flooding through me like a river, halt myself from feeling *those* things.

Sam and I, we aren't... together. But still, I reach, desperately wanting to find out more about his home life, his interests, his past. And I almost ask, almost take my hand and run it through his sandy-brown locks, but I don't. Instead, I just stand there in a daze, wondering what happened to his past lover. But again, I don't ask. That's taking it too far.

The way he's looking at me, pride swimming in his flecked irises, hope filling his eyes makes me slip up, makes me throw out words I don't know I'm asking until I do. "What's home like?"

"Home?"

"Yeah. Home," I say. "You're not from around here, are you? Not with that accent."

Sam looks at me a beat, then nods, like he's ready to tell me more. "Oklahoma is where I grew up. It's a lot... different than California," he pauses, scratching his fingers through his scruff. "It gets real hot there in the summers. There's no ocean, there's not much to do. It's a lot quieter, less traffic, especially out in the country. Old, bumpy roads, flat land, lots of red everywhere, including the politics," he laughs, shaking his head. "But it has its quirks, I guess. And the people are mostly friendly. In small towns, everyone seems to know one another. That's how Shawnee was."

I blink, trying to imagine living in a state with no salty breeze to escape to. "No ocean?" I ask with wide eyes. "I can't imagine being landlocked."

He chuckles. "Don't worry, we have the equivalence of red mud and lakes to make up for it."

I laugh with him, then pause, reaching yet again. "Do you miss it?" My voice comes out in a whisper.

He stops for a beat, his brow knitting, lips forming into a tight line. "Sometimes," he murmurs in a low breath. "Some days I think about what my life would look like if I would've stayed, but I don't regret the move. Not one bit. California's my home now."

There's something dragging through his words, a tiny gleam forming in the pits of his brown eyes. I can't quite catch what it is, but it feels like something he wants to leave alone. So, I leave it, even though I want to reach out and brush against whatever he's hiding beneath his deep eyes.

"I umm—I'm glad you came. To California, I mean," I say cautiously, tiptoeing around what I actually want to say. Like how California might've needed him more than Oklahoma. Meaning, *I* might need him.

Don't go there, Violet. So I stray away, once again, believing meeting him was nothing but a lucky coincidence.

"Me too, angel. Me too." Our eyes lock for just a breath, the room oddly silent as our heated bodies brush against one another. And just when his gaze starts to become too much, he tilts his head to the back of the room, beckoning for me to follow. "Come here. I wanna show you something."

"What is it?" I ask, following on his heels with curiosity racing through me.

Sam looks back and throws me a smug smile. "You'll find out in a few seconds." Biting my lip to keep from laughing, I trail after him until he stops and pulls back a white sheet, revealing pink neon signs that light up the moment he plugs them into the outlet by the window.

My lips part. "What are these?"

"I uhh, saw them online and thought maybe you'd help me decide if these would look good up on the walls of the club." He looks at me nervously, taking a hand back through his tousled hair, his lips pulled into an adorably shy smile.

As I take a step forward, I trace my fingers over the edges of the blush-pink signs, taking in every single inch of them. One is in cursive print that says *Stairway to Heaven* with a curved arrow connected to the letter N. The other one has *Stay Awhile* spelled out in big, bold letters, the outline of ocean waves crashing over the top of the words. I swallow, but no words come out.

He listened. Sam really *listened* to every single word I said the first night I met him. I remember it clearly, like it was last night. Saying how the color pink would balance out all the red lights, that it'd make the perfect blend to make his club look better.

"Do you like them?" he asks through my clouded thoughts.

I blink once, twice, and try to pry my hand from the pink signs, but I don't budge. I'm just too stunned. "Sam," I gasp, trying to form words for the swirl of emotions I'm feeling right now. "They're... perfect," I say, stunned. "Is this what you needed to take care of back here? Is that why you..." He slowly nods at me, his lips curling up as his eyes light up like Christmas trees the moment I put the puzzle pieces together.

He brought me back here to get my opinion on signs he bought not just for the club, but for *me.*

"Yeah," he replies, his body shifting toward mine. "I just couldn't stop thinking about what you said about the color pink balancing out the red. And I figured you'd like these. So I bought them. Just needed your approval before I hung them up" He slides his hand right against mine, brushing over my flushed skin, creating heat in more places than just one.

When I look back up at him, his soft brown eyes are all I can see. So I slip, brushing the back of my knuckles against his, teasing the line between no strings attached and feelings that are trying to spiral out of control. "You bought them for me?" I ask breathlessly, my control slipping from my grasp.

He nods, taking a step closer, flirting with fire that can't be tamed. "For you," he murmurs low, his fingers dancing across my wrist, creating goose bumps all down my arms while the scent of sandalwood permeates all around me.

He looks like he wants to kiss me, looks like he wants to...

And just before he hovers any closer, I break the tension, putting distance between our hands. "Should we... go to the back?"

There's a hint of disappointment, but his eyes light up a second later. "If that's what you want." When I nod my head, he chuckles under his breath. "Alright, angel. There's just one more thing I need to do first."

I tilt my head when he opens the bottom drawer of his desk and pulls out a thin sheet of white paper. He comes back over to where I'm standing and holds out his hand, waiting for me to take it.

"What's this?"

"Just something I hope puts your mind at ease," he says.

My eyes scan the large paper, taking in every single black-inked word that's typed across the page. I read it over about a dozen times because I can't believe what I'm holding.

Central Public Health Center: Sexual Health Clinic is typed in bold letters at the top. Sam's full name and information is under that, along with every single test on the sheet being negative. Not a single positive result anywhere in sight. No history of an STI or STD.

My lips part as I swallow. He got every single test done that he could. And the date says it was done last week. Even when I took his word for it. He still went and got tested for me...

"Sam, what's this?" I ask, knowing full well what it is.

He slides a hand through his dark strands and shrugs. "My test results."

"I didn't ask you for—"

"I know." He smiles, crinkling his soft eyes at the corners. "But I wanted you to have them because you deserve to be comfortable. If we're really doing this, I needed to supply you with words on paper. You know, in case you weren't completely comfortable with just taking my word. I wanted to be fully transparent, so here."

My fingers glide over the paper, hovering over his first name while I read it over a thousand times in my head.

Sam, Sam, Sam.

No one's ever gone these lengths for my comfort before.

Flicking my eyes back up to him, I pull a smile over my lips. "Thanks for doing that, Sam."

He nods down at me. "You're welcome, angel. Wanted you to trust me."

Trust is an awfully big word when it comes to my life, but I think I do trust him. More than I've ever trusted any man.

I smile up at him and blink away any evidence that I might shed a tear, and then he tilts his head to the door and smiles. "Come on, let's go."

Dropping the paper back on his desk, he places his hand around the small of my back, leading me out of his office. When he whisks the door open, I look back once more and watch the glow of pink lights disappear from my view, blurring until he shuts the door with a click.

Sam showed me evidence he wasn't lying. Sam wanted me to trust him. Sam bought pink signs just for me. Sam told me about his daughters.

Sam, Sam, Sam.

I'm about to wear his name out in my mind but honestly, I couldn't care less.

I let the echo of the blaring music thrum through my eardrums, let him hug me closer to his broad body as he twists and winds his way through the thick crowd, let my body buzz with endless possibilities of me and him. All I can see is the mirage of flashing, sparkling lights as he takes me down, down, down the dark hallway that'll lead me to the brink of heaven's gates. There's no more room for second-guessing, no more if's or but's as to whether this is a bad idea. I made up my mind the second I stepped into this club and found those swirling shades of dark brown storming under the bar lights.

Before I know it, I'm inside the room. *His* private room. The first thing I notice is the little coffee table packed with two water bottles, a folded white towel, and two empty glasses next to that. "You really thought of everything, didn't you?" I ask as he snatches a bottle, twisting the lid off and handing it to me.

"Well, hydration is important. Plus, you never know when you'll need a towel." He smirks, untwisting his own water bottle cap as he lifts it to his lips, his gaze still on mine.

A blush paints my cheeks crimson. After I take a quick sip, I set the bottle back on the glass table and click my heels across the polished marble, right to the edge of the large pool table. I let my fingertips run along the side of the wood, gently skating the palm of my hand across the red felt. My eyes roam over every square inch of the table, wondering if Sam's a good pool player.

He breaks through my thoughts. "You like to play pool?" he asks across the room, his deep voice floating like a prayer behind me.

Dragging my nails across the smooth surface, I shake my head. "No, not really. Never played much." I laugh. "You?"

He shrugs. "Sometimes. Me and some of my friends get together a couple times a month to play."

"Sounds fun," I muse, gliding my finger up and down the red felt, analyzing the colorful balls tucked neatly together in the center of the table.

"It can be." His velvet voice materializes next to me as he sets his water bottle on the edge of the pool table. "You think you're any good, angel?" He leans against the side, his eyes directly on me.

Nerves rush down my spine because every single time he's standing this close with his eyes locked on mine, I go weak at the knees. But I play off my nervousness and shrug, acting nonchalant. "I'm sure I'm not as good as you," I chime with a laugh, my heels clicking against the floor as I turn directly in his direction.

"What makes you say that?" His head cocks to the side, eyes lingering over every square inch of my silky dress.

Another wave of heat crashes into me, but I let it simmer like lava, pushing it down for as long as I can. "Well, for one, this is *your* club, *your* pool table. And you seem to be good at everything, don't you?"

"And what makes you think you aren't, hmm?" He takes a step closer, a playful smirk pulling on his lips as strands of his silvery-brown scruff glisten under the dim lights. Suddenly, I feel a little warmer than when he was standing a foot away a minute ago.

"I don't know. I'm not... I just..."

"You're not *what*?" he asks, forming a growl under his breath, like he's upset I'm trying to talk down on myself.

"As experienced..." I finish timidly, my eyes flicking down toward the red trimming of the pool table.

Taking a step forward, he cups my chin with his palm and lifts my face, where deep brown eyes stare into mine like crystal clear pools. Pools I want to jump into. "Then let me show you." He smiles.

Let me show you. Those words rush through me like salty sea air, making my lungs tighten from the meaning.

He slowly trails behind me, grabbing my hips and lining me up perpendicular to the table. My heart is lodged in my throat, knocking the wind out of me the closer the heat of his body gets. "First, you gotta be in position. Eyes right on the target, exactly where you want the cue stick to move to."

Sam backs me against his hips, pushing me flush against the edge of the pool table while I stifle a groan at the sensation of him behind my body.

"Then, you gotta take a deep breath. Imagine you're the cue stick, *feel* exactly where you want to hit." His lips line up with the shell of my ear, enough to where he's teasing my skin with his warm breath. One hand slowly dragging up the backside of my dress, one leg spreading my stance wider as I brace my hands on the edge of the table.

"Then what?" I ask, almost panting from the tension.

"Then," he glides his calloused fingers up my inner thigh, right in the crease where his thumb drags along the edge of my red lace, "you have to brace your shoulders, open your legs just enough so you can snap the ball in the pocket you want it to roll into."

He spreads my legs even wider by putting his leg between mine and teases my wet slit with the pad of his thumb, his teeth dragging down the length of my neck as he coos against the side of my ear. "Just as I suspected. Fucking *wet*." Sam chuckles, moving my panties to the side as he begins teasing up and down my drenched folds.

"Mmm. Been wet since you, *ahh*," I hiss the moment he starts languidly circling my puffy clit, making a wave of arousal spill between my thighs.

"Yeah, is that right, angel? Cat got your tongue, so you can't even finish your sentence?" He chuckles, teasing me relentlessly as he leisurely hikes my dress over my hips. In one breath, Sam is tugging the soaked lace free from my legs, stripping me bare and leaving me in a wave of arousal. He pushes me into the side of the pool table, my mind spinning in a blur as he starts circling my bundle of nerves again fervently.

"Sam," I breathe, hot gasps leaving my glossy lips as two thick fingers curl up inside my dripping hole. Tipping my head back in ecstasy, I lean against his broad chest and *feel* the way he lights a fire in my core with his experienced fingers.

"*Yeah*? You like that, don't you? Think you're ready for more?" He chuckles, sliding his palm from my hip as he undoes the zipper of his jeans.

My eyes grow wide when I hear the clank of his belt and feel the denim material being shoved down, along with his briefs. And then I feel the hardening of his cock digging into the small of my back. Groaning, I let him know how good it feels the way he takes his tip and languidly slides it along my wet folds, coating himself in my slick as I moan against the glorious feel of him. But before he goes any further, I hear him sigh behind me.

"Shit," he murmurs under his breath, his hand rustling deep in his pocket.

"What?" I gasp out, alarmed.

"The condom. I left it in my office," he huffs out. I can hear the grind of his words through the clench of his teeth. "Let me just—"

I clamp my hand around his wrist and beg him to stay. "No," I mewl out. "It's okay. Just... don't leave."

"But I just want to be—"

"Sam," I state, adamantly. "Seriously. It's okay. I'm on birth control. You don't have any STIs. I... I trust you."

There. I said it. I trust him. I trust him enough to be smart about this, which he's definitely being.

I never thought this would happen—me telling a guy it's fine not to use one. But I'm not ovulating, and this is the least likely time I could even have a chance at getting pregnant. So I'm going out on a whim because I'm too selfish to let him leave this room right now. And I can't wait another minute to feel him inside me.

"You sure about this?" There's so much hesitation in his tone, a serious question he's imploring.

"Positive," I breathe out, no hesitation crackling in my clear voice.

"Alright. Well, then..." Spreading my legs wider, he bends my hips slightly over the firm edge of the table and then cautiously pushes the tip through my folds. "Deep breath," he murmurs. I squeak, silently begging him to continue.

Fuck me. Please, just take me.

As if he can hear the plea inside my mind, Sam blankets himself around the back of me and runs his tongue along the shell of my ear. "So you want it all, angel? You want to know what heaven feels like?" he whispers inside my ear, filling my mind with fog and lust and an absolute burning need that singes my core.

"All of you?" I ask, curling my fingers against the red felt of the giant pool table, imagining how *good* it'll feel to have him pound his thick cock deep inside me.

"*All* of me," he promises with the snap of his teeth.

"Ye—" He gives me no time to finish my thought before he's pushing all the way inside, stretching my walls as far as they'll go. I gasp for air as he plunges again deeper, harder than the first time. The stretch has me moaning his name, has more slick running down the bulging veins that surround his massive length. And then he's thrusting harder, *deeper* inside me. I swear he's kissing the back of my cervix.

"Oh, fuck me," I moan as he pushes me down against the table, the side of my face kissing the red felt while my fingers dig into the soft material.

"Isn't that what I'm doing, pretty girl? Or do you want it harder?" he growls, his thick fingers pulling me by the hips until he's repeatedly bottoming out inside me.

I can't think straight, can't even comprehend how I got here. All I can think about is those smoldering eyes and his tower of a cock that's throwing bolts of intense pleasure inside my entire body. And it feels so *fucking* good.

"More," I plead, almost to the point of tears from how much he's splitting me in two right now. But I don't want it to stop. I *never* want him to stop. This feels too good.

"Fuck. Come here then," he groans as he pulls his cock from me and spins me around to where I'm sitting on the edge of the pool table, my legs straddling his hips until he's pulling me to the very edge and lining up with my dripping core again.

"You want more, angel? Then *take it*." He smirks devilishly my way and then thrusts hard into me, so deep that I'm arching my back and calling out his name.

"Sammmm," I call, dragging his name out like the building pleasure that's coiling in the pit of my stomach.

"Good girl. Say my name. Just like that," he demands as he pulls the front of my dress down. He latches his mouth around one of my breasts, his tongue flat against my pebbling nipple as I scream with a wave of pleasure that rides through my core. He does the same to the other one, lapping against it until my fingers are laced through his tousled hair, making a groan slip from his own lips at the feel of me clinging to him.

"Yes, *yes*," I moan as I feel his cock relentlessly driving up inside me at an angle that kisses my spongy spot. The one that makes me see entire galaxies. His coarse hair at the base of him brushes against my needy clit, making me scream his name with each stroke he gives me.

I'm right on the edge of breaking, and he knows it. *He knows.*

"Attagirl, angel. Taking my cock so well," he praises. I try to pant out a response, but none comes. I'm just so gone on his dick, basking in the sensational bliss that Sam is giving me.

"Know you're close, sweetheart. Let it out. Let me see you come on my cock," he growls.

Sam cups my chin between his thumb and index finger and lifts my head to where my eyes are level with his. I gasp, seeing just how beautiful those flecks of onyx and dark shades of chocolate are that coat his eyes, making them almost sparkle around the room.

I'm suddenly feeling vulnerable, like I need to avert my gaze, but I can't. I just... *can't.*

The way he's looking at me, like a starving lion, makes me squeeze my legs around his hips a little tighter. He wants to *devour* me on the spot, but there's something else entirely in his gaze that softens just the slightest. And it has me desperate to run, to hide in the shadows so he won't bring out these growing feelings that are burning through my chest.

Do not fall for him. He's not mine to fall for. I don't need another repeat of before. I don't *need him.* But I'm terrified I *do* need him, and that scares the hell out of me.

His eyes bore into mine so intensely that I swear I can see fireworks going off inside those gorgeous irises, numerous vibrant colors blinding me with shades of dark browns and flecks of gold that I feel them colliding straight into my heart.

He smells of summer and sandalwood and chopped pines mixed into the very fabric of his being. I almost drown in the scent. It's so overly consuming that it threatens to knock me off this very table and onto the floor where I'd drag Sam down with me.

His lips are so close to mine, our foreheads nearly colliding as I feel the sweat from his tousled locks drip down onto my flushed skin. And now, he's staring directly at my mouth.

Oh, fuck.

I *want* to know what he tastes like, *want* to feel that beautiful mouth on mine, *want* to collide my tongue with the taste of his, but I just *can't*. Kissing is intimate. Kissing means this is more. But I want it to be more, don't I? And that thought alone drags me out of the intense trance I'm under.

Just when he's about to go for my lips, I quickly turn my head, and his mouth lands directly on my jawline. His eyebrows furrow a little like he's confused; a little hurt flashes across his eyes. Guilt takes a hold and wraps tightly around my insides, but I push it down as Sam starts kissing down my neck instead. He tangles his thick fingers through my loose curls, his hot breath skating down my skin as he starts to suck ravenously at my collarbone. His hips thrust hard up inside me, continually kissing that sweet spongy part that has my body begging for more. I'm so far gone that my head feels foggy and heavy the moment I start to combust.

"There you go. That's a good girl," he praises the second he feels me clench around his length, ready to spill for him. "Let me see it."

I let go, feel the blinding orgasm wash over me, hear my own ragged breaths surround the shiny black walls. But what sends me over the edge the most is Sam's crooked smirk and deep gravelly voice as he calls me a good girl while I come undone.

I'm exhausted, my body spent, but he's not done with me yet. No. He hasn't finished yet, and I know he intends to wring another orgasm from me.

"Christ. You feel just like velvet coming around my cock, angel. I want to feel you do it again. Want to take you over the edge," he pants out, and then he starts to *climb* my body.

Pushing me back to where I'm sprawled against the middle of the pool table, the colorful balls fly every which way when my arms fall to each side, clinging for anything to hold on to. My legs are spread till I'm basically spread-eagled over the red felt. Sam *crawls* on top of me like he's dominating my very being, claiming what's his for the night. I let out a gasp when he folds my knees into my chest, twisting and contorting my limbs till I'm a pretzel.

"I'm not done with you yet." He smirks. Taking the bottom of his thumb, he starts spreading wet arousal over my folds, and the man fucking moans, like he's reveling in the feel of my body. "So *fucking* soft for me, angel," he groans as he brings his thumb up to his mouth and sucks the arousal down.

"Oh," I murmur under my breath, watching him revel in the taste of *me*. My eyes are blown wide at the mere vision of Sam above me, delving in my taste, moaning my name through each lick of his thumb. It's intoxicating, watching him drink me down like I'm his favorite drink of choice. Just staring at him like this is enough to make my mind all fuzzy—the tousled, messy hair, the rippling muscles that flex each time he moves, the dark eyes that penetrate me into place, the silver threads that lace his dark scruff. He's so fucking beautiful. I could just lay here all night and stare at him for hours. He's just that electric, and I'm afraid I'm falling hard for him. Maybe I can't stop myself from slipping into the darkness, but he'd catch me. At least I'd like to think he would...

"Sam," I mutter, my voice barely a whisper.

"What is it, angel?" he asks softly as he brushes a strand of hair delicately behind my ear.

Intimate. That's fucking intimate. But I'm not sure I have the strength to care at the moment. I just *need* him to touch me again.

"Touch me, please," I beg, my eyes teary as I look up at him, clinging to his broad shoulders like I'm desperate for his touch.

Sam chuckles and leans in, his warm breath blowing over my face. "That's all you had to say, sweetheart."

He quickly pins my arms above my head, his hands lacing around my wrists, and then he's plunging deep inside me like the hilt of a sword, his cock splitting me in two all over again as his dark eyes stare directly into mine.

It's like an entirely different world in this room than out there in the noisy crowd of people. In here it's just the two of us—ragged breaths and tumbling bodies that seem to magnetize to each other. It's nothing I've ever experienced in my life, the insane pleasure coursing down every single nerve ending in my body, and Sam just makes it burn that much hotter.

Sam clenches his teeth the deeper he ruts into me. My high-pitched moans collide with his, and the room fills with a symphony of ecstasy. His hands roam *everywhere* over my body, and I swear I'm about to ignite into flames in this very spot. I might just burn the entire club down.

"So good," he groans through the motions. His forehead falls down on mine, his lips so close, practically screaming for me to let down my walls so he can pull me in for a kiss. I almost want to, almost break as the scent of cinnamon lingers across my face, but I keep my walls high, kicking away the urge that's driving us both insane.

"Sam, I'm not gonna—*fuck*—last much longer," I grit through my teeth as he thrusts into that perfect spongy spot I can never reach myself.

"Then *let go*," he growls, digging his fingernails into my captured wrists as he ruts faster and harder into me, bottoming out time and time again.

Happily obliging for him, I arch my back off the red felt as I slip into oblivion and let the white-hot heat slowly drip down the length of my spine. It feels like warm honey sliding down his cock as my mind turns to mush, my lips moaning his name as I release *everything* for him.

"Good *fucking girl*," he praises me through it, keeping his steady pace of sliding his cock in and out of my pussy that vibrates for him. I indulge in his praise, my body convulsing from the intense climax. And now, I'm just waiting for him to crack, too.

His strong body hangs over mine like a sturdy tower, his flexed jaw clenching as he groans to himself, angling my hips higher as he dives inside. Deep strokes blend into pure need that consumes me whole. I'm surprised the pool table hasn't collapsed at the rate the two of us have been going at it. We're igniting into flames together, uncontrollable ones.

"Violet, I'm about to—" Sam pants out, his breathing erratic with each thrust he gives.

I thread my fingers through his dripping locks, my smile wide as I encourage him just like he encouraged me. "So let go for me, Sam." And he does, in that exact moment. He slides out his cock from inside me, throwing his beautiful head back as he strokes himself, until warm shots of cum paint the inside of my thighs. The way he moans my name makes me melt, has me gripping the edge of his bunched up shirt, until he's finished releasing himself.

He takes his time shoving his softening cock back into his briefs, adjusting his jeans until they're back on his hips and in place. And as he turns his back toward the pool table, my eyes stay locked on his while I try to focus on deep breaths. Out of habit, I cringe just thinking about him letting me lie here on the pool table by myself, his sticky cum between my thighs, leaving me a mess just like my ex had done a dozen times. But Sam surprises me. He's not even away for a full minute until he's carefully spreading my legs, taking the towel and wiping away the evidence that he'd been there.

I watch him like I'm memorizing him. The soft strokes of his hands, the careful way he glances up while he cleans me off, the crooked smile that makes me breathless. He's always so gentle and careful with me, like I'll break any second. He's just so... *soft*. That's something I've never had before. He makes me feel taken care of.

When he's finished pulling down the skirt of my dress and adjusting my top, he collapses on his back next to me, brushing his arm against mine. We just breathe for a few seconds, focusing on deep breaths and getting oxygen into our lungs. I feel like I just ran a marathon, and Sam was the wolf that chased me to the finish line.

"That was amazing," Sam beams next to me. When I turn my head, he's smiling brightly over at me, his chocolate eyes absolutely sparkling. He gazes at me like I'm the only girl in the world he sees. It makes my breath catch.

"Yeah, that was... incredible," I reply, still breathless from the unbelievable sex Sam just gave me. "You did a number on me." I giggle under my breath, feeling heat bloom in my cheeks.

He chuckles and nods his head, smiling over at me. "If I made you feel good, then at least I know I'm doing one thing right in this world."

Sucking my bottom lip between my teeth, I scan his messy hair, fighting myself from reaching out and lacing my fingers through the soft strands. It'd be so easy to roll over and rest my head on his chest, explore the brown flecks of his shining irises, to just fall into him.

He watches me toy with the idea, smiling at whatever it is he's thinking in that beautiful head of his. And as the fire crackles and pops in the corner of the room, a question leaves his lips. One that throws me off guard. "What's your favorite color?"

I knit my eyebrows together and part my lips at the question. He's asking me my favorite color? Right after he just pinned me down and fucked me on the pool table?

Tilting my head to the side, I answer, "Pink."

His eyes light up a little, and a smile encapsulates his lips. "Ahh. Pink. Of course that's your favorite color. It makes so much sense now." He hints at the way I brought up the pink signs the first night I met him, then his eyes flick over my shiny pink dress, smiling like he's got a major crush. But he's not just smiling at the color; he's smiling at *me*.

Butterflies assault my stomach; nerves ripple through my bloodstream. To take some of the heat off, I ask him just as much. "And what about you? What's your favorite color?"

"Blue," he answers without a second thought, staring me deep in the eyes.

"What kind of blue?" I whisper, afraid to break the tension that's hanging like a cloud over our heads.

Throwing me an easy smile, he goes, "Like midnight or cobalt blue. Not just any type of blue. But one that's as deep as the ocean. The kind you'd only find under the moonlight or ten feet under the waves. Blue like I've never quite seen before..."

All forms of breathing stop. He wasn't just telling me his favorite color. He was describing the shades of my irises, all while staring deep into my eyes...

"Oh," is all I can get out, because I'm glued to this spot. My lips part in awe as I stare at his dreamy eyes that seem to soften into puppy eyes. "That sounds so pretty," I whisper out, letting the back of his knuckles brush against mine.

"Never seen anything prettier in my life." He says it so freely, like he's blowing it into the wind, allowing the trees to listen, too.

We stay like that for minutes, just staring at each other, not saying a word. The way he's looking at me says it all. He's got a soft spot for me, just as I do for him. And I don't know how long we can keep this up before one of us breaks or slips up. People shouldn't feel like this in a no strings attached situation, but did I set myself up for failure for saying that in the first place? Will all this come crashing down soon, this charade of a game? Except this isn't a game. This is all *real*.

Will I be able to swim my way out of the high tide before it swallows me whole? Or will it drag me down until I can't reach Sam anymore...

Chapter Nineteen

Violet

Ocean waves crash in the distance as my body tosses and turns in the sheets. My fingers claw into the pillows, and my body rocks from side to side like I'm fighting off a monster. I feel sleep drag me down, feel the black tides slip over me, calling to me like deadly sirens at sea. I try to push the chanting voices away, try to drown out the rock of waves against my head, but nothing works. I'm slipping down into the abyss, body tangled in a net, cast out into the middle of the ocean where no one can hear my silent screams. I'm just mute, a paralyzed skeleton between my sheets.

My body stills for a moment as the waves close in on me. I can't move, can't swim my way out of this one because I know this feeling. This hollow, helpless feeling. I'm being pulled into one of my nightmares. The ones where narrowed green eyes and dirty blond hair fill my vision. The one where I'm at that kitchen table. Where it all began...

No... I'm caught in a place between wake and sleep, but I'm being pulled into darkness. I claw at my nightgown, grit my teeth, whimper as if I'll just wake up. But I don't. I'm too far gone, too lost in the fog of a memory I don't want to relive.

And then I'm just... *gone.*

The edge of the silver fork rakes against the porcelain plate, making my teeth grind at the wretched sound. The pop of the open beer bottle has my nails digging into the wall of the little apartment kitchen.

"Violet," Jason growls from the dining room, his mood enhancing with every sip of alcohol he takes.

I hold my head high and try not to drop the shaking plate of freshly baked brownies. Try to stop my beating heart when I place a gentle hand on his shoulder, holding the plate in front of him.

"Yes, love?" I ask sweetly, holding back the fear on my tongue, masking the absolute terror that's surely swimming through my eyes.

His jaw tics as he grabs a brownie, roughly pushing the plate back where it almost drops from my grasp. And when he takes a bite and looks up at me with heated eyes, I freeze.

"Thought I said dark chocolate." He chews through the dessert, scowling with each rip of his teeth, green eyes flashing anger up at me.

I shudder in place, my voice coming out shakily. "I... I know. I'm sorry. They only had milk chocolate. They were out of the dark. I could just... go to another store." Taking the plate out of his reach and stepping back, he loops a firm hand around my wrist and stops me in my tracks, dragging fear from my lungs.

"Did I fucking say I was done?" he yells, whipping the plate from my hand and throwing it across the table to where glass shatters. Brownies go toppling to the floor, along with his bottle of Budweiser.

"No... no I." He stops me short by jumping up from his seat. There's nothing but hot anger fueling the fire. He shoves me up against the wall and pins my wrists to where I can't escape. And no matter what I say, it doesn't fucking matter because he's drunk and lost to rage. "Jason," I try again, voice muted when he punches a fist through the wall next to my head. Terror eats me alive, has me fearing for my life. This is one of his worst nights.

"You stupid slut. Cooking me a dry chicken. Serving me overcooked brownies that aren't dark chocolate. Making me ask for another beer when you damn well

know I asked for a new bottle over ten minutes ago." His hot breath scorches my face like fire from a dragon's snout and has me whimpering into the wall, praying he doesn't lay a hand across my cheek.

"Jason, please. I—"

"Just shut up! For once in your life, just shut your goddamn mouth and listen to me!"

I fall into a helpless silence while tears slide down my cheeks. My body trembles beneath him, my legs about to give out as his bloodshot eyes stare at me like I'm the most disgusting human on the planet. His eyes aren't even bright green anymore. They're more murky, like a swamp, but filled with blood. My blood.

Just when I think he'll lunge for me, he pushes his strong body off the wall, leaving me to coil in on myself as I slide to the floor in a desperate heap, thanking God he didn't completely lose it tonight. But there's bruises on my wrists from his tight grip, which will probably stain my skin purple by the end of the night. I can't even catch my breath till Jason is right back in his wooden chair, his uneaten half of brownie back in his mouth.

"Clean this mess up," he grumbles out, a deep scowl permanent on his mouth.

With one more deep breath, I push myself off the floor, dragging my body through the entrance of the kitchen to grab the broom. But before I can reach it, a gentle hand tugs on my wrist. Whipping around in fright thinking it's Jason about to tear me a new one, I freeze in place. Warm brown eyes swim in my vision. His lips parted with hurt, concern lathered all through his tanned features.

Sam...

"Angel."

And just like that, I'm ripped from the nightmare. I gasp for air, choking on nothing as I throw the sheets from my bare legs, desperate to relieve the fire that's burning through my lungs. My body shakes violently, my legs wobbly and weak once I hit the light switch in the bathroom. I barely make it to the edge of the toilet before I'm throwing myself on the floor, knees scraping against the pink bathroom mat.

My head pounds with a rolling migraine, my stomach clenching to empty whatever's left in my system. Leaning forward, I death grip the edge of the toilet. All that comes out are dry heaves suffocating my lungs. Heat churns in my gut as I think of those violent, red-rimmed eyes, his fingers wrapped like vines around my wrists.

My skin ignites like I just burned my skin on the stove from the memory. Grabbing a hold of my faded scar on my left wrist, I let the tears run rampant down my cheeks.

"It was just a nightmare," I whimper to myself, my legs giving out as I topple back against the edge of the porcelain tub. Curling my arms around my knees, I rock myself till I'm calmed down, till I know I'm safe again.

"You're safe. You're okay," I whisper out, letting another tear fall down my face. "It was just a dream…"

But that dream was once a reality. Was once something that happened time and time again. As my breathing slows, I let the vision of Sam float through my mind.

Sam. What was Sam doing in my dream? I'm always alone in them. Always stuck cleaning up my own mess. No matter who's been in my life before, it's always just me and Jason in these nightmares. But Sam's starting to imprint his way in them now. Little flashes of his eyes, a soft touch to my skin, something warm to help me find my way out of the nightmares.

He's like my personal guardian angel.

I toss more ideas around, fiddling with my bottom lip while I think. Maybe it's because I've been spending more time with Sam. Or maybe it's because I was texting him before I fell asleep. Or maybe he's…

My thoughts pause, thinking back on my therapy session where I saw him in my hypnotic state. The bottle. He caught it before it hit the ground. Before it could break apart and slash my wrist open. But then this time, he had a loose hold on me. Looked at me with those soft brown eyes of his. Like he wanted to save me.

Groaning, I drag myself off the cold floor and fall back into bed with visions of Sam clouding my mind. A part of me wishes he was right next to me, so I could snuggle into his warm chest. Maybe he'd take all my nightmares away, bottle them up and throw them out to the sea.

Maybe he'll be the one to make them all just stop.

The next afternoon, I'm pretty useless at work. I'm distracted because I didn't get much sleep. I'm still running that entire nightmare through my mind, trying to piece together what happened. Why Sam showed up.

Maybe I'm overanalyzing this whole thing. Maybe I'm just *still* not over what happened. I'm definitely not over it. Healing from it, yes. But over it? I'm far from it.

Janet doesn't even bother me today. She probably knows better by now, even though she keeps sending disapproving glances my way with her beady eyes and pursed lips. I shrug it off and just shuffle around a bin of books, half here and half somewhere far away in my head.

Tension snakes its way into the back of my neck, creating a pounding headache I try to shake off. Working my fingers through the knots in my neck, I sigh and make my way back to the circulation desk, figuring coffee might help this growing migraine. I'm just tired and jumpy. This should help, I hope.

Taking a sip from my sparkly mug, I collapse into the leather chair and unlock my phone. Brianna's always so comforting when I bring up shaky topics. Maybe she could help ease my mind a bit.

I pull up her name and type out a quick message. Well, not that quick, because my fingers are shaking just typing the words out.

Violet: Hey, you busy? Had a rough night and could use a friend.

Flipping the phone down onto the smooth desk, I don't even get one step away before my phone is lighting up.

"That was quick. I wonder if she's..." My breath stops as I look down and see a new message from Sam.

Sam...

Sam: You don't happen to like the movie *Van Helsing*, do you?

My fingers can't quite move fast enough as I type out a reply.

Violet: Hmm. Maybe...Why do you ask?

A quiet snicker leaves my lips as my mouth twitches into a smile.

Sam: Figured pretty girls liked Dracula and werewolves, maybe some action with bits of horror. Ya know, someone like you. :)

Oh, this man. This smooth flirt of a man. Shaking my head, I can't ignore the heat filling my cheeks as a blush stains my face. Biting my bottom lip, I send another text through.

Violet: Ahh. I see. Well, what if I told you I've seen it about ten times?

My phone vibrates in my hand a few seconds later as his text materializes in front of my wide eyes.

Sam: I had a feeling. Guess I was right all along, angel.

Angel. Spinning around in my chair, I hold the phone to my chest, giggling to myself and smiling like I've never quite smiled before. Well, not like I have until I met Sam, that is.

I don't quite know what it is about him that pulled me to him in the first place. Maybe it was his big brown eyes, his Southern charm, the way he can make me blush like no one else can. The way he puts me first before himself. The way he... *cares.*

Yes, cares. That's the word.

It's strange. No one's ever cared about me before. Not like he seems to care. And we aren't even *together.* Well, we're something. Casually dating? No, dating isn't the right word and hooking up isn't, either. A situation-ship, maybe?

Oh, I don't know. But none of that matters now. For now, I'll just enjoy whatever we are and worry about it another day. Right now, this feels right.

Tugging my bottom lip between my teeth, I send another text and then another, until it's just a repeated cycle of this back and forth flirting. And even though Brianna's text comes through, I slide up on the notification and continue texting Sam.

For the moment, all my fears and worries about my nightmare fade away. All my anxiousness floats up to the roof, freeing me of the weights that sat like concrete on my shoulders. Right now is mine and Sam's time. Which is turning into being my favorite moments.

It's only a few more minutes of playful flirting till he asks.

Sam: So, Friday? My office is wide open if you wanna keep me company. Maybe I'll pretend to get some work done. Or maybe I'll just be distracted by an angel.

Leaning back into the office chair, I kick my feet and try to compose the internal scream I'm letting out. Like in *Sixteen Candles* when Samantha finally gets the dream guy, Jake Ryan. Except this time, I'm the one getting him. Whatever getting him means...

Violet: I'll be there :)

And I will. Fridays are becoming my new favorite day. No strings attached or not. I can't lie, I really love spending time with the man with big brown eyes.

CHAPTER TWENTY

SAM

The soft hum of Nirvana plays quietly from my laptop speakers in the background. My fingers tap gently against a sand-colored folder as I place it back in the file cabinet. I'm only half listening to the lyrics of "Something in the Way", placing my full attention on Violet the minute her beautiful voice slips through the still air. Her voice is as angelic as her presence, almost glowing as bright as her soft blue eyes. Eyes I have a hard time looking away from.

"So, how long have you been in San Diego now?" she asks across the room as her dainty fingers slide against the mahogany desk.

"A little over five years now." I skim through another open file, pushing through the mess that sits before me. When did I get so much damn paperwork?

"That's quite a while. You like it, I'm guessing?"

I turn and watch her still trailing around the desk, her fingerprints now imprinted in the leather of my chair. "Yeah, a lot, actually. It's more homey than I thought it'd be." And I continue to stare, my eyes locked on the way she moves. Like she's walking through water. Graceful, easy, like a fairy dancing in the rain. Hips swaying side to side, black heels clicking back and forth against the shiny marble floor. And those legs. God, those fucking long, smooth legs that seem to go on for days.

She's so pretty...

 "And before San Diego? Were you in Oklahoma?"

Her question jolts me out of my trance. I run my fingers through my locks and shake my head. "No. It's been a long time since I've been there."

"How long?" She stops pacing and looks up at me with those heart-stopping blue eyes. I gulp at the sight.

"Ten years."

Jesus. Has it already been a decade? Sometimes it doesn't feel like it.

"All that time in California?" She raises a brow, a piqued interest blooming on her pretty face.

"Yes." I swipe my finger over the sandpaper feel of a closed file, but my eyes never leave hers.

"Where?"

Such a curious girl. Asking so many questions tonight. She's starting to open up a bit more now, even if she's still shrouded with shyness.

Leaning against the wall, I cross my arms and answer. "We started in San Francisco. Stayed there a few months, but it was too expensive. Too crowded." I pause for a second, remembering the little apartment we shared. Me, Kayla, Kelsey, even Bryson. "And then we went to Los Angeles for a couple years. Found a steady job, but it definitely wasn't the most family-friendly place. So we stayed in Irvine a bit after, until I found somewhere more permanent. And we just kinda ended up here on a whim." Shrugging my shoulders, I ponder on the crazy memories over the years. It's good to finally be settled into a permanent home.

"Wow. So you've been around the state quite a bit then," she says in awe as she leans against my desk, both her hands flat on the smooth wood.

I nod and resume the tapping against the folder. "More than I would've liked, but it was an adventure. I'll give it that. Lots of memories."

It's quiet for a minute, the only sounds are faint music floating under the cracks of the closed door and the static from my open laptop. But there's her voice again, breaking apart the noise. "What made you choose San Diego?"

Thumbing my way through the messy drawer, I finally find the right place the folder goes and push it in its place. "I did a little research into somewhere with good schools. Somewhere safe, a place I could settle down with the girls. Somewhere where it was quieter. Close to the beach. Not as much traffic."

"Well," she laughs, "I think you picked one of the best cities then. San Diego is beautiful."

Lifting my head up, I turn my body back to her. "Yeah, it—" I pause momentarily, fixed on the pretty picture in front of me. "It sure is..." But I'm not talking about the city; I'm talking about *her*. She's perched on top of my desk, legs swinging off the side, a photograph of me and my girls in her hands. She traces the edge of the glass, a soft smile forming on her deep red lips. And that's it. I'm speechless now because *this*, right in front of me, is something I could picture myself seeing every night. Violet—in my office, on my desk, smiling like she's won a prize. But I think that's me. *I've* won because she's sitting in my office, choosing to spend time with *me*.

She's easily becoming my favorite part of the week.

"What was it you did back in Oklahoma? You never told me."

I take a step forward, my hands shoved deep into the front pockets of my black slacks. "I had my own pool business. Spent most of my days out in the heat building inground pools, making customers' visions come to life." And then I take another step, and another.

"Were you also the one to do all the paperwork?" She looks up at me, her dazzling smile making me suck in a breath.

Shaking my head, I step forward, into her space. "Nah, someone else did. I preferred being out building the pools."

"So that's where you get your calluses from. I was wondering." She glances down at my hands when I slip them out of my pockets, staring, like she's trying to map the lines of my palms. But then she flicks her eyes back to the photo flat in her lap.

She was wondering about the calluses. Curious how I got them. That means she thinks about the palms of my hands. The feel of the worn calluses gliding against her smooth skin. That's exactly what I want to be doing now, touching her.

"Yeah. That's where I got them from." I smile as I stop right next to her, my eyes on the framed photo in her hands.

Taking my time, I slide my palm up her bare thigh. Just for a second. Enough to hear the quiet gasp she lets out as I inch up her perfect sun-kissed skin. And just as I tease the edge of her midnight blue dress, the one with a light sparkly touch, I draw back and hover in the near distance.

Her fingers still trace along the edges of the glass frame, analyzing every inch of the picture. And out of the blue, she asks, "You miss it?"

A sigh falls from my lips as I lean against my office chair. Of course I miss it. I miss it all the time. "A lot, actually. But I'm not entirely done with it. My neighbors let me take care of their pool."

"I see." She smiles as she places the picture back on the desk where it belongs. When she spins back around, her eyes find mine. "Why'd you stop?"

Folding my arms over my chest, I shrug, searching for words that don't involve bringing up Lois. I'm not exactly ready for that. "I needed a change of scenery. Wanted to try my cards at other opportunities."

"Like opening your own club?" She tilts her head, which makes her long brunette waves tumble over her shoulders.

I'm really trying my best not to reach out and tangle my fingers through her hair. Because all I want to do is sit down in my leather chair and pull her into my lap. Maybe then I'd finally get to feel what those pretty red lips taste like. She'd probably taste like cherries, sunlight, spring waters...

Shaking the thoughts from my mind, I nod. "Yes, exactly that."

"What made you want to start a club?"

"I... don't know," I reply honestly. "When I came to San Diego, I just had this strange feeling when I walked through the Gaslamp District. I liked the feel of the area, like all the lit-up lights at night. It was exciting. And I just kind of wanted a place people could come and be free. Dance the night away and relax, take off some stress. Just wanted a place for them to come and indulge in whatever they needed after a long week. Whether that was meeting someone new or getting lost in their partner's arms. It just felt like a new beginning. What I was meant to do."

She looks at me, her eyes bright as her crimson lips curl into a shy smile. "Well, you certainly were successful. Club Inferno's one of the top nightclubs around Southern California. At least that's what I saw."

"Did you Google that?" I smirk.

"Maybe. I'll never tell." And there she goes again. Blushing and giggling under her breath.

She's fucking adorable.

My eyes slide down her body, assessing her beauty under the dim lights. Her blue dress hugs her body, accentuating the curves of her hips. Thin straps disappear beneath her long brown hair. Her fingers fidget with the bottom of the dress that falls halfway down her thighs. And then there's those long legs that go on for days and days that end in black heels which compliment her outfit, just like her dress matches her eyes.

Man, those eyes. Those blue shades of midnight. I've never seen eyes quite like hers before. So pretty I just want to capture them with my camera.

Gazing up at her, I ask, "Have you always been in San Diego?"

She shakes her head in response. "No. I'm from Napa Valley."

I raise my brows as I take in the information. "The wine region? You're kinda far from home, aren't you?"

Shrugging her shoulders nonchalantly, she drags her index finger across the top of my desk, making circular patterns into the wood. "San Diego's my home now. But my parents still live in Napa. They own this big, fancy winery out there, so they stay pretty busy. Especially in the summer."

"So you must be an expert in wine, huh?" I ask playfully as I grab another tan folder off my desk, letting my fingers brush along her thigh once more. This time I let my hand linger, just so I can see the pink blush staining her cheeks. She's a nervous little thing, but I like it. I like her...

She bats her long eyelashes up at me and smiles. "I can definitely tell you a lot about a glass of Pinot Noir. Might just steer you toward some strawberry wine, though. But that's just my opinion. It's... one of my favorites." She says the last sentence like she's telling me a well-kept secret. A piece of her that not many other people know.

Brushing the pad of my thumb along her outer thigh, I fix her with a knowing smirk. "Now that I know this, you think I need to fix my wine menu up a bit?"

She tilts her head to the side and assesses me for just a second before she says, "I could take a look, yeah." Adjusting her position on the edge of the desk, she twists her lips and hesitates a beat. "I umm... I'm not really a big drinker, to be honest." I don't miss the flash of something fall across her irises, but I can't make out what it is.

Blinking her way, I nod, then swallow. Like something's catching in my throat. "Me either," I confess. "Don't get me wrong, I may like a cold glass of whiskey every now and then to take the edge off after a long week, but that's about it."

"But you own a nightclub." She laughs, but it doesn't meet her eyes. "Isn't that kind of contradictory?"

"Doesn't mean I like to overindulge." I shrug, my hand still placed over her warm skin. "After two drinks, I'm done. Kinda the same with customers. Once I see someone is getting a little too wild, I cut them off and send them home in an Uber, if they came alone."

She blinks up at me and nods, her lips parted just a smidge. "Same," she stutters, "I mean… I'm the same way about any alcohol. I don't really like when people go overboard."

My eyes stay fixed to her for a few more seconds as I try to contemplate the meaning of her wide eyes and the invisible images that dance across her irises. There was something unspoken between us, a hidden meaning that I can't quite decipher, but maybe someday she'll let me in, and I'll do the same.

I let my hand drop from her thigh, already missing the contact of her skin, and then I make my way back to the filing cabinet and leave whatever that was behind. Alcohol and all.

A comfortable silence seeps in as I get back to what I was doing, but work is the last thing on my mind. I really don't want to do anything but sit and talk with her. But isn't that what I've been doing the past hour and a half?

Well, mostly.

Okay, fine. I haven't scratched a dent in my paperwork. Maybe I should just go ahead and bite the bullet. Hire an assistant that'll keep my files in order. But maybe I just want Violet to help me…

"Do you go visit them often?" I ask as I begin to shuffle the papers in the folder. "Your parents."

"No," she murmurs in a low tone. Almost like there's regret in her voice. "I haven't been out there in about a year. I should probably go for a visit soon. Keeps my mom from worrying too much."

Worrying too much. What all would she be worried about? She's got me intrigued, but I don't ask.

"I'm sure they'd love to see you," I chime in, hoping I might sway her to go. Something in her voice catches. She sounds like she misses home.

Does she miss home?

"Yeah, I'm sure they would." She's quiet for a few seconds, and when I turn my head, she's looking down at her dress, picking at the sparkly material with her shiny nails. She looks… sad.

I want to dig more, scratch beneath the surface, ask about her past with them. But before I can, her soft voice echoes another question through the room. "What about your parents? Are they still in Oklahoma?"

"Mhm," I answer. "My dad has a little farm out in Shawnee. And my mom makes goat's milk soap at the house. She's got a good thing going with the farmers market out there. Every Saturday she's out in her little green stand, talking up a storm with the locals."

I place my palm flat against the filing cabinet and smile as memories come flooding back to me. Weekends spent helping out on the farm. The monthly barbecues the county used to put on. The orange sunsets that'd paint the sky like a portrait while I sipped fresh lemonade on the back porch in the rocking chair my dad built when me and Bryson were just kids.

God, sometimes I miss it. The quiet stillness of the country. Makes me want to drive back and stay a week or two. But then again, home brings painful memories. Ones I don't really want to remember.

"That sounds so lovely," Violet says brightly, bringing me back to the present. "Do you get to see them often?"

I shove the folder in my hand into the very back of the drawer, pushing down the guilt that sits on my chest. "Not as much as I'd like, no. Haven't been back there in a couple of years."

"How come?" she asks softly, but doesn't push the subject.

Pausing, I push my fingers through my hair and blow out a breath as I answer, "It's hard to go back, I guess."

She looks at me for a minute, head tilted and curious eyes searching mine. Probably wondering why I haven't been back in so long.

I won't tell her why. At least, not yet. Lois is... a touchy subject, to this day. But I'd like to tell her, when I'm ready. When I'm comfortable with her.

Aren't we well past that point, though? Doesn't sleeping together mean the ball's out of the park now?

But the problem is, I feel like I'm way past comfortable. Something else is getting in the way.

Once again, Violet's voice breaks through my stirring thoughts.

"You must miss them," she says lightly, like she's walking on eggshells.

Guess we both miss our parents.

"Every day," I whisper out, enough for her to hear the crack in my voice.

Before I get too sentimental, I point to an open folder on my desk. "Can you do me a favor and bring me that folder? The dark brown one next to my laptop?"

"Sure." She slides off the side of my desk and carefully picks up the folder in her delicate hands. I watch the sway of her hips as she glides over to me, clicking her black heels along the marble. "Here you go," she says sweetly, handing me the closed folder.

"Thanks, angel." When I pry it from her hands, I make it a point to brush the back of my hand against hers.

I push the folder into the back of the cabinet, right behind the other I just put away. And right as I'm about to close the metal drawer, I hear the sound of Violet clearing her throat.

Turning abruptly, I see a look cross her face that's both appalled and humorous. "What?" I ask, confused by the way she's acting.

Violet's red lips curl with amusement. "Did you put all those in there yourself?"

"Yes?" I shoot her a quizzical look, prompting her to continue.

She just smiles as she assesses the clear mess. "Your organization skills could use some work."

"Calling me sloppy?" I flash her a smile, teasing her.

She giggles under her breath and shakes her head. "No, it could just be a little more put together."

"Go on, tell me more." And I want that. I really do. I'm practically inviting her to call me out. "Think you know better?"

She raises a brow and crosses her arms over her chest, thoroughly amused. "You know I do this for a living, right? Organizing, filing, classifying books."

Leaning up against the cabinet, I nod in response and play along, pushing for more. "Mhm. Well, maybe I should hire an assistant. Someone who could organize my life a little better."

Someone like her.

She darts her tongue across her bottom lip, preparing for a comeback. "Maybe you should." There's a little sassiness to her tone, a little flirting, perhaps. "Why don't you start at the library first? Rent out a room, take some applications, see what pretty girl catches your eye."

Keep it up, angel. She doesn't realize flirting with her is one of my favorite pastimes, and the night is still young.

"Maybe I will. Know any brunettes needing a job?" I retort back with a smirk, watching as she narrows her eyes playfully my way.

Attagirl. Keep going.

"Maybe." Violet slides the palm of her hand over the various colored folders, but her pretty blue eyes stay locked on mine. "Better get the applications out. I'm sure you'll have a pile on your desk before Monday, Mr. Club Owner." She accentuates the syllables of my nickname which makes a shiver run down my back like electricity coursing through the air.

Jesus. Even a nickname as simple as that gets me, but only because it's coming from her. The impish smirk on her lips tells me enough—that she's having just as much fun as I am right now.

She's fucking adorable when she flirts.

"That's the last thing I need. More paperwork." I chuckle under my breath.

She slowly turns her head to the side and looks at me for a second, shyly pushing back a lock of brunette hair behind her ear. I track the movement all too closely. "I could help you, you know," she murmurs quietly, shyly fluttering her long eyelashes my way.

I gulp, repeat what she just said in my mind, and smile, taking a step closer in her direction. "Yeah?"

She shrugs nonchalantly like it's a piece of cake. "It's not hard. There's just a better system you could use. Maybe color coordinate? Label the tops? Not too hard. You just need to... organize."

Organize. It's only a simple word. She's just trying to help me manage my paperwork better, but it's almost like she's saying she'll organize my entire life. I don't need her to, but I *want* her to. She's already proving herself that having her beside me makes my life ten times better. Whether this is going anywhere or not, I want it to.

Dragging my palm over my smooth scruff, I pin my stare on Violet and let the owner of this club do the talking. Smooth, seductive, flirtatious is *exactly* what I'm going for right now. "Keep going, angel. What else would you recommend?"

Violet flicks her eyes over the cabinet and slides the open drawer closed with a bang while she thinks on it. "Maybe a bigger... cabinet?"

Taking another large step toward her, I go in for the kill.

One. Two. *Three.*

Time to turn the heat up.

"And what about ties?" I ask as I loosen the black tie around my neck. "Are you good with these?"

Click. Click. Click.

Her high heels are all I hear as she draws back, but I follow in step with her, *chasing* her.

"I'm not the best," she says breathlessly, gulping down the words while her wide eyes watch my tie fall against my hand.

"Why don't we trade off then? You help me make my files more doable, and I'll teach you... *this.*" I back her up slowly against the wall, right where she can't escape. Right where she's at my vantage point. One of my hands falls against her waist, curves so perfect that it's taking every ounce of strength I have not to rip the dress clear off her, just so I can feel how smooth her skin is.

Her breathing accelerates as she grabs a hold of my white button-up shirt, like she's holding on for dear life. "Sam…"

God. I fucking love when she says my name like that. All breathless and shaky. She makes me a bit dizzy when she does that. Makes it where it's hard to stand up straight. I could just fall to my knees, worship her body like the goddess she is. I could do just that, but I'm not above a little teasing. And that's *exactly* what I'm doing. Working her up so she'll be soaked for me.

Yeah. This little angel will see heaven before the night is through.

"Sam, what are you…"

"Just hold still," I breathe out, gathering her hands together as I wrap the silky tie around her wrists.

She purrs out a whine as I finish tying a loose knot around her wrists. Smiling, I lift her arms high above her head, hook the material around a golden hook, and growl through my teeth when I see how pretty she looks at my command. "Look at you, so fucking pretty."

Her breath comes in waves, in and out like the blood that must be rushing in between her thighs. It makes me groan on the spot. Makes my blood flow to my cock that's already hard as a rock for her. But not yet. I want to play with her first, want to make her drown in sensual tingles as I purr her name against the shell of her ear. She loves the praise, loves the teasing, so I'll give it to her.

"You trying to teach me a lesson or something?" she gasps out as I slide a finger down her collarbone, between her breasts, stopping right at the end of her pretty blue dress.

Leaning in, I drag my lips over the side of her jawline, letting them slide up against the curve of her ear. Then, I whisper fluidly, "Something like that." She nearly breaks at the knees.

She gasps as my hand slides up her thigh, right beneath her dress, just enough to where I graze over the lace between her legs. She sucks in a breath, eyes wide and as blue as the ocean tides, begging me with those pretty irises to continue. But I don't budge. I'll happily indulge all her needs, when the time is right.

"Sam, please…" she begs with those stunning eyes that make me weak. If she keeps this up, I won't be able to hold out much longer.

Sliding my hand back out from under her dress, I press against her hip, my teeth grazing against her neckline, breathing in the scent of her floral perfume and the fragrance of her long locks.

"Jesus, Violet." I sigh into the crook of her neck with my tongue laving against her skin as chills begin to race down my spine. "You're such a good girl, do you know that?"

"*Y—yes,*" she whines out with need.

I could recognize that sound from a mile away. She *loves* the praise, the attention, the *affection.* So I brush my fingers under her chin, tilting her face up as I take a step back, still caging her against the wall.

And when my eyes flick over her perfect, shaking form, it nearly brings me to the floor.

"Sam, I need you to—"

"Do what?" I whisper into her ear as I step back in her personal space, the palm of my hand teasing up her inner thigh, almost where she wants me.

I slide my tongue along my bottom lip, look at her with blown-out eyes, and remind her I want her just as bad as she wants me. Letting my thumb ghost over her clothed folds, I flash her a devilish smirk and show her who's in control.

She tries to speak, but she's cut off when I blow against the shell of her ear, whispering filth into her mind. "I know, angel. Can feel how bad you want it. How *wet* you are for me." I take it upon myself to brush over her clit, featherlike, enough to make her shudder at the touch.

"You make me so… so…" She squirms when I take my hand and place it on her hip instead, my fingers dancing across the blue silk of her dress. But instead of surprise, she looks a bit disappointed as she pouts out, "Why'd you stop?"

Chuckling under my breath, I shake my head and brush my lips against the side of her ear. "Just working you up, sweetheart."

She rolls her eyes and presses the back of her head against the wall, laughing as she breathes, "You're such a tease."

"Just for you, angel." I send her a flirtatious wink and then unhook her wrists from the wall, gently bringing her hands back in front of her.

"If I didn't know any better, I'd say you were a fan of bondage." There's a twinkle of mischief in her eyes, something I want to play with.

"If it means tying pretty girls up like yourself, then yes. Call me the biggest fan." She blushes while I slowly untie her wrists, letting the silky fabric slide away from her warm skin.

"Of course you are," she laughs—one that makes my heart beat a bit faster.

"You know, I could show you some other time how to—" I pause and lose track of my words when my vision catches the faint hint of a scar on the inside of her left wrist.

Long, jagged, exposed like glass might've dug into her fragile skin. It looks old, worn, a trace of something that shouldn't have happened.

My brows form a tight line as I look up slowly, concern etching my face. She parts her lips, and a flash of panic flits across her eyes. But it's only there for a second. Just a fraction, but enough for me to catch it before it fades.

Brushing my thumb over the raised scar, I search her eyes and ask carefully, "What's this?"

Drawing a slight gasp from her mouth, she tugs her wrist away from me in a hurry. "It's nothing."

I pull my lips together into a tight line and stare down at her exposed scar. "It doesn't look like nothing..." My voice drops off again as I look back up into her wide blue eyes.

There it is again. A flicker of fright tumbles across her shiny irises, but she shakes it away. "No, it... it's nothing. *Nothing,*" she repeats it once more a little firmly, trying to laugh it off and cover it with her other hand.

I reach for her, but she yanks away again before I can capture her hand. She acts like I just burned her with my touch...

Curling her fingers carefully around her wrist, she shakes her head in dismissal, brushing it off like it's just a tiny scratch. "I... umm," she hesitates a second, searching for something to grasp as she tugs at the skirt of her dress, "I was being stupid. I had my hands full with some glass cups and wasn't looking where I was going. And my cat, Shadow, he got underneath my feet. So I tripped over him and slipped on the kitchen floor."

She has a cat?

I blink at her as I take in the new information. "I didn't know you had a cat..."

She sniffles, puts on a sad smile, and nods her head up and down mechanically. "He... he died last year. He had cancer." Her words come out broken, shaky, like she's holding herself together by a tiny thread that's frayed and worn. And in that moment, I want to pull her in, wrap my arms around her, and drown out the pain that's tethered through her glassy eyes.

"Oh, I... I'm sorry, sweetheart." Giving her a sympathetic smile, I reach for her, but she stays put.

"It's okay. He was... great. But I—I'm just really clumsy sometimes. It was my fault. I should've seen him. I shouldn't have been carrying so much. I should've just known *better*." Her voice comes out muffled and strained, and there it is again. That flare of hurt streaking across her watering eyes. She's trying to be strong, trying to not drop her guarded walls, but I know her better than that. She's hurting, and it seems like she's blaming herself for an accident that wasn't her fault.

I try to approach her softly, taking a careful step forward as my fingers brush the edge of her dress. "Hey, you okay?"

"Mhm," she hums out, putting on a fake smile—one that's wilted with guilt.

What could she possibly be guilty of?

"It's just..." I gaze back down at her wrist, wondering if that's really the whole picture. That scar, it looks like something other than just an accident. "You did quite a number to your wrist."

"I'm okay, really." She sucks in a breath and blinks away the building tears, like she's afraid to let me see her cry. "I'm fine."

But is she really?

I take another careful step toward her and hover my fingers over her closed hand, but she doesn't budge. She just stands there, looking like a deer in the headlights. "You sure?" I ask, prying for more information.

Come on, Violet. Let me in.

I just want her to talk to me, but she's quick to get the attention off herself.

"Positive." She nods quickly, her eyes still wide as an owl's.

I catch her hand in mine and tell her with my eyes that she can vent. She can let her emotions free around me. "Sweetheart, I..."

Tugging her hand from mine, she takes a few steps back and wipes beneath her eye, hiding more evidence of pain. "Just give me a minute. I need to run to the restroom."

"Violet..." I call her name in a desperate plea, hoping she'll just stop, freeze in place so I can snake my arms around her waist and hold her. That's what she needs, I think. To let some weight off her chest. But she doesn't budge, doesn't even stop to turn around.

"Just... wait." And that's all she says before she's barging through my office door and disappearing down the hall. The door shuts with a bang, and then I'm just left in silence, alone, once again.

Slicking a hand back through my tousled locks, I sigh, let a deep breath out, and think hard on what just happened.

A cat. She never told me she had a cat before. And how did I miss that scar? I had every opportunity to see it, so how the fuck did I miss *that*?

There was something else in her eyes that she was hiding. A flicker of fear, hurt, a flash of a memory?

I pause as the gears start spinning in my head. What if... what if that wasn't the whole truth? What if someone...

No. I stop the thought there, halt the what ifs. Violet said it was her cat that tripped her. She wouldn't lie, would she? No. Not that beautiful girl.

But what if... would someone be capable of hurting her? Would someone *intentionally* put her in harm's way? I can't imagine it, can't put together a scene that would make sense. She's too... *good*. Too pure, angelic. No one could lay a finger on her.

But then again, men like to take advantage of the best ones...

But she told me it was her cat, so I'll believe her, unless she tells me otherwise.

For now, I won't think of any other possibilities.

If anyone ever... I have to stop myself for a second as my hands turn into flexed fists, my jaw clenching at the very thought. If anyone ever dared lay a hand on her, I'd have to fucking kill them.

Nobody hurts *my* girl.

But she's not my girl, is she?

No. But I want her to be, don't I?

Groaning out, I make my way out of the office and forget the what ifs as I fix my tie back into place, putting behind the building questions in my brain.

Violet needs me, whether she wants to admit that or not, and I'm not going to let her down. Not tonight.

Not ever.

Chapter Twenty-One

Violet

Slamming the office door shut, I sprint to the bathroom, pushing past a couple making out in the hall, not even stopping to say sorry when I hear the man yell my way. I have to keep going. Have to keep my breathing even. I can break when I get inside. Can fall apart all over when I'm safe, away from the blaring noise that's distorting my rampant thoughts.

I don't dare turn around. Don't let myself swing my head back to that office in hopes of seeing Sam. I can't... I can't look at him right now. Not unless I want to start sobbing.

Tears prick the backs of my eyes as I tumble into the bathroom and catch myself against the marble counter, my fingers digging into the smooth surface so hard that I feel like my painted nails might split in half.

The scar. He *saw* my scar. His calloused fingers slid over the jagged surface. He thoroughly assessed it, stared like it was made of glass and could see right through me.

He fucking *saw* me. That part of me I keep closed in a tight bottle, sealed so no one can slip inside. But he did. *Sam* did. He broke the seal, saw a flash of my past. My cracked, fractured former life that I never wanted him to see in the first place...

I slipped up, couldn't mask my emotions. Couldn't steer him straight that I was just fine. Because I *wasn't* fine. I'm *not* fine. I'm broken. And he saw that. For just a split second, my gates were wide open, and I led him right to the very thing I can't bring myself to talk to him about.

Jason...

My body starts to shake uncontrollably when I run my fingers cautiously over the raw scar, tracing lines that map back to that dark night. The one where I got this from. Tears splash against my cheeks as I squeeze my eyes shut, reminding myself to breathe.

"You're okay. You're safe. Stop crying," I whisper out as my fingers brush over the faded scar, reminding myself it's over. But the tears don't stop; they just keep rushing down my face like a raging waterfall.

When I open my eyes back up, I wipe away the eyeliner that's smudged beneath my eyelashes, scrub away the raw evidence that I've been crying. "Jesus, pull yourself together. Sam is waiting," I mutter beneath my breath, reprimanding myself for letting this happen.

This should've never happened, but it did because I couldn't control my own emotions. It's still too raw, too fresh, even though it's been a little over a couple years. When will I ever learn to just heal?

My fingers comb through my loose waves, trying my best to put myself back in one piece, to look remotely presentable like I didn't just break down in the bathroom. I don't want Sam to see me like this. Don't want him to think I'm some pathetic mess of a girl who doesn't know how to control my roller coaster of emotions when someone asks me about my past. That's why I don't dare go there. Never bring up the one thing that almost literally killed me.

I freeze as I stare at my red-rimmed eyes, my body turning numb on the spot. Sam... I didn't tell him the truth. Not exactly. I danced around it, tiptoed over broken glass that ended slashing my wrist open.

It wasn't Shadow. Not my perfect boy. My fuzzy best friend who's long gone now. Just shy of six months—when he took his last breath.

I inhale sharply, sucking in a breath while I lean against the firm sink, holding the pain in as I think about all that I've lost.

Shadow was the only thing I could salvage from the broken relationship. The one piece I was able to hold on to. But now, he's gone, too. And now, I'm left with nothing but a permanent scar to remind myself what I should've left behind. What I should've escaped before Jason got his filthy hands on me one last time...

Worrying my bottom lip between my teeth, I take a good look at myself and give myself a pep talk while I pull myself together. I can't seem to straighten my dress out enough. Can't fake a smile on my cherry red lips. Can't hide the watery film over my eyes, but I have to. Sam's waiting for me; I need to go.

With one last helpless sigh and a quick glance over my shoulder in the mirror, I push off the counter and hold my head high while I drag my heels forward, back into the flashing lights of the club.

Breathe. Just breathe.

That's all I can seem to say. All I can do is put a brave face on and pray I don't break down again.

Be brave, Violet.

With one last breath, I pull the door open and push myself through. It's only a couple steps until I see the large shape of Sam looming in front of me. I gasp and stop in my tracks when I see him leaning against the wall—his hands deep in his black slacks, black tie loose around his neck, tousled brown hair a little wavy from running his fingers through it. But what gets me the most is the way he's looking at me—big brown eyes etched with concern, staring like I'm a wounded puppy. It almost makes me break right there on the spot, but I don't. I just hover and let the warmth of his gaze soothe my pain away.

"You alright?" he asks gently, almost like I'll shatter if he's too loud.

I bite the inside of my cheek and nod as I hum out, "Mhm."

With a quick flit of his eyes over my body, he reads me again, probably assessing if it was a lie, but he takes it as it is. "Good. Glad you're okay." It sounds like he wants to say something else, but he doesn't finish, just hovers closer to me.

Feeling the weight of his intense stare, I look in the direction of his private room and nod. "Should we... go to the back?"

When I spin back around toward him, waiting for an answer, he just shakes his head and curls his lips into an easy smile. "Nah. Not tonight."

"Oh." It comes out more disappointed than I wanted it to, but I've already ruined tonight, so why would he want to, anyway? I've already done enough. Shown him a piece of me I never wanted to...

I go to turn away, but he steps in front of me and blocks my path. When I tilt my head up, he's smiling. So easy, so composed. "We're gonna dance instead."

That throws me off balance, makes me widen my eyes to see he's actually being serious. His sincere eyes say it's anything but a lie.

"Dance?" I ask, like the word is foreign to my lips.

"Yes, we're going to dance." He speaks the words fluently, slowly, so I can soak them in, then he's easing his hand in mine and tugging me forward. "Come on."

When we emerge from the dark hallway, the atmosphere turns from serene to untamed and restless. The flash of the fluorescent lights causes me to squint. Crowds of enthusiastic clubgoers make me shrink into Sam's side, suddenly turning me claustrophobic. The music is too loud, too thunderous as it rings across the walls, echoing back at me like chanting roars.

But as I grasp him a little tighter, he squeezes my hand gently and parts the crowd—bodies shifting as they make room for us.

It's like every single head turns and stares when Sam enters the room. Eyes wide, glares sharp at me, whispers swarming around my head like a hoard of bees. I can't focus, can't breathe with this much attention on myself. The flashing lights seem to blind me. And I want to run. Want to bolt to a dark corner where no one can see me. Hide like the cowering kitten I really am.

But then Sam does something. He makes a downward hand signal to the DJ and in the next moment, the room shifts. The lights dim, the fast-paced music turns into a slow, steady rhythm that stills my accelerated heartbeat. And when he turns to face me and looks at me with those big brown eyes, it's as if every single person standing in the room disappears altogether, even my panic. It just dissipates into thin air. For those few seconds, I'm weightless.

"You ready?" Sam asks with the tilt of his head, signaling for me to come closer.

I fiddle with my bottom lip and laugh under my breath. "I'm not a very good dancer," I confess shyly.

"Now I don't believe that for a second," he shoots back with a light chuckle sliding off the tip of his tongue.

I can't help but relax a bit, even if my stiff muscles protest at the notion. His laugh—that sweet, airy sound—is enough to drive me closer. Just a smidge.

He reaches for me, but I step out of bounds, my stomach still flipping with nerves. "No, really. I have two left feet."

"Just... try." It's a request, a formal invitation that beckons me closer. So I nod, agreeing to do just that. *Try.*

This time, he paces a step forward, right into my space. His right hand curls against the curve of my hip while his left palm slides over mine smoothly, creating heat between our bodies.

"A little closer, sweetheart," he murmurs out, smooth as silk. I don't resist his call this time as he pulls me in tighter, enough to where I can smell the thick scent of him permeating all around me like a blowing candle.

Sandalwood, a touch of sunlight, palm trees dancing in the California breeze. That's what he smells like, what his trademark has to be. It seems to be my new favorite scent.

Flicking my eyes up, I send him a nervous smile. "Promise not to drop me?"

He gently squeezes the back of my hand, throws a heart-stopping smile my way, and reels me in. "What makes you think I'd ever let go?"

It sounds like a promise—the way he lets those words flow so effortlessly off his tongue. And I believe him, I really do. If I fall, he'll surely scoop me up in his strong arms and cover me with his guardian angel wings. He loves to call me angel, but really, I think he's been mine this entire time.

His long fingers latch over mine, and then he's moving us in a slow, easy rhythm—just like the song that plays softly through the speakers. "Alright, just follow my lead," he instructs. "It's only two steps. Just stay close to me."

My feet move in sync with his as the outside world starts to blur. I vaguely see the disco ball shimmer through the fog. Can almost make out swishes of pink and purple dresses out of the corner of my eye, but all that seems to be clear is Sam standing in front of me.

He's got this light stance about him. So sure of himself, so confident. I wish I could be like that—fearless, self-assured, steady. But I'm the opposite of those things. I'm just here, floating along the dance floor, trying not to fall flat on my face.

My eyes burn into my old scar, just long enough to trip over my own two feet, but Sam only holds me closer. "I'm really not great at this." I half-laugh, my cheeks turning crimson as embarrassment reaches the surface.

"You're doing just fine, sweetheart," he assures me, his fingers flexing into the material of my dress, guiding me through my rigid movements.

As the song starts to fade off, another one starts to play, just as slow as the last one. Nerves start to bite at my heels as I catch peripheral glances at the edge of my scar, reminding me what happened in his office.

He saw the way I cracked. Saw a flash of pain bolt through my eyes as visions of Shadow and Jason rushed through my mind. My eyes fall to the floor as unease swirls in the pit of my stomach, sending gut-wrenching memories flying through my mind.

The glass, little black paws kneading into my flesh, the awful slurs, beer bottles lining the floor.

Gulping down grief, I start to choke. Start to trip over Sam's leather shoes. Just when I start to slip, Sam's silky voice breaks through the panic and quells my rampant thoughts. "Hey." He places two fingers underneath my chin and lifts my face to his, till I'm face to face with those warm, sappy brown eyes. "Eyes up, angel. Just look at me. I won't let you fall."

I don't dare drop my eyes now. All I can seem to do is stare into those pools of serenity. I've never quite seen such a unique shade of golden-brown in eyes like his before.

The pad of his thumb brushes along the back of my hand, creating butterflies inside my stomach. And the way he's looking at me—like I'm something special—makes it hard for me to look away.

"Look at you. Doing so good," he compliments as he spins me around the dance floor effortlessly.

"All because you kept me upright," I tease lightly.

He shakes his head and sighs. "Like I said. I wasn't gonna let you fall."

I stay close to Sam and hold tight to his hand while my left arm drapes over his broad shoulder, relaxing into his warm touch. Shimmers of sparkles reflect in his honey-colored eyes, creating an entire night sky.

God, he's so gorgeous. Just so *good*. How did I end up in the arms of such a sweet club owner?

He didn't ask me to go to the back with him, he just wanted me to dance with him. It's like he knew I needed this. Needed the safety and security of being near him, to save me from the panic attack that was building when he saw the scar.

But this is... *different*. Much more intimate than being crowded by his massive body on the pool table. This is the kind of soft intimacy where he can just hold me in his arms, pull me close, dissipate any lines that we might've been crossing in that private room.

This is... real. At least, it feels that way.

I fall into his chest, nuzzling my face in the crook of his neck as my fingers cautiously start to intertwine with his. It's so easy, feels right the way they fall into place like puzzle pieces.

"You know, I had a cat once upon a time," Sam says out of the blue.

Pushing back from his chest, I look up with wide eyes, and my jaw drops in awe. "You had a cat?"

"Mhm," he hums. "When I was around fifteen. Her name was Mittens. A white Ragdoll cat."

I open my mouth, but nothing comes out until I force out a laugh. "Really?"

He nods. "Sure did. Me and Bryson gave that cat hell, but at the end of the day, she'd always come curl up on my chest when it was time for bed."

My lips curl into an easy smile, my eyes dreamy as I think about Sam with a cat. "Figured you'd be a dog person."

"Oh, yeah? Why's that?" He angles his head, waiting patiently until I answer.

"I don't know." I shrug. "You just kind of give off Golden Retriever type vibes."

A playful smile reaches his bright eyes as he replies, "Who says I can't be both?"

"You *can* be both." I sigh, happily.

He guides me in slow motion around the smooth dance floor and lets his thumb trace lines on the back of my hand. "Kayla's been asking me lately about getting a cat."

"Oh?" I ask, piqued.

"Yeah," he laughs, "every few weeks she'll subtly bring it up."

Nerves light the inside of my body as I discreetly dance my fingers against the ends of his smooth sandy locks. "Well, why haven't you gotten her one yet?"

He raises an eyebrow at that. "You trying to persuade me, angel?"

I shrug nonchalantly and play along. "Maybe."

"Look at you," he bites with a smug smirk, "being a bad influence, aren't ya?"

Sucking my bottom lip between my teeth, I brush the tips of my fingers across the top of his white collared shirt and bat my eyelashes flirtatiously at him. "Is it working?"

He flicks his eyes over me, takes me in for a beat, and melts as a charming smile curls across his plush lips. "The verdict's still out."

The verdict's still out. He's repeating back what I said to him before I even knew he was the club owner. Before he decided to flip my world upside down.

But nonetheless, my cheeks are as bright red and warm as the relentless sun at the beach. He's got this smooth way of speaking, always knows exactly just how to get to me. That's one thing I like about him. The endless amount he can make me blush.

We fall back into a comfortable silence, and I find myself pressing myself into his chest, my head leaning on his shoulder, fingers laced through his. It's all so intimate, so very exquisite, *delicate.* But I like the way this feels. It feels right to be here—holding Sam's hand, letting him spin me in slow motion under the sparkly disco ball, allowing myself to just enjoy this moment. Sam's so much different than I expected...

Tilting my head up, I call his name softly, "Sam?"

"Hm?" he hums out, his lips ghosting over the crown of my head.

"Thank you," I whisper in a hoarse voice, holding back any tears from spilling.

He leans his head back and takes a good look at me, his eyebrows knitting in question. "For what?"

Gulping away a sob that tries to break free from my lips, I smile and let my emotions run free through my telling eyes. "For asking me to dance tonight."

Pulling his lips into a tight line, he nods, understanding written all over his deep brown irises. He knows the real reason why I'm saying thank you. Well, half of the reason. He knows I needed him. And that in itself says more than any words could right now.

Sam leans his chin atop my head, pulls me close, and slides the palm of his hand across my lower back, the tips of his soothing fingers keeping the lingering pain from breaching the surface. "You're welcome, angel. I'd ask you all over again if I could."

Closing my eyes, I breathe in his sandalwood scent, letting the slow song playing through the room soothe my mind, allowing Sam's hand to run up the back of my spine so he can gently brush his fingers over the exposed skin at the nape of my neck.

For a fraction of a second, I allow the possibility of us to enter my mind. What it would be like if *he* were mine.

Maybe he explores the thought himself. Tosses the idea back and forth like flipping a coin through the air, wondering if it'll land on the side that chooses me.

When I lift my eyes to his, it doesn't take any time to assess the question. The answer is swimming in the starry galaxies of his eyes. He *does* think about what it'd be like if I were his and he were mine.

For a breath of a moment, just a second in time, I wonder what he'd taste like. Maybe sunshine, a sky full of endless possibilities. A sweet dream that never ends.

Pressing myself like a blanket against him, I curl my arm around his back, just so I can breathe him in a little deeper. So I can hold on for as long as I possibly can.

We can both keep dancing around the big elephant in the room, silently slip between the lines before they completely blur. But neither of us speaks; we just spin through the motions, pretending like boundaries don't exist just this once.

Maybe I'll be brave one day. Bold enough to speak the words into existence. *Are you mine, Sam?* I think I'd like to be his...

We stay like this—fingers intertwined, spinning in slow motion, blurring lines that cease to exist in the moment—until the floor clears, until we're the only two people left on the dance floor.

Never mind the music stopped minutes ago or that the flashing lights dimmed till the disco ball turned stationary seconds ago. I like it here—in his strong arms, where it's warm. I like the feel of the slide of his hand in mine. I *like* him. Everything about him, actually.

Whatever this is, it's come to my attention that it's much more than just hooking up. Something clicks in my brain; stars align in the night sky. *This* was meant to be infinite—like the slow tides of the ocean rolling against the shoreline. I won't call it a name. Not yet, but one day, I'll be sure to shout it from the cliffside that he's mine.

"You know, the music stopped a while ago," I breathe out tentatively, my fingers flexing against his just because I don't want to let go. Not yet.

"I barely even noticed," he drawls out in a low, husky breath. One that makes shivers run down my spine.

We keep spinning, keep circulating the big, now empty dance floor. But I don't mind. Not when he lifts his arm and twirls me in slow motion. Not when he pulls me in and tugs me firmly against his body. Not even when he starts to hum out one of my favorite songs under his breath.

I curl my lips up and flash him a soft smile as he holds me tight. "Should we... stop?"

Not that I want to stop. I don't. I *really* don't.

Tilting his head back, he sends me a mischievous grin and says, "You tell me."

That's all the answer I need. So I lean the side of my face into the crease of his white button-up and enjoy this moment in Sam's strong arms.

After another slow spin, I see the flash of movement in the corner of my eye and when I blink to the right, I can't help but giggle silently.

There, in the corner of the room, is Bryson standing slack-jawed, staring wide-eyed at us. In one hand is a clipboard, the other hangs loosely by his side. He watches us carefully, assesses our slow movements—the way Sam curls his fingers into mine, the way we move like a wave, in sync with each other's bodies.

Bryson cards a hand through his blond locks, still staring like he doesn't quite believe what he's seeing. But there, in the next moment, his hazel eyes soften, and his lips tug into a lazy smile—like he's enjoying every second of this as much as I am.

"Bryson's watching," I whisper into Sam's chest, unwilling to demagnetize from his body.

Sam looks over his shoulder and chuckles, sighing as he turns back to me and gazes into my eyes. "So let him watch."

There's a definitive sparkle in his eye—one that makes my stomach do somersaults. He doesn't care who's watching. Doesn't care that the club is already closed for the night, and neither do I. I think I'd dance the whole night away with Sam if I could. Just stay in his arms till he finally lets go.

As a sweet smile curves over my lips, I let my head rest back on his chest, let him continue guiding me around the middle of the dance floor.

He's right. Let Bryson watch. It doesn't matter because this moment belongs to *us.* Me and Sam.

This right here is *ours.*

So we dance, continue circling the inevitable of breaking our interlaced hands apart. I quite like this—holding his hand, a lot more than I should.

And then there's that question. The one whispering wishes into my ear.

Are you mine, Sam?

Chapter Twenty-Two

Sam

Sunlight filters through the open kitchen window, the white curtains swaying in the gentle breeze. As I lean against the granite island and stare at the news app on my phone, my thoughts evade to anything other than seventy-degree weather and traffic stops.

The stupid grin on my lips won't stop tugging at the corners of my mouth. I can't seem to focus too hard because my head's still swimming with flashbacks of Violet in my arms. I pause, biting my bottom lip as my hand slowly scratches down my scruff while I materialize back to that night.

The feel of my hand entwined with hers. The slide of my palm against her soft blue dress. The gleam of her ocean eyes delving deep into mine. How we danced till three in the morning, didn't stop till she told me to. I could've danced with her the entire night, until the sun came up. And if I had it my way, I'd still have her in my arms.

And then I get this crazy idea—one so unlike me that I don't exactly know what's gotten into me. *A cat.* I could finally get Kayla that cat she's been asking for. Maybe, just maybe, I could bring Violet over to the house. Persuade her to stay a little longer, to feel out whatever's happening between us.

But what would I say to Kayla? *This is my friend, Violet.*

No. That doesn't sound right.

How about—*this is the woman I've been secretly hooking up with.*

Nah. Too risqué. Not exactly the whole truth.

Or maybe—*this is Violet, the woman I can't get out of my head. The one that makes me forget how to breathe.*

Sighing, I pull up the San Diego animal rescue website in search of the perfect cat and click on the adoptable cats link. When it opens, my eyes widen.

There's so many different options. Siamese, Persian, Ragdoll, Oriental Shorthair, the list goes on.

Flick. Flick. I scroll through the pages in a daze, my fingers dancing along the screen, my eyes lighting up at the endless possibilities. I let my finger flip to the next page, a stupid shit-eating grin plastered on my face while I absentmindedly think of bright blue eyes and a red-lipped smile that makes me dizzy.

Honestly, I was skeptical about getting a cat. Just another responsibility. Another bill to pay. But the more Kayla asked me, the more I thought about a cat. And now? There's Violet.

I saw that look in her eyes. That gloomy, deep sadness residing in her blue irises. I wanted to pull her in right then, tug her in my lap, and gift her another cat. I was ready to drive her straight to the animal shelter and tell her to pick out whichever one called to her.

Kayla might've been the one to stir the idea of a cat in my head, but now I think I'm giving in for both of them. Violet *and* Kayla.

Just when I'm about to turn the page, I pause on a black and white tuxedo cat. One with deep green eyes and a fluffy tail curled around fuzzy paws. Quickly scanning the description, I see she's a four-year-old female cat. Her qualities involve cuddling, sunbathing, head nudges when she wants attention, and family-centered. Not too attention-seeking, independent, loves to nap on the windowsill.

Whiskers. Her name is fucking Whiskers. That's actually adorable, if I'm being honest.

The more I look at her, the more I feel sure. This is the one. The perfect little family cat I can think of. Kayla would be nuts over her but also, I think Violet would love her, too...

In the next second, Kayla flits through the open kitchen and heads for the refrigerator, grabbing the orange juice off the top shelf and clinking a pink glass in the sanded cupboard.

"Hey, Dad," she throws out while she picks up a piece of toast.

"Hey, kiddo," I reply with a massive grin on my lips, fingers tapping repeatedly against the edge of my phone. No matter how hard I try to hide the excitement in my voice or the glow that must be beaming from my eyes, Kayla will see right through it.

Through a bite of toast, she muffles, "You're oddly cheery today. What's got you smiling so big?"

Shrugging, I act like it's just a normal Wednesday. Just a morning with my coffee, hanging out in the kitchen. "Nothing. Just a nice day is all." But there's that hint of joy in my words, much more animated than I usually am in the early morning.

She tilts her head to the side and raises her eyebrows, her hazel eyes blooming with suspicion. "Mhm. Whatever you say."

See. I knew it. Can't get anything past that girl. She's too damn smart.

She skirts around the kitchen, shuffling her pink slippers over the polished wood, yawning as she scoops up her orange juice glass to take another gulp. She drops the subject completely, figuring I won't really say what's on my mind.

As she turns her back to put away the carton of juice, I clear my throat and speak. "Kayla?"

Spinning around, she pushes back her long hair and leans against the opposite side of the kitchen island. "What's up?"

Easing my way into it, I drag my palm against my scruff and ask, "What do you think about the name Whiskers?"

She stares at me a beat, her eyes wide, lips in a tight line as she contemplates my question. "Dad."

"Kiddo," I respond back, making a good effort not to give myself away just yet with the twitch of my lips.

It only takes her a second to slap her hands on top of the granite in excitement. "You didn't. Did you?!"

Casually shrugging my shoulders, I go, "Was thinking about it."

The green in her eyes shines like clovers as thrill and excitement take hold of her. "Really? Are you being for real right now?"

I nod and slide her my phone. "Here. What do you think about this one?"

She sprints over to my side and snatches the phone, her eyes massive and sparkling when she gets a glimpse of Whiskers. "Oh my God. She's perfect! Her little black and white paws and those green eyes. Can we get her? Pleaseeeee?"

Jesus. I haven't heard her beg like this since she was twelve, insisting I take her and her sister to Disneyland. I gave in, just as I do now. How can I say no to that innocent face?

With the tip of my head, I hum out a yes. "I'll send in an application this morning."

Kayla throws her arms around the back of my neck and pulls me in for a big hug, almost knocking me off the stool completely. "Thank you, thank you, thank you!"

I wrap my arms around her and give her a tight squeeze. "You're welcome, kiddo. About time I caved, I suppose."

She pulls back and smiles. "What made you change your mind?"

"I, uhh... I'm not sure," I pause, dragging my palm over my mouth, spinning reasons why I caved. "Guess you finally convinced me."

But I know that's not true. Not exactly.

Violet. That's who changed my mind.

Kayla giggles through the air and interrupts my thoughts of Violet as she finishes her toast and orange juice, staring dreamily out the window. "Can we go get her this morning? Maybe they'll let us bypass the paperwork."

I take a sip of my black coffee and chuckle under my breath. "Slow down, kiddo. We'll get her when we get her. You just go on upstairs and get ready. Don't wanna get you to school late."

She groans, but throws me a big smile, one that makes my heart swell. "Oh, alright." With one more glance my way, Kayla exits the room, chanting, "We're getting a cat!" all the way up the stairs.

I shake my head and turn my attention back to the image of Whiskers—the cat that might soon be a part of our little family.

Something tugs in my chest, a little hope fizzing against the bubbles of coffee sloshing around in my stomach.

Violet.

Maybe one day I'll be able to stand in this kitchen and make coffee for Violet while she sits in the recliner, snuggling with Whiskers purring in her lap. It's a faint illusion, pieces of anticipation falling into place.

It may not become reality, but this little trace of hope is something worth holding on to. It's a step in the right direction. And I'll keep pacing myself till I have her.

CHAPTER TWENTY-THREE

VIOLET

Fashion Valley is brimming with people meandering from store to store, despite it being early in the day on a Wednesday. Even the parking lot is packed with shiny convertibles and sporty cars that glitter in the sunlight.

Guess I wasn't the only one with the great idea of taking a day off in the middle of the week.

I casually waltz through the open air, admiring the green succulents, the swaying palms overhead, the distant ocean breeze flitting through the blue sky. Closing my eyes for just a moment, I breathe in the rich perfume from Burberry and make my way through the stores.

A little retail therapy to clear my mind of work, my earlier therapy session with Jenna, and a certain brown-eyed man who won't seem to leave my mind.

Sam... I wonder what he's up to today. Is he lounging around the house? Perhaps working up a sweat in the gym? Sifting through piles of paperwork that I promised to help him sort out?

Smiling giddily to myself, I disappear inside American Eagle and leave the thought of Sam at the door. After picking out a pretty yellow sundress, I shift down the row of lit-up stores, zigzagging through the various retail outlets. Grabbing an elegant, fruity Chance Eau Tendre perfume from Chanel.

Browsing over-the-shoulder purses from Coach. Perusing sets of athletic wear in Fabletics. Sliding into Hollister and leaving with a bag of bleached denim jeans.

I'm not a huge spender. Not too much into diamond jewelry or flashy rings weighing on my fingers. But sometimes it's nice to indulge for a day—let my long hair down and take a deep breath of salty sea air.

As I stroll along the walkway, passing benches of people and a flowing fountain, I pause in front of the sparkling lights of Victoria's Secret and flick my eyes into the store.

A whisk of tingles slide down my spine as I gaze at the sheer lingerie, ranging from silky and chic to smoldering and temptress. The flex of my fingers signal me to keep walking, but I'm far too intrigued now. It's like I'm attached by strings, getting pulled like a puppet to move. So that's what I do—move.

Skimming the bottom of my white Converse on the polished tile, I wander around aimlessly. Brushing my fingers over red lace, assessing a matching set of lilac sleepwear, taking in the stacks of lacy thongs on a side table.

Lingerie isn't something I normally buy. Never really had someone to wear it for. Well, there was that one time... I flinch at the reminder. That time when I put on a matching set of crimson lace lingerie. The panties completely see-through, the push-up bra bedazzled and tight. I sat there on the edge of the bed, trying to beckon Jason into the room. But with one flick of his red-rimmed, murky green eyes, he just cat-called me for one second and said maybe later.

He didn't come back later, though. He just passed out on the couch, a beer bottle emptied and tipped over, covering the coffee table in a sticky film of Corona.

That's the last time I tried. Figured it wasn't worth it if he couldn't appreciate me trying my hardest to please him. I should've left right then, but instead, I stayed till he shredded the lacy fabric, just like he did my heart...

I shake off the dull ache that's simmering in my gut and replace it with a splash of hope. Breathing in and out, slow and steady, I think of the sunshine slipping through the glass windows, the feel of new shopping bags in my left hand, the freedom of being off in the middle of the busy week.

He can't continue ruining my life. Not anymore.

Just as I turn to leave the store, my eyes catch on a piece of material. One so pretty that it pulls me in the direction of the black hanger. It doesn't take me long to drop my bags on the floor, my hands instantly moving to the exquisite material.

Light pink. The color of a soft rose, mixed with a hint of bubble gum. My fingers glide over the slim bodysuit, and my eyes drag down the all-over lace. I examine it, admiring the fine details of the tiny flowers sewn into the delicate material. There's silk ribbons attached to the sides, meant as a way to tie a perfect bow with. Thin straps crisscross in the back, pure cotton lines the inside of the gusset, and the small cutouts on the side make for a sexy tease.

There's something about this one. Maybe because it's my favorite color, or maybe because it's delicate and soft and would make me feel a bit more confident. I've never bought lingerie for myself, but today, I almost want to.

The longer I stare at it, immobile to the spot, the more I want to try it on.

Then I get this weird buzzing sensation in the back of my neck, sending signals to my brain. Would Sam like this? The color, the deep V-shape between the breasts, the lace that would climb over my skin and reveal what's underneath the lace.

Maybe I want to get it just so I can wear it for him...

Without another thought, I'm grabbing up the pile of bags from the floor and hooking my fingers over the lingerie hanger, heading straight back toward the glittery pink walls of the dressing rooms.

Once I'm inside, lock latched and clothes thrown in a heap on the stool, I carefully slide on the pink bodysuit until the thin straps are up over my shoulders and situated into place. When I look up into the floor-to-ceiling mirror, I freeze, momentarily stunned as my eyes take in the mirage of a woman. A woman I don't recognize for a split second.

Slowly, tentatively, my fingers trace over the edges of the soft pink lace, dancing across flower patterns and the silk ribbon that's tied in a pretty bow around the curves of my waist. I let them brush across the dipping slope of the intricate material, slide them over the tops of my breasts, completely speechless as I turn in a slow circle to examine the pretty image before me.

And then I stop in front of the mirror, blinking in disbelief at what I'm standing in.

I feel... beautiful for once. Sexy in a demure way. Whatever self-confidence I lost in the downfall of Jason is creeping up again. Sliding up my spine until I'm nearly glowing in the reflection of the mirror. All those condescending, negative words spewed from Jason's lewd tongue are gone, for the moment. In place stands a woman who's taking back her feminism. Dipping into that sex appeal and allure of desires I never thought I could really just enjoy.

But that's wrong. This isn't the first time I've felt desirable.

No. That first night Sam took me down that moonlit hall, I felt it all. I *still* feel it all—just like a surfer crashing into an intense wave, knocking the breath from their lungs. That's how Sam makes me feel every time he looks at me.

He's the impenetrable wave that knocks all the lost confidence back into me. He makes me feel... wanted.

I get this silly idea in my head. Something I never would've done before. I want to slide the lingerie on, perch on top of his pool table, and make him come find me—just like a game of cat and mouse. But really, I'd love nothing more than for him to catch me.

After a few more minutes of staring into the mirror, I change back into my cutoff jean shorts and light blue T-shirt, and make my way to the register, a massive grin tugging at my glossy pink lips.

I'm going to wear this for Sam because he deserves that. Deserves nothing but the best because he took care of me when I was breaking down in his office, tugged me into his arms so he could melt all that pain away.

He deserves good things, and maybe I do, too...

When I get back to my SUV, I throw the various bags in the backseat, taking extra care to tuck the pink striped Victoria's Secret bag underneath the back of the passenger seat. Don't want that to get far from me.

As I flick my eyes in the rear-view mirror and buckle the seatbelt securely around my body, I slip the key in the ignition and turn, expecting the rifts of a Breaking Benjamin song to slip out from the speakers. Instead, I'm disappointed to find that there's only a high-pitched squeal from the engine as the dash lights flicker and die in the next second.

"What the…"

I try again, snapping the key to the right until the engine almost turns over, but I'm left with nothing but the click of my fingernails scratching down the leather steering wheel.

Puffing out a cloud of air, I unbuckle my seatbelt and swing the door open, popping the hood with the click of a button. When the shiny hood is propped open, I gaze over the numerous wires and electrical parts, pretending I know exactly what I'm looking at. But really, I don't have a clue.

"Uhhhh." Slamming the hood down with a bang, I lean back against the warm body of the car, squeezing my eyes shut as I slide my iPhone from my pocket. When I take a nice, steady breath to calm down, I take it upon myself to flick through my contacts and try to find someone that can help.

My dad was always the one to call first when I had car trouble, but with him being in Napa, that's almost impossible. I can't reach Brianna, she's in Los Angeles for a conference. And Taylor's near Malibu, tending to endless errands from her client who's an upcoming actress. I don't really have any family near here, just an aunt who lives a couple hours east and a distant cousin idling between the border of Northern California and Oregon. Which leaves me with absolutely no one.

Tucking a lock furiously behind my ear, I press my lips into a tight line and thumb through my contacts again. I could call a tow truck, try my luck with the roadside assistance number I have shoved in my wallet, but that could be hours of waiting around.

Just as I decide to almost give up and track down a security guard in the parking lot, my fingers stop moving, thumb hovering over three distinct letters that stand out like an orange cone in the middle of the highway.

Sam...

I could call him. Tap my thumb against his number and let the line ring till he picks up. But there's a nagging feeling in my gut that's pressing against my nerves, signaling to drop it. I'd be asking too much of him. Stepping over boundaries that shouldn't be crossed. I'm outside his club. That means lines would zigzag, get thrown out the window. But really, it's just a small favor. Something I'd happily pay him back for.

So I slowly drop my thumb, breaching thin lines, and then the line clicks, sending a monotone ringing noise as I press the phone to my ear and hold my breath.

Don't pick up. Just let it go to voicemail. That's what half of me says. The other part desperately wants him to. And just when I think he won't, the end of the line clicks and out comes a deep voice that's thick with gravel. "Angel?"

God. His voice, that nickname. Two things that can make my knees weak.

"Hi, Sam," I drawl out, hoping he can't hear the shakiness in my voice.

"Well, what do I owe the pleasure of a call on a Wednesday afternoon from you?"

I can hear the chuckle under his breath. I almost ask him to repeat it just for me.

"I, umm... I kinda have a favor to ask." The toes of my Converse dig into the cement, kicking absentmindedly to shake off the jitters.

"Oh? What kind of favor?" There's a bit of amusement in his tone, laced with another deep laugh.

Smiling at the sound, I push my free hand into the pocket of my shorts, scratching absentmindedly at the frayed denim. "Well, it's my car. I tried to turn the key, and the ignition wouldn't turn over. I didn't know who else to call and—"

He stops me right there, halting my words with a direct question. "Where are you?"

Biting my bottom lip, I answer back, "Fashion Valley."

"I can be there in about fifteen minutes. What kind of car do you drive?"

"A RAV4. It's light blue, and there's a white hibiscus sticker on the back window. You can't miss it."

"And you're parked where?"

I look out through the bright sun and shield my eyes as I stare up at a looming palm tree that's next to some red poppies springing up from the patch of green grass. "The south side of the parking lot. Close to a parked yellow sports car."

Chewing down more nerves, I don't have to wait for his response because it comes immediately.

"Alright, angel. Just hang tight. Be there soon." And then I hear the click of the receiver as the line goes dead.

Standing there with wide eyes, my breath starts to shake. Sam is really coming to help me get my car going again. That man really is my hero…

Shortly after the call, a shiny black Chevy pulls up next to my parked car. The windows are tinted, a little hard to see through the shade of black, but I faintly glimpse the trace of his large figure through the windshield.

He doesn't leave me hanging. He arrives precisely on the dot, just like he said. Not even one minute late.

I dangle the car keys from my Laguna Beach lanyard, swinging it back and forth like a pendulum against my thigh, my eyes widening as he steps out into the sunlight.

He's got a white T-shirt on—one that sticks to his broad chest, accentuating muscles under the thin material. A light blue flannel hangs over that—sleeves rolled up to his elbows, exposing the traces of black ink that swirls across his right forearm. Tan khaki shorts are donned against muscular thighs, with clean white tennis shoes to compliment the outfit.

I have to swallow down nerves and ground myself to the cement so I don't topple over.

There's a gentle smile curving over his lips. Brown eyes glistening like stars in the sunlight, tanned skin glowing like gold dust beneath the heat. And his hair—mussed to perfection. Messy, untamed sandy-brown locks blowing in the wind. Hair I want to lace my fingers through.

He looks... *good.* Maybe better than in the black slacks and sleek ties he wears. I like him all fancy and good-looking, but seeing him in normal, casual clothes makes my heart skip a beat. Makes me breathe a little deeper because we're outside the club and he's here, standing before me, *saving* me from being stranded.

He came when I called—just like he said he would.

"Hey," he says casually as he walks up to me, brown eyes giving me a once-over. I don't miss the way he lingers there—on my legs, my *eyes.* It makes nerves flush hot in my cheeks, especially when he flashes that sideways smile of his.

"Hi," I breathe out quietly as an easy smile meets my lips.

"Looks like I found you." He grins, his big eyes shining against the sunlight like gold marble.

"You found me," I voice as quiet as a mouse, tongue sticking to the roof of my mouth as I repeat his phrase in my head.

I found you. Figuratively and literally, three simple words mixing together like swirling wine.

"Mind if I take a look?" He nods toward the driver's door, asking for permission. I happily pave the way for him.

"Oh, yeah. Go ahead."

He steps around me, brushing his arm against mine. I feel the fire singeing my skin.

"Just gotta pop the hood," he huffs out as he plops into the front seat, reaching for the lever to the hood.

A shiver runs straight down my spine as I see him crane his neck, almost far enough to see the little striped bag with pink tissue paper spilling over the edges. Victoria's Secret letters slithered in bold across the front. It's a surprise, something I'm not ready to reveal yet. But to my advantage, he doesn't turn completely around, just slides from the white leather and shuffles to the front, popping the hood open.

He knows exactly what he's doing, looks like he's done this a million times as he shifts crossed wires and bulky parts around that I could never understand.

I watch him work, eagerly lapping the view of beads of sweat against his tousled brown locks, biceps flexing against flannel, black ink prominent against the thick veins that wrap like vines down his forearm. It's like I'm mesmerized by watching this beautiful man taking time out of his day to help me sort out my car problems, and I can't take my eyes off him for even a second.

But he seems to be watching me, too. I see the way his eyes flit to mine every couple of minutes, feel the heat building as the hot sun beats down on our backs. But it's not just the sun I'm feeling. It's whatever *this* is. That electric buzz humming in my ears every time he's near.

Sandalwood, warm sand, saltwater misted through his silky hair. I smell it all.

As he continues working—thoroughly inspecting the engine—my voice slips out softly, "Thanks for coming."

He stops working, looks up with those big doe eyes, and steals my breath once more. "Couldn't leave you stranded, could I?"

"No, guess not." I laugh, my fingers toying with the edges of the frayed denim nervously.

After a few more minutes of diligent work, Sam's wiping sweat from his brow and nodding toward the keys dangling from my pocket. "Go ahead and try to start it. Think I got it figured out."

When I slide against the seat and slip the key into the ignition, I quickly turn it and squeal when the engine turns over, ecstatic that whatever he did worked. Shutting the engine off, I jump up from the front seat and emerge back into the sunlight as he slams the hood shut.

"You fixed it!"

Sam takes a step forward and leans against the side of the car, his thick arms crossed over his chest. He shrugs, acting like it was nothing. "Wasn't that hard."

"What was wrong with it?" I ask, cocking my head to the side.

"There were a couple wires that came unhooked. Just had to put them back where they needed to go. Nothing big," he replies. "But, you might want to get your oil changed soon. Looks a little past time."

"Ahh," I say. "Quite the mechanic, aren't you?"

He flexes an arm back, sliding his fingers through his locks. Something I want to do...

"You could call it that, sure. I work on my truck, so I know the ins and outs."

Letting a laugh leave my lips, I kick against the concrete, nervous once again. But I'm always nervous around him, aren't I? "Figured. Well, looks like I should schedule to have the dealership change my oil."

He pushes a hand in his khaki pocket, looks up, and pauses for just a second before he murmurs, "I could do it for you."

"Oh?" I question, my eyebrows raising.

He nods. "Sure. Might save you a pretty penny. I change mine all the time. Wouldn't mind taking on one other car."

"Oh. I... okay."

The warm breeze brushes through my hair, blowing in that faint line once again—the one we keep tripping over. Another hint, another step toward *something* where boundaries don't exist anymore. And that's a scary thought to think about.

Breaking the moment, I lean into my open door and fish out a crisp twenty-dollar bill from deep inside my purse. I can't just let Sam come all this way and help me start my car without gifting him something. He deserves this.

When I stand a few paces away from him, I extend my arm out, revealing the green bill. "Here. Something for fixing my car."

He flexes his jaw, shaking his head as he tries to push my hand away. "No. I can't accept that."

"But I want you to have it," I insist, taking a step closer to him as I wave the twenty toward him.

"Nah. Keep it," he asserts, finality in his tone.

"Please, Sam," I press, adamant he takes it off my hands. "Just... take it."

"Violet," he sighs, taking a large step forward as his large hand closes around mine, fingers flexing till the twenty is crumpled in my palm. "I don't want your money." There's an edge to the way he says it, but there's softness swirling in his brown eyes.

"Well..." I pause, staring up at him in a trancelike state. "What do you want?" My voice comes out meek, whispering the question like I'm walking on eggshells. It sounds like I'm asking something else. Something in uncharted territory.

He stares at me a beat, answers flashing through his brown irises. His jaw unclenches, mouth parting like he's just as mesmerized as me. There's a softness in his features, eyes swimming with something I can't quite trace. But there's that thick tension blowing through the air—the one I always feel when I'm around him. Then he's really looking at me with those soft brown eyes, drawing me in like a moth to a flame. I see it for just a second, feel it in the way my heartstrings play like violins against my chest.

He wants *me*. That's what his eyes give away, what my heart whispers to me. For just a second, I see it all so clearly.

"Just..." he whispers, "your time."

Your time... Sam wants *my* time...

We both stand there, arrested in the moment, melting those blurred lines away for just a minute.

"Okay," I reply, my voice hoarse and quiet.

Another silent moment goes by, until he rustles in front of me, hand flexing back through his hair. "Hey, are you busy?"

Cocking an eyebrow up in question, I loosely shrug. "I mean, I'm standing outside my car in a parking lot. So, no?"

He flashes me an *easy, smartass* grin and tugs at his pockets, hesitant. "Can I..." he starts, pausing to clear his throat, "I want to show you something."

"Show me what?" I cross my arms and tilt my head in curiosity.

"It's a secret." He smirks, his eyes swirling with mischief.

I rock back and forth on my heels, smiling. "What if I don't like secrets?"

Another smile, one that makes my insides hum. "You trust me?"

I think it over, chewing the gloss from my bottom lip, nervously twirling a finger against a loose string on the bottom of my jean shorts.

Trust is an awfully big word for me, one that doesn't come easy. But as he looks at me, big brown eyes full of hope, I can't help but to trust fall right into him.

With a slow nod, I take the leap. "Yes." It's a ghost of a whisper, but loud enough that he hears me.

He gives me a carefree smile and beckons me to follow. "Come on then, angel." And I follow, right on his heels.

As I climb into his truck—seats all black leather and the cab smelling of pinewood—I flick my eyes back to my vacant car, then over to Sam as he slides into the driver's seat. And I smell him *everywhere* now; his sandalwood trademark scent mixing with the pine.

He smells like mine.

When the engine roars to life and his hand flexes over the leather steering wheel, he gives me this jaw-dropping smile, and then I'm gone.

I just sealed my fate, tethered myself to a rock that'll send me soaring over a cliff, right into the deep ocean. By getting inside this truck, I just took a step closer, jumped right over that boundary line.

There's no going back now.

CHAPTER TWENTY-FOUR

SAM

The soft hum of Tears for Fears plays low through the speakers as the tires track over smooth road, nerves spinning in the back of my mind. Violet's in my truck, in my passenger seat, in *my* space outside the club.

I can't help but glance over at her every few seconds. Can't help but to stare as sunlight shines over her glossy lips. She's got this big smile on her glowing face as she hums along to the track, her hand bouncing on her thigh to the beat. I don't think I've ever been so distracted while I was driving before. Not until now.

As I near the exit to the beach, adrenaline pumps in my veins, echoing the thick rush through my ears. I'm about to show Violet my secret hideout. A place I haven't even shown Kayla or Kelsey because it's a sacred place. One so special that I might be slipping into uncharted territory if I give it away.

But what am I doing now? Exactly that. Giving that secret away to *her*.

My fingers flex tighter against the steering wheel the closer I get. My heart beats as loud as a tropic thunderstorm, all lightning and gusts of winds dragging me into the cyclone. I could turn this truck around this very instant, tell her something came up. I could take her *anywhere* but my special place. But Violet...

she's special to me. And as scared as I am about opening my darkest part of myself up for her, I want to do that. *Need* to do that.

Time won't go any slower. This might be the only shot I have.

Slowing the truck to a halt, I cut the engine and stare out at the open expanse of my little hideout—a private beach where no one seems to come. My sweet escape. Practically a little island of its own. It's just a few miles west of Sunset Cliffs Beach. A place where the tourists never seem to find. But I found it and now, it's mine.

Violet looks out the windshield, then back at me, blue eyes intrigued by the sight. "Come on." I smile as I slide out of the truck and beckon her to follow. She does, and I can't seem to stop the warmth serenading in my chest.

I'm really showing Violet my special place.

"Wow, this is beautiful," she gushes as she scans the wide open area, taking in the view like she's staring at a masterpiece.

Tall palm trees sway behind us. A flock of seagulls sing their song through the bright blue sky, disappearing for a moment behind fluffy white clouds. The salty breeze blows gently through my hair. Calm waves crash against the surface, creating puddles of water down by the tidepools. Cavernous alcoves line both sides of the beach, making this place look like an enchanted Neverland. The sand is golden and soft, and a vast blue ocean lies ahead just feet from us.

I take a deep breath, breathing in the salty air, letting it serenade my lungs with fresh oxygen, then I close my eyes for just a moment. And when I open them, Violet's staring right at me with wide eyes.

"What is this place?" she asks, wonder filling her dreamy voice.

"I call it my special place," I reply as I slip my tennis shoes off and pat the warm sand next to me, inviting Violet to join me.

She slides down beside me and does the same, taking her Converse off to slip her toes beneath the sand. "How is it that I've lived here for years and never even knew this place existed?"

I shrug and flash her a small smirk. "Guess you just weren't looking hard enough."

We sit there a moment in comfortable silence, glancing out at the incoming waves, watching the top of the blue water glisten like diamonds under the sun, listening to the sea lions in the far distance.

Twisting my wrist, I look at my watch and curl my lips up, smirking to myself that it's exactly the right time. Two-thirty in the afternoon. Just about time for the show to begin.

I hear them before they appear, their high-pitched whistles in the distance. And when I notice the first splash offshore, I nudge Violet's shoulder and point to the sea. "Right on time," I smile, "look."

As she looks up, her eyes light up like fireworks, eyes gigantic when a pod of bottlenose dolphins start leaping from the water. There's probably over a hundred of them. Small calves flipping beside their mothers, showing off their tricks like they're on a stage. And then more come, joining in with the other ones. Their tails shine against the water, gray colors ranging from dark to light shades. This is always one of my favorite things to see, something that keeps me coming back. It never gets old, watching them enjoy freedom in the wide open ocean, loving life.

When I look over at Violet, she's got this huge grin on her glossy lips—one that pulls at my heartstrings. "Sam..." she whispers in awe.

"I know," I reply, joy filling my voice. "Isn't it beautiful?"

"It's breathtaking," she gasps as she watches another dolphin fly out of the water, busy with its routine of catching fish. "You've seen them before?"

"Mhm. They usually come about the same time of day. I've seen them over a dozen times. Never gets old."

"Wow..." She's all awestruck and stunned, and I can tell she's loving every bit of this, as much as I am. But I think I'm enjoying watching her more...

I can't help but to stare as she watches the marine animals disappear into the far distance, her eyes as blue as the deep sea, brunette curls flying in the wind, sun-kissed by the golden rays. She's absolutely sparkling, her smile making me speechless. I don't think a woman has ever had this effect on me before, and I'm not sure how to take that.

As the salty breeze blows through my tousled locks, I fix my stare on her, watching as she gazes dreamily at the sea. Digging my fingers into the soft sand, I bite the inside of my cheek, trying to refrain from spilling all my dark secrets. But the way I continue watching her—all starry-eyed and contempt by the water—makes me loosen my tight jaw.

If I want to be with her—*really* be with her—then I have to take the leap. So I do.

This is it. I'm about to tell her *everything*.

With one last gulp, I say her name over the crashing tides of the ocean. "Violet?"

"Hmm?" she hums, still locked onto the shining waters up ahead.

"There's something I need to tell you."

She cranes her neck to the left and flicks her eyes over at me. "What is it?"

Taking a deep breath, I gently blow it out and stare at the sea. "I didn't just come to California to try my hand at better job opportunities." I feel her gaze on me from my peripheral vision, furrowed brows and eyes full of questions.

"Oh?' she asks. "What else did you come here for then?"

Inhaling a lungful of crisp air, I close my eyes and let the words fly out. "To escape."

She snaps her head to mine and parts her lips. "Escape?" she ponders out.

I nod, shaking my head up and down slowly as my eyes drift to the sand, counting the grainy texture until I'm brave enough to murmur out, "I was married before."

She shifts next to me uncomfortably, until she's leaning against her left arm and spurring me on. "Married?"

Dragging my tongue across the top of my teeth, I swallow back any chance of backing out and sigh in return. "We got divorced before I moved here."

There's a moment of silence, not even the seagulls dare to interrupt me. But Violet looks at me with those big blue eyes and softly nudges. "What happened?"

I take a moment to prepare what I'm about to share, tell myself to keep breathing, but it's hard when it feels like I'm choking on salt water. "She, uhh," I stutter and try again. "She turned out to not be a safe place for me and my girls anymore."

When I flick my eyes up at her, she's patiently waiting, intent on me to continue. She's not rushing me or demanding answers, she just sits there in the sand until I'm ready to say more.

Digging my heels deeper into the smooth sand, I decide to start from the beginning. Violet deserves that—the truth. "Me and Lois, my ex-wife, were high school sweethearts. Shortly got married soon after graduating. Everything was perfect, or so I thought. Till we had Kelsey."

Violet's fingers melt into the grainy sand, fidgeting through her question. "What happened after you had Kelsey?"

I gnaw at the inside of my cheek, feeling blood run down the back of my throat when I swallow. This shouldn't be so hard to talk about, but it still feels fresh. That deep wound sitting in the back of my chest, still bleeding like it was just yesterday when I left Oklahoma. When I left her.

With another sigh, I drawl out, "She lost herself..."

Violet treads carefully and asks, "Lost herself?"

I thread a hand through my hair and watch the sand crinkle beneath my feet, trying to settle my covered sadness. "She was first off, a narcissist. Didn't show her true colors till years later. And then she started drinking, heavily," I whisper out.

Violet shifts next to me, as if she's trying to get closer. "She drank around the girls?"

"Yes," I murmur through my teeth. "Even though I tried to get her to stop, she just kept *drinking*."

Her eyes fall to the ground when she asks, "Did she get the treatment she needed?"

"For a while, yes. Got her to go to some counseling sessions with me, and then her doctor prescribed medication to help with the cravings. But then she started slipping. Started having these big setbacks. Refusing the medication, saying she didn't need therapy, blaming me when I tried encouraging her that she should go. But it only got worse after we had Kayla…" Flexing my hand into a fist, I drag my clipped nails against the inside of my palm, squeezing till I flinch in pain.

It's not fucking easy talking about this, but I have to try. I have to try for Violet…

She curls her fingers in the sand and stares at the ground. "Did the medicine help?"

"Mmm," I groan. "Half the time. Until she started downing them with bottles of wine."

Violet flinches at the mention of the term bottle and turns her body toward the incoming waves, staring mindlessly into the open ocean.

Did that strike a nerve in her?

She's quiet for a few seconds, out of bounds until she speaks again. "She never pulled through?"

I shake my head, confirming my nightmare all over. "No, not really…"

"Where, umm," she rasps. "Where is she now?"

"Still in Oklahoma, as far as I know. Living with her folks, in their guest house. Last I heard, she wouldn't listen to them, either. Just got addicted to the high of it all somewhere down the line."

The part when the dopamine kicks in and you feel like you're on cloud nine is what she liked most, but there's nothing euphoric about being so gone that you can't even control what's going on around you. It's like a disease, eats away at the brain like a cancer. That's what the alcohol did to her. Rotted her away till she was unrecognizable. Not the woman I fell in love with all those years ago, and it still hurts because a part of me still loves her.

"Does she still see your daughters?" Violet asks, gently bringing it up.

A grimace twitches over my lips as I tether myself to the sand. "No. Not after the incident where she forgot them in the car and blew through my credit card at the mall." The memory makes me sick. Makes me want to grab and pull a fistful of hair out to know that I could've gotten there too late. That was the final straw. Anything could have happened to my girls. "But she still tries, when she's having an episode. Lashes out through the phone that I got full custody of the girls and not her. Never mind that they don't want to speak to her. Besides, they never really had a mother. Not for long, at least..."

Pain twists in my gut, creating a wrenching agony that zaps through my chest. She could max me out, buy all the stilettos she wanted, but she had no right to put *my* girls in danger like that. If I wouldn't have called her, she would've forgotten they were there in the first place. I wouldn't have raced there from work to snatch Kayla and Kelsey up into my arms, to take them home where it was safe.

That was the last time I left them unsupervised with her. I just never knew she'd go so off the deep end like that...

"Sam..." Violet's voice is strained the way she speaks my name. There's pain slipping from her echo, dragging all the way out to sea.

Blinking away a tear that threatens to spill, my strangled voice breaks against the crash of waves hitting shore. "Even decided to ruin my pool business when she was having one of her episodes. Fuck... I should've just... I should've known better. But I believed she'd get better because she promised. She *promised* she'd try, but she didn't really do that. Every day, I thought she'd *just* get better. But she didn't. And my expectations that she would just ended up hurting me more. And now, I blame myself because maybe I should've tried harder."

Not even the ocean's tides seem to calm the storm that's brewing like a hurricane inside me. There's anger, bitterness, and hurt laced through every single word that I let slip off my tongue. What if I just tried harder...

I'm still not over what happened. Even though I'd like to believe I am. Maybe I'll just wear it on my sleeve forever, till I'm laid to rest in the cold ground.

"That's... horrible. Oh my God, I'm so sorry..." Violet's hand lingers against her side, fingers curling in the sand, almost like she's trying to reach out for me. "But you can't blame yourself, Sam. It's not your fault."

I hang my head, stare directly at my feet, close my eyes, and count to five in my head. But then, I'm spilling more of my heartbreak to Violet. "You know, I tried. I really *tried.* I fought every fucking day for her, was there every step of the way, holding her hand. But it wasn't enough. I was *never* enough." Just like our vows at the altar weren't enough.

"No," she whispers through the wind, dragging her hand closer to where I can practically feel her warmth through the fabric of my shorts. "Don't say that."

She wraps her hand around my wrist, making some of my pain disappear by the way she's latching on like a sloth. But her warmth fades the second her fingers slide from my skin.

I already miss her touch...

"But it's true," I reply, firmer than I intend to come off. Maybe it's just the held-in emotions I've been suppressing all these years. Maybe I'm just still torn apart. "In the end, she didn't want me. She didn't want the girls. She didn't want *us.*"

Violet stares ahead, as quiet as a mouse. But she's listening, waiting.

My voice barely comes out a whisper, hushed from silent tears. "And you know one of the worst parts? She flat out told me she didn't want to give up the alcohol. She'd rather be consumed by that than be there for her family."

Violet presses her pink lips together in a tight line and curls her knees up till she's hugging them to her chest. She seems lost to the high tide, blue eyes gone into another dimension that's far from my reach. She looks like she's hurting, too. Maybe it's just my imagination, but there's a flicker of something searing behind her shiny irises. Like she's holding back tears of her own.

She stays silent, her thoughts miles away from me. So I lean forward and sling my right arm over my knee, sliding just a bit closer to where my shoulder brushes hers.

"Lois really loved Chardonnay. I still have a hard time thinking I maybe could've stopped her from drowning herself in it," I murmur under my breath as weights crush against my lungs. "Never thought it'd be one of her breaking points."

And what a contradiction I am, with an array of wine on my club's drink menu. It's not the wine that bothers me, though. Not really. It's just the memory of what it did to her.

Violet wraps her arms tighter around her knees, almost as if she's shielding herself from the ocean spray. But there's that same faraway look in her eyes, a hint of understanding the way her lips twitch back and forth.

She finally nods slowly, signaling that she heard me loud and clear. "Alcohol's a really hard habit to break once you're deep in the trenches. Sometimes it can't be helped..."

"Yeah, you're absolutely right. A really hard habit to break..."

There's another pause between our conversation as heaviness blankets the cool air, tying strings around my ankles so I can't move. But neither of us so much as flinch for that moment. The only thing that seems to be ours is the shared silence permeating thickly around the perimeter of the beach.

A lone seagull lands in the water a few feet from where we sit, and that seems to stir Violet from her trance.

She scratches along her arm uncontrollably, her blue eyes fixed intently on the horizon. And then, her soft voice slips through the still air. "You know, sometimes the things we love the most have a way of fading away. And no matter how hard you fight for them, sometimes that just pushes them further, till they're miles away from shore. Sometimes..." she pauses, pushing herself to finish, "you just end up more hurt than the other person you're trying to help."

"And all you can do is set them free," I finish for her.

"Like ashes in the wind..." she whispers, letting her own words blow out to sea.

She sounds exactly like she understands me. Looks as if she has some pain she's holding onto as well...

"But through all the pain, I found something I love. Something I enjoy waking up and going to. Even if it's not building pools," I laugh. "My club... it's something I built from the ground up. It's a place that's mine, and it's just..." I shrug, losing my words through emotion. "I really love it, Violet. I turned my pain into something beautiful. In a strange way, it helped heal me."

Violet's eyes get a little foggy, and she's got this big smile that makes my heart skip a beat. "You sure did, Sam. You turned it into just that—something beautiful. And it *is* something special. Something you're so good at. And I can see how you touch it with a bit of magic. You've got a special touch."

I'm a little speechless, a little breathless because what do I say to that? Thank you? You make the place feel like magic? Or maybe, you belong there with me...

Just before I have the chance to say anything, I pause the moment I feel her fingertips brush along my forearm, gliding gently over my inked skin.

"This tattoo," she articulates, intently studying the swirls of waves on my skin, "what's the meaning behind it?"

"See this here?" I point to the shaded watch. "The pocket watch symbolizes a shift in my life. Seven o'clock on the dot—the moment I left Oklahoma and drove straight out to California. Didn't even stop to rest, just kept driving till I saw mountains. It means the minutes kept passing, but time didn't stop. The gears kept going, ticking while I kept moving."

"And the waves?" She traces the curved lines perfectly, imprinting herself into my skin like the black ink. Goose bumps follow with every pass of her fingertips.

"See how it crashes over the watch?" I take her hand in mine and guide her fingers along the outline, tracing slopes across the water that consumes the time.

"Mhm," she hums, eyes fixed intently on the glass that's cracking underneath the pressure of the inked waves.

"Well," I begin, "it means a new beginning. Starting over and leaving behind what I left back in Oklahoma. California was the start of something unknown, exciting, a place I could raise my girls in peace. So I guess it just comes down to a symbol of healing. Something lost but not forgotten. It means there's hope for me and my girls. There's *life* through the salty waves besides pain."

"That's beautiful, Sam," she whispers, her breath hot over my skin. I let her hand go, but she keeps tracing over divots across my arm, like she's mapping out every line, every scar that leads straight to my heart.

"Thanks, angel," I smile, "I think it is, too."

Time passes slowly as she trails her fingertips up and down my inner forearm, nails gently scratching the surface. She's quite enthralled with my ink, but I'm more mesmerized by the sight of her sitting next to me, replacing pain by the hearts she etches into my skin.

She didn't run when I told her about my dark past. Didn't judge me or call me a betrayer for leaving my wife. She stayed when I needed her most...

When her fingers fall from my skin, I look out toward the horizon as blue waves crash against shallow rocks covered in dark green moss. "You know," I pause. "I've never brought anyone else here before."

She snaps her head up, her lips parted in disbelief. "Not even your daughters?"

I shake my head and chuckle under my breath. "Not even them."

"Then... why me?" she asks faintly, barely breathing the words out.

"Because you—" I have to stop for a second. Have to peer down into pools of soft blue eyes that make my insides liquid. It's there, swimming in her sea of stars that I feel it. The real reason I brought her here. "You make me feel like there's hope worth fighting for."

She blinks a couple times, her lips parted like she's speechless. And her eyes—dark cobalt splashes of water—soften at the edges.

Jesus. She really does know how to take my breath away.

Before I know what's happening, she slowly leans her head against my shoulder and wraps her arms tight around my forearm, like she doesn't want to let go. And I hope she won't. She can hold on for as long as she wants. I won't make her let go.

Taking my time, I rest my chin atop her head, gently tilting down till my lips are ghosting over the crown of her brunette locks. And then we just sit there in silence, watching the mist of a whale's spout in the distance, listening to the slow waves lap at the shore. Violet wrapped around my arm, gently humming against the crook of my neck as the salty breeze blows through her lilac-scented curls.

I see it so clearly now, like a still, glassy lake. I was meant to find Violet.

Falling for her was as easy as watching the first snowfall of the season. Slow, effortless, and altogether breathtaking. But also, it was as fast as lightning, blinding me in ways I didn't see coming.

I think I'll just stay right here for a while. Right next to Violet, while the lapping waves break the surface. Until the sun slips away from the horizon.

Maybe we'll stay till midnight, watching the stars twinkle and fall across the night sky.

Or maybe I'll stay forever, so I can get the chance to love her.

Yeah... I think I'd love nothing more than to fall in love with her. But I'm already there, slipping my toes under the swirling waves, drowning in her lilac scent, getting lost in her shades of blue.

She'd be so easy to love...

Chapter Twenty-Five

Violet

I don't wait a minute, not even a second before I decide tonight is the night. The night I surprise Sam with a little scavenger hunt. One that'll lead him right to me...

After he showed me his sacred, secret place three days ago, I couldn't hold back any longer. I want to do something special for him because he shared the most vulnerable side of himself with me. Opened up his darker past and let me inside.

He let me in, even though I'm still not fully throwing my guarded walls down for him.

I wish I could do that. Shed a little of my closed-up trauma into the light. Let him inside like he did for me. But I'm not ready yet. So I'll just show him how much I appreciate what he did on Wednesday for me the way I can.

When I pull up into the crowded parking lot and step out into the cool air, I fling a flowery tote bag over my shoulder and curl a small smile across my red lips, laughing at what's inside—a striped Victoria's Secret bag and yards of sheer pink ribbon. And of course, underneath my velvet black dress is the new pink lingerie I picked out from the store. The one I bought just for me, but also for Sam...

The club is just as I suspect—packed, warm with the scent of musk and leather, flashing lights throwing different shades of vivid shapes across the sparkly walls. I turn my head from side to side, sweeping my gaze across the crowded floor, searching for Sam. I don't see him, but I do see someone familiar. Someone that could help me accomplish my task of the night.

Bryson.

He sees me out of the corner of his eye on the staircase, his hand flexed around the black railing, twinkling fairy lights beneath him. I hear his deep drawl before I get the chance to say anything.

"Well, well, well. What do we have here? Violet, once again?" He smirks, his hazel eyes shining with mischief as he chuckles on his way down the stairs. "Gonna have to get you a member's card since this seems to be your new favorite hangout spot."

"Ha-ha, very funny." I roll my eyes and grab the dark green straps of the tote, clutching it tighter to my body. "Where's Sam?"

"In his office," he states casually, brushing his fingers over his dark navy suit.

"Think you could do me a favor?" I ask as I lean against the handrail of the staircase.

"Depends." He quirks a thick eyebrow up and studies me for a second, eyes roaming over the bag mysteriously and then back up at me.

"I need you to unlock the back room for me."

"Oh, you *need* me to." He chuckles, amusement carrying through his tone.

"Please?" I ask nicely, shining him my best puppy dog eyes I can conjure up.

"What's in the bag?" His eyes fall back to the bag while the back of his hand gently knocks against it.

I tug it closer to my body and shrug. "It's a surprise for Sam."

"Hmm." He looks me up and down and smiles. "Gonna have to get you your own key."

"Oh, no. That's not necessary," I laugh. Would he seriously get me my own key or is he just joking with me?

"Sure it is. You're here often enough, back there with my brother." There's that wink again. And now my face is beet red with embarrassment.

I roll my eyes and shake my curls out. "Can you just get him out of his office for like five minutes? I need to put something in there."

Bryson drags a hand over his clean-shaven face, eyeing me precariously. "What are you up to, Violet?"

It's not like I can show him what's in the bag without mortifying myself, so I keep it as a casual response. "Look, he did something really nice for me on Wednesday. And now, I want to do something nice for him. So will you just—"

"Alright, alright." He sighs, giving in to my asking. "I'll help you. Just give me a few minutes. I'll make sure he doesn't see you."

"Thank you, Bryson. I owe you." I give him a quick hug in thanks, and he just laughs when he pulls away.

"Don't owe me a damn thing, darling. Just promise me one thing?"

"What's that?" I cock my head and listen.

"Be good to him. He's uhh... he's pretty taken with you."

My lips part in awe, and for a moment I'm speechless. "Oh, umm. Yeah, okay. I promise."

He sends me one more friendly smile. "Wait here." And then he's disappearing through the thick crowd, leaving me alone with my little tote bag and big hopes that tonight I'll make Sam's night.

Bryson's nice. He's got this really infectious personality that's easy to be around, and I can tell how much he cares about his brother. I think we could be friends. I'd like that. Maybe he'd introduce me to his girlfriend. Maybe even...

The word double date crosses my mind for a brief second, but I send that thought flying into the middle of the packed dance floor. Me and Sam, we aren't dating. Not yet. That word, that *thing* gives me the jitters. Maybe because I'm not ready for that word to make its appearance yet. Or maybe I'm just scared of what could happen if we did.

But nonetheless, I shake off those hesitant feelings and wait for Bryson's signal. I don't know what it is, but he said to wait here, so that's what I'll do. Wait, like I always do.

The disco lights shine across the ceiling, creating star patterns against the red and pink silhouette of lights that blur across the room. It doesn't take me long to notice just how much pink Sam's actually added. It's almost as equal to the red flash of signs that are hung around the club. Now there's pink neon signs flaming against the sparkly walls, mixing perfectly with the shades of crimson.

A pink flamingo, some pretty palm trees adjacent to the DJ's booth, a sign that says *This Way to Paradise* strewn across the top of the hall that leads to Sam's office.

I get stuck in the haze of it all when I notice a familiar head of tousled sandy-brown locks turning to the right. Bryson's blond strands and tall stature shield Sam's eyes from me, and he nods my way and winks, signaling me that it's go time. I don't waste a minute till I'm slipping behind him, whispering, "Thank you," while I scurry along to Sam's office.

My black heels skid across the floor as I rush into Sam's office, quickly closing the door so he won't see what I'm up to. When I turn around, I can't help but smile as my eyes roam around his inviting office. He let me color code his entire filing cabinet, and one of the sky-blue folders is open on his desk, right next to his charcoal coffee mug.

I glide my fingers over the glass, my eyes flitting over the various rock albums. Albums I happen to love. As I saunter over to Sam's mahogany desk, I take my time with setting the tote bag down at my feet and pause for just a second. Deftones is playing softly through his Bluetooth speaker, and the air smells just like Sam.

Sandalwood, a touch of ocean breeze, sunshine slipping over freshly mowed grass.

It's intoxicating, really. His scent is everywhere, even clinging to the fabric of my velvet dress.

And then, there's his coffee mug, simmering with a fresh brew of hazelnut. I let my fingertips swirl around the rim, imagining what his lips might taste like. His tongue probably tastes like honey, lips sugar-coated in ecstasy. I almost want to drop my mouth against the edge of the ceramic, seal my red lipstick against the invisible marks he's left from his lips. Maybe then I'll know exactly what he tastes like, and he'll get a flavor of me, too.

But for now, I'll just imagine the scenario till I'm brave enough to play it out myself.

One day, hopefully soon, I'll just drown in his sweet kisses.

Dreamily, I pull out the black and pink striped Victoria's Secret bag and place it in the center of his desk. Then, I hum along to "Rosemary", getting lost in my starry-eyed stare as I uncap a black ink pen and start scrawling in cursive letters across pink card stock paper. I take my time, curving the letters with perfection.

Come find me – Violet

I seal it with a kiss, leaving my crimson lipstick outlined on the bottom right. If I can't bring myself to just unwind and reel him in, leave my mark against his mouth, then at least he'll have this. That's all I can give him, for now...

Spritzing the paper with a dash of vanilla perfume, I place it inside the bag, right underneath the pink decorative tissue paper, and smile at my work. But I'm not done yet, not even close.

Taking one more good look around the room, I clutch the tote bag up over my shoulder and hover my fingers over his warm coffee mug, caressing the edge where his lips were just minutes ago, then I turn and head out the door.

Stealing one more glance toward the front of the hall, I smile as I grab the pink sheer ribbons out of my bag and get to work. I coil the pretty fabric over dimly lit lights, string them over the silver frames of mirrors, and teether them with my scent as I linger the ribbon over the collar of my neck, where the vanilla perfume wafts like candy. I do that all the way down the opposite hall, decorating the walls in swirls of pink and tying a pretty bow over the gold handles of his private room.

Slipping through the doorway, I tug the door closed and throw my bag over the side of the coffee table. Along with that, I unlatch the straps of my heels and throw them on the floor, and then do the same with my dress, sliding it off till it's draped over the back of the leather couch.

Now, it's just me and my pretty lingerie snug against my skin, shining under the dim lights. Gently hoisting myself up onto the pool table, I place myself in the center to where my legs are dangling off the edge, where Sam could easily slide between my legs...

Then, I take my phone and type him out a little text and send it off with a whoosh, positive I'm in way over my head.

Violet: Deftones and coffee? Think you might be missing just one other thing...

He's going to love this. I smile to myself and wait for his entrance, hoping he'll devour me like he downs his coffee.

Chapter Twenty-Six

Sam

The deep echo of the booming music slides through my ears, enough to create a throbbing pulse in my wrist. I was happily content in my office with my cup of coffee, listening to Deftones while I sifted through paperwork. Paperwork that's now in color coded folders all because Violet thought that might help organize my constant mess of papers.

God, I wish she was here now, keeping me company, talking to me with that sweet, perfect voice of hers.

And there I go, thinking of Violet for the hundredth time tonight.

Groaning to myself, I slick a hand back through my hair and raise a brow to Bryson, who's ranting about shit we need to get done in the next month for the club.

"And then we should—"

I have no problem interrupting my brother. "Can we just continue this later? Really need to get back to that paperwork."

He throws a sinister smirk my way. "Why? You got a hot date with your girlfriend?" Bryson winks, and I swear I can see mischief implanted in his hazel eyes.

I shake my head in denial. "She's not my girlfriend."

He gives me a skeptical look, like he sees right through me. "You sure spend a lot of time with her for her not to be."

Shrugging, I throw him a confused glance. "Yeah, well. It's complicated."

"Complicated my ass. I see the way you look at her."

My fingers lace through my dark strands, and I huff out in annoyance. "You sure are nosey."

Bryson smirks my way. "Have to be, Sammy. Gotta watch out for my little brother." He slaps the back of my shoulder and chuckles over the music.

"You do that," I murmur through the air. "I'll text you when I'm done cleaning up in my office."

"Don't think you'll need my help in a few minutes…"

"Huh? What do you mean—" He's gone before I can get the words out.

Why wouldn't I need his help?

Oh, whatever.

Just as I start heading back to my office, my phone buzzes in the side pocket of my black slacks. When I pull it out and see Violet's nickname lit up across the middle of the screen, my heart skips a beat. Wasting no time, I slide it unlocked and read the text as I walk through the thick crowd.

Angel: Deftones and coffee? Think you might be missing just one other thing…

Doing a double take, I read it over just to make sure my eyes are working properly.

Think you might be missing just one other thing…

Is she… is Violet here?

I don't stop to think; I just move. When I make it to my office, I shove the door open in hopes of finding her, but instead, I find a perfectly placed striped black and pink Victoria's Secret bag in the middle of my desk.

"Sneaky girl." I chuckle to myself, wondering how she ever slipped in through my club without me noticing. I think I'd smell her the second she walked in, just like I smell her now, blending in with the fresh brew of coffee sitting idle on the mahogany desk.

Vanilla permeates the room as I toss the pink tissue paper to the side and find a note at the bottom of the bag. Pulling it out, I smile the second I read the perfect cursive letters across the pink paper.

Come find me – Violet

My eyes peel over every inch, slope, dip, and curve of her words until they blur through the paper. My breath escalates the moment my fingers trace over the imprint of her perfect crimson lips, sealing the note with her kiss. Even through the paper, I feel how soft they must be. Like velvet. Perfect for kissing... And I'm dying to kiss her, if only she'd just hold still long enough for me to.

When I place the paper back on top of my desk and spin around, I find some pink ribbon tied around the back of the door handle, giving me a clue for where she's at.

If she wants me to come find her, then I'll chase her down, and I won't stop until I catch her and she's mine.

Twisting the door open, I follow the trail of sheer ribbon that's draped over hanging mirrors and thrown over muted lights. My fingers drag over the thin material, caressing the feel of it like it's Violet's soft skin.

There's another pink ribbon strung over the staircase railing, and I have a feeling where this is all leading me to.

My private room.

I scoot past crowds of fancy dressed clubgoers, the beat of the fast-paced music hypnotizing me in a trance. Violet's all I can hear, all I can see, and I won't stop moving till I have her pressed against me.

Another trail of pink ribbon strings me along down the darkened hallway, the black walls glittering in the reflection of the mirrors with each pass of bright color.

She's near. I can smell her through the air—vanilla and lilac scents mixing together to create a magical concoction that'll only bring me to my knees. Forget the sweat of the dancefloor crowd. Forget the pop of champagne bottles and the aroma of expensive liquor floating through the air. The only thing that remotely matters to me right now is getting to Violet.

I think she's my new favorite attribute of this entire nightclub.

And just as I suspect, there's a big pink bow tied neatly around the golden handle to the room. The one that'll lead me straight to my pretty angel.

Found you.

Wrapping my hand around the handle, I twist it and enter the room, relief flooding my system when I see her out of the corner of my eye.

"Violet?" I ask as I click the door shut and look up. My gaze automatically goes to her silhouette underneath the warm light in the corner of the room.

"Surprise," she says shyly, a pretty blush staining her cheeks when she nervously smiles my way.

"How did you—" I stop and stare, momentarily struck speechless as light basks around her, creating a glowing effect over her smooth skin. I gulp, my mouth parted in shock.

She's fucking gorgeous.

Crimson red lips curled into a soft smile. Long beachy waves cascading down her shoulders. Her legs swinging back and forth over the side where she's perched on the edge of the red pool table.

And that outfit. *Fuck.* Light pink lace hugging her curves in all the right places. The low V-shaped cut of the lingerie revealing the outline of her breasts. A pretty satin ribbon tied around her waist, finished with a big bow in the back that's calling my name to undo. And her legs—long, smooth, glistening under the soft lighting in the room.

But her eyes—big sapphire irises twinkling like stars—are what get me the most.

She makes me weak. Makes me think heaven really did open its gates. She's the guardian angel who dropped right into my lap, and I think she was sent just for me.

"Bryson might've helped me." She laughs under her breath as she flutters her long eyelashes up at me, cheeks still pink from nerves.

She's so fucking cute when she's nervous.

"Of course he did." I smirk as I move toward her across the marble flooring.

"Only with unlocking the door and keeping you out of your office, though. I did the rest," she says proudly, like she's content by the magic she just conjured around my club.

She should be so proud, because I'm enamored by her art. Maybe I should let her decorate more often—turn my club into whatever she wants.

"And you did so good," I commend with the twitch of my lips.

"Thanks." She giggles, her eyes flickering toward the floor for just a second. I step between her legs and place the flat of my palms on her soft thighs. She looks up with a gasp, eyes wide when she meets my sly smirk.

The things I want to do to this woman...

"Look at you, angel. So goddamn gorgeous." I trace the outline of the pink lace, slowly dragging my finger all the way from her collarbone, down to the curve of her hip, till my hand's right back where it belongs.

"You like it?" She lifts her pretty eyes to me, and I'm momentarily stunned into place.

"Like it? No, I love it," I breathe out, my hands gently massaging the tops of her creamy thighs while I ravish over her beauty.

"Picked it just for you." She smiles up at me and blushes again, and that's all it takes for the breath to be sucked out of my lungs, deprived of any and all oxygen once again.

Oh, she's laying it on thick. Like butter—soft and melting any self-restraint that I have left. When it comes to her, all that is gone. I just can't control myself around her.

"Did you now?" I inquire, raising a brow playfully.

"Mhm," she hums.

I tilt my head and let my fingers dance across her skin. "So, you're telling me you did all this for me?" I circle the pad of my thumb softly across her inner thigh, silently chuckling when I feel her jump from my touch.

Oh, the sweet sounds I'll be making her sing tonight...

"That's what I'm saying," she confirms.

"All because you just wanted to?"

She shrugs and hesitates a breath. "This is kind of a thank you, I guess, for Wednesday. You know, for helping me with my car and for taking me to your secret beach."

I shake my head and smile. "Well, I think you sitting all pretty on my pool table with a pink bow wrapped around your waist is the best thank you I've ever gotten."

"Thought you might like it." Her shy laughter makes me dizzy.

She's so fucking adorable.

"Now, let me take a good look at you, angel." I take a step back, letting my hands drop from her thighs, and suck in a deep breath. Nothing could've prepared me for this right here. "Fucking stunning."

"Am I ready for my closeup?" She flips her hair across her shoulder and poses for me, bringing one of her knees to her chest while her other leg drops over the edge of the table, creating the perfect angle for a snapshot.

If it were up to me, I'd fill this entire room with framed photos of her, just so I could stare into the blue eyes of the angel who came and knocked me clear off my feet. I'd call it heaven sent.

"Think I need to snap a few photos so I can remind you how gorgeous you look right now," I tease as I pull out my phone from the pocket of my slacks.

"Sam," she warns, her eyes following the line of my thumb that's unlocking the screen.

"May I?" I ask respectfully, my thumb hovering over the camera app in case she says yes.

Please say yes.

Violet chews her bottom lip in thought, but ultimately agrees. "Alright." My eyes light up with excitement the second she says yes.

Opening up the app, I position the camera at the perfect angle, exactly where I can capture her flirtatious, suggestive pose that's just for me. "Smile, angel."

Click. The camera shutters, and I go again, hovering closer so I can zoom in and snap her stunning blue eyes and her smile that makes me dizzy.

Snap. Snap. Snap.

I lose track of how many I take. Maybe well over thirty by now, but I don't care. She could fill up my entire camera roll, and it still wouldn't be enough. She's all I want to see.

"Gorgeous," I whisper, watching her shift, brushing her long hair across her shoulder. I nearly drool when she winks my way, making my eyes starry with the shine of her eyes. "Think you're ready for the cover of Vogue."

"If you say so." She rolls her eyes and gives me this *be for real* look. But I'm being dead serious.

"I *do* say so," I snap playfully as I hear the shutter of the camera app the moment I lean in and get a closeup of her pretty face.

This one's going as my background on my laptop. Or maybe I'll frame it in my office, put her right next to the picture of me and my girls. Claim her as mine, too...

"Haven't you taken enough yet?" She laughs carelessly, throwing her head back and giving me those eyes that make me weak.

I capture one more and smirk her way. "Not a chance." Before she has a moment to respond, I throw my phone onto the red felt and tug her toward me. "Now, come here." I scoop her up, slide my arms around her hips, and lift her off the pool table till she's in my arms as I take her over to the couch.

"Sam!" she squeaks out, laughing. "Put me down."

I shake my head. "Not a chance, angel."

We go tumbling into the couch. My back against the cool leather, her legs straddling my hips. My hands roam across her body—one toying with the bow's ribbon against her low back, the other twirling around a highlighted strand where sunshine left its mark.

I smell her *everywhere*. Vanilla wafting in waves, lilac dousing my white button-up shirt in the sweet scent of her. I swear I could drown it in, and I'd be completely fine with suffocating on the trademark scent of her.

"Did I tell you how stunning you look?" I ask, dragging my finger over the top of her breasts, tracing lines against the thin lace that glitters with every pass of my skin.

Violet gasps when I drift my hand lower, my fingertips dancing down her body, skating further until I'm teasing across her hip bone, thumb toying with the edge of her lace in the crease of her inner thigh.

"More than once," she whispers against my ear, her warm breath blowing tingles across my skin. "But I wouldn't mind hearing it again."

Heat coils in my gut, shifting lower until a hot wave of feral need drives through me. She makes my blood run like a rushing river; desire floods my insides.

I've never quite wanted anyone this badly before. Not to the point where I'd run through forests barefoot or brave stormy waves just to get a taste of her. Not even Lois made me feel this way, but Violet? She makes me feel it all, like everything all at once.

"You're breathtaking," I breathe out as I stare into her beautiful blue eyes, sucking in a breath when she doesn't turn away.

She smiles as she reaches out and laces her fingers through my tousled hair, disheveling it with every stroke of her fingertips. "I like your hair like this."

"What, all messy?" I groan out, relaxing into her touch as her nails scrape over my scalp. It feels good, feels like I could just lay my head in her lap and have her do this all night long, but I have other things in mind...

"Yeah." She smiles contently. "Means I can play with it and mess it up."

I chuckle under my breath and run the tip of my tongue across my bottom teeth, staring in awe at the pretty angel sitting in my lap. "You do that all you want, sweetheart. I won't stop you." And I don't. She just keeps mussing her fingers through, situating herself closer till she's sitting right on top of me—right where I'm fucking burning for her.

My left arm wraps across her waist, pulling her in until she's chest to chest to me, where I can feel her erratic heartbeats. My right hand brushes a lock of hair behind her ear, and I linger there just waiting for *something* to happen. But something is happening. I can feel it in the air like the crackling fireplace behind us.

She's studying me, searching deep inside the depths of my eyes while her hands rest on top of my chest. A corner of her red lips twitch up in a smile. "Hey." She pauses a beat and opens her mouth. "Your eyes. There's a little green in them."

My heartbeat ceases. "Yeah." I breathe out a laugh and smile softly at her. "Just noticed that, did you?"

"Guess I wasn't looking hard enough before," she whispers into the air.

I stare at her, absorbed in the way she focuses on the little details, like how I'm counting the dark blue flecks in her shining eyes.

No one's ever mentioned the couple of green specks in my irises. You have to be looking extremely close, have to have the right lighting, otherwise my eyes just come off as brown. But Violet noticed that tiny little detail, enough to say something, and that stirs something deep inside me.

"Funny, because no one ever notices that," I murmur out in a hushed tone.

"Well, I did," she chirps.

I smile, slow and warm. "Yeah, you did..."

The shift in the room is stifling, the air blanketed in a thick coat of tension. I let my knuckles graze against the side of her cheek, my fingertips ghosting over the bottom of her crimson lip.

I move without thinking, completely blind with a sudden need to have her closer. She gasps when my arm drags her tighter against me, where there's no room left between the two of us. My forehead falls against hers, our noses brushing against one another, her breath warm as she exhales and breathes across my mouth.

Her lips are so close, only mere centimeters from mine. It'd be so easy to pull her in all the way, and I'll be damned if I don't.

"Sam…" she whispers, her fingers flexing against my shirt, bunching the stiff material up beneath her grip.

"Hm?" I could answer her, call her pretty name in this very room, but I'm too gone in the haze. Too far now where I can't stop. I have to kiss her. Just once, so I can say I finally got to. I need to know what she tastes like. Need to know how fluent she twists my name around my tongue when I'm dripping over her taste buds.

Her lips hover across from mine, breath faltering when I slowly splay my palm across the back of her neck, giving me more leverage so I can reel her in close enough to collide with her lush lips.

"Violet," I murmur out, my voice wrecked from how close she is now. "What are you doing to me?"

"The same thing you're doing to me…" It's a trace of a whisper, only enough for me to grasp those few syllables. The words sound like a sweet melody coming from her.

I'm affecting her as much as she is me, or so it seems. Maybe we're both burning for the other's kiss, but I think my flames will bring down this entire club.

My eyes flick down to her cherry lips, glossing over the shine of them, drowning in her lilac waves of hair that tumble across her shoulders. I move my hand down to her chin and lift her eyes to mine, so I can see that longing look coat her depths of blue. I lean in, bringing her with me, my heart thundering against my chest. I'm so close, can already feel the silk of her lips grazing over mine.

This is it. She's mine.

And just when I'm about to seal the kiss, she moves her head to the side and leans back, till she's crawling off my lap. A long drag of a sigh leaves my lips because I *almost* had her. She was right there waiting for me, and I wasn't fast enough.

"Wait." I catch her wrist and keep her from going any further. "Where are you going?"

Her eyes soften, and then there's that flirtatious hint of a smirk on her lips, inviting me to play a game. "Come catch me." She snatches her wrist from me and trails away from the couch as she sprints off in the opposite direction. But before she gets too far, she stops at the coffee table and turns to look at me. There's a look in her eye that tells me she wants me to go after her, so I will.

Letting a deep sigh out, I lean my head against the back of the leather and crane my neck just enough to see her dazzling smile under the glow of the dim lights.

If she wants me to come get her, then that's what I'll do. I'll chase her all over the entire state of California if that's what I have to do to catch her. And once I catch her, *she's mine.*

Not wasting a second, I push off the edge of the couch and make a run for her, twisting and zigzagging around tables and fancy decor. I almost knock over an ornate glass lamp that sits close to the pool table, but I dodge it just in time.

Violet leans against the side of the pool table on the opposite side of me, giving me a frisky look as she bats her long eyelashes my way. "What's the matter? Can't catch me, brown eyes?"

Brown eyes? Is that a new nickname for me? If so, I hope she continues to call me that, because Jesus, that's fucking cute.

"Brown eyes?" I smirk as I watch her flirt back with a smile.

"Yeah, *brown eyes*," she accentuates the name. "Am I too fast for you, or should I slow down? Let you catch your breath?"

Oh, she wants to play, does she? That's fine with me because I intend to pounce right on top of her when she's in arm's reach.

My lips curl into a devilish smirk as I drag my hand across the smooth wood panel of the table. I narrow my eyes playfully, alluding to this cat and mouse game. She has to know I'm going to win.

"Oh, don't worry, angel. I'm gonna catch you if it's the last thing I do."

"Is that a promise?" she asks with a lilt to her voice.

"You've got my word." I nod, trying my best not to barrel over the top of this pool table like a prowling wolf. "Now *run*."

Violet squeaks when she turns and makes a run for it, bouncing away from my reach like she's the bunny and I'm the fox. I circle around the left side of the pool table and dash after her. She's fast, but she's no match for me. Not even a chance.

Grabbing her by the waist, I pick her up and spin her in a circle. She yells my name playfully, and then we both go toppling to the floor in a fit of laughter. She's pinned with her back against the cool marble, wrists captured above her head by my hands. It's all fun and games until the heat blankets the air again, turning the moment into fiery streaks instead of playful amusement.

"I caught you." I smirk, my eyes staring into her bright blue irises.

"So, what are you going to do with me, Sam?" Her voice is a little hoarse when she asks, a fit of nerves tangled in her vocal cords.

This woman has no idea what all I'd like to do to her. Like how I want to kiss every square inch of her body, including her ruby red lips. But for some reason, she's holding back, so I'll just put a pause on that insatiable need I have to ravage her mouth. For now, I'll kiss every other part of her and give her everything that I possibly can.

"There's a lot of things I'd like to do to you," I smile. "But right now, think I'll just take my time with you..."

Her breathing slows when I start to undress her, slipping one thin strap over her shoulder and down her arm, till the other one follows. Licking my bottom lip in anticipation, I steadily latch my fingers over the middle of her cleavage and suck in a deep breath when I pull it down, baring her full breasts on display.

"Beautiful," I whisper out in a haze.

She keeps her big blue eyes locked on mine when I lean down and run my tongue across the shell of her ear, nipping as I trail lower across her skin. I'm sucking at her collarbone, licking my way down her chest, pawing at her perfect breasts as I knead moans from her pretty mouth.

"Oh, that's—" I cut her off the moment I lap my tongue against one of her pebbled breasts, feeding the flames inside my body with every touch of skin I can indulge on. My other hand squeezes her; thumb flicking across the hardened bud as blood rushes to my cock.

I'm as hard as a rock, my erection stretched taut against the zipper of my slacks, but I'm not worried about that at the moment because right now, my only mission is to get her as wet as possible with my mouth.

I slink my way down her soft tummy, unraveling the pink bow in the back, pulling the lacy piece of fabric *down, down, down* until I end at her hips. My fingers tease what's underneath, my smirk wide as I look up at her with heat in my eyes.

Sending her a flirtatious wink, I drag the thin fabric down her legs till she's completely bare before me, legs spread wide, the shine of her slick on full display.

I sit back on the balls of my feet, dragging a palm across my open mouth, staring at a goddess before me. My heartbeat kicks up a notch as my eyes peel over her perfect form, and I just can't quite grasp that this is my reality.

Her breathing's erratic, breasts full and supple, blue eyes wide as marbles, summer skin glowing under the dim lights, pussy sopping just for me, long legs splayed side to side, gentle hands brushing through her beachy brunette waves. She looks like a summer dream, looks like she's waiting on me to do more than just admire her from a distance. But she has no idea the things I have in store for her...

This right here is mine.

Mine to fawn over.

Mine to pleasure.

Mine to take my time with. And I'm going to take my goddamn time, right between her legs.

"Do I have some lipstick on the side of my cheek or something?" she asks, shakily.

I shake my head and chuckle under my breath, letting my hand drop from my mouth. "No. Just taking a good look at you, angel."

"And what does the verdict say?" She smiles.

And there she goes, hitting me with those flirty questions, making my heart skip beats.

Leaning down, I wrap a hand firmly around her ankle and tug her toward me, causing her to gasp at the action. "The verdict says you're fucking gorgeous, and that I need to take you nice and slow..."

Before she can say anything, I bend over and start peppering her with little kisses, all the way up to her inner thigh in teasingly slow motion. She groans when I spread her wide, gently nipping at her soft skin, fingers dancing over her hip bones.

I'm just getting her riled up, and it's working because her center is all sticky, dripping like a faucet that's ready to be fixed.

Smiling up at her from the floor, I lay on my stomach and scoot her up higher, where her hips are off the floor and her legs are thrown over my shoulders.

"So fucking wet," I groan out as the top of my nose drags over the soft carpet of hair above her clit, catching whiffs of her distinct scent that smells intoxicating. It's like I'm a starving wolf, imprinting on the smell of its mate, reveling on what I'm about to feast on.

She smells like fucking paradise.

"You make me wet," she chokes out when I run my lips teasingly over the seam of her drenched folds, enticing her to cover me in slick. "Sam—" she cries as I run my thumb across her clit, languidly circling while I feed on her pretty moans.

"That's right, pretty girl. You just lay back and enjoy this. Gonna make you pour for me." I smirk.

With one last breath, I dive in, tongue first. I lay the flat of my tongue against her, running impossibly slow up the entirety of her pussy as she chokes on a moan.

"Attagirl. Keep doing that," I praise her affectionately.

Taking my time, I meticulously suck on her clit till it's puffy and swollen for me. Then, I make out with it, twirling my tongue in repeated circles while my hands grip the tops of her thighs.

"Oh, shit. *Sam,*" she whines out as her hands card through my locks, grabbing on for dear life.

That's my good girl. Keep doing that for me, just like that.

My nails scratch along her plush thighs as I eat her ravenously. Her slick coats the bottom of my scruff, sending me into hyperdrive as her sweet tang covers my taste buds.

I hold her in place, swirling my tongue in circular patterns while I spell her name out in relentless motions. And just for keepsakes, I twist the letters of my name into her bundle of nerves feverishly, just so she won't forget who makes her feel good.

That's me. *I* make her feel good. *I* eat her like a ripe plum, leaving nothing but the seed behind. And I'll continue devouring her like this, tongue-fucking and sucking her down like my favorite brand of whiskey. She'd make a hell of a flavor—all sweet and shiny like the gloss of her lips.

I'm just a man. A man who's addicted to her staccato moans as I lap up slick between her thighs. Making her come is one of my favorite hobbies, but the pretty sounds that leave her lips is probably my new favorite soundtrack.

"Sam, I'm not gonna. I'm gonna—" She throws her head back, her half-lidded eyes rolling as she squeezes her legs around my neck, jutting her hips up as I crush my mouth against her wet core.

She's fucking drenched, soaking my face, her scent invading my nostrils like a field of flowers. She's all panting with her red lips parted, repeating my name like a prayer to the sky.

I release her clit with a pop for just a second, just so I can growl out a final demand before she spills for me. And with a devilish smirk, I narrow my eyes and puff out the words, "Good. *Fucking.* Girl. Now come for me."

That does it right there. She loves the praise, loves me calling her a good girl, so I revel in it. Smirking through the action, I lean down and swirl my tongue around her swollen mound, giving her one more unabashed lick as I take her bundle of nerves into my mouth.

She's fucking gone now.

She squeezes her eyes shut and screams my name as she releases the flood gates, coating me in her sticky slick. I lap her up like she's the only water source in the hot desert, swallowing the taste of her sweet tang like it'll give me eternal life.

Violet's my favorite drink of choice. Loaded with the sweetest flavor that no one else will get to taste. She's mine to indulge in, for now. Or maybe forever, if I'm lucky.

When I'm finished licking away the evidence of her orgasm, she slowly comes out of her dreamlike state, eyes all bright and shining like diamonds under the lights. She's still breathing hard, chest going up and down in waves. But the smile she gives me knocks the breath from my lungs.

"Your head stop spinning yet?" I laugh through a lopsided grin.

"Mostly." She smiles up at me, still catching her breath. "You've got a gift with that tongue, brown eyes."

"What can I say, angel? It was meant for eating pretty things…"

Like *her.*

"You're…" She pauses to look at me with a tilted head and curious eyes.

"I'm what?"

"Good… at making me blush," she smiles.

Speak of the devil. Her cheeks are as rosy as her red lips now.

"That's not all I'm good at," I challenge with a smug smirk.

She lifts a brow and smiles. Before she can question me further, I snatch her up around the waist and trade places with her—me on my back while she straddles my hips.

She gasps. "You're fast, Brooks, I'll give you that."

"Faster than lightning," I tease.

"That your next move?" She tilts her head and eyes me with those striking eyes that send my heart thumping against my ribcage.

"Nah, don't think so." I chuckle.

"Then what is?"

"It's your move."

"Mine?" She looks taken aback at that.

"Yeah."

"What do you want me to do?" She giggles.

I want her to do lots of things, but there's one particular move I want right this second.

"Want you to ride me, pretty girl," I say, flashing her my best smile.

"What makes you think I'm any good at—"

I stop her from finishing that sentence and nod down at her legs bracketing my hips. "Go on, angel. Show me what those wings can do. Know you must be so good, don't sell yourself short."

She looks down at her position and then back up at me, hesitant.

She's adorable when she's nervous.

Placing my hands gently on her hips, I push her further down, till she's sliding across my bulge. It's hard not to moan when the friction between us is making the veins in my cock flood with heat. And then she's so fucking wet, rubbing over me like that.

"Be my good girl?" I smirk as I watch her still against my hips, eyes flicking up to mine with a clear answer swirling in those blues.

Her answer is yes.

Languidly, she reaches over and starts unbuttoning my shirt, popping one button off after the other. She flits her gorgeous eyes up at me through every other button, a curl of a smile over that pretty red mouth.

It's so sensual—her undressing me in slow motion, like a work of art on display in a museum. Every move, every stroke of her fingers is like magic, and I can see the track of sparkles running through her fingertips. She doesn't stop till my shirt's flung open, my chest exposed as she runs her hands skillfully down my skin.

She can take all the time she wants, and my eyes would never stray from hers. She's certainly my Mona Lisa.

Gingerly, she unhooks my silver belt buckle and effortlessly slides the belt through the loops in my pants. She bites her lower lip when she drags the zipper of my slacks down and tugs them down, along with my briefs, freeing my erection from its confines.

I'm a mess. Precum spilling over my swollen tip, hard as a rock just for her.

Violet just stares at me, a look in her eyes I can't quite discern, but there's stars swimming in her blue irises, telling me she's just as hypnotized as I am.

"Is this what you wanted?" She whispers it, her voice clear as day in my ear. And when she wraps her hand loosely around my shaft and starts guiding it to her entrance, I forget how to breathe.

"Yes." It's barely a scratch of a sound, but she hears me. "Want you to—"

"Ride you," she finishes for me, with a smile that makes my heartbeat cease.

"You read my mind," I tease, letting my fingers drape over her hips, softly scratching my nails against her smooth skin.

"We seem to do that a lot." She smiles.

"Yeah, we do. Don't we?" I'm momentarily lost in her eyes, drowning in the sound of her pretty laugh, the flutter of her long eyelashes each time she throws me that nervous blush.

I seem to do this a lot, too. Get lost in all her different shades. She really is such a beauty...

Keeping her eyes locked on mine, she lines my tip up with her folds and slowly slides down, groaning at the stretch till I'm bottomed out inside her. I moan at the feel of her silky walls clinging to me, sucking me in like a vacuum each time she moves up and down in a steady rhythm.

"Fuck, Violet," I groan with my head against the cool marble, my fingers gripping her skin with each glide of her hips.

She's a natural at riding, and she's making me feel so fucking good.

"Am I doing okay?" she chokes, her own moans falling from her pretty lips when I hit the back of her walls.

"Oh, *yeah*. Doing all the right things, angel. Just like that," I praise her through her fluid motions, driving her own chase for release.

She tosses her spiral curls over her right shoulder, throwing her head back when she hits that sweet spot. I'm just as lost in my own ecstasy as she rocks her hips faster, causing my cock to swell inside her.

"*Fuck*," I growl out through clenched teeth, already so fucking gone as her tight cunt squeezes me. This feels too good. *She* feels too good, and I'm about to be a goner before long.

"S-Sam," she stutters through a whine, her hand outstretched, desperate for something to hold on to. She's reaching for the edge of my open shirt, but I give her something else to grasp. My hand.

I lace my fingers through hers, tethering myself to her while we both ride out our pleasure. She's everywhere all at once. Running through my bloodstream, pulsating through my mind, reaching inside to wrap around my heartstrings.

My eyes are half-lidded, body spent as I watch this ethereal goddess move in waves above me, lips parted, her slick coating my cock again and again with each thrust she makes, her full breasts bouncing up and down, her body absolutely shrouded in glitter under the dim lights.

She's fucking divine.

I can feel her squeezing me, suffocating me in the best possible way. So I do what I do best—make sure she releases first.

My thumb brushes over her swollen clit which earns me a melodic moan from her deep red lips.

"*Sam,*" she gasps, her nails digging into the back of my hand with each stroke to her bundle of nerves.

"Let go, angel. Wanna feel you," I murmur out, watching as she falls apart beneath my touch.

Her back arches, mouth parts as she sings out the prettiest moan I've ever heard, with my name tied to her song. I work her through it, hissing when she squeezes around my cock, her motions still fluid as she bounces up and down on top of me.

She shudders again, releasing her slick over me, the lewd noises of our bodies moving in tandem, echoing through the room. She's so fucking pretty when she falls apart, just like the angel that she is. Divine and radiant through the glow of her orgasm.

When she's coherent again, she leans into me and rocks her hips harder, coaxing me to come undone each time I kiss the back of her cervix.

Blood rushes through my hardened cock, my balls tightening, her snug walls driving my own release as she slides up and down, inclining me to break.

"Violet, I need to. *Fuck*, need to—"

"Then come." She smiles sweetly through the rhythm of her movements.

She presses the flat of her palms on my chest and leans forward, sliding all her weight down till I'm about to lose it.

"You're squeezing me so—so *tight*," I growl through my teeth. "I'm not gonna last. You gotta—"

She tramples over my stuttering and hovers over me, her blue eyes locking with mine. "Come inside me, please. I... I want you to."

My eyes widen as I thrust my hips against her, riding out the last of my control. "You sure?" I need to know she's absolutely positive before I do something selfish.

She nods her head up and down, giving me the okay. "Yes. *Please.*"

Without another thought, I rub my thumb across her swollen clit, let her moans fill the room with each deep thrust I give her. Her voice is angelic, a symphony playing inside my head with each circular motion I rub into her needy clit.

I hold on just long enough until we're both coming together, letting our releases wash over each other. Our eyes stay locked in a trace, both our tongues moaning each other's names like we're calling out for destiny. My seed spills deep inside her, hot ropes of cum filling her up as I claim her as mine.

Mine.

Then, she collapses on top of me, and I pull her in, hugging her to my chest like we've done this a million times.

This is so *intimate,* and it feels so very right. My cum spilling down her inner thighs, her body pressing into mine, her nails grazing down my neck, blue eyes dancing beneath her long eyelashes, cheeks flushed from the exertion of riding on top of me.

I blink up at her, chest heaving with exhaustion, but I'm too enamored by the angel that's curled around my body.

And it hits me like a tidal wave, throws me off balance while I'm tethered to her strong current.

I think I love this girl...

She flicks her pretty eyes up to me, blinking through each exhale from her lungs, catching her breath in the moment. "How was that?"

A smile slowly curls over my mouth as I look at her affectionately. "Best damn ride I've ever been on."

She giggles and nuzzles against the cotton of my collar, her fingers gently scratching up over my scruff, making me groan through her slow motions.

I could stay like this all night, splayed over this intricate marble floor with Violet tucked against my body. I'm sure my low back will be screaming at me in the morning, but I don't fucking care. Right now, all I seem to care about is *her*.

"Violet?"

"Hm?" she hums out, gently scratching her nails across the sweat of my skin.

"Are you busy Tuesday?"

She tilts her head up and looks at me with wandering eyes, questions swirling off the tip of her tongue. "Umm. I don't think so. How come?"

I smile, knowing exactly what I want to say to her. I want to take her out, on a real date, to my favorite little diner in San Diego. It's not really a place I've taken anyone else before, except my girls. But Violet? I want to take her there, too. Show her another piece of why I love this city so much.

"There's this little diner out on the coast. I wanna take you there."

"Like, to dinner?" She's holding back the word *date,* but I see that question brimming in her eyes.

"Yeah," I chuckle. "Dinner."

There's a little hesitation there, maybe a flash of apprehension, but it's gone in the next second. "Oh. Uh. Okay. Yeah, I like dinner."

I smile down at her and brush my fingers down her back in a soothing way, getting lost in the sea of her eyes. "Six o'clock work for you?"

"Sounds perfect," she answers with a smile.

It's a date, I think to myself, elated that she said yes to dinner.

It's a step, another inch toward something more. And I'm ready. Ready to enter into that next level, even though it seems like we've passed that point days ago.

I want Violet, that I know. And even though there's that slight tug of hesitation, that reminder that me and Lois are officially through and that I'll have to slowly introduce the girls to Violet, I'm ready.

And there's that funny feeling swimming deep inside my chest as Violet nuzzles back into my side, fizzling all the way up to my brain. I've completely fallen head over heels for this girl...

CHAPTER TWENTY-SEVEN

VIOLET

Tuesday evening appears in the blink of an eye, faster than I imagined it'd come. It's not like I've been freaking out or anything. Nope. Not at all.

I sigh and try to relax, but it's virtually impossible.

I'm a chaotic mess. Apprehensive, unsettled, a fucking bundle of nerves.

Why am I so nervous?

Oh, right. Because this is a *date*.

I pat the side of my forehead with a white towel, dabbing a bead of sweat away, careful not to ruin my makeup. I really went all out tonight. A fresh, contoured face, shimmery eyeshadow that makes the blue in my eyes pop, smooth red lipstick painted over my lips, diamond studs in my ears. I took extra time curling perfect spiral waves into my hair and spent an hour picking out the perfect outfit—a white strappy sundress with lilac flowers sewed into the fabric, topped off with slip-on Converse. Not too fancy or casual, but the perfect mix of both.

Taking a good look at myself in the mirror, I press my lipstick together and twirl a highlighted strand of hair around my index finger nervously.

"This is fine," I tell myself in the mirror. "I'm perfectly *fine*." But I'm still nervous as hell.

I jump when my phone buzzes on the side of the bed and sprint to see who it is. When I glance down, there's a FaceTime call from Brianna. Sliding the phone open, I smile when both Taylor and Brianna appear in the frame of the screen, a double call of encouragement.

Before I get a word out, Brianna shouts through the phone. "Okay, let's see!"

"See what?" I ask with a nervous smile.

"Your outfit!" Taylor bellows. "Go on. Stand back and give us a twirl."

I balance the phone on top of my dresser and back up into the glow of the bathroom, spinning slowly as I run my fingers through my curls, stopping abruptly after two spins so they can assess my makeup.

They both gasp in unison, but Brianna interrupts Taylor, like usual. "You are such a BABE!" She boldens the last word through a high-pitched scream, her blonde curls bouncing against the air as she stands outside her apartment balcony.

"Really? You think I look okay?" I ask hesitantly, my fingers running over the top of the flowery material, suddenly nervous that I picked the wrong outfit.

"More than okay, Vi!" Taylor shouts through the receiver. "You're fucking gorgeous, and Sam's going to flip his lid when he sees you in that dress."

Tugging on the end of my dress, I bite my bottom lip and get lost in a haze of worry.

Sam. I'm going on a date with *Sam*. This is real. It's really happening.

"Vi," Brianna calls through the end of the phone. "What's wrong?"

"Nothing," I mutter, but they see right through me, like always.

"Mhm," Taylor huffs out, her fiery ponytail flipping with the toss of her head. "You can't hide from us. What's the matter? You nervous?"

More than just nervous. I'm terrified.

"Yes," I whisper out, my eyebrows threading together in worry.

"Why?" Brianna asks, tilting her head to get a better look at my face through the screen.

"I... I don't know. I'm just nervous." I shrug, crossing my arms across my chest for a sense of security.

"About what?"

"Things."

"Like?" Brianna doesn't back down, just keeps nudging at the question.

I sigh and drag a finger across the edge of a purple flower. "What if I'm not ready? What if he hates this dress? What if... what if this was all just a bad idea?"

"No, Violet. Don't you dare go there. Get out of your head," Taylor grounds out, like she can cement over those scary thoughts.

"But what if it's true? What if I'm really not ready?" I say again, fear etching my tone.

What if I'm not ready to take that next step, even though I want that more than anything?

"Vi," Brianna calls to me, dragging my attention back to the screen. "You've come so far. Don't miss out on the chance for a great guy to take you out. Where's all this doubt coming from, babe?"

"The nightmares..." I state, wishing I could just leave my ex in the past, right where he belongs.

"You're still having them?" Taylor asks, her green eyes turning tense when she stares at me, looking for answers.

I told Bri, but not Taylor yet. Guess I just didn't want to bring them up again like a broken record.

"Yeah." I swallow. "A lot more lately. And they've been really intense."

"I thought they slowed down?" She leans against her kitchen counter, and Brianna just stares through the screen, silent.

"They did... but then I met Sam. And well, since last week especially, they've been bad. Like, *really* bad. The worst they've been since..." I cut it off there, afraid to relive the horrors of my past. Now is not the time for another panic attack I can't control.

"I'm sure they're just you being nervous," Taylor tries, but I don't take her word. It's not just nerves. Something is wrong.

"No. Something feels... off." And it does. Chills ripple across my skin at the unsettling feeling. It feels like I'm standing in the middle of a horror film, and the killer is hiding with a knife behind my sheer curtain, ready to attack at any moment.

"What feels off?" she tries again.

"I don't know. It feels..." I almost don't even want to say it, afraid to speak it into existence. "It feels like someone's breathing down my neck. Like maybe I shouldn't go."

"Oh, you're going, alright! You are not skipping this date," Brianna cuts in like a knife.

Date. Right. This is a date. I'm going on a date. It's not like I'm attending my funeral, I think...

"When you say someone's breathing down your neck, do you mean..."

"Jason." The word tastes like tar across my tongue, and it leaves an aftertaste that lingers like death.

"Babe. He's in jail," Brianna speaks slowly, composed. Like she's walking on thin ice.

Jail, right. He's locked up tight. He can't hurt me. But what if he got out...

"I know. Just... something doesn't feel right," I say, my teeth chattering like the room is ice cold.

"What did your therapist say about this? I assume you told her?" Taylor pours herself a glass of water while she listens.

"She said I'm regressing back..." I look down at the carpet, ashamed that I'm going backwards again.

"Because you're scared?"

"Extremely."

"Of Sam?" Brianna pries, trying to slip into my mind.

"No, no." I shake my head, flitting the question away. "Not Sam... just—"

"Hey, relax. It's going to be fine. You're going to have a great time with Sam. And Jason can't ruin it. Not anymore. This is your chance, Vi. Take it and run with it. You deserve it." Brianna smiles at me, and Taylor follows her lead, holding her glass up as she cheers through an agreement.

"She's right," Taylor says eagerly. "Everything's going to be fine. I know it."

Then why do I have this awful pit in my stomach like everything's going to implode on me?

Through my racing thoughts, a text notification from Sam chimes across the top of the screen.

Sam: Be there in about five minutes, angel.

My heart thunders in my chest at the message.

"Guys, Sam's going to be here in five minutes. I need to go." I stumble across the floor and pick up my phone, already dizzy with anticipation.

"Right. Go have fun, bestie!" Taylor shouts.

"Yeah, what she said. And Vi?" Brianna halts me before I hang up.

"What?"

"Fucking kiss him this time." She smirks savagely.

I roll my eyes and shake my head. "Goodbye!" And then I end the call, stopping her from egging me on any further.

It's not like I don't want to kiss him. Trust me, I've thought about his lips more than a dozen times and what they might feel like. But again, that's sacred territory, and kissing means much, much more...

But this is more. Sam and I... we're *more*.

Tossing those slippery thoughts aside, I race back into the fluorescence of my bathroom, run the brush through my waves a couple more times, and perfect the crimson shine on my lips. And just when I take one last spin in the mirror, assessing my work, there's a couple of quiet knocks at the door.

With one last look at my wide eyes in the mirror, I swallow and head for the door, slinging my purse over my shoulder.

This is it. It's really happening.

Taking one last long breath, I twist the doorknob and throw the door open, eager to see the man who waits patiently for me on the other side.

When I look up, my heart stops.

There he is. Hands in the pockets of his light blue jeans, a hunter green flannel stretched across his biceps, sleeves rolled up to his elbows, exposing that dark, twisting ocean ink I really love running my fingers over.

He looks like a daydream. His sandy-brown locks all slicked back, a few strands falling across the sides of his forehead. Making me want to brush the strands back in place or maybe just card my fingers through those soft locks.

And his eyes. Big, sparkling pools of warmth that glitter in the sinking sun.

"Hi," he says warmly as a lopsided smile slips over his lips in greeting.

I bite my bottom lip nervously, hands behind my back so I don't fidget in front of him. "Hi."

"You look…" His eyes trail up and down my body while another breathtaking smile takes me out. "Beautiful," he finishes as he slides a hand back through his hair, his eyes still lingering over my summer dress.

"Thanks," I giggle out nervously, feeling the sting of a blush coat my cheeks. "So do you." My face reddens the moment I realize what I just said.

He chuckles out an infectious laugh and rocks on the balls of his feet. "Beautiful, huh?"

"You know what I meant." I roll my eyes and push him playfully in the arm.

"Yeah. Just giving you a hard time," he jokes, catching my wrist before I can let it fall back to my side.

"You like to do that a lot, don't you?" I crinkle my nose at him and smirk, hoping I'm coming off as cute instead of a smartass.

"More than anything," he chuckles. He lingers his fingers on my skin for just a few seconds more, his eyes in a trancelike state as he watches me carefully. I don't move, can't even breathe when he's looking at me like I'm the only girl in the world.

As he places my hand slowly back down to my side, he brushes the edge of my dress, letting his thumb trace over one of the sewn flowers, almost like he's memorizing every piece of my outfit.

When he looks back up, I'm lost in the pretty shades of his marble-like brown eyes, capturing a visual memory of those few flecks of dark green in the back of his irises.

He really is beautiful. Inside and out.

There's a moment. The same one I felt when he found me in his private room. The one where he looks like he wants to kiss me…

With one more tug of my wrist, he smiles and nods his head in the direction of his parked Chevy. "Come on, pretty girl. Let's go." He lightly places a hand on the small of my back and leads me off the sidewalk, even opens the passenger door like the gentleman he is.

I latch the seatbelt across my body when I climb in and lean into the cool leather, hoping he can't hear my racing heartbeat.

"You going to tell me the name of where we're going?" I giggle when he's situated in his seat and starting the engine up.

He looks over at me before he pulls away from the curb. "Ever hear of Nicki's Diner?"

I shake my head. "No."

"Well, think you're gonna love it." He gives me one of those lazy sideways smiles and melts my heart while he's at it.

This man. How is he so smooth and yet so sweet at the same time?

"How is it that you know more places than me, and I've lived here longer?"

He shrugs his shoulders and bites down on his bottom lip, tugging a smile on when he glances my way. "Guess I was just meant to show you them."

Guess I was just meant to show you.

"Maybe…" I place my elbow on the side of the door and cover my mouth as a massive smile curls across my lips. Warmth somersaults through my stomach, the butterflies scattering through the silent giggles I'm making.

How is it that even when I'm feeling nervous, he can still make me laugh?

Maybe tonight won't be a disaster at all. Maybe it'll just be perfect, like Sam…

When we arrive outside the little diner, my eyes light up when my feet hit the ground. Lights are strung all around the outside. White lilies decorate the front garden while palm trees sit on each side of the building. The diner's made of a rusty-colored brick, and big windows line each side. Blinking, bold letters slope across the top that spell out *Nicki's Diner*.

This place is already perfect.

"After you." Sam nods, his hand on the small of my back as he opens the glass door and leads me inside.

When I step in, an old jukebox sits at the entrance, lit up in neon green colors. An Elvis song vibrates through the overhead speakers. Leather booths line the fading brown walls; pictures of The Beatles, Marilyn Monroe, and old movie stars hang around the cozy diner. The dining counter has black leather stools, some taken by an older couple sipping on cups of coffee. Next to them, there's a huge glass display with various pies and desserts behind it, just waiting for someone to take a bite out of.

Yeah, I definitely like this place.

"Wow. How'd you find this place?" I ask, all starry-eyed as I take in the glowing diner.

"Just found it while I was driving around the city one day. What do you think?"

"It's perfect."

Sam looks over his shoulder at me, a crooked grin tugging at his lips while he says, "Thought you might like it, angel."

Angel. He gets me every time with that nickname. Makes me all tingly inside.

His fingers brush along my inner wrist, igniting sparks of electricity under my skin.

Just as he looks at me again with yearning eyes, the sound of a chipper voice interrupts our moment. "Hey, Sam! Table for two?" a perky brunette asks as she waves two crisp menus our way.

"Kat, hi. Yeah, table for two, please."

"Right this way, then." She smiles, throwing her ponytail over her shoulder when she turns.

I smirk up at him. "Come here a lot?"

He gives me a playful smile, flicking his brown eyes over me. "How'd you guess?"

When we make it to the leather booth, he keeps his fingers lingering on my skin till I'm sliding across the seat. He takes the opposite side, knees brushing against mine as he situates himself.

Kat takes our drink order before disappearing into the kitchen. Two glasses of ice water, with lemon wedges on the side.

Scanning the plastic menu, I'm frankly overwhelmed by all the choices. Too many home-cooked options to pick from, but my eyes linger over the burger section. "So, what's your go-to here? Since you obviously come here a lot."

Sam chuckles, slowly lowering his menu so I can see that playful glimmer of onyx shimmering in his eyes. "Usually just get the old-fashioned cheeseburger and a chocolate shake."

I let the corners of my mouth tilt into a smile. "Not bad, Brooks."

"And you? What kind of shake girl are you?" He leans his elbow on the polished table top, gazing into my eyes.

I have to catch my breath when I stare at him—his hair slicked back, grey threads of scruff catching under the lights, his dark green flannel hugging his muscles, the top two buttons undone, leaving room to flirt with the idea of that tanned skin shining underneath. He's just too good looking, and he makes it hard to concentrate on anything else.

I fold my arms on the table and gaze into his honeysuckle-colored eyes. "Strawberry is my favorite, if we're talking classics."

He gives me a warm smile, but before he can say anything else, a different blonde waitress comes up to the table and takes over while the brunette helps a couple by the window. "Well, what do we have here? Sam Brooks bringing a young lady to the diner? My, thought I'd never see the day." She laughs as she sets our waters down.

Sam's face reddens as he rakes a hand slowly over his scruff. "Guess I just had to find the right one first." He smiles, flicking his eyes over in my direction. My breath catches at his words.

He's never brought anyone else here before? Oh…

"I see." She trails her eyes over to me and then back at Sam. "She's pretty," the waitress mouths at Sam, and now it's my turn to blush. "Well, what'll it be? Your usual?" she asks, taking out a notepad and a black pen to write with.

"You know it." He chuckles. "What do you want, angel?" he asks, looking over at me with that gleam in his eye.

I catch the waitress giggling and covering her mouth when he calls me angel. And now my cheeks are as red as her painted nails.

Clearing my throat, I look up from the menu. "Can I get the classic cheeseburger with French fries and a strawberry shake?"

"Sure can, sugar. I'll get that order in and be right back. My name's Carla, so don't hesitate to holler if you need me." She stuffs the notepad back in her white apron and winks at Sam before she disappears around a corner.

I take a generous sip of water and swish the bendy straw around nervously, looking up from under my dark eyelashes at the dreamboat that sits across from me. "So, first girl you've brought here?" I ask, smirking flirtatiously.

Sam taps his right index finger on the edge of the table and nods. "Besides Kayla and Kelsey, yeah. First girl." My eyes lock with his for a few seconds, and my heart skips a beat at the intention that burns in his brown irises.

The questions slur through my mind. *Are you mine, Sam? Do you really want me? Do you feel that undeniable spark between us that I've felt since the moment I met you?*

All those questions are valid and realistic. But I see it in those swirls of cinnamon that gloss over his bright eyes. The answers are all there, but am I brave enough to cross the line I've already tripped over numerous times?

The tension that's crackling through the air gets interrupted when Carla comes back with two milkshakes in her hands—one strawberry, the other chocolate. "Here ya go! Food should be out in a few." She whisks away, leaving the two of us alone again.

I pull my eyes off Sam and slip a straw into my strawberry shake, mixing it around until my nerves dissolve into liquid. "How's the book coming along?"

Sam wipes the corner of his mouth with a napkin and dips a silver spoon into the chocolate shake. "I've got like fifty more pages to read."

Cocking an eyebrow up, I ask, "And?"

He drops the spoon from his mouth and spins it around the shake meticulously. "Honestly, I'm really enjoying it. The fighting scenes, the ongoing war, the—"

"The banter, the spice?" I tease him, watching his cheeks turn red at the implication.

"Ahh, the spicy scenes. They uhh…" he pauses, laughing to himself as he shakes his head and slides a hand through his hair, "they don't live up to the real thing, do they?"

"No, they don't." My cheeks heat, just like the inside of my thighs do. "Just wait till the second book comes out in a couple months."

"The second book? Already think I'm gonna read the second one?" He smirks, one eyebrow stretched up as he licks his bottom lip clean of chocolate. The sight makes my stomach flip.

I take my chances with my next choice of words. "Figured you'd read it for me…" I whisper, just loud enough for his mouth to tug up in a full-on grin.

"Well, when you put it that way, of course I'll read it. I'd read anything you put in my hands." He smiles. His knee knocks against mine, causing my heart to hammer in my chest as I engulf myself in the scent of him, in his gorgeous brown eyes. Even from the wafts of burgers and fries, I still smell him—that sandalwood cologne floating around my senses. I think I'd like to drown in it and in him.

The next half hour is spent delving into the food, flirting back and forth, brushing knees against one another, blushing and smiling more than I have in my entire life. And it's all because of this man. This sweet, incredibly dreamy hunk of a man. How did I ever end up in a diner talking about life with Sam Brooks, the charming club owner?

I learn he's a Pisces; his birthday is March 20th. His is right before mine, May 12th. Taurus and Pisces, almost the perfect combination...

He likes the 80's rock bands. His favorite movie is *Jaws*, funny enough, and said he was always drawn to the sea because of it. His dream was always to travel the world, visit Italy and the Egyptian pyramids. He likes late walks on the beach, where he can think under the moonlit sky. He loves animals, pretty much grew up on a farm with all the goats his father raised. He also played lead guitar in a self-made band in high school.

He's just so easy to talk to, like I've known him my whole life.

"You were in a band?" I laugh incredulously as I look at his gleaming eyes.

"That's what I said." He smiles and leans back against the booth, spreading his legs wide, like this is the most casual conversation ever. He looks like he's enjoying himself.

"Do you still play?" I ask with hope glittering in my eyes.

He shakes his head and puffs out a laugh. "Haven't in many years. Tried to get my girls to learn, but they didn't have an interest. So, my acoustic's just sitting in the garage, hanging on the wall."

"You should take it down, try to play again."

He taps his index finger on the edge of the table, and a small smile curls around that beautiful mouth. "Why? You want to learn?"

I bat my eyelashes up at him nervously and ask quietly, "Are you offering to teach me?"

He shrugs his broad shoulders casually and leans forward, stretching his hands out just enough to graze my outer forearm. "If that's what you want, angel. I've got some free time on my hands. Wouldn't mind showing you a thing or two on the strings."

Goose bumps race across my skin with every graze his fingertips leave against my arm. The more I stare at him, the more I want to reach across the table and melt into his glowing soul. "Okay..."

"Is that a yes?" he pines, trying to twist his thick fingers around my skull, searching for an answer that's right on top of my bashful tongue.

"Like... at your club?" I ask, hesitantly.

"At my club, sure. But preferably, my house," he states.

His house. I don't know why, but the mention of that has something that feels a lot like bile rising in my throat. His *house.* That's different than meeting at his club, even different than this right now.

I swallow a shot of water, suddenly realizing this is so much more than just a casual dinner. This is *the* date. The one that'll set everything in motion to be much, much more than what it has been. My stomach's clenched in a tight knot at the very thought of what comes next.

A relationship.

When I don't answer, he brushes his fingers along the outside of my wrist, and my vision starts tunneling.

"I've been thinking..." He blinks a couple of times and drops those beautiful brown eyes on me, giving me that million-dollar smile that makes me weak at the knees.

"About?" I tilt my head, playing dumb because I know what comes next. He's about to ask me. Fuck...

He strokes his fingertips against my clammy skin and sighs. "What are we doing here, angel?"

I know *exactly* what he's asking. I'm just too scared to hear those words come out of his mouth.

My heart halts and for a second I can't breathe, but I play it off. "Eating dinner?"

"No," he chuckles, "that's not what I meant." He slides his free hand down his salt-and-pepper scruff. His eyes are piercing through mine like the morning sunrise on a rainy day, sending my heart soaring out the window. "I mean... *us.*"

Us. There it is, the million-dollar question of the night. Us...

"Us?" My voice shakes at the word, and my breathing is anything but normal.

He places his hand on top of mine and looks at me all doe-eyed. My breathing escalates, and I'm momentarily trapped in the nightmares of my mind. Fear consumes my thoughts, sending them into overdrive.

Don't do it, Sam. Please, don't.

I'm panicking internally, a catastrophe about to split me like the Titanic.

I'm not ready. *Fuck.* I can't. Not tonight.

"Look, these past couple of months I've had a lot of fun getting to know you. And I've been thinking a lot lately. Violet, I..."

"Don't." The word's out of my mouth before I can reel it back in.

His face drops, his smile gone as his eyebrows thread together in confusion. "Why not?"

"Just... don't." I rip my hand away from him, hoping that'll get the message across loud and clear, but I think I've already given him tinnitus with my words.

He tries to reach for me and catches my hand again for a moment, until I shove it underneath the table where he can't. "Listen. I've started developing feelings for you, and—"

"I never asked you to." It comes off louder than I intended it to, more stern than I wanted.

I should just shut up, silence my voice so I can't hurt him because I don't *want* to. But I already did, didn't I?

His lips twitch down at the corners, like I just slapped him across the mouth. "*No*, but it happened, okay?"

Oh, it happened alright, just like it happened to me.

I feel it, right at the back of my neck—a little spider weaving its crystal-like web against my skin, burrowing into my vocal cords so I can't speak.

The room turns deathly frigid as goose bumps gather across my skin, turning me ice cold. Everything's too loud. The crackle of the static coming from the overhead speakers, the clank of fine china in the back of the kitchen, the slide of a wooden chair across the room, the intense throbbing in the back of my head.

It's too much. *This* is too much.

"Is this why you never let me kiss you? Because you don't..." His face is contorted in pain, just like he fought tooth and nail to get to the front of a concert hall, only to end up at the very back with a blocked view.

"I have a thing with kissing," I breathe out, shaking my head like that'll dismiss the answer I just gave.

Kissing is affection. Kissing means this is *real*. But it is real, so why am I trying to ruin this? Oh right, because I'm a fucking coward who can't talk about my past.

"Oh. I kinda suspected," he answers, his words garbled over the sound of the front door chimes ringing as a young couple walks in.

I bite the back of my tongue till I feel blood in the back of my throat, quickly swallowing the tang of disappointment of my words. Shaking my head, I look down at my lap and let the words fall off my broken voice. "You don't want me, Sam."

"Yes, I *do*," he says adamantly, trying to prove his point.

I curl my fingers into the tops of my thighs, leaving crescent moons imprinted in my skin. Maybe the pain in my legs will outweigh the anguish I feel in my chest.

"No, you really don't..." I whisper, praying he'll take the bait.

Everything I've learned in therapy comes to a crumbling halt, pieces of my lessons now laying in broken shards on the diner floor, just like my heart.

I'm not good for Sam. He doesn't want a girl like me, all broken and unhealed from a past abusive relationship. He deserves someone that's whole, who knows how to say exactly what they want. I'm not that, and maybe I never will be.

I struggle with my internal thoughts, feeding myself lies so maybe I can just run. I never was good at running, not until Jason went to jail. Then, I was a free bird, fleeing anything that tried to cage me again. But Sam doesn't do that, does he? No. He doesn't try to hold me down or chain me. He freed me...

Just when I think of taking back my words, flits of my nightmares from the last few days come to life in my head. There's Jason holding me back, his jagged fingernails imprinting scars in my skin, my screams drowned out by his incessant drunken slurs. Sam's taking his place, sharp green eyes being replaced with deep brown eyes. The bottle slips, glass crashes against the coffee table, sending Sam flying through the door, and all that's left is my frail body underneath Jason's.

My nails dig into the soft material of my dress, almost ripping clear through as I shove the nightmares out of my head.

What if...

No. That couldn't happen.

But what if Jason got out somehow? What if he's watching me, prowling outside my apartment, just waiting for the perfect time to pounce?

What if he tries to hurt Sam? I can't think like that, but it's plausible. If Jason got a hold of Sam, he'd try to kill him. And I can't be responsible, can't accept that I could be the reason Sam could get hurt. So I have to push him away. For his own safety. He's better off without me, even though I don't want that. Not really...

I don't deserve Sam. He deserves safety and honesty, and a girl who can fucking *kiss* him. I can't do any of those things apparently, so I need to take my leave, for his own good.

"Look at me," Sam voices across the booth, adamant that I look up.

I shake my head, purse my lips together, and stand my ground. "No." I can't bear to look at him, not when I'm holding the sword above his heart.

I don't *want* to hurt him, so why can't I just come out and say it? Say what I *truly* feel about him. How he's saved me in every way, but I can't do the same for him.

"Violet, look at me," he states defeatedly as pain laces through his vocal cords. "Look me right in the eyes and tell me that you don't want this. That you don't want *me*."

My lips quiver, but I shake my head and hold myself together. "Just leave it, Sam," I murmur under my breath. There's no use. I'd rather walk out that door and never see him again than look up and see how battered and bruised I've colored him.

"Violet. Look. At. Me," he growls out, but there's no anger in his words, just torture. A cry of mourning.

Hesitantly, I blink away tears, holding myself back from spilling all my emotions in front of him. My fingers stay locked around the fabric by the middle of my thighs, using it as an anchor so I don't drown in the middle of the ocean. But the ship's sailed when I look up and see how *wrecked* he looks—big brown eyes that hold back tears, a strained expression on his face, deep lines on his forehead, and a clenched jaw.

He looks like I just ran over his favorite pet, and I can't take back the pain I just inflicted on him.

Licking the bottom of my teeth, I put on a brave face and tell him a lie. "I... I don't want this."

Liar. You're such a fucking liar! I scream at myself internally. I've wrapped the noose around my own neck, and now we're both dead.

"Then maybe we should've never started this whole thing in the first place."

I break at his words, cracking at the seams as the threads come undone around my heartstrings.

My fault. My fault. My fault. It's all I can think, all I can seem to repeat in my mind. I did the one thing I never intended to do—break his heart.

Maybe I'll learn not to wear my heart on my sleeve when I can't even talk about my past trauma. Jason ruined me and now, he's ruined my chance with Sam, too.

"Can you just take me home, please?" I whimper out, hanging my head in defeat. I want to fucking cry, but I can't let him see me weak. I'm already fragile enough. What's the point in crying when I can't even show him why I'm such a goddamned wreck?

"You want some pie, sugars?" Carla interrupts, her giddy voice dancing across the heavy silence that sits between me and Sam. I look up just enough to see the tic in his jaw, his eye still swimming with pain. Pain that I caused him...

"No," he says hoarsely, clearing his throat as he speaks again, a little harsher. "Think we're done here. Just the check, please."

I die at the scene, the broken glass shattering across my feet from his words. He didn't catch the bottle after all. Or rather, I made him drop it...

"Oh, um. Alright. Be back in a minute." She gives me a crooked stare, her eyebrows threaded together in question, but she brushes it off as she hurries to get the check.

I keep my eyes cast downward, fingers tangling into the fabric of my dress. I'm surprised I haven't ripped it clear off yet with all the fidgeting I've been doing, but I'm just trying to keep myself in one piece, at least till I'm back home, safe in my walls. I can fall apart there after this is all over.

Sam's shoe brushes mine, but he quickly drags it back, like I just scorched him in the flames. But that's exactly what I did. I burned him alive.

I dare to sneak a peek under my eyelashes, but I regret it the moment I see that weathered stare—that stonelike face that tells me enough. He's just as devastated as me because he thought this was more, and it *should* be more. But I'm just a girl with a fucked up past who just can't seem to let go, so I ruin everything I touch.

Flicking my gaze back down to my dress, I let my curled fingers shred a line through the delicate material, creating a fractured piece of a memory I'll surely remember for the rest of my life.

This was a special dress, one I thought Sam would like. And I was so excited to wear it because his eyes lit up the moment he saw me standing in it. And now? Now I just feel like Cinderella when her stepsisters tore her favorite ball gown to shreds. I'm nothing but fire ashes that burned out long ago.

When she drops off the check, Sam leaves a fifty on top of the bill and doesn't even bother waiting for change. He doesn't say anything to me, barely even flickers his cinnamon eyes my way as he waits by the door, delaying the inevitable.

Once we walk out this door, it's over. Me and Sam are *done.*

I feel lifeless when I slide through the diner door and climb into the passenger seat. Shame's written all over my face as I buckle the seatbelt and wait for him to start the engine. I turn my head toward the window, watch the glow of the outside lights disappear in the rear-view mirror, silently saying goodbye to the one chance I had to make things right.

Craning my head to the left, I see him flexing his fingers against the leather steering wheel, clenching his jaw tight, raking his hand back through his now disheveled hair. He looks like he's been through hell, looks like he just lost his favorite person, and I guess he did. Except I'm not his favorite person. I can't be…

The rest of the truck ride is soundless. The only noise is the faint hum of the engine and the spin of the tires across pavement. His music is even muted, and it feels like he's giving me the cold shoulder. Maybe I deserve that. I don't blame him if he never wants to talk to me after this. If I were him, I wouldn't.

He deserves better. Better than me, at least…

When he finally pulls up to the curb by my front door, he puts the truck in park and keeps one hand clenched around the steering wheel, only facing forward with his lips formed in a tight line.

Slowly, I unbuckle my seatbelt and look at him with swimming eyes. My vision blurs, but I hold it together and try to compose my shaky breath. "Thank you for dinner."

"It was no trouble." He flexes his fingers, his jaw clenching into a fist. No *"You're welcome, sweetheart."* No *"Angel."* No sign of life in his droning voice.

My hand stretches to the side as I reach for the door handle, but I stay put and stare at him while my stomach churns.

Say something, Violet.

"Sam, I—"

He stops me mid-sentence and cranes his neck to the side. I almost don't recognize him. He's so... *broken.* "Can I ask you one thing?"

"Yes."

Ask me anything. Make me take back what I said. Reach into my soul and take what's yours—like my heart.

"Did any of this mean anything to you?"

My eyes blow wide at the question. Dropping my hand from the door handle, I gaze at him, praying he'll see the desperation that's brewing in my eyes. "Of course it did!" I don't shout, not really, but my voice is higher than it normally is.

Sam, please. Tell me you see it—that hunger for more.

"That's all I wanted to know." He nods, dropping his far-off gaze to his lap.

There's an uncomfortable silence permeating through the thick air, fogging my eyes up with each second that ticks by.

Fucking tell him, Violet. Tell him how badly you want to be with him. But I can't get my words to work, so I say the only thing I can. I have to try to make this right.

"If you ever want to—"

"I don't think we should continue this." He sighs, dragging his hazy eyes back to mine. I see the crack of torment in his flecks, and it makes me want to crawl into his lap, wrap my arms around him, but I can't even do that. So I continue staring ahead, covering the held-back tears in my eyes. "You know, since…"

"Since what I said at the diner…" I whisper out, locking my fingers together, desperate to break out of these chains I'm in, but I can't. I can't say what I really want to because I'm just a scared little mouse who never seemed to prepare for this moment.

"I can't do casual anymore, Violet. Not after…" He drags a hand down his jawline, covering his mouth as a long sigh leaves his lips.

He doesn't really mean what he's saying, does he? He doesn't want me anymore. Because I'm the one that messed up. I hurt him, and now I'm just as devastated as he is.

"I understand," I murmur through my teeth, clawing for some of the excess weight to be lifted from my chest, but the relief never comes. It just sits like cement, holding me back from saying what I truly mean.

"Alright." He shifts in his seat, clearly uncomfortable, like he wants me gone. *He wants me gone…*

It's like I get kicked in the chest with a flying soccer ball. All the air is sucked from my lungs and suddenly, I can't even breathe.

I pry the door open and slowly step out, dragging the balls of my feet against the concrete. When I turn back toward him, my hand sliding over the edge of the door, I muster enough courage to speak. "Well, I guess I'll see you around?"

"Yeah, maybe…" He doesn't look in my direction, only stares ahead at the empty road.

Dropping my hand from the door, I scratch along my left arm and pause once I get to my faded scar. It fucking burns tonight, just like my eyes do.

"Sam?"

"Yeah?" He lifts his gaze to mine, and hope swims in his brown irises, like maybe he's waiting for me to do something, but I don't.

"Never mind," I shake my head and look toward the ground, scuffing the bottom of my shoe against the white surface.

"Well, I guess this is it?" I ask hesitantly.

"Guess it is..."

I reach for the invisible thread between us, coil my fingers around that splice of hope, but the cord snaps when he speaks. "I... just," he hesitates, struggling to get the words out. "Take care of yourself, Violet."

I sway where I stand and grab the door to keep from toppling over. Swallowing my sadness down my throat, I flick my eyes up to him and try not to cry. "Sounds a lot like a goodbye."

He leans against the steering wheel and drags his palm over his mouth, smothering his words when he says, "I guess it is..."

Nodding sadly, I take a step back, clear the space between us, and watch my world crumble in my palm. This isn't what I wanted, but I can't fucking use my voice. All I see are flashes of Jason through my eyes, like a bolt of lightning. He'd hurt Sam, and I can't watch that happen. Even if he's gone, he's still there simmering like stale alcohol.

I want Sam. God, I want him so much, but he doesn't deserve this. Doesn't deserve *me* when I'm not even finished healing from past trauma. So I'll let him go.

"Goodbye, Sam..." I whisper, straining the words through my teeth like they're poison.

Please don't hate me, Sam.

He gives me one last long look, his eyes flickering with sadness, drinking me in one last time. I've never seen him so... lost. There's a splash of a tear licking at the corner of his eye, but he wipes it away before it can fall.

With one last lost glance my way, he chokes on his words. "Goodbye, Violet."

My ears ring through the goodbye, the low cadence of his Southern drawl tugging me away. I step back and slam the door closed and just stare blankly through the tinted passenger window, wishing he'd just stay. But why would he? I've made my bed, now I have to sleep in it.

The black Chevy rumbles to life and before he pulls away, he glances once more at me with a look of pain smothered in the tears he holds back. One word, one movement. That's all it'd take to stop him from leaving, but it's too late. He pulls out and drives away. I stare through the building fog in a daze and watch his tail lights disappear around the corner, exiting my life forever.

I stare, hoping he'll come back, praying he'll find it in himself to turn around, chase after me, but he doesn't. He's gone, just like my heart is.

Suddenly, I can't breathe, can't fill enough oxygen in my lungs. He's gone, and I can't seem to get that straight in my head.

Come back.

"Sam," I murmur, feeling the wet teardrops slip down my cheeks like fresh snowflakes. "Come back..."

My feet hit the ground running as oxygen depletes in my lungs. "Come back. Come back," I whine, sprinting till I trip over brick and go crashing to the ground. Pain erupts in my body, my scraped knee bleeding onto the sidewalk, just like my heart. And when I look up with tears pooling in the backs of my eyes, I realize he's not coming back. Maybe not ever...

Thunder rumbles in the distance. Heavy rain clouds cover the night sky. Even the wail of the ocean tides seem to hear my cries. Rain splashes against my skin, the soft pattering lands against the bunched fabric of my dress, lighting pain across the fresh wound of my scraped knee.

Rain's been dormant in San Diego for months now, but it came tonight, sprinkling its own splashes of sadness across my tainted skin. It must've heard my cries. Must've slipped against the cracks in my heart and tugged at the frail strings. The heavens heard my plea, and they're mourning with each teardrop that falls from the sky. And then I drown in a pool of my own tears.

I curl in on myself, pressing my knees against my chest to help settle the ache, but it still stings. So I let the tears run down my legs, watch my dress get ruined, rock myself to a lucid state until numbness takes over.

"Sam. He's gone..." I whisper into thin air, succumbing to the static that hollows me out.

Sam's gone. He's fucking *gone.*

I just lost the best thing that ever happened to me...

CHAPTER TWENTY-EIGHT

SAM

Rain pelts against the windshield. Fog slips across the night sky, creating a thick layer of haze outside the side window. My eyes burn like fire; pain sears in my chest the further I get down the road, away from Violet.

Violet.

She was supposed to be mine. I thought she was. Thought we crossed those lines long ago, maybe even in that first week. But I guess she's not, and all this was just *fun*.

It wasn't just that to me, though. It was real. *This* is real. The feelings, the way my heart soared each time I held her in my arms. It felt good, felt like heaven every time her blue eyes melded with mine. Like sparks coming off a lightning strike.

Those sapphire eyes I already miss...

I can still feel her—the way her body clung to mine when we danced all night under the glittering disco ball; when her hand folded against mine. Or when she'd run her fingers through my hair and get it all ruffled and messy. But I liked it, every single second I spent with her. Especially when she smiled at me. Those perfect, painted red lips that I never did get to kiss.

I kissed every other part of her, but not the one place I really wanted to. She never let me...

Her scent still lingers in the passenger seat, making that ache tug and pull inside my chest. She's still there—on my fingers, crawling up my flannel shirt, sticking to the ends of my hair, curling her way inside my chest. She's all around me still, painting her swirls of purple and pink colors into the dying sunset, hanging around just enough for me to reach my hand out and catch them before they disappear behind the dark rain clouds forever.

I should turn back, reverse the truck and go chase after the one girl I never wanted to lose, but I can't. She said *no*. She doesn't *want* me like I thought she did.

Fuck. She doesn't want me...

I paw at my now disheveled strands of hair, clench my hand around the leather of the steering wheel till it's bleach white, gnash my teeth till I can practically taste blood running down my throat. But what does it matter? I can't turn around because she *doesn't* want me. Not like I want her.

"*Fuck*," I growl, pounding my fist on the steering wheel as I surge to a stop at the red light. Rain pelts across the windshield, creating fog on the side of the road where the ocean rages stormy waves.

I close my eyes for just a second, wincing when I see the flash of her diamond eyes and breathtaking smile. But when I open them back up, she's gone, just like her ghost in the passenger seat.

A cold, wet tear slides down the side of my face, ending on the thigh of my jeans. I don't dare try to stop the next one that falls; it'd be useless to try. I'm allowed to cry, allowed to break down for just a second because I just lost something I wasn't quite ready to let go of.

Huffing out a deep breath, I step on the gas when the light turns green and try to figure out why tonight ended like it did. Our date was going so well. She knew it was a date, didn't she? It was implied, but I never actually said the word.

Maybe that's why she looked so shocked when I asked her that question. I kind of just threw it out there.

But it was there. That chemistry, the mingling feelings that hung in the air like blankets of falling snow. Conversation came so easy, just like the smiles and that bubbly laughter of hers. But then I asked her *that* question, what we were doing, and I spilled my guts all over the table.

I told her I wanted more, and she didn't...

But where did I get it wrong? I *felt* it, that pull between us like an elastic string attached to one another. The way she looked at me that first time I held her in my arms. The way she smiled when she found out I was a father. And even when she decorated my club in pink ribbon and sat perched atop my pool table, all dolled up just for me in her favorite color, I felt it.

I thought she felt it, too. But maybe I was wrong. Maybe I've been wrong this entire time.

Dragging a hand over my mouth painfully slowly while I pull into my lit neighborhood, I try to play back what happened tonight. Try to conjure up where exactly I went wrong. But I can only spin up so many scenarios in my head until I break apart. I'm just a man, and there's only so much I can take. Losing Lois through the years was painful enough, but this cuts deeper somehow. Losing Violet is something I never thought about because I didn't think it'd happen. God, was I wrong. Because look what I just lost... my angel.

When I park the truck and turn off the engine, I run a hand through my messy strands and try to pull myself together just long enough to get to the front door. I practically have to drag myself, scuffing the bottom of my shoes across the driveway, until I'm back in the safety of my home. The lights are low, no static of the TV in the living room, no padding of feet upstairs. Kayla must've fallen asleep. I told her not to wait up, so she's probably lost in a cozy dream. Whereas I'm stuck in a nightmare.

I collapse into the leather of the couch, let the sound of thunder crackle in the distance as I sulk in silence, ticking my jaw each time I think about *her*—the angel I let slip away.

There's this twinge in my gut. This deep pull that's tugging at me, telling me to go back, but why should I? I'd only make things worse.

As I let my head drape across the back of the couch, I close my eyes, trying my best to block out the entire world. I wish it'd just stop spinning, stop tilting its axis so I could stop feeling this awful pain. It's a feeling I never wanted to feel again, but I took that chance knowing it might happen, and it *fucking* did.

I sit there for hours, till my body starts to give out. Till darkness tries to swallow me. And just when I'm about to doze off, my phone vibrates to life in my pocket. I jolt up straight and grab the phone out, my eyes alight with hope that it's Violet, but those feelings are cut short when it's not her. Instead, it's my mother.

Wiping my eyes with the back of my shirt, I take a steady breath and pray I can get through this without bringing up Violet. She doesn't even know I've been seeing anyone. Why ruin it now when I've already done that myself?

Clicking the call to life, I lift the phone to my ear and calmly say hello. "Mom?"

"Hi, sweetie," she answers in that sweet, motherly tone. "Sorry if it's late for you. I was just hoping I'd catch you before bed."

I turn my head and look at the glowing digital numbers on the stove and see it's now a little past midnight.

"No, it's fine, Mom. I'm still up," I say in the best way I can, but I can't hide that little shakiness in my voice.

She pauses on the end of the line. "You okay, hun? You sound kind of sad."

"No, no. I'm just tired." I'm lying through my teeth, but what else can I do? It's hard enough as it is.

"You work hard, Son. You should get more rest. I know you like to wear yourself out." She laughs.

"Yeah…" Work hard. Just like I worked to ruin the one date I didn't want to fuck up.

"How're the girls?" I hear her ask through the echo of her crochet needles being put to work.

"Oh, you know. Kelsey's staying busy with her classes, and Kayla's busy with soccer and school. Can barely keep track of them sometimes." I chuckle under my breath, feeling a bit of relief bringing my daughters up instead of thinking of *her*.

"That's good. They're keeping you on your toes then."

"All the time," I answer back, letting my head fall against the back of the couch.

"I sure do miss them. And you and Bryson." She's got that melancholy tone, the one she gets that makes guilt coil like a knot in my stomach. She's still sad we both moved so far away. Even though she's proud of us for chasing after something together, she wishes we could've done that back home.

"We miss you too, Mom," I confirm, trying my best not to shed another tear. I've already done that enough tonight.

"And how's the club going? I suspect it's been as busy as opening weekend?" she pries out, searching for answers.

"It's been… eventful. Chaotic, in a good way. Just a lot more than I thought it'd be to take on." I'm up to my ears in responsibilities, but Bryson helps. And Violet…

Fuck. Violet… She's helped me more than anyone has. Came up with a system that made it more manageable for me. But now, that's all gone…

I choke back a sob as my mother speaks through the other end of the phone. "Well, I'm sure you and Bryson have it under control. I sure am proud of you boys. Always were so successful, no matter what you decided to do."

A curl of a smile pulls at the side of my mouth. "Thanks, Mom. You always know just what to say." Just like she'd know what to say about Violet, but I don't have the heart to bring her up. Not this second, at least.

"You'll have to make a trip out here soon. Come see me and your father. Maybe give your old man a hand on the farm."

That faint tug pulls against my heart when she brings up home. I haven't been back there in a long, long time. "Yeah, it's been a while since I've been home."

"Too long." She sighs before pausing a second, and I hear her drop her crochet needles. "Listen, before I forget, there's something I wanted to say."

I jolt up from the back of the couch and sit at alert. "Is Dad okay?"

"Your father is fine, Sam. The doctor's visit was just a scare. He's back out in the barn, just like normal. Can't keep that man in bed past sunrise." I can hear her smile through the phone.

I blow out a held-in breath and relax against the leather, letting my spine slouch against the cool material. "Oh, good. That's good."

"But, you may want to sit down for this."

I straighten up again and grip the edge of the couch. "What's wrong?"

"Nothing is wrong. Just..." She takes a breath and blows it out. "Something happened over the past week. Lois, she came to the house."

My eyes widen in horror. "What? Are you okay? Is Dad—"

She interrupts my unending questions. "Sam, we're fine. Nothing happened, I promise."

"Then why did she—"

"Her parents, Miranda and Eli, dropped by."

"Why?" There's a sharp edge to my tone. They've stayed away for years. Why is she suddenly hovering over my childhood home like she's plotting something?

"I don't know how to tell you this, but I thought you deserved to know. *She* wanted you to know."

I paw at my face, grinding my teeth together as I grit words out. "Deserved to know what? Mom, just spit it out, please."

She draws out a sigh before she continues. "She's going to an inpatient rehab, sweetie. Her parents finally convinced her, and she's willing to try this time. *Really* try."

"What…" She's really going? By her own choice?

"Lois, she wanted me to tell you how sorry she was. For everything, and she hopes you're happy."

"Happy. But she…" I'm stunned speechless. Honestly, I don't even know what to say. I never thought I'd see her pull out of that deep fog—the one that held her back from trying to get better. But she wants to get better, or she wants to at least try?

"I know it's tough bringing her up. And I know it's over, but they all thought you deserved to know. Lois wanted that, to tell you how sorry she is, and she hopes the girls forgive her one day, if at all."

"Mom, she… *what*?" I can't believe what I'm hearing. Lois is apologizing?

"I'm sorry if I just sprung that on you, but I wanted you to know. And I'm sorry. I'm sorry the whole thing didn't work out. You're brave, Son. And I hope you know I'm always here if you want to talk about anything, even her."

My lips twitch as I speak, and my eyes are just as big as they were the second she said Lois's name. "Yeah. That's uhh… thanks, Mom. For telling me, I mean. Definitely threw me off guard, but glad she's finally trying. I umm… hope she finds happiness too…" I mean that, truly. Even if we both couldn't find it together, I do hope that one day she gets that again.

"You sure you're okay, hun? There's nothing else on your mind?"

I open my mouth, hovering over Violet's name, but I stop myself. There's no use bringing up what's gone. "No, just… No. I'm just tired." And I am tired. Tired because of the painful goodbye, and now I find out my ex-wife is apologizing for all these years of back and forth arguments and fighting for something that's long lost?

Actually, I'm more than tired. I'm fucking spent.

"Oh, alright. Well, go get some sleep, and tell the girls I said hello, will you?" she asks brightly.

"Yeah, I will… Night, Mom," I murmur out in a hoarse voice, trying my best to keep all the weighted emotions grounded on the floor.

"Good night, hun. Call me soon."

"I will. Bye, Mom…" I end the call and let my phone drop to the couch.

Staring at the wall, I try to replay the conversation with my mom, still shocked by everything that was said.

Lois apologized. Not directly to me, but to my mother. She probably knew I wouldn't answer her texts, so she went through the one person closest to me.

As a matter of fact, Lois hasn't even tried to reach out in the past week. Actually, I haven't heard a peep from her in a couple weeks. But then again, maybe she was having a good week and didn't feel the need to. Maybe, just maybe she's having a breakthrough…

Hunching over, my elbow hit my knees and the back of my hands cover my eyes. This is all too much to handle in a night. I can't think straight, can't cope through all these painful emotions.

I sit there another hour, wallowing over broken pasts, grieving the loss of two people I deeply cared about. Lois and me, we're over, but I still have those lingering feelings for her shoved in the pit of my stomach. I think I'll always love her, a part of her, but I'll never go back there again. We're through, and it's better this way. And really, I pray to God she finds happiness and healing. I just wish I can heal from losing someone else. Someone I thought was *the* one. Violet…

After groveling on the couch, I drag myself up the stairs to take a cold shower, scrubbing away the evidence of loss and heartbreak. It doesn't help, but at least the sweat of the night is off my skin. And once I'm collapsed into bed and dragged down into darkness, all I hear is Violet's last goodbye…

The next day, I'm barely breathing. Only able to drag myself downstairs and stomach a glass of water. Kayla left a text message for me, said Nicole was dropping her off at school and that they'd be catching a new movie later. I texted Bryson, asked him to handle things at the club and said I wasn't feeling good, which I'm not. I feel like my heart's been ripped clear out of my chest, and there's not much I can do about it.

I spend half the day dozing off, clearing my head of what ifs. But the other half, I spend flipping through photos of Violet—the ones I took of her. Pausing on my favorite close up of her, I linger the pad of my thumb over her big smile, slowly tracing the curve of her perfect red lips. Her blue eyes sparkling like diamonds under the pool table lighting, the red hues mixing in the background, creating the perfect glow around her spiral curls.

God. I miss her. I can still smell the lavender in her brunette hair. And her laughter. That soft cadence of hers, it's still echoing in my ears.

Just as I start to get lost back in her glittery blue irises, Kayla's voice over my shoulder jolts me out of the memory.

"Dad?"

I quickly lock my phone and place it face down on the coffee table, hiding away Violet's pretty face from her view.

"Hey, kiddo. I thought you already left for the movie?" I turn my right wrist and glance down at the hour and minute hands, seeing that it's fifteen past seven. "Wasn't your movie supposed to start at seven-thirty?"

"Yeah, but I'm not going," she says unbothered.

"Why?" I turn my head and find her shrugging, as if it's no big deal.

"Told Nicole to reschedule to another night."

I clear my throat and watch her pad across the end of the couch, her light brown ponytail thrown over her shoulder and her pink fuzzy slippers sliding across the floor. "Can I ask why?"

She shrugs again, but this time she smiles. "You looked like you could use some company."

I shake my head and let out a low chuckle. "Kiddo, you really don't have to—"

"What are we watching? *Jaws*?" she asks brightly, interrupting me yet again.

I tilt my head to the side and give her a suspicious look. "You want to watch *Jaws* with your old man instead of going out with your friend?"

She throws me the sleek remote. "Why not? It's your favorite, right?"

"Right." I give her a tight-lipped smile and raise a brow, still in disbelief that she'd rather stay in than go out with her friends.

"Well, turn it on then," she giggles. "I need to grab something in the kitchen. Be right back." She flits away, disappearing into the kitchen behind the living room.

Flipping through the movie channels, I click on *Jaws* and let the ominous shark theme song float through the speakers.

"Two root beers and a pint of chocolate chip cookie dough ice cream coming right up!" Kayla sing-songs as she joins me on the couch, placing the sodas on top of the coffee table and handing me a spoon. A large pint of ice cream sits between us, and she's already ready to dig in.

"Kayla." I stop her mid-bite.

"What?" She throws me an amused look as she shoves a spoonful of ice cream in her mouth.

"What's all this?" I nod to the ice cream, the sodas, the movie that's ready to play on the screen, and to her as she curls up on the couch with her favorite fleece blanket.

"Some of your favorite snacks made by your favorite daughter?" she quirks out.

"Favorite daughter, huh?" I chuckle as a sideways smile meets my lips.

"Don't tell Kelsey," she whispers through a giggle.

"Never." I laugh, feeling that warm, fuzzy feeling creep in, replacing the cold that set in last night.

My girls are the best. And Kayla, she's like my little built-in best friend. I wouldn't trade them for the world.

"Alright, push Play. Let's get this movie night started." She shoves the remote in my hand, and I can't say no, so I press Play and let the sea of beginning credits roll.

As the camera zooms in and out of coral reefs and splashes of water, I look over and smile at the one girl who can always make me feel better. No matter what it is—whether it be I wake up on the wrong side of the bed or am going through a heartbreak—she always seems to know, and she'll do anything to make me feel better.

I'm the luckiest dad in the world.

"Thanks, kiddo," I say, nudging her with my elbow while I pick up the silver spoon and dig it into a chunk of cookie dough.

"For what?" She turns her head to the side and smiles up at me, knowing damn well why I'm saying thank you.

"For choosing to hang out with me. You already made my night ten times better."

"That's why I'm your favorite daughter, right?" she teases.

"Sure, kiddo. Whatever you say." I swallow a bite of the ice cream and savor the sweet taste on my tongue.

We fall into silence, focusing on the flitting images of the first shark attack, but Kayla's voice interrupts just before the first bite.

"Hey, Dad? Are we still going to get Whiskers tomorrow?"

My back goes rigid against the cool leather. Whiskers. That's right. Pick up day is tomorrow, and I already put her on hold.

I run my fingers through my hair and nod through the ache in my chest. Violet. She was supposed to meet Whiskers...

"Yeah, we're still gonna get her..." I croak out, clearing the large knot that's tangling in the back of my throat.

"Yes!" She pumps a fist in the air and shrieks. "I'm so excited! I already know she'll be the most perfect cat. You're the best." Taking me by surprise, she throws her arms around me and smothers me in a warm hug. I can't help but laugh as I hug her back.

"Easy now. Gonna spill the root beer," I chuckle out as she lets go and eases back into her spot, grabbing another spoonful of ice cream.

As the movie goes on, that ache still tugs in my chest, but Kayla makes it better. She makes me forget just for a little while what I just lost. So for now,

I'll just sit and watch the movie while I enjoy my daughter's company, sipping on soda and drowning in sugary ice cream. For now, I'll let Violet float in the ocean of my mind for a little while, until I'm ten feet under the crashing waves, chasing after her again...

Chapter Twenty-Nine

Violet

The week blurs like mixed paint, bright colors fading into dark remnants of my mind. The first three days after the dinner were spent in bed, curled up in the comfort of the cold, now wrinkled sheets. I called into work, told them I had something contagious. They didn't ask what I had; they just left me alone, like I wanted them to. Brianna and Taylor even let me be after I told them I was sick and just needed to sleep it off. I didn't tell them how things went with Sam, just said it was fine. But it's not fine. *I'm* not fine.

The truth is, I'm a wreck. I've barely gotten a solid hour of sleep without waking up in a cold sweat or screaming Sam's name after those awful nightmares swam through my head. Tears stain my sheets, my eyes are still swollen from endless crying, getting myself to stomach a full meal is almost impossible, and I miss Shadow more than I ever have. I wish I could just scoop him up and snuggle him into the side of my neck, but he's gone, just like Sam...

That first night after we said our goodbyes, the nightmares flooded my system like a death omen, and they haven't stopped since. They've all been different, flashing various shades of red behind my eyelids. Except now, my dreams have shifted. Instead of Sam catching the bottle before it crashes into tiny pieces on the floor, his face is what hits the hardwood floor, and Jason's the one that's shoving him down...

I should've told Sam about my dark past. Should've warned him I'm still working through my trauma because now it's eating me alive, and I can't do a damn thing about it. I can't bring myself to tell him. Even if I've stared endlessly at his name on my phone with my thumb hovering over his number, I just can't do it. He probably hates me, just like I hate myself now.

So like a sloth, I drag my lifeless body through the grueling days, until I can't hide anymore. I have to face reality—one where Sam's not in it.

Mondays are hard, but coming in on a Tuesday is even worse when you call in the day before. The light's too harsh, the noise of whispered voices in rows of books is too fucking loud, and I already have a growing migraine from being dehydrated.

I was supposed to have therapy today, but like a coward, I canceled that too because I can't talk about it. Not now, not next week, maybe not ever. Jenna would be so disappointed in me. I had the best thing splayed out in the palm of my hand, and now I ruined it, just like I ruin everything I touch.

Janet made her famous homemade chocolate chip cookies, the ones I love. She offered me a couple when I wasn't actively giving her a hard time. I always joke around with her just so I can see her scoff and roll her eyes while she lectures me, but I can't even throw a smart remark her way today. She must know something is going on because we always have that playful co-worker banter churning in the library, but not today. Not this week. I'm not in the mood.

"You sure you're feeling okay?" Janet asks with sincere eyes.

"I'm fine, just not hungry," I murmur as I drag a finger over the circulation desk, lingering against an edge that's sharp.

"Hmm." She gives me a once-over and pushes her rimmed glasses against the curve of her nose. "Okay. Well, I'll save you some to take home anyway. Make you a little to-go plate for later."

"Thanks," I reply quietly, circling my finger against the same spot I've been fixated on for the past five whole minutes.

She starts to walk away, but she stops and flips her dark bob of hair my way. "Violet?"

Slowly, I look up, keeping my hand in place on the desk. "What?"

Janet throws me a sweet, caring smile my way, like she knows something is going on that I'm not telling her. But obviously, she doesn't pry. "Take it easy today, yeah? Maybe leave a couple hours early?"

"I'm fine, Janet. Thanks though," I state with a bite to my tone. I don't mean to be harsh or short with her, but my mood can't seem to be tamed at the moment.

She nods, giving me one more apologetic look before she disappears. "If you change your mind, let me know. I'll be in the history section if you need anything."

I let her trail off without so much as a thank you from my lips as my fingers still trace over the smooth, jagged surface of the corner. Maybe if I dig deep enough into the pointed crevice, my pain will slowly ebb into the cracks so I don't have to feel like this anymore.

Just as I start to spiral back into the depths of my mind, a meek voice behind me grabs my attention. "Excuse me. Do you work here?"

"Oh, yes. How can I help you?" I mask the misery in my tone and replace it with the best customer service voice I can muster up.

"I just needed to return this book."

When I whip around and find the familiar hardcover flash across my peripheral, I freeze for a second and then reach out, taking it from the young customer. I let my fingers trace over the patterns of the winding trees, letting flashbacks of me and Sam's talks of the book arrest me in the moment.

"One of my favorites..." I whisper as I feel a tear sting in the back of my eye.

"Sorry, it's going to come up as late when you scan it into the system. You see, I had to keep stealing it away from my dad so I could finish it."

I pause and drag my eyes up to the smiling girl who stands in front of me.

"Your dad?" I ask, scanning her features from where I stand.

"Yeah." She giggles. "Kind of a strange thing to say. He's not really even into fantasy books, but this one had him hooked."

Wait.

My eyes dance over her features. Long brown hair falls across her shoulders, and she's tall. Almost as tall as me. Bright hazel eyes, a few freckles dusted across her button-shaped nose, and a white T-shirt adorned with black and red colors that spell out *Canyon Crest Soccer*.

Kayla.

She's so pretty. Her eyes remind me so much of Sam's with those flecks of brown sinking into green. She even looks a little like Bryson.

"I wonder who gave him the idea to read *Incinerate the Darkness*, because it wasn't me." She laughs as she twirls a piece of hair absentmindedly.

"Yeah. I wonder who..." I murmur out, still stunned that Sam's daughter is standing right in front of me, and I can't even introduce myself because I ruined that chance.

Sam. My stomach knots at the thought of him. God, I miss him.

"But anyway, I have some money to cover the late fee." She pulls out a five-dollar bill and starts to hand it to me, but I refuse and shake my head.

"No, it's okay. I got it," I confirm with a push.

She tilts her head and knits her eyebrows together. "You sure? It's no trouble. It's my fault it's late. Well, maybe my dad's, but—"

I set the book on the circulation desk and nod. "I'm sure. I'll take care of it."

"Umm, thanks." She's looking at me strangely, like I'm overstepping by not charging her, but I can't. I'll just clear it in the system. I can't let her pay. Not Sam's daughter.

"So you read it?" I ask as I slip behind the desk and slide into my office chair, clicking the computer to life with the push of a button.

"Well, most of it." Kayla leans against the counter, her elbows on the smooth surface, like she's chatting with a friend. "Dad wouldn't let me read chapters eighteen and twenty-seven. Said I wasn't old enough for the steamy scenes, but whatever."

I silently chuckle under my breath as a small smile tugs at my lips. "Of course he did." Sounds exactly like something Sam would do. He watches over his girls, after all.

My heart stops momentarily when I see Sam's name light up across the screen. Five days late in the system. Late because of me, probably...

I clear out the extra charge and wipe the evidence that he was here away. Like he never came into my life in the first place, and it hurts. It hurts like hell.

Biting my lower lip to keep from crying, I shove myself up from the desk and circle back around to where I'm standing next to Kayla. "You're all clear. Got the late fee taken off."

"Thanks." She smiles.

I try to flash her one back, but I don't have the strength. Not when Sam's hanging like a dark cloud over my head. Instead, I shrug nonchalantly and hope she doesn't think I'm rude. This isn't how I wanted my first encounter with Kayla to be. I thought it'd be over a dinner one day, but I already went and screwed up that possibility.

"Hey, wait." She focuses in on me and squints her hazel eyes as she assesses me closely. "Do I know you?"

"Oh, no. I don't think so," I quickly reply, shaking my head as I cross my arms over my chest.

"Hang on." She steps in front of me, and it's like a lightbulb flashes on in her head. Her eyes widen, and she opens her mouth in awe. "You're her. The girl in my dad's phone."

What?

I'm a little speechless, so I stutter out and shake my head in dismissal. "No, no. That can't be right." It just can't.

"I'm positive!" she says firmly. "You're the one I've caught my dad staring at in his photos."

I open my mouth, but nothing comes out. No, this can't be right. He can't be thinking of me, can he?

"He's been... looking at my picture?" I ask cautiously, my eyes just as wide as hers.

She nods. "Every day for the past few days."

"Oh."

What do you say to your ex-hookup's daughter you just met? Clearly I don't have any practice in this area, and I'm still completely shocked from when I realized just who she was.

She turns her head toward the entrance of the library, maybe searching for Sam, but then she flicks her bright gaze back to mine. "Look, I don't know what happened between you two or who you are to him, but maybe you should talk to him?"

I curl my hands deeper into my sides and shake my head sadly. "He doesn't want to talk to me."

"What makes you so sure?" She leans her head to the left and stares at me with hope in her hazel eyes. Just when I'm about to say something, the sound of a truck's horn blares out front, startling us both. "I, umm, gotta go," Kayla sighs. "But real quick, can I say something?"

I swallow and nod, my nails embedded into my skin now. "Sure."

There's a light smile playing on her pink lips, but there's also something somber weighing in her eyes. "Sometimes things we lose have a way of coming back to us, even if we think they're gone forever."

I open my mouth and then snap it shut, a little jolted from the meaning of her words. My eyes fall to my feet as I detangle her words.

Would he come back?

When I look up from the shiny floor, her brown hair's disappearing through the sliding glass doors, and then she's just gone.

Taking a moment to process what just happened, I hesitantly drag my feet to the large glass windows and pause right next to a large palm tree that shades me from view. I scan the busy parking lot and stop when I see Sam's truck in the far-left corner as Kayla climbs in. Even if the window's tinted, I can still see the outline of his face—that sculpted jaw with the salt-and-pepper scruff, tousled sandy locks, and that soft smile that lights his face when he's talking to Kayla.

My chest aches the longer I watch, but I can't turn away, even when he flicks his eyes this way. He can't see me, but I can see him as clear as still water. There's a longing tugging in my chest, a sway to my posture that tilts me off center, a hammering in my head that tells me to run, but I don't. I can't move.

It should be so easy. Just walk out there, open his truck door, and tell him to stay.

Stay. That's what I really want to tell him, but with one more flick of his eyes to the entrance, he's pulling out of the parking lot and disappearing down the street. Just like that night I told him goodbye.

My palm presses against the clear glass like I can reach right through and brush my fingers against his black swirls of ink. Like I can draw invisible lines of my name into that permanent tattoo. But like the night of the diner, I let him go, let him drift off through the ocean mist. Maybe he'll find my message in a bottle someday and remember what it was like when he held me in his arms under the warm lights of his club, where it was safe.

"Goodbye, Sam," I say through the glass as a tear slides down my face.

But like the coward I am, I find myself wishing he'd turn back around, just long enough for him to see me still standing here...

Chapter Thirty

Sam

Sunlight warms my clenched fist around the steering wheel, seeping through cracks on my calloused palm that splinter with pain. The cold, stale coffee sits in the cup holder, forgotten after I pulled into the parking lot of San Diego Central Library, too busy trying to hold myself together in one piece.

My other hand tracks along my jawline for the thousandth time in the last ten minutes, scratching absentmindedly down my scruff, holding in sighs as my eyes drift to the sliding glass doors of the entrance. And I'm watching, waiting, hoping she'll just magically materialize in front of me, or better yet, flutter her long, dark eyelashes while blue eyes shimmer in the sunlight, coaxing me to come inside and stay.

I scrub a hand over my eyes, fighting the urge to throw my seatbelt off and march right inside those doors, seek Violet out like I did as I followed her into close quarters of wooden bookshelves. That's how I found her before, surrounded in her niche of comfort with stacks of books all around her. And I remember it so well—her warm laughter that glided around the book-filled room, the beautiful smile she wore against her glossy red lips, her big blue eyes blanketing me in waves of hope. And then there was that adorable blush—the one she always painted on just for me when I'd tease or make her smile, like I was the only one that lit her up a million shades of red.

But then she said goodbye, and all the twinkling stars she put in my skies all fell into the ocean, leaving me stranded and left for dead. I said it, too, when I should've treaded water to get back to her. But now she's miles away, and I can't get myself to fight the current.

I can't fucking do it. Not today. And I hate myself for it.

But something tugs at me, prods me inside like a baited fishing hook, urging me to throw the line back into the water. Chase the diamond eyes that float in front of the sinking boat.

Honking the horn to get out of here faster, I'm jolted from my scattered thoughts when Kayla swings the passenger door open and hops inside, buckling her seatbelt with a click.

"You get the book returned okay?" I ask, turning to her while she kicks the soccer ball against the side of her pink cleats.

"Yep." She nods, still focused on the shiny ball at her feet.

"Late fee wasn't too much, was it?" I turn the key in the ignition, enough for the engine to rev to life.

Kayla tucks a piece of brunette hair behind her ear and looks up at me with a waning expression. "She actually didn't charge me."

There's that tug in my chest: hard, unsettling, pulling me toward the sliding doors.

Violet. It had to be Violet. No one else would've just waved a late fee away. Just like when I pushed away her hand with the folded twenty, she pushed Kayla's away, too. Her voice shreds in my ears like sharp nails on a dry chalkboard.

Take it. Please.

And then I clasped my palm over her hand, pleading for something else in exchange.

I don't want your money, Violet. I just want your company...

It stings. The memory. The feel of my thumb dragging along the back of her hand repeatedly, permanently ingraining her into my skin like a tattoo.

"Didn't charge you?" I ask a little hoarsely.

Kayla shrugs. "Said she'd take care of it."

"Oh, I see," I murmur as my hand slides against leather, creating deeper calluses into my palm. "Was nice of her..."

What do you want then, Sam?

Your time. Your time. Your time.

Like a song stuck on repeat, all I can think about is that moment in the mall parking lot, with my hand curled around hers, tugging her to follow me to my special place. The place I chose *her*.

My head's spinning. Fog's filling the cavernous parts of my brain, but Kayla's voice pulls me out of it.

"Dad?"

"Yeah?" I fix my set jaw and look at her, just as her hazel eyes grow a bit darker.

"I saw her," she whispers through the front of the truck. My heart stalls.

"Who?" I lick my bottom teeth, pretend I'm asking the unknown, but I know exactly who she's talking about. She's talking about the angel who lit up my club.

"The one you've been looking at in your phone." She drops her eyes to my phone sitting on the console, and my eyes grow wide.

"You've been spying on me over my shoulder?" I raise a brow and watch her lift her big eyes, apologies written all over her flecks of green.

"I wasn't trying to," she says softly, nervously tracking a finger over the black edges of my phone. "But I couldn't ignore it. Not when you kept staring at her more than just once."

I close my eyes, breathe out a solid breath, and pinch the bridge of my nose like it'll lift some weight off my stiff shoulders. I didn't want her to find out this way. Actually, I didn't want her to know at all. If I wasn't going to introduce Kayla to Violet, I wanted to dodge that bullet of pain.

"Who is she?" she asks curiously, tilting her head to get a better look at me.

Dropping my hand to my thigh, I huff out through clenched teeth. "Umm, she—"

"Is she your girlfriend?" she interjects as hope bubbles in her bright eyes.

Girlfriend. The word sears itself through my boggled brain.

"No, Kayla. That's not—"

She cuts me off and smiles over at me with shiny white teeth. "She's really pretty."

Pretty. More than that. She's the sun that set me on fire. She's ethereal.

"Yeah, she is..." I sigh, curling the edge of my lips up to where I feel a dimple cave deep into my cheek.

The most beautiful angel I've ever seen.

"What happened?"

I curl my fingers into my denim jeans until I feel nails bite my skin.

"It's complicated, kiddo." It's barely a whisper, but it's there.

"What's so complicated?" Her mouth hangs open as she waits for an answer. An answer I can't give her.

She didn't want more. She didn't want... us.

I sink my fingers against the warm leather of the steering wheel, my jaw ticking with each moment that passes.

"It's just. I don't know. She—"

There she goes, cutting me off again, just so she can get her words in. "You don't have to hide her, Dad. It's okay if you date. In fact, I want you to. I want you to do what makes you happy. Does she make you happy?"

Happy. She made me so fucking happy.

"She did..." I feel the sting of a tear behind my eye, burning to be set free.

"Then go in there," she urges, pushing my shoulder. "Talk to her."

I shake my head, refusing to move. "Kiddo, like I said, it's complicated."

"Mom didn't deserve you." That stops me in my tracks, makes my eyes widen as she presses on. "You deserve someone like her." She points to the entrance of the library, where roses line the sidewalk and clear glass reflects back at me. "If she really makes you happy, then you deserve her. You deserve *good* things. She seems good."

She is good. More than good.

My teeth bite into the flesh of my gums, soaking in crimson at the back of my throat.

Fuck. Even my own daughter is pushing me to go talk to her. But I can't make my feet move, can't muscle enough energy to pry the door open.

I let a chuckle fall from my lips, shaking my head as a sad smile tugs at the corners of my mouth. "Thanks for that, kiddo. Really. But I can't."

Kayla scrunches her eyebrows together and thins her lips in a tight line. "She looked sad," she mumbles under her breath. "Just like you've looked the past few days."

My throat constricts against a sob, but I swallow it down.

"I'm... I'm fine," I lie as my tongue prods against the inside of my cheek, feeling the weight of it sting the back of my eyes.

I'm far from fine, but I don't want to appease the notion.

"Are you?" She leans against the middle console, really looking me in the eyes, trying her best to conjure all my emotions onto a plate.

Kayla always sees right through me. Always has, always will. She won't drop the investigation of me and Violet, but for now, I silence the questions.

"Yeah," I say with no emotion. "Let's just get you to soccer practice, okay?"

She drops it, for now, and leans back into her seat, staring out the passenger window at a passing white car.

Before I pull out of the parking lot, I glance at those sliding doors, do a double take when I see a figure hidden in the corner, right next to a looming potted plant. I stop once I recognize the shape—the curve of her hips, her long legs, that chestnut dark hair with the sun-kissed highlights that sweep past her shoulders.

Violet.

A single tear streaks down my cheek, but I wipe away the evidence, pushing down sparks of pain that ignite in my chest. Part of me wants to turn off the truck and run in there, wrap her tightly in my arms till the pain just stops. The other part of me tells me to leave, so that's what I do.

I pump my foot on the gas and start to drive toward the exit of the parking lot, but it's hard to see straight when my eyes keep flicking in the mirror to see if she's still watching.

Stay. The word eats me alive, pulls at my teeth the closer I get to leaving.

Just stay.

My heart breaks, cracks like the glass of my tattooed watch the second I flick my eyes to the rear-view mirror, reminding me how painful it was to drive off that rainy night and leave her behind. But I'm doing it again. Leaving, just like I left Violet standing in the rain, staring absentmindedly as she watched me drive off. It stings like a fresh cut. Burns like a knife sliding into raw skin. I'm just opening that vacant wound—the one I ripped open, mixing saltwater tears and dry sand into something that can't be sewn up. Violet's the only one who can sew it shut, take the pain from my deep cuts. But like a knife, I pushed till she let go, allowing the cut to bleed out into the rusty water.

This is all my doing, so I should just soak in the pain, let it sink me into the ocean's waves. I think I'd allow it to if it meant I could forget her for just one fucking second. But she's tattooed herself into my swirls of black ink, and I can't seem to wipe her clean.

So she'll stay. A memory of what almost was. Maybe if I would've kept my damn mouth shut, then she'd still be here, whispering sweet nothings into my ear while she hangs around my neck. But she's not, and I have to let her go. But I don't want that. I don't want to let go.

But like the pinpricks eating into my skin, I pull away and let her go.

Chapter Thirty-One

Violet

I barely make it home in one piece, zigzagging through street lines, eyes burning with held-back tears. I thought I was stronger than this. Thought I'd be able to be tough and let him go, but after seeing Kayla and the outline of his face through the passenger window, I cracked under pressure and waves of hurt.

I just can't get over how he made me feel—like zaps of cosmic energy that he brought back to life in me. No one has *ever* made me feel the way Sam makes me feel—like I'm worth it to him. Like I'm something special in his eyes. But he's that to me, too. Something I wish I hadn't let slip away.

Now, I made him break, too...

My vision swims, and I barely make it through the front door until I'm collapsing onto my velvet couch and pulling my phone free. I mindlessly open an old text thread with Sam and stare at the screen, looking for any sign of life behind the flicker of the phone, reaching for just an ounce of reassurance that he isn't really gone, but I get none. There are no bubbles typing, no thumb pressing Send, no heartbeat behind old texts.

He's just... *gone.*

It hits me then. That fear of abandonment. The sick feeling sliding up my throat that he won't come back. The emotional turmoil of a choice in the wake of panic. A decision I made recklessly all because I was scared. But now, I'm more than that. I'm terrified that I lost him forever. A person who makes me feel whole, seen, complete. Someone I considered to be my new favorite person.

That's what Sam was to me—my favorite. *My* person. But he's not that anymore, is he? I shattered him...

I click Brianna's number so fast that I drop my phone from my shaky grasp and pick it up frantically, fumbling with the flimsy case until it rests against the side of my ear. It rings, echoing around my head as panic sets in.

Pick up, Bri. Pick up. Pick up.

Just when I'm about to give up, she picks up the end of the line. There's a giddy ring to her voice. "Vi! Hey. Are you feeling better? Also, tell me everything! Give me all the details."

"Bri..." I breathe out, in hopes she'll stop probing.

"Wait, don't tell me." I can visually see her holding up a flat palm, with a big smile lit across her face. "You kissed him, didn't you?"

Crack. A visible tear splits across my heart. I feel it, and it's deep, encumbered inside my rib cage.

"Bri," I try again, my voice hushed, distorted.

"It was perfect, wasn't it?" She just keeps digging, shoveling her way all the way down to my grave. "Was it in the diner, outside the truck, or?"

Snap. And just like that, my heart shatters like dust, crumbling inside like black ashes.

"Did he ask you to be his girlfriend?"

Rip. And he's gone.

"Bri, stop!" I scream, letting my wrecked voice echo around the living room. She goes silent. "Just stop..." I'm tired. So worn down. I'm barely hanging on by a thread.

"Violet? Are you okay?" Her gentle voice pushes through the speaker, but she's asking the wrong question. She should know by now. I'm far from okay.

I choke down a sob and shake my head through the salty tears. "No. No, I'm not." And it's finally the truth. I'm not anywhere near okay. I wasn't three years ago, and I'm still not.

"Babe, what's wrong?" Brianna reaches through the phone.

"I just..." I start. "He left. He... he's gone. And... Bri. I need you. I need—" I break down, sob through the pain, wear my heart on my sleeve like a tattoo. I hear her car keys jingle through the phone.

"Stay put. I'm coming over. Be there in ten minutes. 'Kay?"

"'Kay." It's enough of a response, all I can seem to get out.

"Don't move. Be right there. Just... hang on." And then the line goes dead. All I hear now is silent static and my shallow breathing through my stinging tears.

Hold on. I should've held on, but I let go. I let him go...

Hugging my knees to my chest, I wrap my arms around my legs and soak my black pants with the sting of salt, clinging to a reality that I just don't want to deal with. I don't want to think about anything. Don't want to think about how crushed he looked. Don't want to linger on the gloss of those sad brown eyes. Just want to forget any of it ever happened—like how I just lost the best thing that ever happened to me...

I sink into the middle of the couch, squeezing my eyes shut as tears ricochet down my eyelashes. The faint sound of distant ocean tides crash against the gray sky outside, drowning the pain rolling through my body. It's just me, the flickering light of the vanilla scented candle, and my muted cries that keep the ghosts away. Ghosts I scared off long ago.

My fault. My fault. My fault.

I did this to myself. And now, I have to swim through the ache. The ache of losing him.

I'm so busy replaying the tainted scenes after the dinner that I barely hear the creak of the door open, too far gone in the wash of drowning memories. But Bri pulls me up, stopping the sting for just a second as she gently tugs my knees down.

"Hey, it's me," she quietly says, keeping her voice still so she doesn't alarm me. Her hand squeezes around my kneecap, a touch of her sweet energy comforting me.

"Bri," I choke out, wiping the back of my hand against my red eyes, holding out for the sun to burst its streaks of warm sunlight through the curtain, but it doesn't come. It's just overcast, cloudy. The sun's gone.

"I'm here." Her voice is dulcet, and the familiar cotton candy perfume on her skin pushes a little more comfort my way. "Did Sam hurt you?" she asks as she kneels in front of me, her brown eyes shimmering with sympathy.

"No. No, he didn't." I shake my head through the tears, adamant that she knows that's not the case.

Sam would never hurt me. Not him. Not ever.

"Then what happened?" She tilts her brown eyes up at me, and I immediately feel the sting of remembering looking into Sam's somber eyes the night I cut him loose.

He didn't hurt me, but I hurt him...

I close my eyes and breathe before I answer. Let the Band-Aid rip right off. "Last week, when me and Sam were at dinner, he asked what we were doing. He asked for more. Said he had feelings for me, and I... I told him that's not what I wanted. That I didn't want *him*..." More tears gather in the back of my eyes and then they fall to my lap, like the rainstorm that soaked me that very same night he left.

He left. I let him drive off. I told him goodbye...

I wish I would've told him to stay. I wish I could've been that brave because the truth is, I want him, more than anything.

"Oh, babe." She grabs my hand and squeezes, holds it there to comfort me. "You said you didn't want him?" she asks, hesitantly, like she's walking on a tightrope over my prone body.

My face falls, and I fight to mutter words through my grinding teeth. "He looked so wrecked, so broken, Bri. I just... I got scared. I choked, and now I ruined it." I fumble my words, fiddling the tip of my thumb into the velvet cushion absentmindedly as waves of hurt tumble inside my chest.

"Scared?" She tips her head and looks at me as she pulls for more information. "Of Sam or something else?"

More like *someone*, not something. That someone being Jason. That charming, smooth-talking blond mop of a surfer who reeled me in. Five years older than me, a slithering snake that twisted his scaly body around my neck, suffocating me until he shed his skin and showed the real monster hiding behind those layers. A monster who hurt me...

I should've never let him in. Now look at what's become of me—a broken woman who can't get her shit together, who can't fucking heal the wounds on her own. I was doing okay for a while, until Sam showed up. Until he took me by the hand and showed me what a slice of heaven could look like. But I chose purgatory instead. Chose to shed my wings for lakes of fire. And then, I let him go...

Swallowing down the ache, I grab a hold of Bri's hand and clutch it for support. "Scared of putting him in a position where he could get hurt by me or even... Jason." His name feels like ash against my tongue. "But I already hurt him, so I guess I was right. I'm not *good* for him. I'm not good for anyone."

Brianna joins me on the couch and shakes her blonde curls, brushing my words away. "No. *No*, don't even think that for a second. You're one of the best. No, actually, the greatest. Sam would be so lucky to have you."

A curt chuckle bubbles out of my throat. "Lucky."

Yeah. Lucky he got away from the awful mess I am.

"Yes, *lucky*." There's a firmness in her voice, but it softens the next second. "Violet, you're so kind and genuine and full of love. Don't ever sell yourself short. Babe, you are *so* worth it."

Worth it. The words cut deep like a stab wound. I never felt worth it. At least, not after Jason started emotionally manipulating me. Not after he twisted spiteful words he used against me to make me stay. I should've never fucking listened to him in the first place.

Pressing pause, I shake my head at the words. "Stop. Really, I'm a mess and—"

Bri halts me before I can interject. "Jason's a piece of shit for what he did to you. That narcissistic, abusive asshole tried to break you. But Vi, you've come so far, mentally and emotionally. And I'd hate to see you lose someone who seems to light you up in ways I've never seen before."

My shoulders slump as I look at the edge of the couch, fixating on a single hanging thread. "He said goodbye, though. *I* said goodbye. And I don't think he wants to talk to me. He wouldn't have had his daughter run a book into the library today if he wanted to see me."

She pauses and crooks her head to the side. "You saw his daughter?"

"Kayla?" I nod. "Yeah. I saw her..." A small smile tugs at the corners of my lips. Even if it wasn't a formal introduction and was the only time I'll ever get to see her, at least I got to meet her once. Once is enough to know that she's a special girl, and Sam raised such a beautiful, smart daughter. I really wish I didn't mess things up with Sam, because I would've loved to get to know his girls, too.

"You talked to her?" There's a trace of a smile on her shiny pink lips.

"Mhm," I hum. "For a couple minutes. She seemed... lovely, actually. But Sam, he didn't come inside. Not this time." Sadness blooms once again, replacing that fraction of happiness with something deeper, heavier.

He didn't come find me.

"I think..." she pauses, methodically thinking before going on. "I think he might be hurting just as bad as you are right now. And maybe, just maybe, he wanted to give you a little space? Maybe he needed it to sort out his own feelings. Because from the sounds of everything that's gone on the past couple of months, I think he really wanted it to be more the entire time."

More. I wanted it to be more, too, if I'm being honest with myself. I think I've always wanted more, the moment he walked up and took the bar stool next to me.

Sliding my tongue across the top of my teeth, I still and shudder out. "I couldn't even tell him how I really felt. I just let him drive off..."

I let him get away when all I wanted was for him to stay.

She turns her knee inward, looks me dead in the eye with her sparkling brown eyes, and asks, "Do you want to be with him?"

"Yes," I breathe out with no hesitation. The easiest yes I've ever said in my life.

"You *really* want to be with him?" She knits her brows together and searches my eyes, just to make sure it wasn't a lie.

"*Yes.* Bri, I..." I pause, letting the built-up feelings thrum through my bloodstream. Sam's all over me—swelling inside my chest, hugging every smooth curve, sliding his fingers through the strings of my heart. He's *everywhere,* and I can't ignore the longing that's buzzing in my body. It's crystal clear now. It's always been him. And like a dove, I release it through the air, letting my wings spread once again as I say it out loud. "I love him..."

"You love him?" She says it in awe, with happy tears shimmering in her eyes.

I nod, showing her it's true. "Ever since that night he danced all night with me..." That's where it happened, where my heart belonged to Sam. It was when he gently pulled me against him, told me to look up, and promised he wouldn't drop me.

Promise you won't drop me?

What makes you think I'd ever let go?

"Then you're going to get him back." She squeezes my hand giddily.

"How?"

"Tomorrow night, you're going to walk straight into his club, and you're going to tell him *exactly* how you feel."

"No. Bri, I can't," I murmur as I shake my head. "He won't talk to me."

"*Yes,* you can, and he *will* talk to you," she promises with encouragement. "You can do this."

I can do this. I can do this.

It's just a few sentences. An apology. Three little words that threaten to spill through the air like painted sunsets on the horizon.

It's just Sam—my safe haven.

I can do this, I think.

"You really have a lot of faith in me, don't you?" I smile as tears gather in my eyes.

She flashes me one right back. "I've never doubted you for one second."

Brianna. My best friend. The one who always encourages me to be brave. The one who's always here, even if it's three o'clock in the morning. Even if I can't pull myself out of bed. She's always right there when I need her. And right now, I'm grateful she didn't talk me off the ledge. I'm thankful she pushed me into Sam that first night. And now, I'm completely indebted to her that she's encouraging me to chase after something I want. *Someone* I love...

I have to go tell him.

I pull her in for a tight hug and squeeze my arms around her. "Thanks, Bri. For everything. You're the best."

"Don't I know it." She laughs. When she pulls away, she stands up and holds her hand out in front of me. "Now come on, get up. Let's go."

"Go where?"

"I'm taking you out for ice cream. And then we're going to sit on the beach and have us a nice chat."

I sigh as I take her hand, let her pull me up, then pad after her. "What would I do without you?" I ask.

She looks back at me as she opens the front door and smirks. "You'd be lost without me."

She's right. I would be lost. I may have been drowning through the healing stages of Jason, but she was always right there. And now, I hope she'll be there through the rest. But she will be. I just know it.

So with the lock of my door, I leave the grief behind, wearing a new smile that's filled with a little more hope. Tomorrow will either go two ways: he shuts me out and breaks my heart, or he chooses me like I choose him.

Sam. It was always Sam.

Chapter Thirty-Two

SAM

The pool lights shimmer under the glow of moonlit water as I stare at the ripples of blue in a blur. My thumb traces absentmindedly against the condensation building on my glass of whiskey, the ice melting into the amber shades of alcohol. Just a sip to take the edge off the pain. Just a social gathering outside Laura's house after Kayla's soccer practice. A gathering to discuss *me*.

Laura's sitting right next to Caleb on a tan lounge chair, her fingers interlocked with her husband's. Bryson's in the next lounge chair over with his girlfriend, Serena, snuggled up against him, her legs swung on top of his while his hand rests on her tan thigh.

I feel like I'm interrupting something, like I'm intruding on a double date. And I'm just here, alone, sipping some chilled whiskey from a glass that's barely touched. It feels like I'm missing something, *someone*. And I know exactly who that someone is.

Violet.

"Wait, say it again," Laura says across from me, her auburn hair swinging over her shoulder the more she leans forward.

"I already told you." I sigh, pushing my fingers back through my hair. "I drove off."

"And you just left?" Caleb asks as he tips the neck of a beer bottle to his lips, keeping his eyes on me as he swallows.

My jaw tics, and my tongue pushes against my teeth. "That's what I did, yes."

I just... *left*.

"She didn't try to stop you?" Serena fishes for answers with her big doe eyes while Bryson combs his hand through her straight, long black hair. He's listening quietly to the conversation, all while he showers his girlfriend with affection.

My stomach churns at the sight, makes regret bubble up inside me. That should be me and Violet right now—her on my lap while I lazily draw heart shapes over her smooth skin. If only she would've told me to stay. If I'd just turned the truck around and fought for her. But I didn't because I took her goodbye as a clear answer.

I shake my head slowly, with my eyes glued to the concrete of the porch. "I didn't turn back to check."

There's a heavy silence in the air, only the tune of the radio floating through the open sliding glass door. It's like they're all judging me, but I know they're not. Not really, it's just all in my head.

Laura carefully interrupts my spinning thoughts. "From everything you've told us, I just don't see why she told you she didn't want more."

"Yeah," I mumble out as I hunch over the edge of the lounge chair. "I thought she wanted me, too, but I guess I got it wrong." But *how* did I get it wrong? I must've missed something from the start.

"She seemed like she was enjoying the date, right? I mean, it sounded like you two had a lot in common." Serena bounces another question off to me.

"We were and we do, but once I told her I had feelings for her and wanted more, she switched, just like that. Like a light died inside her or something."

That's what it was. Once I brought up the question, the big smile she had curled across her red lips slowly dropped, and those sparkling blue eyes seemed to darken when I told her how I felt.

What did I miss?

I've been pulling my hair out the past few days playing the date over, all the nights we spent together in the club. The long phone conversations, the flirtatious banter of texts back and forth, that deep connection I felt teether us together like a bond.

I just don't understand what happened or where I went wrong, and it's been driving me mad.

"And she got really hesitant, really quiet?" Caleb asks through another gulp of alcohol.

I nod. "Barely said a word after that. We uh, didn't really talk again till I dropped her off."

"What'd you say then?" Laura questions.

I shrug. "Told her I couldn't continue to see her or keep hooking up if I couldn't give her more. So we both said goodbye and—"

"And you just let her go?"

I flick my gaze up and stare at my brother, my mouth parted from the burning question. Those are some of the first words he's said this entire night. His hazel eyes narrow just the slightest, and he's got his mouth pursed together while his hand tightens around Serena's thigh.

Rubbing my lips together, I nod my head up and down. "I let her go..."

"That doesn't sound right," he says with defiance in his tone. "No, that's... that can't be."

"What do you mean, Bryson? Did you not hear what I just said?" There's a bite to my words, a bit of frustration leaving my lips.

"I heard you loud and clear," he states, shaking his locks of blond out. "But you're wrong. She wanted you."

"No, she told me she didn't want—"

"You really believed her?" He stares at me with a knowing look in his eye—one I'm all too familiar with. I twitch my lips as I look back at him, reluctant to say anything. "Sammy, listen to me for a minute, will you?"

"Alright," I huff out, straightening my spine at full attention. Whatever he has to say must be important. And even though he loves to get on my nerves, I know that's not what he's doing. He's older than me, so I've always known him to be the wiser one. Maybe I should listen this time.

"Look," he starts, "I don't know everything that went on between you two, but I can tell you one thing: every time she walked into the club, her eyes lit up the second she set her eyes on you. Could practically see stars in them."

Looking out toward the shimmer of the pool lights, I clench my jaw and continue to listen.

"And I don't think Violet was telling the whole truth. There had to be a reason she said that, because I know her well enough to know that she *likes* you. Sammy, she might just be—"

I snap my head back toward him so fast that I almost fall off the edge of the lounge chair. "Then *why* did she say she *didn't* want me?" It comes off angry, a deep growl from the back of my throat. And maybe it's just because I'm hurting and confused, but I'm not a victim here. I'm also at fault.

Bryson breathes out a sigh and relaxes back into the brown cushion. "You're gonna have to ask her that yourself."

Hanging my head, I rake a hand slowly across my scruff and think about that night all over again. I thought I did it all right. Thought I went slow enough and eased into the conversation. I wish I could go back in time and do it all over. Maybe I should've waited for her to say something. But Bryson is also right. Her eyes did seem to sparkle every time I looked at her under the glow of the red lights in the club.

I just wanted her to be mine...

Laura cuts into my sulking. "Did she ever talk about her past relationships, her most recent ex?"

My thumb drags along the cold glass while I stare past ripples of water, my eyes catching a glimpse of the full moon in the sky.

Her ex. Now that I think of it, no. She barely said a word, if ever.

Turning my head back to Laura, I look at her with a blank stare and whisper, "Actually, no. Not really…"

There was only that one time before I went down on her. But then again, was she dropping me little hints, hoping I'd pick up on them? Like that night I danced with her.

"And you said she was hesitant after you told her how you felt, when you asked if she wanted more?" Laura asks.

"Yeah. What are you getting at?" My eyes lock with her green eyes, and there's a glimmer of hesitance in them.

"Think there might be something she's not telling you? Maybe something she's scared to say? Maybe someone did something to scare her?"

I gulp down on nothing as I remember that flash of horror in her scared eyes. Right when my fingers skimmed across the old scar on her left wrist. She yanked away so fast that I barely registered the silent cry of help she was sending me. But she brushed it off and gave me a small smile, promising that she was fine. Said she tripped over her cat and cut herself on broken glass, but is that what really happened? Has she been hiding something about her past this entire time that she didn't want me to know about?

I scrub a hand down my face and blink up, but my voice is in a faraway place when I answer. "I think someone hurt her…"

And the question stirs inside me like a tidal wave. *Did someone hurt my angel?*

"Go after her, Sammy." Bryson tips his head toward me, nudging me to move.

"What?" I ask, frozen in place.

Go after her?

"You're in love with her, aren't you?" Bryson questions, but it's not really a question. He's stating a fact.

"I…" I lose my voice and stare across the yard at a swaying palm tree, fixated on the rough texture of the trunk.

In love with her? Yeah. I think I've been in love with her since the moment I laid eyes on her.

I feel it then—the way my heartstrings pull and prod every time I think of her blue eyes. The way her laugh makes me dizzy, and how I feel complete when she's in a room with me. How lost I feel when she's out of reach.

"Sam, I know that look. He's right, isn't he?" Laura says through the wind.

Dragging a hand back through my locks, I prod at the inside of my cheek until I can muster up the words that I've been holding in. "I... *yes*. I'm in love with her."

There, I said it. Set the words free through the California sky. Said the one thing I've been too scared to think or even speak after Lois. But Lois is the past, and if I want to make Violet my future, then I need to move fast.

"Answer this for me," Bryson says. "Do you think you can live without her?"

Live without her? No. I can't even last a week without her without feeling like my heart will implode.

"No..." I answer in a whisper.

"Then what are you waiting for? Go after her!" he yells, spurring me to get up from my chair and run.

I quickly stand, leaving the glass of barely touched whiskey on the side table. Fishing for my keys in my pocket, I snatch them and start moving towards the back gate. "I—umm. I gotta go."

"Go get her, Sammy." Bryson smiles my way while the others cheer me on.

I don't stay any longer. I just move, practically sprinting to my trunk until I feel the engine roar to life and hear the click of my seatbelt. There's no time to wait any longer. I have to get her back. One way or another.

"Hold on, Violet. I'm coming, baby."

Speeding out of the tucked away neighborhood, I peel out of the entrance, chasing moonlight as my foot presses hard against the gas pedal. I can't stop, can't slow my racing heart down, so I zip through yellow lights and make a dash for her.

"Come on," I growl as I nearly miss my turn and race through a red light.

I'm being reckless, the way I'm zigzagging through traffic and coasting stop signs. But I don't care. The only thing I remotely care about is *her*—Violet. I *just* have to get to her. This may be my only chance.

After fifteen minutes of impulsive driving, I screech into her apartment complex and park right outside her building. Cutting the gas, I tear the seatbelt off and bolt for her door—the one that's painted white and has a number twelve hanging in the middle. The one with the overflowing flower pots and butterfly stickers across the brick that leads to *her*.

Wasting no time, I hurry up to her door and knock four times, calling her name with urgency in my shaky voice. "Violet, open the door. Please, just open up." I bang my fists against wood, each knock reverberating with longing.

Come on, Violet. Open up, baby. Let me in.

When she doesn't answer, I lean my ear against the smooth surface and try again, easing my knuckles against the door. I listen for any shuffling of feet behind the wood, but there's nothing. Not even the tap of her nails against the other side of the wall.

"Violet?" I try again, this time lowered, as I rap my knuckles once more.

Nothing. Not a peep.

Violet...

I pull my phone from the pocket of my jeans and thumb through my contacts till I land on her name. Pressing on the call button, I lift the phone to my ear and hope she answers.

Pick up. Pick up. Pick up so I can tell you how I feel.

I don't even get one ring in till it drops off to voicemail. I still when I hear her melodic voice slip through the speaker. *"You've reached Violet. Sorry I couldn't get to your call, but leave a message and I'll try to get back to you as soon as I can."*

The loud beep rings in my ears, blaring white noise through my eardrums. I take a deep breath, think about spilling my feelings, but I end up dropping the phone and ending the call before I can say anything. My heart beats steady in my chest as I slip the phone back into my pocket and rest my head against the middle of the door. I could've said a million things over the phone, could've told her how much I miss her and how nothing's the same without her there in my club.

But it's not just the club I'm missing her at. It's here, in my arms, where I miss her the most. And for once in my life, I feel as empty as a cavern on the shore that's been deprived of saltwater for months.

Groaning, I flatten my palms against the white wood and pretend I can reach inside. Go incorporeal so I could find Violet and pull her into my arms like the ghost that I feel I am. I'd hug away every doubt that's eating her alive, kiss away all her fears and scars that she doesn't speak of out loud. I'd rock her like the gentle waves of the sea and tell her how much she means to me, how much I love her...

Or maybe I should just do what they always say. If I love Violet, then maybe I should set her free. If she comes back, then maybe she was always mine. And if not, she never was...

But I don't *want* to let her go. And maybe I should, but I just can't. Because I don't want to live without her. So maybe I'll just stay a while, laze in the ocean waves till she comes back around and shines a little sunlight on me.

Violet was always worth it. To me, she's worth waiting for. So I'll wait, as long as I have to.

I slink down on the porch and tilt my head back against the door, hoping she'll call or open the door or appear on her porch step. But minutes turn into an hour, and she's still not here.

She didn't show...

So I lift myself up with a grunt, shake off the ache in my lower back, and press my palm once more to her door. I smell her, even if she's not physically here right now. I still breathe in her scent like she's right *here.* Lavender, a touch of vanilla, citrus fruit sticking to my clothes. She's everywhere, even if she's gone.

With one last sigh, I drop my hand to my side and drag my feet to my truck, leaving behind the one thing I came to find. Violet's not here, and waiting for the rain to fall isn't going to bring her back to me, even if I want it to.

When I climb in the truck and glance back at her closed door, I hold back tears and drive away, just like I did last week when I left her standing in the rain...

I'm such an idiot. I should've never driven away, but here I am, doing that exact same thing once again.

With one last glance in the rear-view mirror, I whisper through the air. "Come find me, Violet. Come back to me. I'll wait forever if I have to."

I let you go once, but once I get you again, I'll never let go. Never, ever.

CHAPTER THIRTY-THREE

SAM

The headache pounds against my skull like a steel hammer as I work my fingers through my messy hair, pulling at the ends till I get a moment of relief from the incessant thumping against the side of my head. I took a Tylenol, tried nursing two glasses of water down my throat, but none of it helped.

I've spent the past half hour flicking through my phone, glossing over text messages and phone calls that aren't from Violet.

Violet. She never called back, and I didn't even see the blue bubbles of her typing out a text just to decide to not say anything. It's only been one night, but it feels like weeks ago that I was at her porch, pounding my fists against her door while I called her name.

Violet, Violet, Violet. She's all I can fucking think about. Forget about the unanswered emails on my work laptop or the stack of papers I need to organize. What's the point of all this if I can't pull myself out of the trenches? Why am I making myself suffer when I can just drag my ass up and try again? But wouldn't Violet have called me back if she wanted to? Wouldn't she have smelled my cologne or felt my handprint against her door? Wouldn't she know that I did try to find her?

Maybe she just doesn't want to be found. Maybe I should just let her go…

"Sammy?" Bryson's voice floats through my office, muffling the sounds of blaring music inside the club when he shuts the door to my office.

"What is it, Bryson?" I groan out, dragging a palm roughly through my scruff.

"Jesus, are you feeling okay? You look exhausted." He makes his way beside my desk and eyes the mess I've made.

"Thanks for the compliment," I scoff. "But I'm fine. Just didn't sleep well last night." It's not a lie. I haven't slept in days, especially last night. Just tossed and turned, hoping she'd call, but I only got static.

"She still hasn't called?" He tilts his head and looks at me with concerned eyes.

"No, she hasn't..."

"Just give her time." He places a hand softly on my shoulder and gives it a light squeeze.

"Easier said than done," I sigh. "Did you need something?"

"Actually, yes. There's uh, someone here to see you." My head snaps up, and my heart beats wildly against my chest. But to my dismay, he slashes the hope in my chest. "Not her."

"Then who the *fuck* is it?" I growl. I'm not in the mood for customers or business talk. I *just* want *her*.

"It's Chelsea."

My jaw tics. "Chelsea? We didn't have an order for tonight."

"I know," he states as he brushes off a piece of lent on his black suit. "She's not here on business, just for fun."

"Oh, I see."

"She umm..." he pauses. "She's asking for you."

"Well, tell her I'm busy," I snap out.

Asking for me? Why on Earth would she be asking for me when she's not here doing a job?

"I tried. She's persistent," he states with a blank face.

"I don't want to—"

He holds up a palm. "I know. Just go talk to her. You know she won't stop. Not until you cut the cord. She's been crazy about you since that first delivery. Just... let her down gently, yeah?"

"But she's not Violet. And I don't—"

Again, he halts me from continuing. "That's exactly why you need to tell her. Because Sammy, she's not gonna stop asking me until you walk out this door and tell her your heart belongs to someone else."

I slide my tongue along my bottom teeth and clench the edge of my glass, letting the condensation drip until I make a decision.

Finally, I sigh and agree. "Right... alright, fine. I'll talk to her."

He flashes me a smile and points my way before I exit the office. "Remember, *easy*."

"Yeah, yeah," I roll my eyes. "I'll go easy on her, for the love of God."

Twisting the door open, I step out into the dim hallway and enter into the chaos of the club. It's too fucking loud, too crowded in every corner. I have to slide past packs of women who are grinding against men dressed in fancy suits and gold Rolex watches, indulging in their own ecstasy.

When I make my way through the sea of clubgoers, I have to blink away the flash of pink and reds that tunnel my vision, have to keep moving in a drag as my feet stick to the floor spilled with alcohol.

Violet, Violet, Violet. I chant her name through my lungs, swallow her syllables back down. I'm about to run out of the club when all of a sudden a hand catches my arm.

"Sam?"

I turn in a blur, ready to shake off whoever's got a hold on me, but then I see a flash of blonde hair and realize just who's standing there. "Oh, hey. Chelsea, what are you doing here—" My sentence drops off, and my mouth opens as my eyes drink her in. There's no T-shirt or casual jeans. There's just glitz and glam.

Her bleach blonde hair is curled and pulled across her right shoulder. Diamond studs shine through the waves of blonde. The red dress she wears clings to her body like a glove. Big breasts spill from the V-shape of the front of her dress; the flashy material barely covers her dark tan thighs, and clear stilettos finish the outfit.

I swallow and keep my eyes from drifting, distracting myself as I loosen the white collar of my shirt.

Fucking hell.

She stares up at me with a glint in her light blue eyes and smiles sweetly. "Oh, you know. Just hanging out. Thought I'd stop in and see what the fuss was all about for once."

She's seen my club a million times. Why is she suddenly so intrigued now?

"Ahh, I see." I cross my arms uncomfortably, looking around to find something to pull me away.

Any day now, Bryson. You can come out any time and lead me away.

Just as I'm about to give her an excuse, she asks with a curl of her pink lips, "You want to grab a drink?"

"I uhh..." I look around, unable to come up with a realistic excuse and sigh. "Umm, sure."

"Perfect," she smirks.

Fuck.

She leads me to an open set of bar stools and taps on mine as she climbs up and perches her elbow on the bar top. "What are you drinking tonight?"

"Whiskey on the rocks," I reply with no hesitation. Whiskey's easy, smooth, my drink of choice when I need to relax a bit. And maybe having one sip will ease the voices ringing in my ears.

"Could've figured that," she laughs.

"Hey, Sam. What can I get you two? Whiskey on the rocks?" Hailey asks from the other side, flipping her blonde ponytail and throwing me a smile.

"Yep!" Chelsea interjects, answering for me. "One of those, and can I get a martini?"

"Sure thing. I'll... get those right out." Hailey flicks her gaze my way, then back at Chelsea. She eyes me suspiciously as she trails off to fetch the drinks, like I've been caught cheating. I'm not cheating, just having a drink, but I can't help the sick feeling that bubbles up my throat—like I just swallowed poison.

"You come here with friends tonight?" I ask, turning my attention back to Chelsea.

She swirls a painted red nail across the sleek surface and shrugs. "Actually, they're at the bar next door. I told them I'd just drop by for a little bit and see if you were here. Guess I got lucky."

My mouth runs dry. *Guess I got lucky?*

No, I don't want this. I don't want Chelsea. Not like that. Not like I want Violet.

Hailey drops off our drinks and leaves us in a hurry as she helps other customers. I watch Chelsea take a sip of her martini as she flutters her eyelashes my way.

I try to steer her the other direction, away from me because I know what she wants. "You should go back to your friends," I push. "They're probably missing you right now."

"They can wait," she purrs. "Besides, I'd rather get a drink with you. And maybe steal a dance?" She rests her hand on top of my wrist, dragging her long nails over the back of my hand until I feel spiders crawl down my back.

There's that feeling—the one where my lungs start to collapse. Suddenly, the room's too hot, too sticky, and I need to find a pool to jump in quick.

Her eyes are dancing with flits of danger, mixed with champagne bubbles and heart-shaped patterns. And I see it—the lust in her gaze. She's trying to make a move, and I'm about to dodge her love spell she's trying to cast.

I don't want Chelsea. I just want the woman with the stack of books and big blue eyes that knocks the breath from my lungs.

Fuck. I have to make this stop right now.

"Chelsea, stop. Just stop." I push her hand away and almost spill her drink.

Her bright eyes widen into saucers. "Did I do something?"

"No, you didn't." I shake my head and hold my hands up. "I just… I can't. Okay?"

"Why not? Am I not your type or something?" Chelsea muffles out a nervous laugh and twists a strand of blonde around her finger.

"Chelsea, look." I drag a palm over my mouth and sigh. "You're beautiful, and somebody's gonna make you really happy someday, but I'm not the one. I'm sorry."

"I don't understand…" She places her arm against the bar top and leans into it, staring up at me with heartbreaking eyes.

"I'm seeing someone, okay?"

There. I said it. I finally got it out of my system. Something I should've told her long ago. Instead, I had her hanging by a thread, hoping one day I'd take the bait and finally ask her out. But the truth is, I never wanted to do that. She is beautiful and charismatic, I'll give her that, but nobody's ever hooked me quite like Violet did…

"Sam Brooks is taken?" She clicks her tongue and stares at me with wide eyes and a thick smirk across the gloss of her mouth. "I had no idea."

I chuckle and rake a hand through my hair. "Well, it's a long story," I confess. "And right now we're kind of in a bind, but I'm crazy about her, and I need to go find her so maybe we can fix things. I'm really sorry, Chelsea. I'll take care of the bill," I say as I scoot off the edge of the bar stool and prepare to stand.

"No worries." She smiles. "What's her name?" It's a genuine question. There's no jealousy there, just general curiosity. Friendly, even.

"Her name's Violet." The corners of my mouth twitch when I say her name.

Violet. The girl I'm fucking crazy about. Violet. The one I'll always chase after.

She swirls her slim straw in her glass and nods. "Well, Sam, she's a lucky girl. Really lucky, actually."

I smile and tip my head. "Thanks, Chelsea. But I think I'm the lucky one. And if I don't get up now then—" My sentence is cut off from the clash of broken glass on the floor. The entire crowd around the bar turns their heads and looks in the direction of the disruptive noise. And when I look up to see what happened, my heart halts in my chest.

Big, watery blue eyes swim in my vision. A blur of brunette curls with soft highlights clashes with the fluorescent pink colors across the way. Red lips open and close, but no sound escapes. And the halo that usually eliminates the top of her head dies.

Oh, fuck.

"Violet?"

And then, she's running.

Chapter Thirty-Four

Violet

Just go in there and do it. Tell him how you feel.

I've tried talking myself out of it for the past half hour, even turned back around to go home just to end back up in the parking lot of Club Inferno. And then I started pacing, fidgeting with my fingers, and walking back and forth in front of the double doors.

Come on. Pull yourself together, Violet. Go in there and get your man.

My man... That's what I want Sam to be, right?

The flashing red lights outside the club shine bright against the glow of the full moon. A brisk breeze cuts through the cool air, blowing my long waves of hair back against my shoulders. It sinks underneath my dark blue dress, chilling my spine, making me squirm. My body hums with nerves, with desire, with *need.*

I want Sam.

Sam, Sam, Sam.

He's all I've been able to think about. He's all I *want* to think about. Even when I'm at work, or talking to customers, or in my therapy sessions, my mind always goes straight to *him.*

Maybe at first I didn't want to blur the lines. Didn't want to mix feelings with pleasure. Didn't want to fall head over heels, but look where that led me. I tripped head first into the ocean, and the only thing that kept me afloat was Sam.

So, now's my chance to tell him exactly how I feel—that I'm deeply, madly in love with him and want to be with him. A relationship was never off the table. Not really. I was just too scared to let my walls down. But for Sam, I'll do just about anything.

All I have to do is apologize first. That should be easy enough, right? If I don't walk in there in the next minute then I may lose him for good. I've already lost him once. I'm not sure I can handle losing him again. Not this time.

Taking one last deep breath, I take the plunge and step through the glossy black doors. Time to face my fate.

The club is buzzing with crowds, all painted under tinges of red and pink blurs of color. The music blares, loud and heavy over the bass. Even the second floor is packed with bodies.

My anxiety's in overdrive, but I lock in and focus on my mission at hand. Sam. I need to find Sam.

I stop at the corner of the bar and brush my hand over the smooth bar top, letting the cool material suck away the anxious thoughts. Scanning the crowd, I look for the handsome man who stands out amongst the rest. The one with dark brown eyes who makes every single nerve ending vibrate inside me every time he sets his heated gaze on me. That smoldering, captivating, charming man who lights my heart on fire.

I'm so stupid for letting him go.

A group of women in short, elaborate dresses get up from their bar stools and scamper off to the busy dance floor, leaving me room to see the rest of the crowd at the bar. Glasses clink together, bartenders rush to grab drinks for patrons, all while the mirror behind the bar reflects back at me.

Out of my peripheral vision, I hear an easy laughter, see a flash of blonde curls and familiar tousled brown hair. Quickly, I turn my head and zero in on brown eyes I'd recognize anywhere. My heart gets stuck in my throat at the sight.

Right there at the very end of the bar sits Sam, all muscle in a button-up crimson shirt with the top three buttons undone to expose his broad chest and tan skin. The sleeves are rolled up to his elbows, like usual, accentuating the defined veins that wrap around his forearms, and the black watch clasped on his right wrist just sets them off even more. But what paralyzes me the most is the fact that he's sitting at the bar with another woman. Someone who isn't me...

Big blonde curls fall across her pink blush-filled cheeks, and her tiny dress exposes large breasts that spill from the low-cut design. Her pink, sparkly mouth opens as she laughs freely, beaming at Sam. She caresses his wrist, fingers brushing lightly across tan skin, probably whispering sweet nothings to him over a drink.

I flinch and look down at the ground because I can't watch this. I can't stand here and stare at what's unfolding before my eyes. It's just like that first night I met him. The same charming smile, sweet-talking, tooth-aching rot of smooth, enticing words. And he'll have her by the end of the night, just like he got me.

Clenching my stomach, I cough, dry heaving on nothing. I'm going to throw up.

A week and a half without him and he's already wrapped around another woman's finger. Go fucking figure. I told him I didn't want more, so what did I expect? Him to wait around? No. I just didn't know he'd move on so fast...

When I force my eyes back up, she's still staring at him, enthralled by his conversation. She's not touching him anymore, but I still see that shimmer of something, a spark in her eyes. She wants him, and I'm sure by the end of the night he'll have her perched on top of his pool table with his hands all over her golden skin.

My blood runs cold, and it feels as if I just got hit by a metal bat in the center of my gut. I tightly dig my manicured nails into the bar top, holding on to something to keep me upright.

Another laugh. Another light touch to his shoulder. Another smirk meeting her pink lips. And he just sits there, like he wants to be there. Like he wants *her*.

I can't watch this. I can't *fucking* do this tonight. He was supposed to be mine, but I'm too late...

And there I go, falling apart at the seams. I feel a hot prick against the back of my eyes, and my vision starts to blur. Fiery tears bleed into my eyeliner as I back up, my hand still clutching the edge of the bar for support.

Not watching where I'm going, I end up spilling an entire glass of bubbling alcohol and knock into the back of someone. The beverage slides off the edge and onto the floor, shattering and sloshing liquid as it splashes against my black high heels.

The clatter of the broken glass stirs memories. Takes me back for just a second to that dark blur of a night. I blink, try to shake off the feeling as I slip back into the ambience of the club and away from the terror that's trying to pull me under.

The crowd around the bar goes silent for a beat as they turn to face me. Some whisper in each other's ears as they carefully eye me, but I can't hear them. Their voices are all washed out, all faded in the background. It's just me and the smashed glass littering the marble flooring, crunching beneath the slick of my heels.

I brush the back of my hand under my eye and sniffle as I look up, trying to forget that broken glass is a trigger for me. And suddenly, my world starts to spin because Sam is staring back at me with big brown eyes, his hands clenched, mouth partially open, and then he's abruptly standing, pushing back the bar stool with his legs. He's mouthing my name, but I can't hear anything besides the ringing in my ears. Another crunch of glass beneath my heels and I'm fading fast.

Run. Leave. That's all I know now. All I've seemed to learn from that awful relationship that left me in tattered pieces. And now, I can't move fast enough.

I feel Sam's heat against my back, reaching for me with his voice, but it's drowned out by all the noise in my fuzzy brain.

Tripping over my own two feet, I claw my way to the double doors, ripping through black and white suits, stumbling against the backs of sparkly dresses. I can't seem to suck in enough clean air; it all just feels polluted, contaminated with poisonous gas. I need to get to safety *now*.

Sucking in a sharp breath, I let it all out once I'm through the entry doors and back outside in the cool air, away from all the noise. I still feel the shards of glass in the bottom of my shoes, even though they're not there. It's just remnants of my memory, tugging me back to sharp glass and broken bottles.

The bottles. They broke—just like my heart.

Just when I start to catch my breath, Sam comes barreling through the double doors and shouts my name loudly. "Violet, stop!" he yells. "Didn't you hear me calling your name?"

"Guess not," I mumble as I dig my heel into the cement, crossing my arms against the chill that slips down my spine.

I want to tell him to go away. Want to shove his chest till he disappears through the doors and lets me just breathe for once.

I start to turn the other way, but he halts me. "Hey, stop. Wait!" he calls after me, running toward me and stopping two feet in front of me. "Angel, talk to me."

"Don't call me angel," I snap, retreating a step back from his advances.

"Wait." Sam takes a step forward and reaches his arm out to try to catch my wrist. When he starts to curl his fingers against my skin, I pull away.

"*Don't,*" I warn sharply.

He looks taken aback by my warning. All wide-eyed and mouth parted. "Will you just let me explain?"

I shake my head and hold back tears. "What's there to explain? Looks to me like you were on a date. You don't have to explain that to me, Sam. That's *none* of my business."

But I want it to be my business, don't I? Or maybe I just want to leave, forget he even exists so he can move on with someone who won't hold him back like I do. But I don't want that either.

"A date?" He furrows his brows together in confusion. "No. Violet, no. That's not—"

"No?" I laugh in disbelief. "Because it sure looked a lot like that first night you bought me a drink." I fold my arms over my chest and fight the ice of the wind against my bare arms.

"No, that's—No. That's not what that was. She works with me."

"So you buy your coworkers drinks and let them put their hands all over you?" I cock my hip out and stand my ground, digging my heel into the cement.

"That's not what happened." He sighs as he runs a hand frantically through the back of his sandy-brown locks.

Rolling my eyes, I steer my gaze to the ground and press my red lips together. "Why don't you just go back to your date, Sam? I'm sure she's waiting for you."

"She's not my date. She—"

I wipe a frustrated tear from my cheek and pierce my eyes on him. "Did you talk her up like you did me? Give her that irresistible smirk while you gave her a nickname? Get her all worked up just so you could spread her legs on your fucking pool table!"

The elastic snaps and splits my patience, pulling apart pieces of what held me together this past week. Everything I had bottled up inside just breaks—like carved glass on the floor. *I* break.

"Whoa. Easy there," he says softly, lifting his palms in the air to try to calm me down. "I wasn't gonna sleep with her."

"No? Because it felt like she was ready to drag you back there herself." Another frustrated tear slips from my lashes and lands with a splash against the back of my hand.

"Violet... no. No, I wouldn't do that to you." There's something in his eyes. A glint of emotion, a hint of regret, reflecting the grief floating in those flecks of onyx. His voice is wrecked, and I almost believe him. For a second, I do.

He wouldn't lie to you, one part of me whispers. The other part screams he would, so I believe the deceit instead of the gut feeling that's churning deep in my stomach.

"But you would," I whisper, defeated.

"No, I wouldn't!" He fights back, taking a step forward as he pleads for me to listen. "Just... Fuck. Just let me explain. Okay?"

"Why?" I throw my arms up, giving up the battle between us.

"Just, please," he grovels in front of me, almost drops to his knees with big brown puppy eyes that beg to be listened to. I can't say no to that, so I stay put and let him speak. "I know how it must have looked, but I can promise you it wasn't what you thought it was."

"What was it then?"

Carding a hand through his disheveled hair, he frowns. "Look, she showed up unannounced tonight. Her name's Chelsea. She works with the club, delivering and ordering alcohol." He catches his breath and continues. "Bryson said she was asking for me tonight, so I went, and then she wanted to get a drink, and I thought it'd be easier to let her down gently that way. I didn't want to be rude and—"

"Let her down?" I blink as thoughts scatter around my boggled brain.

"Yes, let her down," he confirms with a nod. "She's had a thing for me ever since she started working with us. And tonight she just sorta went for it, even though I never went there. And fuck, I know it must've looked bad to you," he says with defeat in his tone.

Twisting my lips together, I contemplate for a beat. "She was touching you, Sam. She was touching you like she... like she wanted to take you home." There's tears pooling in the back of my eyes, making the night air all foggy.

"I know," he sighs, "and I stopped her from continuing. I stopped her because I told her about you."

"You... what?" I mutter under my breath.

He stares at me with so much longing in those cinnamon eyes that it makes me want to reach for him, but I don't. I just stay put and let him explain. "I told her my heart belonged to you. Christ, I told her how crazy I am about you! And I'm sorry if it looked any different. But I promise you, it was nothing. She means *nothing* to me because... Well, because of you."

There's that silver string wading in the distance, pulling on heartstrings that don't want to beat. But I hear it—a melodic harp that floats through the air, all soothing and gentle. A soundtrack that plays back memories of me and Sam—all euphoric laughter and endless smiles. But the track scratches, skips once doubt seeps in and breaks the record in half, leaving me in pieces in the parking lot.

"Me?" I whisper, letting uncertainty rock me against the concrete.

She must be so fun. All filled with light and carefree thoughts, probably flawless with no cracks in her skin. No fracture in the ends. She's probably not breakable like me. Probably doesn't have piles of unhealed trauma weighing on her shoulders like I do. She's probably perfect while I'm just... not. Why would Sam pick me over her when I've already shown my true colors by shoving him away? By telling him to run, leave, and just slip away. And I let him, just like that. I'm the one that let him go...

Sam's insistence rings through my ears, tearing parts of my self-doubt away. "Yes, you. She's not you, Violet. Nobody else can replace *you*. You're just... you're unlike anyone I've ever met before. You're so..." He stares at me with tears licking at his waterline, brown flecks all starry and submersed in drifts of green—like he's waving a white flag in the distance, giving up his will to fight anymore. Like he's giving it all up for *me*. "Goddamn it, Violet. You're so fucking special. You've *always* been that to me, no matter what was said after dinner."

Feelings blow all around me, tangling through my hair, lacing through the ends of my dress, blurring those same lines again. My eyes sting, vision gets foggy as I stand there, just staring with my lips rubbing together, fighting words from spilling.

Say something, anything. But I don't. I just stand there, mute as an empty room, tugging at held-in words that threaten to slip at any moment.

"I went to your apartment last night," he says softer, easier.

I blink up at him, completely speechless. "What? When?"

Why would he do that?

He nods slowly. "A little after nine o'clock."

"I wasn't home..." My eyes drop to the ground, but he's right there in front of me, lifting my chin with the cup of his palm. I lean into the feel of him, letting his calluses soothe me over, allowing his careful touch to warm my insides from the bite of frost.

"I waited there, Violet. I waited over an hour, and I called you."

"My phone was dead. I didn't see the missed call..." I whisper out, barely there, holding on by a thin thread.

"I tried finding you, angel. Fuck, I tried." He brushes the back of his knuckles against a falling tear and wipes it away like it was never there in the first place. And it feels good, feels right against the cool air.

"You left..." I cry, stepping back out of his space, where I can't smell the earthy, ocean scent that drips off his clothes.

He shakes his head and squeezes his eyes shut like he's pushing past pain. "I didn't want to. I *never* wanted to leave in the first place."

But he did. He left because I pushed him away.

"I said goodbye…" I confess as I dig my fingers into the fabric of my dress, holding on to something that might ground me from the wave of emotions that's taking me down.

I said goodbye…

"But you came back." A small, sad smile curls across his plush lips. "Why did you come back, Violet?"

"I… just," I choke out. "You drove off. You—"

"I thought you wanted me to." There's a gleam of a tear in his eye that he won't let escape, a sting to his words that pricks my skin.

"No…"

"No?" He tilts his head, his expression all melancholy and pensive as he looks at me with a sliver of hope in the twinkle of his brown eyes.

"No," I repeat. "I didn't want you to go…"

Sam stares at me a beat, then he takes a step toward me, and another, until he's right in front of me. "What is it that you want?"

I freeze on the spot. "I, uhh—"

"*What* do you want?" he asks again, accentuating each word carefully.

The question taunts me, throws me off center. Words build in my throat, but they're all jumbled and distorted. I can't think straight. Not when his sandalwood scent crashes right through me. Not when his big chocolate eyes are staring straight through me like glass. Not when he's standing right in front of me, making me want to drop all pretense and jump straight into his arms and never let go. Not when he's looking at me like he could piece together every broken part of my unspoken past.

"I… I…" I can't get anything out. Not one single word.

For fuck's sake, just tell him what you want!

When I don't say anything, he shifts his weight and scrubs a hand over his mouth like he's losing patience. "I can see this isn't easy for you. But angel, if you don't tell me what you want, then I can't give you that." He takes a step forward, serenading me in whiffs of him—mahogany and licks of whiskey across his lips. "Now, do you want me to turn around and walk back in there, and—"

"No!" I shoot my hand out and halt him from retreating. It's a desperate cry for help.

Help me, Sam. Show me how to let go.

Just *let go.*

"No?" he asks with a raised brow as he catches the back of my hand. "So tell me. What is it that you want?" he repeats again, brushing the pad of his thumb against the back of my hand. "Is it me? Do you want *me?* Do you want more, *need* more? Because I can give you more, angel. I can give you *so* much more if only you'll let me…"

The slow strokes of his touch ease my thundering heart, but I'm still shaking, still speechless.

Teach me to let go.

"Sam, I…"

"Yes?" he asks as he steps into my space, breaking barriers with each blink of his brown eyes.

"I… I want…" I gulp, breathing in the scent of ocean tides, letting them drown me as I fist the front of his crimson shirt and hold on for dear life.

"Say it, angel. It's okay. Say what you want," he coaxes through that silky, smooth voice of his. His fingers move gently over the curve of my jaw and climb up until he's pushing a lock of my hair behind my ear, tenderly twisting around the smooth curl. It feels good, feels like he's tethering himself through the highlights the sun left across dark strands. Feels like he's touching me again for the first time. But this time, he leaves his heart in the palm of my hand and waits for me to take it.

Take it, Violet. It's yours. It's always been yours.

He's always been mine to take…

Looking up into the cinnamon flecks of his eyes, I see reflections of myself swirling in them. See promises of forever tied into the warmth of his smile. And for a moment, I remember how to use my voice. Remember a time I didn't have to bite my tongue and fear blood would spill on the carpet.

Sam's hand slips down my arm till he's brushing the back of his knuckles against my hand, nudging me to take the leap.

Jump, Violet. I'll catch you. That's what his soft brown eyes say as they crinkle at the edges, the crow's feet pulling till my heart skips a beat.

Taking a step forward into him, I sink, starting my descent into the swimming pool of Sam's heart as I latch on.

"I want y—" My confession is cut off by the loud slamming of the front double doors. I jump back and let my hand drop from Sam's shirt as pounding feet cut through the thick tension of October air.

Fuck. He was right there, eating from the palm of my hand. I was *right there*.

Cursing under my breath, I let my eyes fall to the concrete as car keys jingle from the slide of jeans, letting my lips purse until whoever interrupted me leaves the perimeter. But whoever it is goes stagnant and stalls to the right of me.

"Violet?"

I freeze on the spot. My blood runs cold, and time ceases to exist. That voice. That rugged, slurred, husky voice paralyzes me into place. I'd know that scratchy bass of vocal cords anywhere.

Jason...

When my eyes lift, they go wide, and the breath from my lungs gets knocked away. "Jason?"

"Well, well, well," he whistles out, low and long, dragging the snap of his teeth with a smirk. "I can't believe my fucking eyes."

He's just as I remember. Except he's different somehow, more monster than he is human. More lethal than before.

"What are you doing here..." My eyes flick over the new, fresh black ink that covers the entirety of his left arm. Sweat coats the back of my neck as I drink in the body of a man who almost ripped me apart.

Tall, he's so fucking tall—just over six foot three. He's still got long, shaggy blond hair that reaches the tips of his ears, with greasy strands that shade the yellow in his muddy green eyes. Eyes that could kill. Strong, bulky muscles line his shoulders and sunburnt arms. Arms that could snap a man in half. A gold chain glints around his neck, and worn hands that used to tear into my flesh flex into fists at his sides, almost like he's ready to snap at any second.

He doesn't answer my question, just glares my way with a wide smirk on his lips. "Miss me, buttercup?"

Buttercup. The nickname he branded upon me like a lash of glass. It burns, churns inside me like a thunderstorm, seeps into my skin like drops of blood. It makes me fucking sick.

This can't be happening. This *can't* be real. I'm going to blink, and he'll be gone. But blinking does nothing. It only drags along my conscience that this is very much real life, and he's corporeal enough to snap.

He *fucking* found me.

"I thought you were in jail..." I whisper quietly, just loud enough for him to hear as he stalks toward me with wide strides, scuffing his white Vans across the cement. Each footstep has my heart thundering.

He chuckles and opens his big mouth, sneering out, "They let me out on good behavior." Pieces of blond hair fall into his darkening eyes, making my stomach sick at the sight. He pushes them back and pierces me with an icy stare.

Sam stands a few feet back, watching the scene unfold with his eyes wide and mouth partially open. Confusion stirs in his eyes as he flicks back and forth between us, trying to unwind what's happening before him.

"You... you're not supposed to be here." I gulp nervously, taking a hesitant step back. He keeps advancing, keeps prowling my way with a fierce hunger in his murky eyes.

"Baby, I can be anywhere I want to be," he croons sickeningly. I can smell the strong alcohol blowing off his chapped lips, can see how wasted he already is by the way he sways and slurs.

I take a step back to get away from the beer sticking to his jeans, but he wraps his predatory fingers around my left wrist and tugs me hard toward him.

A deep gasp leaves my lips when he drags his rough skin across the outline of my scar, flaring phantom pain against my wrist. "I see you still have this old thing. Look at that. Nicely healed, a clean cut, but look at that scarring. Shit." His eyes flash bright green like he's admiring his own work of art, smirking deviously as he sinks his jagged nails into the past, pretending it's oozing with blood he can play with.

"Let go," I demand with a desperate attempt to pull free, but he only tugs me closer. Only conjures another whine from my lips.

"No. I don't want to let go, buttercup." He chuckles sinisterly as red carves out splotches of yellow in his eyes. "Think I'll keep a hold of you this time."

"Get off her!" Sam growls, pushing Jason away from his tight hold on me. His hand peels away from my skin, leaving behind crescent-shaped nail marks in my wrist. I gasp for air, covering the burn of my skin from the evening breeze.

Sam looks at me with concern laced through his gentle eyes. "Are you okay?" he asks as he looks at the way I hold the inside of my wrist. Like I'm wounded. I drop my fingers and reveal the faded scar. He stares, and his jaw clenches as realization sets in. "Did he... did he do that to you?" he whispers, brushing his fingers lightly over the numb area.

I clench my teeth together and nod, revealing the truth to him. Now he knows. It wasn't Shadow or me being clumsy; it was Jason who marked me permanently in red.

He stills before me, staring my way. Our eyes meet, blurring together in understanding. Now he knows I was only trying to protect him from Jason. I was just trying to save him from *this*.

"It wasn't Shadow. It was... him," I murmur out through chattering teeth. But Sam doesn't look mad. He looks like he just put together all the missing puzzle pieces.

Sam tries to reach out again to grasp me, but Jason shoves his way between us and glares at Sam. "Wait a goddamn minute. Is this who you've been fucking since I've been gone?" Shallow green eyes make their way to me.

"That's none of your concern," I seethe.

"Oh, I see." Jason throws back his head and laughs like a maniac. "You think you can replace me just like that? You don't think you still belong to *me*?" He grows possessive and angry as fire heats his gaze.

"She's not *yours*," Sam snaps back at him, stepping between us like a guard dog.

"That's hilarious. You're killing me here," Jason doubles over and bellows out.

"Wasn't supposed to be funny," Sam snarls.

Jason pushes Sam out of the way and snatches my wrist, pulling hard. "Come on, let's go."

"No, I said let go!" I scream in his face and push against his muscular chest, but that only makes him angrier. Sam yanks me back, and it's like I'm in between a game of tug of war. Whoever pulls tighter gets to have me, and Sam won't let Jason win.

"I'm only going to tell you this once. Turn around and leave before I call the cops." Sam flares his nostrils and shows his incisors as a warning, but Jason barely flinches.

"Who the fuck are you to tell me to leave?"

"I'm the owner of this club, asshole. And I don't take kindly to strangers threatening me or Violet."

Jason scoffs and points a finger at me. "She isn't *your* girl."

"And she isn't *yours*," Sam declares with a growl.

Tension lights through the air, creating rifts in both directions. I strain to keep a hold of gravity, praying to whoever will listen that this ends with no blood. But I know better. It *always* ends in blood when it comes to Jason, and this time won't be any different.

"You've been messing with her, haven't you?" Jason accuses, narrowing his eyes into thin slits. "I can practically smell her on you like a wet dog."

"Jason, leave him alone!" I step forward, cutting the rope free, but Jason always finds a way to cheat.

"No. I think I need to teach him a lesson. Something like don't fucking touch another man's property." He steps forward and fists the middle of Sam's crimson shirt like he's about to fight him.

No, no, no. This can't be happening. My nightmares were supposed to be that—*just* dreams. But I'm afraid this will only end how every scene in my nightmares concludes—with Sam's face smashed on the ground.

No, not Sam. Not my sweet Sam.

Sam slaps Jason's hand away and barks out, "She's not your property, you sick bastard. And she certainly isn't yours anymore."

Jason pushes the edge of his tongue into the side of his cheek and smirks. "Not mine, huh? We'll just see about that."

I try to intercept, try to stop the brawl from happening, but it's too late. I can't stop what's already begun.

It'll only end in blood...

Jason's jaw clenches, and his bloodshot eyes grow impatient. They circle each other, feeding the flames as they start their engines. And once I see that killer look in Jason's glare, I jump. "No... Jason, stop!" But it's too late; he doesn't hear me.

The next thing I see is Jason throwing his fist in the air. It comes down like lightning, ending in a crack once it meets Sam's cheek. I gasp in horror and cover my mouth when I hear just how hard Jason hit him.

"Sam!" My voice is drowned out by the pounding of flesh, the blur of punches flying through the air. I can't watch, but I'm stuck staring as my fight or flight instincts kick in.

Sam takes a second to recover, then he's moving fast. He shoves Jason up against the brick wall and throws a punch to his curved nose. The snapping of bones catches my attention, but that doesn't stop Jason. He's a killing machine, and he's out for Sam's blood.

He dodges Sam's advances and grabs a hold of the collar of his shirt, throwing him back against the hood of a black Mercedes and down to the ground. Sam shakes it off and runs toward Jason, tackling him back against the brick wall.

I can't stand this. Can't stomach watching them tear each other apart punch by punch. Flinching at each hit, I drown out the noise, make myself small as I cover my ears and breathe. I *just* want all the loud, violent sounds to stop.

Taking my hands down from my ears, I fix my posture and hold my tears in, knowing exactly what I have to do. I have to make it stop. They're fighting because of me, and I won't have any part in picking out a gravestone.

This is all my fault, and I have to fix it.

As Jason begins to throw another punch at Sam, I hold my breath and step between them and push Jason away as the back of Sam's head slams against the bricks with a crack. "Jason, I said *stop!*"

Before I know what's happening, Jason slaps me hard across the cheek. So hard that I see stars in my vision. And then he shoves me down against the ground, making the bottom of my blue dress tear across the seam. Dirt cakes my scraped kneecaps, pain flares like fire through the palms of my scratched hands, and my vision goes spotty.

"Violet!" I hear Sam scream my name through the fog as I cup my stinging cheek, wincing through the pain. There's a flash of Jason being thrown against brick in my peripheral vision, but I'm too far gone to do anything. Too light-headed to move.

I fade into the background, shutting the outside world out. All I can seem to focus on is the numbing ache across my skin. Fire never bothered me until I got burned in the end.

Squeezing my eyes shut, I try to flush the memories out, but they roll across my eyelids like a movie clip. And then, I remember *everything*. I remember it like it was just yesterday.

Rain pattered across the kitchen window. The apartment was still, quiet. But then the atmosphere changed, flicked like a light switch once he caught me off guard. The snap of his teeth, a broken bottle, alcohol smothering the cream carpet that quickly stained red. Three numbers were dialed on the cracked cell phone before he snapped it and draped his heavy body over me, smothering me in sharp glass as he sliced deep into my wrist. Shadow faded when he wrung his hands around my neck, injecting venom in my slowing body with the spew of drunken slurs. But then sirens wailed, uniformed officers kicked down the door and dragged him out in handcuffs.

That's all I really remember from that night. All that really sticks with me from when I passed out from blood loss and woke up in the hospital a day later.

Jason took everything from me and now, he's trying to take it all again, just like the night he tried killing me. But he can't have Sam, I won't let him.

With all the strength I can muster, I lift my heavy eyes and freeze the moment I see Jason's body looming over me, casting down a nasty glare through swampy green eyes.

He tsks and clicks his tongue as he fishes inside the pocket of his blue jeans. A piece of long silver glints under the moonlight and when he holds it up in the air, my eyes widen in horror when I realize just what it is—a pocketknife.

"I should've known you'd try to leave, buttercup," he hisses. "And I should've ended it there. But I guess now will have to do. Say goodbye to your little boyfriend, Violet."

The shine of the blade hovers high above his head as he positions himself over me, pointing the knife downward before he plunges it through my skin. I make myself small and cover my head, hiding myself in the ripped fabric of my dress.

This is it. He's finally going to end it, like it should've back in that suffocating apartment where I couldn't escape. I could fight back, kick my legs and shove him back, but there's no more fight left in me, no energy to extend. I might as well make it easy for him and let him carve through the scars on my wrist, let him finally tie an anchor around my ankle and submerge me underwater till I can't breathe.

He's already damaged me beyond repair, so what's one last slash that'll silence me for good? That's what he wants, so maybe he should just end it.

"Goodbye, Sam…" I whisper through chattering teeth, caving in on myself as Jason lunges at me with the knife.

Maybe in death I'll blow through the palm trees and slip through Sam's doorway, whisper *I love you* in the autumn breeze. Maybe then he'll know the words I never could say out loud.

"No, Violet!" Sam shouts through the blur of violence.

But before I can open my eyes, my world fades to black.

Chapter Thirty-Five

Sam

"Violet!" I scream through the night air as I lunge for Jason.

Not my girl. Not my sweet angel.

I move on autopilot, racing across the parking lot just as he's about to jab the knife through her back. Right before he attacks, I body slam into him and wrestle him to the ground. The knife waves through the air as Jason grabs a hold and aims it right at my chest, but I dodge the sharp edge.

Slapping his wrist away, the knife falls to the ground with a clatter. Jason kicks me in the gut and I double over, unable to fight from the gut-wrenching ache that's churning inside.

He catches me off guard and snatches up the knife while he's still on his back. Grabbing me by the collar, he holds me over him and turns the blade on me, determined to kill me, too.

"Hold still," he grinds through his teeth as I fight back, my hands pushing his wrists away from the sleeve of my button-up shirt.

I cough up saliva as he knees me in the groin, doing anything he can to make me drop my hands. But even through the excruciating pain, I still fight back. He ends up nicking the rolled-up cuff of my sleeve, almost draws blood across my forearm, but with every ounce of strength I have, I grab the knife from him and throw it far across the parking lot, where he won't be able to reach it.

He fists the top of my hair and slams me against the ground as he rolls on top of me. Pain flares in every inch of my body, but I can't stop fighting. He won't win this war; I won't let him.

Just as he's about to go for my throat, I twist his wrist till bones pop. "Fuck!" he yells, lunging again for anything he can grab. But to my avail, I'm able to dodge his advances while I kick him in the kneecap. I shove him to the ground and pin his shoulders as I straddle him, making sure he can't escape.

"Go ahead." He chuckles darkly, spitting blood in the air from the front tooth I knocked loose. "Break me like I broke her, and don't you fucking hold back." He glares at me, daring me to take the bait. And I will. Oh, I fucking will.

Ticking my jaw, I stare daggers into his bloodshot eyes, radiating the same hate I see swirling in that muddy green color.

He hurt Violet, almost killed her with the silver edge of the knife. And I can't let that slide. Can't turn my head and brush it off because he just messed with the wrong guy. He broke my girl, now I'm going to break his fucking face.

I growl through my teeth and snap as I raise my fist in the air. Without wasting another second, I swing.

"This." *Punch.* "Is." *Crack.* "For." *Smack.* "Violet." I let him have it, using my fists like they're punching gloves.

Jason sputters through a bloody cough and cackles. "You can do better than that, prick."

Taking all my anger out, I keep punching, keep bashing my knuckles into his face, even though they've gone numb. I can't stop, won't give up till he's knocked out entirely. I don't want to hear another snide remark from his slurred voice.

"This is for hurting *my* girl!" I bring my fist down once again, hearing the crack of his nose as blood spews against the concrete. He chokes for breath, still smirking and laughing through the pain like he's actually enjoying this. But I think I'm enjoying it more.

The way he talked about Violet has my blood boiling over. And the way he smacked her around has me ready to break both of his hands so he can never hurt my girl or any other woman ever again. How many has he abused mentally, emotionally, *and* physically? Probably more than Violet knows.

Now I know why Violet's always been so reserved, why she hid part of her past from me. She was terrified of *him*—the one who helped break her. If only I would've known then I would've done things differently. I would have been more careful with her, and I never would've driven away in the first place.

I punch through the pain, adding to his black eye and bloody mouth. But it's not enough. I'm not finished yet. Just when I'm about to go for his other half-closed eye, someone tugs me back, restraining me from hitting him again.

"Stop, Sammy. Enough!" Bryson barks through an inhale, out of breath from running over to us. "You got him. Now stop."

I suck in a breath, panting through the sweat of the fight, coming back down from the adrenaline rush. Snapping my teeth, I growl, "Get him out of here, Bryson."

"I already called the cops," he confirms, still kneeling at my side to make sure I don't lunge again. "You alright? Never seen you get in a fight like that before."

Huffing a breath out, I narrow my eyes at Jason's supine body in front of me as he doubles over in pain, cradling his bloody face like that'll give him a lick of relief.

"I'm fine, just got a little knocked around," I groan. "But he tried to hurt Violet. He tried to—" My mouth goes dry at the thought of Violet.

Fuck. I need to get to Violet.

Crawling over to her curled up body, I gently touch her arm, but she pulls away. "Violet, it's me," I say soothingly, hoping she'll look up.

Please, look up.

She stays curled in a ball, shaking, reluctant to do anything. It hurts to see her like this, hurts to know how much he did to her. All I want is to scoop her into my arms and tell her it'll all be okay, but it's not that simple. Not this time.

I try again, more delicate with my movements and words. "Hey, sweetheart. It's me, Sam. Can you look up for me?" Gently brushing my fingers under her chin, she slowly looks up from the ground. I almost break when I see tears spilling from her eyes and her red lips trembling. She looks so lost, so broken at the seams—like she just lost herself entirely.

"Sam?" she asks, hesitantly hooking her fingers around the ruined sleeve of my shirt.

"It's me, sweetheart. I'm here," I coo as my fingers cup the back of her head gently.

She takes a long look at me, examining the depths of my eyes and every square inch of my face. Her eyes grow large when she traces her fingers over the corner of the left side of my face, where I'm bound to be hurt. It stings where she brushes her palm over, but I barely flinch.

The light dies in her eyes when she whispers, "You're hurt…"

Catching her hand as it falls, I squeeze it and shake my head. "I'm okay, angel. I'm fine. Are you okay?"

Her bottom lip trembles as she shakes her head, spilling another tear that slides down her quickly bruising cheek. Brushing the pad of my thumb to catch it, her eyes dart to the side as the bouncers drag Jason toward the front door, securing his hands behind his back as he laughs through the pain.

Turning my head back to Violet, I see her lost in a faraway place—somewhere that I can't reach her. "Sweetheart, talk to me," I beg, my hands clasping her shoulders as I plead for her to look at me.

When she finally flicks her gaze up at me, her eyes swim with violent storms, and this time I can't pull her out of the hurricane. She throws her arms around my back and sinks into my chest, her tears soaking the fabric, sobs echoing through the night air.

"It's okay, baby. I've got you," I coo, wrapping my arms around her as I envelope her in warmth, desperate to give her a semblance of peace. "I've got you."

Twisting my head to the left, I wince at the whiplash and stare at Bryson as he slowly picks up the knife. He furrows his eyebrows and looks at me and then Violet, questions churning in his eyes. "Did he try to—"

I nod, cringing through the words. "He tried killing her..." Violet squeezes me as the words leave my lips, and I cup her head to my chest, holding her through the storm.

Bryson's mouth drops open as he looks down at the knife in his hand, then back up at me. "Is she okay?" There's so much concern swimming through his eyes, like he's just as shocked as I am.

Shaking my head, I rest my chin atop her head and hold her close, shielding her from the outside world. But it's not safe here. Not till he's locked up. Not till my girl's inside, where I can protect her from anymore harm. I won't rest till he's gone for good.

Looking back up, I murmur, "I need to get her out of here, Bryson. I need to take her home."

He rakes a hand through his blond locks and nods in agreement. "Yeah, that's a good idea. You go on, I'll take it from here."

Narrowing my eyes, I deadlock on the path Jason was dragged off to. "I want to press charges. *All* of them," I growl out through clenched teeth. "Think you can handle that?"

Bryson frowns and crosses his arms over his chest, nodding. "Fucker won't ever step foot in our club again," he promises with cold eyes. "I'll turn the video footage in, but I'm sure they'll want to talk to you as well."

My jaw tics and I nod. "They can call me. I'll happily go down to the station. Whatever gets him tried with attempted murder."

Violet hugs me closer and hides her face in the crook of my arm, signaling it's time for me to leave. Bryson gets the hint and says goodbye. "Go on. I've got it.

Just get her home safe." He paces back to the front of the club to clean up the mess of this horrible night.

Flicking my eyes down to Violet, I try to stir her to look up. "Sweetheart, hey. We need to get you up. Do you think you can get up?" Not a sound comes out of her. She just hugs me like a koala, unwilling to let go. I try to pry her from my body, but she doesn't move, she just sticks like glue.

Letting out a long sigh, I run a hand gently down her back and whisper, "Alright, come on. Up you go." Stooping down, I pick her up and cradle her against my body, resistant to drop her. I'd never let her hit the ground.

Snatching the keys of the truck from my pocket, I unlock it and pry open the passenger door, carefully setting Violet down in the leather seat. She's reluctant to let go of me, but she finally releases her tight grip when I ease her to let go.

"I'm gonna take you home with me, baby. Gonna take care of you," I whisper against the top of her head as my lips brush against her soft hair. She doesn't say anything, just lets me buckle her seatbelt into place. Before I shut the door, I linger my fingers over the top of her hand, wishing I could quell the flashbacks that must be flying through her head.

Give me your pain. Show me your scars and I'll kiss them away till they're replaced with something good.

I *just* want my girl to be okay because right now, she's far from it.

When I climb into the driver's seat and start the engine, I put my foot to the gas and drive far, far away from the club, leaving the sparkles of red to blur in the rear-view mirror.

Dragging a palm over my mouth, I flinch through the pain, ignoring the burn of my swollen knuckles. Black and purple colors bruise the back of my hand, but it's not broken. I can still move it, which is good. And my face feels intact, aside from the dots of blood lining my left eyebrow and the growing migraine, I'm fine. It could've been much worse. But I'd gladly beat Jason into the ground another dozen times till he's ten-feet deep underground. He deserves nothing less after what he did to my sweet girl.

Speaking of Violet, when I'm stopped at a red light, I look over to check on her. My throat tightens when I see her curled against the side of the door, her knees tucked to her chest, the blue material torn at the bottom, her body trembling beneath the weight. And the tears don't stop; they just keep running like a waterfall as she gets lost in her head.

My left hand grips the steering wheel tight while my right arm reaches for her, but I stop right before my fingers graze her dark material, not wanting to alarm her. Tipping my head back, I blow out a breath and let my eyes stray back to the empty road ahead. Comforting her is all I want to do, but I'm not quite sure how to manage that without setting her off, so I whisper soothing words through the front of the truck and hope that's enough for now. "We're almost there, angel. Not much longer. I'll get you somewhere safe."

Violet whimpers like a wounded puppy and folds in on herself, but she lets her left arm slide down, just enough for me to brush the side of my hand against. That tells me enough—that she hears me, even if she's not all the way there right now. She knows I'm here, and I'm not going anywhere ever again. And when I get home, I'm doing nothing but holding her all night long, if that's what she needs.

For her, I'd do just about anything to make her smile again, to see the light of those blue eyes pull me under her waves. For Violet, I'd cross entire oceans.

"Almost there, baby. Just hold on…"

CHAPTER THIRTY-SIX

VIOLET

I numbly return to reality once the truck's parked and the engine's cut. Outside floodlights illuminate the edge of a tan garage, cut grass lines, the paved driveway, and the moonlight slipping across a curved palm tree against a house I've never seen before.

This is Sam's house. I'm at Sam's.

I'm barely coherent through the soft brush of Sam's voice slipping through my ears, but I don't make a sound, can't manage to scrounge up the tiniest voice at the moment. I just let him unbuckle my seatbelt and pull me into his arms, lifting me out of the truck and up the winding path to his front door.

Sinking my weight into him, I curl my fingers around his silky shirt and breathe him in like that's what's keeping me afloat. Earthy tones, fresh soap, sandalwood that lingers against the scattered silver in his scruff. I drink him in, let him soak me in safety and comfort, crash against him till I'm tucked against his side. He wraps me up like a knight in shining armor would, but that's exactly what he is, what he's always been.

Sam saved my life tonight, and I don't think I'll ever be able to show him how much that meant to me. Even though I stumbled the past week, almost going over the edge of the cliff, he *still* decided I was worth it. And I really don't understand why. I'm the reason he fell...

Squeezing my eyes shut, I block out the echoes of punches and drunken slurs, trying my best to forget the way Jason grabbed my wrist and jammed the edge of his thumb into my scar. It still burns like he held my hand against the hot oven.

Flinching at the swing of the front door, I bury myself in his chest as he whispers soft words into the shell of my ear, promising me it's going to be alright.

It's okay, sweetheart. You're safe now. I've got you. I'm not going to leave you.

I lock those promises inside my chest, hold on to them like they might blow away in the San Diego breeze. If there's one I hope he keeps, it's that he's not going to leave.

Don't let go. Never let go.

Even though my eyes are squeezed shut, I still feel the warmth of the house as his footsteps creak up a staircase. Feel how safe and comfortable it must be. If Sam's here, then I know I must be safe.

When I hear a door being swung open, I hesitantly sneak a peek once he flips the light switch on. Muted gray carpet lines the flooring. A large window overlooking the backyard sits in the middle of the back wall, with earthy curtains draped over the sides that remind me of sand. A king-sized bed sits in front of that, layered in a navy-blue comforter and fluffy white pillows lining the top. The walls are cream-colored, covered in San Diego art and old rock and roll bands that have played down at The Rady Shell. That's all I can take in, all I seem to be able to register at the moment, but something tugs in my chest because this room is very... Sam.

Gently, Sam unlatches me from his body and sits me down on the edge of the bed. The back of my thighs brush the feel of the soft comforter as I twist my fingers into it, fastening myself to the bed while numbness seeps back in.

When I unwind my fingers from the comforter, I tug at the ends of my torn dress, wanting to rip it clear off my body so I can just breathe. The room feels humid, too sticky for the ripped material. But I'm also as cold as ice, shaking from the chill of Jason attacking Sam. I just need to get out of this dress, need to free myself from the confines of Jason's hands still tugging at my wrists.

I pull and fuss with the itchy fabric, but I can't seem to make my hands work fast enough. It's useless. *I'm useless.*

Almost tearing the entire skirt apart from fidgeting, my breath falters when a gentle hand lands on top of mine, stilling me from panic that rolls through my body. Slowly looking up, I see Sam holding out a long-sleeved flannel—one that's dark brown and looks soft as velvet. One I'd slip so easily into.

"Here, let me help you." His voice is so gentle, eyes a million flecks of painted brown shades. It's so easy to say yes to him. My lips pull firm as I nod, allowing him to help.

"Okay."

Carefully, Sam tugs the zipper down my back, prying the suffocating material away from the heat of my skin. He ever so slowly drags the blue material down my body and over my feet, and then he unclasps each buckle of my black heels and tugs them free as my feet hit the plush gray carpet.

Fiddling with my bottom lip, I watch him slide my arms through the sleeves of the dark flannel and meticulously thread each button through the loops. The soft material falls against my knees, warms the chill down my spine. It smells just like him: clouds of sandalwood and shapes of comfort that swallow me inside the flannel material.

His calloused fingers skim across my knee like waves of water, and the way he's looking up at me with those doe brown eyes makes me want to cry. But also, I wish he'd stay like this all night.

Pushing himself off the floor with a grunt, he says, "Be back in just a second." Then he's padding off in the direction of his bathroom and throwing on bright lights. I hear spurts of water from the sink come to life next.

Drip. Drip. Drip. The crash of the water against the sink makes my heart slow, makes me rethink what all went down tonight, makes me cringe a little more.

Jason's murky, bloodshot eyes cast shadows in my mind. His husky voice slurs curses. The feel of glass brushes the back of my neck, almost embedding itself down my spine.

Twisting my fingers against the flannel, I latch on until crescent-shaped moons mark my thighs. Squeezing my eyes shut, I count to ten to block out the noise and focus on deep breaths, meditating on something good, something healing—like Sam. But Jason's still there, just like the ghost of him that still lingers in the back of my mind.

When I open my eyes back up, Sam's kneeling in front of me with a damp washcloth in his hand. The chocolate flecks in his eyes sparkle and pop as concern lathers them into gentle ocean waves, soothing me from the ghosts that whisper through the air.

Gently, he lifts his arm and brushes a strand of hair behind my ear before the warm washcloth meets the right side of my cheek. Wincing from the sting of Jason's slap, I swallow a cry and allow him to continue the slow motions.

He's so careful with me. Brown eyes flicking every few seconds to assess my face. Making sure I'm okay and that I won't slip like sand into the cracks. That's what I would be doing if it wasn't for Sam taking care of me. I'd just fade into black.

"Is it bad?" I ask as he swipes the damp washcloth over my skin, cooling the burn of the hit.

"Not really." He brushes the pad of his thumb across my skin and looks me right in the eyes. I swallow on the spot. "It's just a little bruised and irritated. Shouldn't last longer than a couple days."

I nod silently and let him continue the slow ministrations of his wrist, working the cotton material hesitantly over my skin. My eyes fall on the colorful bruise that paints the side of his left eye purple and shades of red. And right above that is droplets of blood from a small scrape across the edge of his eyebrow.

Quietly, I pry his fingers from the washcloth and take his place, tenderly rubbing the blood from his face. A deep wrinkle forms above his nose, but he doesn't recoil, just stays put against my legs.

"Does it hurt?" I whisper out, my voice garbled in guilt.

This is all my fault. I'm the reason he's hurt...

Sam's fingers lightly brush against my knee, soothing the ache in my chest.

Your fault. Your fault. Your fault.

Flashing me a sideways smile, he shakes his head. "It's not so bad. Hardly feel a thing."

I frown when I look down and see the top of his right hand. The tan skin's all speckled in black and purple bruising, his knuckles swollen from the hits he gave for me.

Wavering for just a beat, I slide my fingertips across the sea of purple, whisking through the injuries he so unabashedly took for me. That same guilt I felt singe me the night of the diner returns with fire, and it's about to burn me out.

My vision begins to blur as I trace over each swell of his knuckles, slipping over the peaks of each crevice of skin like I'm able to take his bruises and tuck them away into my scar as my own. Vibrations hum through my body, causing me to start shaking.

Your fault. Your fault. Your fault.

Sam's brown eyes widen the second he picks up on the shift of my energy. His big hand's squeezing around my thigh, desperate to get through my bricked walls. "Hey, hey, hey. What's wrong? Did I hurt you?"

Twisting my lips together in a tight line, I blink away tears and shake my head. "No. No, you didn't. I just—"

"Talk to me," he says with urgency, his eyes swarming me for answers.

A single teardrop falls onto the back of his hand, covering the dark bruises with a splash of salty water. It just brings everything together, the whole picture of why we're in this situation in the first place. It's because of *me.* "You got hurt,"

I whisper, afraid to bring it all to light. "You're hurt because of me. This is all my fault."

"No." He cups each side of my face with his warm fingers, staring at me with those brown eyes that reflect implicit need. "Don't you dare for one second think that any of this is your fault."

My eyes fog over as I let the tears rain down, releasing copious amounts of grief I've held onto for the past few years. There's nothing chaining me down anymore, nothing holding me back from crashing against the building glass inside me. It finally breaks, gallons of salty water soaking the carpet, and with it, so do I.

"Then *why* do I feel like it is?" Dropping my head, I let the tears fall like sprinkling rain, soaking the fabric of Sam's flannel shirt.

"Oh, sweetheart. No. Come here." Sam kicks off his shoes and crawls onto the bed, scooping me into his strong arms. He lands on his back and brings the warm comforter over me, smothering the chill of the night away.

Burrowing my face against his chest, I sob into the silk of his shirt. "I'm sorry."

"Shh. It's alright. I've got you," he coos, soothing me over with his thick fingers stroking the back of my hair lightly, easing me of the tension I hold in my shoulders.

"But I... He... You..." I blubber out nonsensical words, my teeth chattering through each syllable.

"Easy now. Easy," he whispers, pulling me closer against him. I nuzzle my face into the crook of his neck, where it's warm and smells of summer days.

I breathe him in, grasping on to the scent of salt water, sinking as deep as I can against his broad chest. My fingers curl possessively against the material, clawing for a balance against the rolling waves. I find a semblance of stability against the steady beat of his heart pulsing through my ear. Sam's the anchor I needed long ago, and right now, he's the only thing keeping me from drifting.

The slow, meticulous circles he drags across my back ease me into a blissful state. His deep, gravelly voice whispering sweet nothings into my ear makes me float off into big, billowing clouds. And then I succumb to the sleep I desperately need, eyelids fluttering shut as darkness takes me under.

I'm safe, wrapped in Sam's arms, and I have no intention of letting go this time.

"You're safe now. Safe here with me." That's the last thing I hear before I drift off into a dreamless state.

The sounds of chirping birds and the light breeze tapping against the window stir me from sleep. A yawn falls from my lips as my eyes slowly peel open to sunlight filtering in through the glass. Deep, slow breaths roll off Sam's chest like ocean waves, and his sandalwood scent sticks to me like his warm flannel wrapped around my body.

Slowly, I blink up and see warm brown eyes sprinkled with sunlight looking down at me, and my heart stops. He's even more beautiful in the morning. All sleepy-eyed with a lopsided smile and tousled sandy-brown hair that I could easily slide my fingers through. He's a reflection of everything that makes me warm and fuzzy, and he makes my head dizzy.

The sound of his sleep-ridden, gravelly voice does nothing good for my racing heart. "Hi." He curls a lock of hair behind my ear gently and lingers his calloused palm against my jawline, warming my skin like sunlight.

"Hi," I repeat, fixated on the way his eyes pop like embers.

"You sleep okay?" he asks, his fingers slowly dancing up and down my arm, creating ripples of warmth with each graze.

"Mhm," I hum with content. "Did you?"

He hitches my leg over his thigh and gently scrapes his nails across my bare skin, smiling like an idiot when he drawls, "Best sleep I've gotten in a long time."

The way he's looking at me, like I'm made of stardust, makes me fall harder, makes me reach up to glide my fingers against the silvery-brown scruff along the side of his face. This feels good, *right*. It feels like I was always meant to end up here with him. Jason never made me feel like Sam does—like a butterfly who got to spread her glittery wings over the sea for the first time in her life. He makes me feel so beautiful and safe, and I don't think I want to fly away now.

"What time is it?" I ask, snuggling deeper against his side while he continues the slow strokes over my skin.

He tilts his wrist up and looks at the glint of silver flashing across his watch. "A little past ten."

"Jesus. I still feel like I could sleep another ten hours," I say through a yawn while rubbing sleep from my eyes. "But wait," I lean my head back and look up at him, "I'm not keeping you from anything, am I?"

"Nah," he chuckles out. "Nothing on the schedule today, and Kayla's staying the weekend with her friend from soccer, so the only plans I have is spending the day with you."

"With me?" I ask, tilting my head to the side.

"With you," he confirms with a nod.

Something stirs inside me—like lapping waves on the shoreline. I feel funny, a little lightheaded, but it's not because I'm scared. Sam just makes me feel everything all at once, and I don't think I'll ever get used to that.

All of a sudden, there's a pitter-pattering noise tapping down the hall, and then the door nudges open partway. Knitting my brows together, I tip my chin up to see what the sound is coming from. But in the next second, a big black and white tuxedo cat jumps up onto the edge of the bed and sits there, staring straight at me with the biggest green eyes I've ever seen.

I open my mouth, but nothing comes out. This cat silhouettes Shadow entirely with its big, fuzzy paws kneading into the navy comforter, the swipe of its long-haired black tail, and the way the purrs echo off the bedroom walls.

"You got a cat?" I ask, almost speechless as I watch this beautiful cat curl up into a little ball by Sam's feet, completely content in his presence.

"I got a cat," he murmurs against the crown of my head.

"When?" He never told me he was thinking about adopting one. Except there was that one moment, when he was slow dancing with me. A moment he teased me with that playful smirk of his, saying how I was trying to persuade him.

"A few days ago," he answers as he makes circular motions into the side of my thigh with the pad of his thumb, gently soothing me from the shock of a cat that brings up memories of my Shadow. "Her name's Whiskers. Got her from the shelter up the coast."

"Whiskers..." I whisper, still staring in awe at her glittering green eyes. "What made you—"

He smiles down at me and slows the motions of his hand on my thigh. "Well, some pretty girl with blue eyes might've persuaded me."

I roll my eyes playfully and giggle. "She sounds like a lot of trouble."

"Not more than I can handle." He tugs on a lopsided grin and plays with the end of my hair, curling a highlighted strand around his index finger.

Throwing my shields down, I gaze up at him and soften my eyes. "Why'd you do it, Sam? Really."

He shrugs nonchalantly while he plays absentmindedly with the collar of the soft flannel I'm wearing, like he's somersaulting with the question. "I gave it some thought since Kayla's been asking me. But also, I, umm..." He pauses a beat and clears his throat while he looks down at me with warm, brown eyes. "I did it for you, too. You know, since you said you lost your cat. And well, I thought maybe you'd come back, so I got her... for you."

Parting my lips, I stare at him, speechless, completely knocked off balance that the thought of me came to his mind, even when I wasn't around. "Sam, that's... You really did that for me?" I blink up at him, swallowing words that I almost let slip.

I love you.

God, I'm so in love with this man.

He nods, smiling down at me as bright light bathes him in angelic waves. "I did, angel. I'd do anything to make you smile."

I blink up at him as tears gather and splash in my eyes. Emotions roll off my fingertips, creating sparks of lightning each time his tan skin grazes mine. I let the tears bleed down my cheeks, crimson stains mixed with leaking mascara, but he wipes them all away with every stroke of his thumb, taking my grief right out of the palm of my hand.

"You still want me? Even after I—"

He catches another tear from falling, and his glistening eyes dive inside mine as he says, "I never stopped wanting you, Violet."

I swallow, batting my eyelashes his way, both perplexed and enamored. This man. This incredible, extraordinary man. *My* man. He never ceases to take my breath away.

"You wanna go take a bath? Could make some breakfast after and then laze around the house. Whatever you want," he drawls, all sleep-coated and starry-eyed.

Smiling, I sigh happily. "Sounds perfect."

"Come on then, pretty girl." He scoots out of the bed, careful not to disturb the now sleeping Whiskers, and tugs me up with him. With my hand in his, he leads me across soft carpet and into the master bathroom as he flicks on the fluorescent lights.

It's all spacious, white tile flooring that seems to glitter. A massive double sink vanity sits to the left, with white marble counters and navy-blue painted cabinets. The lavish mirror with gold trim reflects sunlight through the window next to the acrylic jetted bathtub, covered in white bottles of soap and shampoo next to some folded towels. I flick my eyes back and forth, taking in the neutral toned wallpaper where framed photos of ocean waves and sandy beaches hang across.

This feels like Sam, even smells like his sandalwood-scented soap. All painted in blue and neutral brown tones. This all screams *him*, and I love it. I think I love everything about him.

I work the buttons of the flannel through the loops, watching him fill the bathtub with hot water and scented soap. The bubbles quickly emerge, popping and blowing across the top of the clear water like clouds. When that's all done, he helps me slip out of his flannel, leaving me bare once I shimmy out of my strapless bra and panties. He's right behind me, throwing off his clothes until he's completely bare in front of me—all thick muscles and tan skin.

"In you go, angel," he says. Taking my hand, he guides me into the tub. The bubbles sway and shift as we cut through the water. Sam settles behind me as he pulls me against his broad chest, his thick arms enveloping me like a warm blanket.

He hums into the shell of my ear, caressing his lips against my jawline, slowly dragging the soft washcloth scented with fresh soap up and down my arms in soothing motions. I lean into his body, groaning each time he brushes his mouth against my sensitive skin as he washes the memory of yesterday off.

After he's done, I take the washcloth from his hand and lather it with more soap from the bottle on the edge of the tub. Taking my time, I work it along the cords of his muscles, cleaning all the dirt from last night down the drain. I give his face special attention, drawing smooth lines over the bruised skin by his left eye, carefully attending to the wounds he took in my place.

He watches me closely, big doe eyes staring at me like I'm the prettiest thing he's ever seen. But I know I must look like a hot mess. My curls tangled and wet at the ends, eyes watery, lips half stained with slept-in red lipstick. But here he is, still gazing at me all starry-eyed like I'm the one he's been waiting for all along.

Have you been waiting for me, Sam? Like I've been waiting for you?

With one last swipe of the washcloth to his skin, he picks me up gently and cradles me over his lap, my legs splayed over his submerged thighs. His fingertips gently skate down the length of my arm and end at my wrist, pausing where the edge of the scar begins. It feels like fire when he hovers against the marked area that still feels fresh, makes me flinch when the tip of his thumb brushes cautiously over the jagged length.

"You wanna talk about it?" Sam asks quietly, like I'll break if he speaks too loud or presses too hard on the bruise of the past.

Rolling my bottom lip between my teeth, I sigh. "Not really." But when I flick my gaze up and stare into those concerned brown eyes of his, they draw me in like a moth to a flame, enough for me to swallow back fears and push myself to speak. I *have* to tell him. "But I want to tell you. I've wanted to tell you for a while now. I just didn't know how. So let me try?"

He smiles down at me warmly, encouraging me to be brave. "Take your time, sweetheart. There's no rush. Just whatever you're comfortable with. I'm listening."

A shy, sideways smile curls across my lips as I look up at him, grateful for how patient he is. I slide my hand into his and hold on for support. This isn't going to be easy, but I'll be okay. Sam's here, and he deserves the truth—all of it.

Taking one last breath, I finally release what I've been holding in for so long, setting it free to fly high in the sky. "Jason was my ex-boyfriend, and we've been split up for about three years now. He was still supposed to be in jail. He wasn't..." I hesitate, shaking my head from the sting. "He wasn't supposed to be anywhere near me or a bar, but he did. He broke his restraining order, anyway."

He tenses his jaw and sits up a little straighter. "Why was he in jail?"

Drip. Drip. Drip. The droplets of water trickle from the faucet, so loud that it almost drowns the past screams from my ears.

I slide my tongue across my teeth and tense when I whisper, "He tried to kill me..."

Sam's lips part, and his eyes widen in horror. "That's what this is from? He tried to—"

Nodding, I confirm his worst fears into existence. "Yeah. He made sure I'd never forget him."

Taking the edge of my thumb, I slide across the wet scar that's still tinged in red, even though it's been fully healed for two years. I still see splotches of red coating my delicate skin. Still see his face flickering through my mind each time I stare a little too long at something that never should've happened in the first place.

"Oh, angel. I'm so sorry," Sam whispers, placing a comforting hand on my back as he rubs light circles into my skin. "How long were you two together?"

"Two and a half years too long," I spit out, ashamed I stayed that long when I should've left the first time he screamed in my face.

"Was he always abusive?" He treads on thin ice, careful not to break me, hesitant to finish the last word of his question.

"No." I shake my head slowly and look down into the popping bubbles, pretending I'm floating through unscathed, like Jason can't touch me again. "About halfway through is when it started getting bad. He was in the military, and he started going out with his buddies to the bar multiple times a week. And he ended up just picking up a bad habit of drinking."

Silently, I swish my fingers through the water, concentrating on not falling apart, but the slow motions of his knuckles against my skin keep me from drowning.

"He started getting mean when he drank. Like throwing stuff or kicking over flower pots when he got heated about something. But then it was *me* he started taking his aggression out on. Pulling my hair, getting in my face, pushing me up against the wall..." I feel the prick of tears line the back of my eyes before they begin to fall in the tub full of bubbles.

Sam's fingers curl against the side of my ribcage as he tugs me closer, like he's trying to soften the blow for me. He's so *good*. "Angel..." he murmurs against the crown of my head, his voice like silk coating my insides. He's really the only reason I'm able to hold myself together right now.

I lean against his warm chest and breathe in the smell of fresh soap and *him*. "I wanted to leave so many times, but he'd just suck me right back in, promising he'd change, swearing he'd stop drinking. But he never did. He just kept *going*."

"Did you try to leave? Is that how he—" His eyes flick to my wrist as his voice drops off.

Swallowing back a sob, I nod. "When he was in his room, on the phone, I tried to slip out with Shadow. I was halfway out until he pulled me back in and slammed the door closed. I tried to lie, but he called me out and caught me in the middle of it. And then he ripped Shadow out of my arms and threw me down on the carpet."

Shutting my eyes to the sting of memories, I flex my fingers and squeeze until I feel the edge of my nails biting my flesh. I have to keep going. Have to tell Sam exactly what happened.

"Jason went on a rampage after that. He knocked over the sofa, shattered the coffee table into pieces. There was so much glass and noise and chaos... And then, he pinned me against the carpet and broke a beer bottle in half, started lashing out at me like I was the problem. I tried calling for help, but no one heard me. And when I grabbed for my phone and dialed 911, he smashed the phone and wrapped a hand around my throat so I couldn't scream. I couldn't make a sound when he slashed my left wrist open with the broken beer bottle. Couldn't even blink when everything started going dark..."

The bathroom's shrouded in silence now. Not even the drip of the faucet or bubbles dare to pop. It's just me and Sam together, the side of my face pressed deep into his chest, his arms curling me closer into his body like a thick blanket. I see the way he's looking down at me, even through my peripheral vision. He's got this horror-struck gaze stamped across his brown eyes, like he just saw a ghost float atop the water. But I guess I am a ghost. One who's still haunted from my past with someone who never truly loved me.

"Jesus fucking Christ," he murmurs, shock coating his deep voice. "He did that to you?"

"Mhm," I whimper out as another tear slips down my cheek. "I vaguely remember the drown of the sirens and the police that knocked down the apartment door. How I faded in and out in the back of the ambulance and didn't wake up till they had me all bandaged up and hooked up to some IVs. And I remember screaming for Shadow because I thought... I thought Jason got him, too, but they ended up saving him, just like they saved me from dying. I was two minutes away from bleeding out. Two fucking minutes..."

"Oh my God. That's... that's traumatizing. Baby, I'm so, so fucking sorry you had to go through that." Sam wraps his strong arms around me and cups the back of my head, pressing me into him until I feel nothing but warmth and comfort enveloping me. I don't hesitate to sink into him so I can let the tears pour, so he can see me in all my shades of fucked up.

My teeth chatter as I open my mouth, but I mumble my way through shaky tears, even if it's hard to speak. Sam's got to know why I'm so broken. He has to know why I am the way I am. "He always said I was hard to love, that no one else could but him. But he made me feel so worthless every time he said I was nothing special. That I was just... baggage. And I guess that's why I'm the way that I am, because of *him*." Sucking in another breath, I blow it out and keep going. "He never listened to me, so putting my feelings out there for anyone has been hard. *This* has been hard because I haven't been able to say what I want. And maybe he was right. Maybe I am hard to love."

Sam lifts my chin with two fingers and runs the pad of his thumb under my eye, catching a big tear from falling. "Oh, no, no, no. Don't you believe him for one second, sweetheart. You're beautiful and you're strong and you're definitely not hard to love. You're worth it all."

You're worth it all. Those words, the meaning behind them. It makes my eyes gloss over, makes my heart skip a beat when I stare into his big brown eyes.

"Thank you for making me feel safe and... wanted," I say in awe, my eyes never leaving his.

"Always." He smiles as he runs his thick fingers through the back of my hair. "Thank you for trusting me with that information. I know that wasn't easy for you telling me all that, but I promise it's safe with me. *You're* safe with me. And you know what else?"

"What?" I ask, mesmerized by the cosmic waves flashing through his eyes.

His fingertips brush across my cheek, and he sends me a side smile that could make me melt. "You're the bravest woman I know."

Brave. He thinks I'm brave. I choke back a sob. "You really think so?"

"Mhm. I do, angel. I really do." His voice is so warm, almost like a brassy baritone sound that glides through my ears, like I could listen to it forever.

I melt into him all over, my eyes glistening up at him as I swallow my tongue and force more explanations out. "I'm sorry I couldn't say how I truly felt about you at the diner. I just... I got scared. My body shut down, and I couldn't—"

"Hey. It's okay," he coos into the shell of my ear, sending a wave of relief down my body. "Please don't apologize. I understand you now. I understand why you did it."

"I wanted to protect you, but I couldn't do that, either. I just ended up hurting you, too," I mumble, letting my eyes drop back down to the bubbles surrounding us, but he lifts my chin and stares softly at me.

"Baby, it's okay. Trust me, I'm okay. And so are you. That's all that matters. I'm okay because you're here now. You came back." He chuckles a sigh of relief, like he's afraid he might've lost me for good.

Twisting my bottom lip between my teeth, I blink up at him, ready to say how I truly feel about him. "Sam, can I tell you something?"

"Anything." He nods as a lock of hair falls against his forehead. Carefully, I push it back in place and get lost in the flecks of green hidden behind shades of caramel.

I drag my fingertips across the path of silver in his scruff, tracing lines that look a lot like hearts against the corner of his lips. And it's funny—this fuzzy, static feeling inside my chest. Like zaps of electricity flowing through the water.

"The truth is, I've wanted you this entire time. From the moment I met you, actually. Since you quoted Jane Austen to me. I just... I felt a spark. But even though I was scared and unsure about everything, you were never really a question in the back of my mind. Not really. I was just terrified to bring those feelings to life."

"Oh, sweetheart." His glittering brown eyes delve into mine, and it's written all over them, starry flecks that say he wants me, too. "I've wanted you since the moment I saw you looking at me with those pretty blue eyes of yours. I've wanted you from the second you first smiled at me and told me all the things you hated about my club."

I stifle out a giggle and blink back tears. "Like the lack of pink signs and the absence of a food menu?"

"Pink signs and all," he confirms as he pushes back a piece of hair behind my ear, knuckles falling softly across my jawline.

The bubbles shift all around us when I lace my fingers through his tousled locks, memorizing flecks of onyx and green like they're my favorite shades of color. This man—this extremely sweet, kind, and handsome man—wants me. He *really* wants *me*. And for the first time in my life, I know what it should feel like to be cared for, to be wanted, to be... loved? At least that's what it feels like. The slow, sensual way he says my name. The longing gazes he steals that make me feel like I'm back in high school with a giant crush. The way he takes care of me, listens to me, makes me feel safe.

Love. It's what I'm feeling blooming inside my chest, like a rose garden that just won't stop spreading. I love this man, and I just really want to kiss him because he's looking at me all doe-eyed, like I'm the only girl in the world he wants to look at. And that's it. The rest is history. I'm finished, done, smitten.

I *really* love this man.

Blinking up at him, I slide my hand down his face and brush the edge of my thumb across the side of his scruff. "I'm a little broken, but if you can deal with a few missing pieces, then I'm all yours."

He smiles, and tears lick at the edges of his eyes. "Angel, I'm not exactly whole, either. Got a bunch of chips and cracks in this old coffee cup of mine, but somehow, you glue the pieces back perfectly."

Sam plays with the end of a curl, wrapping his fingers absentmindedly through my hair as he smiles. I can't help but to lean in closer, just so I can see the stars swimming through his glossy eyes.

"And you'll be patient with me?" I ask, pushing another fallen lock away from his forehead.

He grabs my hand and brings it down to the water, so he can intertwine his fingers through mine. "I'll be so patient. I'd wait forever for you if I had to."

"And you still want me?" I inquire, even though I know the answer. I just want to hear him say it out loud again for me.

He brushes the pad of his thumb across the back of my hand and flashes me a breathtaking smile. "I want you every minute, every second, and every breath of every day. I *always* want you."

That's enough confirmation for me to know this is real. *All* this is real. He's mine, and I'm his now.

"Then I'm all yours," I smile, incandescent and overflowing with happiness.

The next second, it's like the world stops spinning on its axis the moment I reach up and slide along his chiseled jaw as I push up higher onto his lap, my forehead connecting with his as I lean into him.

Sam breathes me in deep and hooks one arm around my lower back, his other hand cupping my chin, letting the tip of his thumb graze along my lower lip. He lets it sit there, memorizing every crevice, every line that connects my lips, and it's like a fire singes right through my body. Like no one has ever touched me before. Not like this. Not like he's mapping out every single trace of my soul, reaching and stroking places that have never been touched before. He touches me like I'm art, like I'm his masterpiece that he'll never break.

I see it so clearly now, like he's the ship offshore that threw the lifeboat out before I drowned in the middle of the sea. He's the light that was always meant to find me. He's the one I was always meant to fall for, and now I'm free-falling.

This is it. *He's* it. Sam Brooks is *the* one.

"Do you know what one of my favorite things about you is, angel?" he whispers in a deep, gravelly tone, shaking my very core as he continues to explore the lines of my lips.

"What?" My voice is scratchy, and I almost don't recognize it. I'm just very aware of how close his lips are and how intimate this moment is in the bathtub, on his lap while he tells me how much he wants me. And it's so much. So very paralyzingly too intimate, but I don't care. I don't have the strength to deny him any longer. Not when he wants me just as badly as I want him.

"How brave you are," he says. "After everything you've been through, you were still able to wear your heart on your sleeve and trust me. That takes a whole lot of courage, Violet. Takes a lot of guts, but look what you did. You spread your wings, baby. You lit up the sky and flew above the waves with that pretty halo shining down on those beautiful blue eyes of yours. You did the impossible, and I'm so proud of you."

I'm utterly speechless, rendered silent as I lean into Sam's body, threading my fingers through his tousled hair. I grasp at his beautiful words that fell off his tongue so easily, completely mesmerized by this incredible man who keeps me breathless with every word he speaks.

I breathe in his rich mahogany scent and cling to every word that wraps around my mind. As I lean forward, as far as I can go, I brush the tip of my nose against his and feel the warmth that radiates off his skin, his lips, his very essence that seems to crash into my own body. And it's like every single sound in the world falls away as my lips brush his. Like this is what I've waited my entire life for—to kiss him.

The slight tug of his large hand cupping the back of my neck is all the motivation I need. Letting my hand brush against his slackened jaw, I fall into him, and then my lips are on his.

Warm. His lips are *so* warm, soft as velvet, incredibly perfect. Like they were molded just for me. I lean into the kiss and hum against his plush lips as I circle my arms around the back of his neck. It's like the Earth stops moving and gravity doesn't exist. Even the bubbles in the bath seem to come to a standstill as the kiss permeates throughout the room, like sparkling firecrackers booming and ricocheting across our molded mouths.

I part my lips, inviting him to slot his tongue inside. And when he does, I melt as his honeylike tongue explores my mouth slowly, sensually. He tastes like sips of freshly brewed coffee and warm summer days. But most importantly, he tastes like mine.

This kiss is nothing like I've experienced before. It's warm, slow, inviting, and it's written with Sam all over it. It's ours, and right now, it's infinite like stars.

Sam doesn't rush with this, and neither do I. We only take our time delving into each other, swallowing each other's flavors like it's the only air we'll ever breathe again. And I *drown* in him, in his entire essence. Our bodies move in unison, fingers threading through one another's hair, hearts beating impossibly fast against each other's chest—like a slow staccato rhythm that lights hearts on fire. Everything about this is just so damn romantic and perfect. *He's* perfect.

Eventually, our lips hesitantly disconnect, and the world starts spinning again. Gravity and all its particles come back to Earth.

Sam traces his thumb across my lips and looks at me with the most beautiful shades of deep brown eyes that I've ever seen in my life. He looks completely smitten with me, almost like he's in love.

"Sorry I made you wait so long," I apologize with a smile, my cheeks red as shyness creeps in.

"You don't have to apologize, angel." He chuckles as his fingers linger like fire on my skin. "I would've waited forever if you needed me to. You're worth it, and that kiss was definitely worth waiting for."

My lips part, and my eyes glisten as I stare at the man who has my entire heart in the palm of his hand. There's that tingling sensation again, creeping through the tips of my fingers, crackling like magic through the air. It's right on the tip of my tongue, so I'll set it free, let it float till the words land on the piece of his heart that's mine.

"Sam?" I ask shakily, my hand curling over the damp ends of his soft scruff.

"Yeah?" He tilts his head, getting lost in my eyes all over again, just like I'm lost in his.

"Sam, I..." *One. Two. Three.* Let the words fall like rain. "I love you."

His eyes soften into molten chocolate, and I've never seen him smile this big and bright before—like he's seeing me in a new light. "Angel," he drawls out in a whisper. "I've been in love with you since that day I took you to my special place. But I think I knew even before that. When I first saw you smile at me across the room. I had this feeling, like you were exactly at the right place, at the right time."

My mouth parts open, and I suck in a deep breath, all my guarded walls and insecurities dropping on the spot as I play his words on repeat in my head, until I can fully comprehend what he just said to me. He's in *love* with me.

"You love me?" I ask, blinking up at him in a mesmerized state.

"Yes, my sweet girl. I love you," he purrs as he stares at me with stars twinkling in his eyes. "You take the breath out of me."

I map out every fleck of amber in his eyes, every crevice of pure, syrupy colors that call my name like a siren offshore. And I fall, crashing into his lips until I can only breathe him. There's no oxygen left; there's only *him* and his cinnamon taste that drips off his tongue.

My body molds to his like glue; my fingers glide and tear through his tousled locks, chest flush to his. I climb him like I can't get close enough, can't be satiated when his tongue dances with mine. I drink him down, let him mark his taste where I need him the most, so it can slip down and wrap around my heart where I burn like wildfire for him.

This right here is everything I've been waiting for. *He's* what I've waited my entire life for.

After a few minutes of heated tension and messy kisses, I untether myself from him, only dropping my lips from his mouth. We sit there in each other's space, just breathing each other's air, floating through bubbles and lukewarm water.

Tilting my head, I beam at him as I tousle the back of his hair through my fingers. "Kayla said you finished the book?"

"*Twice*," he states, accentuating the word in bold print.

Blinking, I take a second to register what he just said. "Twice? But why? I thought..."

He lifts my chin and brushes the pad of his thumb across my jawline. "It was the closest thing I could get to having you in my arms."

My mouth parts in surprise, but nothing comes out except his name. "Sam..."

"Two days after the diner, that's all I did was read. Finished the entire thing again in a single night because I could *smell* you on the pages. You smell like freshly printed books on a warm summer's eve. And it had your scent all over those pages, angel." His lips brush over mine, just long enough for me to breathe his fresh scent in, and I feel like I'm falling through thin air, but Sam's on the ground, ready to catch me before I collapse.

"You read it again because it reminded you of me?" I whisper, awestruck in a thick haze of wonder and love.

"That's right, sweet girl. Just for you." His fingers lace with mine, lips caressing the back of my knuckles as if he's drinking me in.

"I... God, I love you." I jump up and tangle my arms around him, just as he wraps his arms around my waist. Then his lips are on mine again. Soft, gentle, magnetic, *electric.* And there I go, floating off into the clouds as his touch and taste send me into a euphoric trance.

When his lips leave mine, he brushes them across the shell of my ear and whispers, "I love you, too, pretty girl."

This is magic, *he's* magic. And I don't think I'll ever get enough of him.

"Come on," he finally says when the water gets too cold, his lips dragging across the crown of my head. "Let's get dried off and go eat some breakfast, love."

Love. I like the sound of that, especially when it comes off his lips.

Taking the cotton towel in his hands, he wraps it around my body and leaves a gentle kiss across my cheek. "You can wear some of my sweats, and I'll grab you a clean shirt."

"Alright," I smile, watching him waltz off through his bedroom with a white towel draped low across his hips, accentuating tan muscles and broad shoulders that encompass him.

I lean against the bathroom doorway and stare mesmerizingly at this beautiful man while he tosses a light blue shirt over his bare shoulder, his hands searching through the walk-in closet for a pair of sweats. It's not long before he emerges with some gray ones and a T-shirt just for me. Handing me the clean clothes, he pulls me in and drops a kiss to my forehead, lingering there for just a second before he pulls free.

"Here you go, beautiful. Might be a little big, but they should work."

"Thanks, Sam." I smile as I take them, brushing the back of my hand against his.

He goes with a simple white T-shirt and a pair of faded blue jeans. His hair's all tousled and unkempt, and he's still got fading bruises covering his right knuckles and above his left eye, but he's still the most beautiful man I've ever seen. He's still *mine.*

After I've slid into the pair of sweats and oversized T-shirt, I comb my fingers through my loose curls and follow him out of the bathroom, my hand in his. Before he walks through, I halt at the door and pull away, hesitant in my stance.

Sam turns back and knits his eyebrows together, tilting his head. "You coming?"

"I'll be down in a minute. Go ahead, I'll meet you down there."

He chuckles as he slips through the door, lingering a few seconds to look back at me. "Alright, angel. Meet you downstairs." And then he disappears, leaving me to wander through his house unsupervised.

I don't want to rush. I just want to take my time and soak up my surroundings, so that's what I do. I wade through his space, slow and leisurely.

Blinking, I take in his sunlit room in full, carving my eyes over a bin full of old records and an acoustic guitar next to that by a mahogany dresser. I smile as I float through the door, leaving behind slept-in bed sheets and sand-colored curtains that blow gently against the open window.

Wandering aimlessly down the long hallway that's lit with natural light and cream-colored walls, I meander my way to the wooden staircase, stopping at the top where picture frames cover the length of the wall. Taking my fingertips, I drag them along the bottom of the frames, pretending I could materialize myself inside them, insert a little piece of me in his past. There he is, in between his daughters in the middle of the beach, with his arms draped over each girl's shoulder. And there's another one next to that: a blue high school graduation gown ironed to perfection and a tasseled hat on top of Kelsey's curled blonde hair. And then there's another: Kayla on top of Sam's shoulders when she was little, right in front of the Monterey Aquarium sign with a plush sea turtle stuffed animal in her right hand and rosy red cheeks cheesing up at the camera. Sam's got this infectious smile floating through the camera, his eyes sparkling with amusement as Kelsey wraps her arms around her dad's back, her blue eyes just as bright as his.

My heart clenches as I peruse each captured memory with glistening eyes, consuming every little detail I can ingrain in the back of my mind. It's all raw, beautiful, a piece of him I want to explore even deeper. And before I get to the last step, I pause at the framed photo before me. My eyes skim the glass over three times until I piece together who's standing in the frame. There's two little boys, one with tousled brown hair and the other with blond, floppy hair. They're in a pair of blue overalls while a woman with a polka dot dress and dark brown curls stands behind them. Next to her is an older man: tall, short blond hair, tan from the sun's yellow rays. And there's a little wooden barn behind them, along with chickens and picket fences.

Gasping, I linger my fingers over the little boy with big brown eyes and the same lopsided smile I know by memory. That's *my* Sam. That's his home, his older brother, his parents, his hometown, his entire childhood in a state I've never been to. But looking through the glass, I feel as if I've been there, just long enough to write my name on a handwritten letter that says *Come find me in California*. I guess he got the message, because he found me when I needed him most. He found me tied in crashing waves and sprawled out across warm sand, waiting till the day he took my hand and taught me to float.

I smile and wipe a tear from the corner of my eye, still hovering over the silhouette of Sam's past. I feel like I've known him my entire life. Feel like I was destined to love this man. It was written in the stars, all sparkly and glittery flits of cosmic rays that spelled his name out just for me in the twinkling night sky. He feels like home. *This* feels like home. Maybe that's where I am now. *Home.*

Padding across smooth wooden floors, I take in the open floor plans, blinking at the light and airy spaces of sunlight. This house feels like it's full of love, sprinkled with care and put to good use. I don't miss a second of it, not even a beat as I flit my eyes across a well-loved soccer ball by the front door, a collection of classic movies next to the flat-screen TV, exposed wooden beams across the high ceilings, hanging art of Malibu beaches and crashing waves across shorelines in the living room, potted plants lined across the back sliding door, soft curtains blowing in the California breeze. It's all so homey and cozy and full of life. It's full of Sam and the smell of sandalwood, and maybe that's why I feel like I belong here. Maybe I finally found a safe place where I can rest my head after all.

I'm home. I finally found where I belong.

A faint tapping sound clicks on the wood behind me. When I turn to look down, there's Whiskers at my side, rubbing up against the cotton material of Sam's sweats. She zigzags between my legs and then sits right in front of me, gazing up with big green eyes that make me melt inside. It's like she's imprinting on me, marking her scent just enough to make me stay. She's Sam's and Kayla's cat, but I guess she's also mine now, too.

Smiling, I lean down and scoop her fuzzy body against my chest as she purrs and nuzzles her pink nose against my shirt. "Come on, Whiskers. Let's go find Sam."

I make my way into the open kitchen, where Sam's tossed silver pans, syrup, flour, milk, eggs, and pancake mix across the granite island. He's still gathering items, even when he's busy holding a phone to his ear while his other hand is mixing strawberries into a glass bowl.

I sit back and watch him, leaning against the counter while he shines like gold in the sunlight. Tan skin glowing, T-shirt bunching around his broad back, a small crease between his eyebrows as he talks quietly on the phone, making sure he's not missing any ingredients from the refrigerator.

Honestly, I could watch him all day while Whiskers lounges in my lap. That sounds like a slice of heaven I'd like to taste.

"Yeah. She's okay. She—" He stops when his gaze flits to mine, eyes warm and melting when he sees me holding Whiskers. He looks like a man in love. "I gotta go, Bryson. I'll call you later." And then he ends the call, drops the bowl of strawberries on the kitchen island, and walks over to me.

"I think she likes me." I smile, placing her back on the floor so she can click back over to her food bowl.

"Yeah?" Sam chuckles as he slides his arms behind my waist and pulls me in. "I think she adores you, just like I do."

I giggle when he brushes his lips across my neckline, ending with a sweet kiss to the side of my cheek. "Guess she wants me to stick around then."

Sam leans his forehead against mine, smiling. "I'm counting on it."

Snaking my arms around his neck, I hesitate. "Was that Bryson on the phone?"

He nods, creasing his brows before he speaks. "That was him."

"Did he—"

"Jason's behind bars," he states firmly, snapping his jaw shut.

A breath I've been holding the past fourteen or so hours leaves my chest, relieving the ache of having to carry weights for too long. "Thank God."

He pulls me closer and looks down at me, a hint of worry twinkling in his eyes. "I'm gonna have to go down to the station tomorrow and give my statement. They wanna talk to me. I'm gonna see if I can get him max times behind those bars."

Flinching, I nod and suck my bottom lip between my teeth, dropping my arms to my sides. "I should probably go, too. You know, since he—"

Cupping a palm against my face, he looks me straight in the eyes. "Baby, are you sure? You don't have to."

I shake my head, firm on my decision. "Just hold my hand and be there for me? I need to do this. Need to lay him to rest for good." Even if there's anxiety trying to creep up my spine, Sam washes it all away like I was never afraid in the first place. He makes the scary monsters stay in old, dusty closets that won't emerge again, and he won't let Jason haunt me again.

Sliding his lips across my forehead, he pulls me in for a tight hug and whispers in my ear, "Okay, angel. Promise I won't let go."

And he won't; he won't ever let go again.

"You hungry?" he asks, entwining his fingers through mine.

"Starving."

He chuckles and pulls me toward the kitchen island. "Let's get you something to eat then, pretty girl."

We move in symbiotic waves, hands brushing one another's while we stir pancake batter and crack eggshells over mixing bowls. It feels so natural, like this isn't the first time we've done this. Making breakfast together, sipping warm coffee out of ceramic mugs, laughing like two best friends who have known each other forever. It's so easy, domestic. It feels like coming home after being gone for months.

This right here is my new favorite thing, and it's all because of Sam.

Spinning me around, I squeak out a laugh when he tugs me into his body, tan skin glowing and brown eyes sparkling with love. He curls a lock of hair behind my ear and smiles. "I want you to meet my girls."

"Already?" My eyes widen into big orbs.

"Mhm," he hums, lingering his warm knuckles against my jawline. "Next Saturday? Kelsey will be home that weekend from college."

"Are you sure? What if they don't like me, or it's too soon, or—"

"Shh," he whispers, soothing me of the anxiety rolling through my stomach. "If there's anything I'm absolutely sure about, it's you. It's *always* going to be you. And they're going to love you, just as much as I do."

Blinking up at him, I tug on a smile and nod, flexing my fingers into the cotton of his shirt. "Okay then. Saturday it is, brown eyes," I tease, batting my eyelashes flirtatiously his way.

Pulling on a smirk, he reels me in like a fish on a hook, taking the bait. "It's a date then, my perfect angel." Then his lips are on mine, soft and warm as I bottle up the taste of him.

I'm not scared anymore. Not now that I've found Sam. Our dark shades of the past bled together, crimson waves that turned into the warmest sunset of colors. Sparkling hues of orange, yellow, and flashes of pink. There's no more blood, no more pain. There's just *us*.

I think I'll stay here a while, until the moon slips into the star-filled sky. Maybe I'll stay a year, until the rain decides to fall again. Or maybe I'll stay forever, slipping my hand through Sam's and never letting go.

441

Chapter Thirty-Seven

Sam

Today's the day. The day my daughters get to meet the love of my life.

I won't lie, the thought is a little terrifying, but it's also the most sure I've ever been about anything in my entire life. Violet's the one, and I don't want to wait another month, week, or day to introduce both parts of my heart that make me whole.

Kelsey's surprisingly ecstatic for me. She even came home early to get all the details in person. And Kayla, she's already smitten with the idea of me having someone around the house. They think I've been lonely, have worried about me all these years I've tried to heal from a broken marriage, but that's not the case anymore. Violet took the shattered pieces of my heart and glued them back together, even handed me a piece of hers. And now, I'm completely whole again.

Sweat beads across the collar of my blue jean shirt as I stuff my phone into the front pocket of my khaki shorts, fidgeting with anything I can get a grip on. My other hand slides through my hair, tousling it enough to make me look like a mess.

"Dad, relax." Kelsey laughs, shaking her long blonde hair behind her shoulders. "You look fine."

"Thanks, Kels." I smile sheepishly. "Just a little nervous, that's all."

"Why?" Kayla asks, peeking her head over Whiskers' fuzzy head that's nuzzled against her neck. "Is it because you really like her?"

"Yeah, kiddo." I laugh, ruffling my hair once more. "She makes me really happy."

Both of my girls turn to me, their eyes shining with hope, smiles beaming across the clean kitchen. And I know what they're thinking. They want this to work just as much as I do.

When I hear tires spinning across the driveway and the sound of an engine cutting, my heart skips a beat. I snatch the red rose off the counter—the one I picked from the garden—and smile at my girls.

She's here. This is it.

Turning, I basically sprint to the door, my heart thumping like horse hooves against my chest. Once the first knock comes, I twist the doorknob and throw the door open, ready for what's on the other side.

The breath is knocked from my chest immediately. There she is, my girl. My gorgeous angel with sunlight framing her in a soft glow. Her long brunette curls fall in waves over her shoulders, blonde highlights kissing her skin like a halo. She's got on a light pink sundress that flows over her soft curves. And her smile. God, that fucking beautiful smile is going to bring me to my knees.

"Hi." I smile, letting my eyes rake over her outfit once more. Sundresses never looked so good before.

"Hi," she says shyly, fluttering her long eyelashes my way.

"You look... gorgeous," I gush, brushing my hand against the skirt of her dress.

"You like the dress okay?"

"Like it?" Giving her a once-over, I sigh. "Angel, I love it. You're stunning."

"Thanks. I picked it just for you."

I shake my head and blow out a laugh. "Of course you did. You know how much I love these sundresses on you. Always look so perfect," I say, letting my hand slide over her waist.

She giggles, blinking those beautiful blue eyes my way. "You look pretty handsome yourself."

Raking a hand through my hair, I use my other to hand her the single red rose. "Umm here. This is for you."

She brushes her hand over mine, igniting sparks under my skin, and takes the rose. "You got me a flower?"

"Mhm. A pretty rose for a pretty girl."

She twists it in her hand and brings it up to her nose, smelling the red petals. "You're sweet."

I push a lock of hair behind her ear and tug on a smile. "You nervous?"

"Very," she replies quickly, her eyes growing into blue orbs.

Shaking my head, I smirk. "Don't be. They're going to love you."

Violet nods and flashes me a genuine smile. "Oh, I have something," she murmurs as she throws open her lilac tote bag, pulling out hardback books. "I might've stopped by the bookstore before I came over. And I got them each something."

"You got them books?" I smile, falling even more in love with her with each minute that passes.

"Yeah, I hope that's okay," she says nervously, chewing on her bottom lip that's painted dark red.

"That's more than okay," I reply, letting the back of my hand trail down the side of her face as I admire everything about her. "God, they're gonna love you."

"I hope so," she whispers faintly.

"But wait, you didn't get me anything, did you?" Lifting a brow, I smirk playfully, seeing if I can pull that nervousness out of her system.

"Of course I did!" she replies in a fit of giggles. "Saved the best for you." Searching deep in her bag, she pulls out a smaller book that's deep blue like the ocean and hands it to me. "Here. Thought you might like this."

Lingering my fingers on her skin, I slowly take it from her and hum as I flip through the crisp pages. Amity Island is all scrawled out on the front cover, with the famous great white I've loved ever since I was a kid.

How does she do it? It's like she already knows me inside and out. Once a blank page, now a filled diary with every locked secret I've ever kept. It's like she reached in and sprinkled life inside, colored me shades of every single color of the rainbow.

"You got me a book all about *Jaws*?" I ask, tilting my head as I stare at ocean-blue eyes I could dive into.

She shrugs and wraps a pretty finger around the end of a curl. "It's your favorite, right? I saw it and thought of you, so I bought it."

She's got me in a vice grip, both dizzy and breathless. It may just be a book, but it's way more than that. And it's not even the fact that she bought it, but the way she thought of me the moment she saw the cover. And I love that, love the way she thinks of me even when I'm not around, and the fact that she did the same for my girls.

I'm gonna keep this one. I'm gonna keep her so no one else can steal her away.

"You're so sweet," I purr. "I'll put it right next to my *Jaws* Blu-ray collection."

After I set it down on the wooden shelf by the door, I tug her into my body and fuse my mouth to her pretty red lips. Those soft lips that I love kissing. She tastes like sunshine, long walks on the beach, strawberries, and my favorite drink of choice—*her.*

When I pull away, I slide my hand into hers and smile. "You ready?"

She takes a deep breath and swallows. "Mhm."

She's adorable when she's nervous.

I squeeze her hand encouragingly and lead her through the entryway, to the kitchen. "Come on."

My heart's beating a million miles an hour, but not all from nerves. I'm just excited, hopeful, and overly ecstatic because this is what I've been waiting for. For my girls to finally meet the woman who's flipped my whole world upside down in the best way possible. And I just have this feeling that it'll be perfect. *This* will be perfect.

When we emerge into the sunlit kitchen, Kayla and Kelsey are both silent, staring bright-eyed at Violet as she nervously smiles their way. "Girls, without further adieu, I'd finally like you to meet my girlfriend, Violet," I say. "Violet, this is Kayla and Kelsey, my best girls."

Kelsey's the first to move. "It's nice to meet you," she says shyly, reaching out to shake Violet's hand.

Violet's just as timid, but her blue eyes light up when she takes Kelsey's hand. "And it's nice to meet you." She smiles. "Your father has told me all about you and your engineering projects. You're very talented. And straight A's? You must be at the top of your class."

Kelsey brushes it off and shakes her blonde hair out. "He likes to brag, I see." She rolls her eyes playfully my way and looks back at Violet with an easy smile. "He's told me a lot about you, too."

"Hopefully only good things?" Violet giggles nervously.

"Only the best." Kelsey nods in confirmation.

I lean against the back of the counter and cross my arms over my chest, eagerly watching the scene unfold in front of me. And again, this woman couldn't be any more adorable than she already is. She always does this thing when she's shy. She twists her index finger around her hair, and her eyes get real big, as big as the moon's. But she's also settling down, getting into a comfortable ease like she's casually talking with a friend from the library.

And then, Kayla hesitantly takes a step forward, blinking her hazel eyes at Violet. "Hi, Violet." She's a little bashful, a little reserved, but her eyes are sparkling with wonder. Hope fizzles against the green flecks in her eyes.

"Kayla," Violet beams as she turns to Kayla. "It's so good to meet you properly."

"Thanks for coming to have lunch with us. We uhh…" she blushes, pulling on the edge of her jean shorts, "we've been excited to meet you."

"I wouldn't miss it for the world." Violet tugs on a grin, and there's this little moment where they're back in that library, meeting each other for the very first time.

I let the breath that I was holding slowly release from my lungs as a weight lifts off my chest. I was always so nervous to bring someone else into my life, afraid my girls would have a hard time accepting anyone, but I was wrong. I was so very wrong. They're accepting her, and I can see how badly Violet wants them to like her.

"Oh, I almost forgot." Violet hurries back into the entryway and emerges a few seconds later with the books behind her back. "I got you two something from the bookstore. I thought maybe you could use them."

"You got us gifts?" Kelsey questions while Kayla stands on her tiptoes, trying to see around Violet's back.

"Hopefully you don't think it's cheesy." A lilty laugh falls from her lips, and she hands each of the bright books to Kayla and Kelsey.

Kelsey turns the pages, her blue eyes big as she takes in each word. "Wait, a book about the Art Deco style bridges? This is actually perfect! I can use this for my upcoming research paper. Thanks, Violet!"

"You're welcome." She smiles. Relief floods her eyes, like she made the right decision about the books.

Kayla blinks, her pink lips parted, almost speechless as she whispers, "Sea turtles…" That happens to be her favorite animal, Violet just doesn't know that. Not yet, at least, but she'll know soon.

"Your dad may have told me you've been interested in marine animals, so I got you a book on aquatic veterinary medicine." She plays with the side of her dress, hesitant to say the next part. "Also, I hear UC Davis has an amazing college program that specializes in that field, and I may know one of the professors."

Kayla's eyes shoot up, like her future just flashed before her eyes. "Like, you mean you could introduce me?"

Violet hums, nodding her head once. "I bet I could pull some strings. She's always looking for high school interns who may be interested in shadowing her when she's out doing fieldwork in the summer."

"You'd do that for me?"

My throat bobs up and down as I see hope flash through her hazel eyes again, like she's just met a new best friend.

"Sure. If that's okay with Sam then—"

Before I know what's happening, Kayla flies forward and wraps her arms around Violet in a tight hug. "Thanks, Violet. You're the best." Violet opens her mouth, but nothing comes out. She just stares down at Kayla in surprise. But slowly, surely, she brings her arms around Kayla and squeezes her back.

I feel the salty burn behind my eyes as tears lick at the corners. I'm smiling like a madman. A man who's in love. A father who finally sees the light at the end of the tunnel. Too long I've been running, chasing away the demons from the past. But now, I'm seeing something I never thought could happen. My girls. My sweet, beautiful girls get a taste of something they never really had. Violet's going to love these girls like they're her own, and I can already see they'll love her right back, especially Kayla. It's all I've ever wanted. *She's* everything I've wanted.

"Here, come on. I want to show you my book collection upstairs real quick." Kayla takes her hand and pulls her out of the room, but not before Violet turns her head to flash me a smile, her blue eyes swimming with life like I've never seen before. And then they disappear up the staircase, leaving me and Kelsey alone.

Kelsey comes around the island and bumps her hip with mine, beaming up at me with a genuine smile. "I like her already."

"Me too, Kels. I really like this one." But more than that. I really fucking love this girl.

"Kayla seems fond of her."

"Yeah, think you're right about that." I chuckle, sliding my palm down my face, still in a daze that this is real life. I'm really bringing another woman into my life, into *their* life.

"She's even prettier in person, plus she's sweet. How'd you get so lucky?"

How did I get so lucky? I guess the universe decided it was my turn. I was never looking. Not really. She just appeared out of thin air, flashing those beautiful blue eyes my way, across my own club.

I shrug, just as unsure as her. "The universe decided to grace me with her, I guess." Sliding a hand back through tousled hair, I sigh, breathless about the whole thing. "I dunno, Kels. All I know is I got super lucky. Never met a woman like her before…"

She tilts her head and flicks her eyes to the empty staircase. "You think she'll stick around?"

Pulling my lips into a huge grin, I nod. "Yeah. This one's not going anywhere." It's like a lightbulb flickers on in my head, flashing bright and sounding alarms through my ears. And the words flicker through my mind like bubbles.

I'm going to marry that girl.

I don't know when. I don't know how, but I know it'll happen, and I have an idea where I might ask her. Somewhere special. Somewhere where water's crystal blue and sunlight shines like diamonds over waves.

My special place. That's where I'll ask her. One day, I'm going to get down on one knee and ask her to be my forever.

I see it like a bolt of lightning flash before my eyes, cosmic rays exploding in the distance. Saturday morning soccer games with Violet cheering Kayla on next to me, the last day of high school party with streamers hanging over my fence, college graduations and long summer road trips on the coast. A diamond ring, wedding bells, doing the rest of my life with Violet by my side, all while watching my girls grow into the beautiful, successful women they'll become. I'm going to do it all, and Violet will be right there, right next to me, holding my hand through it all.

Violet's the one. I think she was always meant to be. I just had to find her through crimson tides that blurred my vision. She took my hand and pulled me out, made me see color like I've never seen before. Vivid blues, bright pops of fuchsia, lights of a rich technicolor world I've never been able to clearly see. Not till I saw *her*.

I've found my forever. It was never in Oklahoma like I thought it'd be. I found it in a big coastal city, inside a club, riding crashing ocean waves where it led me right where I belonged after all this time. I found it in soft red lips, sparkling blue eyes, and the most angelic voice I've ever heard in my entire life. Violet Emery and California sunsets is where I'll find peace for the rest of my life.

This is only the beginning. We still have a lifetime to go, and this time I think I'll finally get it right. *We'll* get it right. Together.

Epilogue

VIOLET

Eight Months Later

The vibrant colors of pink and shades of ruby reds fill my peripheral vision as I make my way through Club Inferno. A place that's become like a second home. Somewhere I love because this is Sam's, and he's made it just as much mine, or so it feels.

As I pass the lit-up bar, I nod to Bryson. He's standing behind the counter, one empty glass in his hand and a cell phone in the other as he tries to juggle two tasks at once. He smiles my way, completing an invisible cheers motion while he smirks that same old shit-eating grin he always has stamped on his face. Waving a hand at him, I smile and keep on walking.

Bryson feels as much a part of my family as Sam does now, and I can't imagine not having either of them in my life. From double dates—and sometimes even triple dates with Laura and Caleb—to movie nights, to long evenings at the club, and long conversations, it's all just been great. Bryson's also been teasing me, calling me his new sister-in-law. He's got his jokes, but oddly, I like the sound of this one.

As for Jason, he's gone. For good this time. After Sam and I went down to the police station and pressed charges, they ended up adding ten plus years on his sentence. And for my own safety and request, they ended up shipping him off to a prison in Florida—the complete opposite side of the country from me. And now, I'm officially free from him. Sam held my hand the entire time, whispered affirmations in my ear, calmed me down enough to face my fear. And I love him for that. He made me brave after years of being scared. He made me finally see the light.

And then, there's the girls—Kayla and Kelsey. We've been bonding the past few months, taking weekend trips to Disneyland, going shopping together, and just having girl time. It's been... nice. I love them like they're my own, but Kayla's got a special place in my heart. Me and her have really gotten close, and sometimes she comes to me more than she does Sam. But he absolutely loves watching her bloom, and I've never seen him smile as much as he's been lately. They all just feel like mine, and I've never been this happy in my life.

They anchored me when I was slipping under stormy waves, pulled me free from the darkness that tried swallowing me. And I can never thank them enough for showing me what a real family feels like and for that stability I needed. Ten months of Sam and eight with the girls, plus Bryson. I kind of wish time would slow down, just a little, so I could savor it like I do every minute with them.

I push my way through the thick crowd and enter into the long, dark hallway that's draped with muted pink lights and hanging mirrors. My heart thunders in my chest the closer I get to Sam's office, eager to see my most favorite person in the entire world. Sam Brooks has my heart, and I might as well scream it on stage so the whole club can know that he's mine, and I'm so in love with him.

When I make it to the glossy black doors in my silver stilettos and sparkly, pink strapless dress, I latch my hand around the door handle and step through to his office. I'm immediately met with the smell of fresh cologne—sandalwood and mahogany—Sam's signature scent. *My* favorite scent. I waft in his presence and lean against the now closed door, staring at the handsome man in the middle of the room.

He's wearing a silky button-up, the sleeves rolled up to his elbows, like always. And there's those thick, veiny arms I love to get wrapped in. It's one of my favorite things. His tousled sandy locks are a little unkempt, but he looks so damn good like that, like I just laced my fingers through his hair, got it all messy just because I like the way he looks like that. And God, he just looks so handsome, even with his nose stuck in some paperwork. I still can't believe he's mine.

Sam sighs and flips a stack of white papers over, groaning into the air. "Bryson, can you just wait five more minutes? I'm almost—"

"I'm not Bryson," I giggle behind my hand.

Sam glances up from his paperwork and a wide grin slowly spreads over his plush mouth. The mouth I *love* to kiss. "No. You sure as hell aren't, sweetheart."

"You busy?" I ask sweetly, letting my hand linger across the wall as I pull away and start to head straight for his mahogany desk.

He shakes his head, watching my every move, his eyes flitting up and down my body. "Never too busy for my girl. Now come here." He pushes the stack of papers to the side, not even caring that some fly off the desk and onto the marble floor. Sam coaxes me forward, curling a thick finger in a *come hither* motion until I'm close enough to where he can reach me. Wrapping an arm around my waist, he pulls me onto his lap and brings me flush to his broad chest.

"Hi, pretty girl." He smiles, pushing a loose curl behind the shell of my ear.

"Hi, handsome," I purr back, my arms locking around his neck. "I missed you today."

"Not as much as I missed you, angel. Been dreaming about kissing those pretty red lips of yours all damn day." He smirks, his fingertips trailing down my skin and lingering across my cheek, making me blush from the affection that's slipping off those glistening brown eyes.

"So kiss me," I whisper, parting my lips in a smile.

He chuckles and bites his lower lip as he looks at me in awe, like I'm a diamond in the rough. "Come here." He tugs me forward and presses his lips against mine, eliciting a deep sigh when his mouth melds with mine. He tastes like coffee, long summer nights, and mine.

"God, I'll never get tired of kissing you. You're sweeter than anything I've ever tasted," he pants through messy kisses, reeling me back in to lick inside my mouth.

I open wider, allowing him to swallow my moans whole with every stroke of his tongue. My hands roam through his tousled hair, making him groan as my long nails scratch against his scalp. His fingers dig further into my back, and it's like the room is on fire, and both of our bodies are the cause of the growing flames.

"You're so fucking beautiful, angel," he mouths as he nips at my bottom lip and teases me on.

"Sam, stop. You're making me blush." I giggle, nuzzling my nose against his in an affectionate way.

"Well, it's true. And I love you." He flashes me a lopsided smile and kisses my cheek, dragging along the shell of my ear, nipping and teasing me more as he elicits another giggle from my lips.

"I love you, too." I curl my fingers through the soft white material of his shirt and stare into his shining brown eyes.

"Not as much as I love you, angel. You really know how to light a man's life up with that pretty glow of yours." Sam pushes my hair over my shoulder and slowly plays with the strands like they're guitar strings, his fingers expertly working as they drag along the back of my neck.

Another groan and I'm tugging him forward. Our mouths meet again, hot and fiery like the first time I kissed him, simmering sparks flying across the warm air like fireworks. There's a hunger in his kiss, like he wants to devour me whole, but he's also so gentle, and I think that's the perfect combination. *He's* perfect, and he's so fucking soft for me.

When our lips break apart and our ragged breaths start to lessen, he cups my cheeks with his large palms as a soft smile curls across his mouth. "I wanna show you something."

I tilt my head and give him a suspicious look. "Show me what?"

He shrugs nonchalantly, acting like it's nothing important. "Just want to show you something in the back. It's a surprise."

Smirking, I crawl off his lap and hold out my hand. "Take me to the back then, Mr. Club Owner."

"Follow me, angel." He pushes himself up and takes my hand as he leads me outside his office and into the dark hallway.

I gladly follow behind him, my heels clicking against the polished floor, his eyes twinkling against the flickering lights. My heart pounds impossibly fast, skipping beats as the sound of thumping music halts once he's pulled me into his private room.

Dropping his hand from mine, he grazes his lips across my ear and whispers, "Wait here." I do as he says, staying put as butterflies flit around my stomach. How is it this man still has this much effect on me?

As I shift my weight side to side, letting the crackle of the music outside soothe my roaring heartbeat, I pause when I hear the faint noise of static above. When I lift my head to see where it's coming from, a faint glow flickering above catches my attention.

"There weren't lights here before," I mumble to myself.

When the flickering stops and a soft glow illuminates above the door, my heart goes straight to my throat. Light pink-colored wings expand against the glittery black walls, and inside the wings spell out words that paralyze me to the spot. *Angel's Place* lights up the middle of the sign, the cursive letters shrouded in a pink hue that sparkles across the room, reflecting off hanging picture frames.

"Oh my God," I whisper as my mouth drops open, my eyes becoming glassy as tears lick at the back of my lids. With barely a breath to spare, I smell his sandalwood scent before I feel Sam's large arms drape around my waist.

"You like it?" he asks, whispering into the shell of my ear, lips dragging against my heated skin while he blankets me in his warmth, his hands tugging me flush to his chest.

"Sam... what did you do?" My voice is hoarse, and it's like he just stole every breath of oxygen I've ever had in my lungs.

"Thought the club could use a touch of you, angel. So, I had it special ordered, and I hung it up earlier. Thought I'd surprise you. I really hope you like it." His lips skate down my jawline, leaving me soft kisses against my skin.

"I... I love it," I say, speechless. "But why did you..."

"Because I love you. This club is as much yours as it is mine, and I want you to be a part of it." He smiles against my jawline. "You've molded this place into something special, and you've changed my life, made it beautiful."

Beautiful. His words stick to my skin like the sweat coating the back of my neck, and it's suddenly like the room is a hot sauna. I'm overwhelmed, and he just keeps surprising me like he does every day.

"Sam, that's the sweetest thing anyone's ever done for me." I squeeze his hands and lace my fingers through his while I breathe in the musk of him.

He chuckles into my ear and says, "Oh, I have one more question to ask you."

Turning slowly toward him, I raise my eyebrows and look into his deep brown eyes. "Oh, what's that?"

He licks his bottom lip and smirks. "What would you say if I changed the name of the club to Angel's Place?"

I blink, speechless at the question.

Did I just hear that right?

"Angel's Place?" I ask slowly, parting my lips in awe.

"Mhm. That's right. I think it suits the club and has a nice ring to it, don't you?" He tilts his head to the side and tugs on a lopsided grin that makes me weak in the knees.

I smile dreamily up at him and let his hand cup my chin as he pulls me close. "Sam Brooks," I giggle, completely smitten by this man, "I love the sound of that. And you're incredible, did you know that?"

"That's all you, angel. You're simply incredible." Sam's thumb trails across my lower lip, his breath warm and blissful, making me want him more and more with every second I'm in his space.

"You really mean it?" I whisper, letting my hands fall against his chest.

"Yeah," he smiles, "it's our place now, baby."

"Ours?" I blink up, my attention on the way his eyes twinkle under the pink fluorescent lights.

"Ours," he confirms. He seals it with a kiss, his mouth falling against my lips. I melt right then into him as our bodies collide like thunder.

I let the kiss burn like fire, heating every single nerve ending in my body. My skin buzzes for him, and his name drags from my lips as he licks inside my mouth, creating a need only he can satiate.

We somehow end up on the pool table—his body crawled over me, my legs wrapped around his back, his lips brushing softly against mine. His strong arms cage me in, his broad body crowding my space until I can't smell anything but *him* crashing over me like rolling waves. My body hums with electricity, my blood pumping through my veins violently, and I'm already completely drenched for him.

"Look at us. Right back where it all started," he hums, the pads of his fingers brushing stray locks behind my ear as his other hand trails *down, down, down* until he's hiking my dress up and teasing me slowly.

"Look at us," I whisper back, my eyes glistening like gold when he looks at me with those soft, sappy brown eyes. His lips brush against mine as light as a feather, and I melt into the pool table, letting my fingernails trace over silver strands in his smooth scruff.

"You gonna be mine forever, angel?" He smiles, leaving a trail of wet kisses across the side of my cheek.

It sounds like a promise wrapped up in his silky-smooth words, but it's something else I can't quite pinpoint. It's something big, exquisite, only something Sam can ask me.

I bite my lower lip and nod, smiling like a lovesick crush. "Mmm, forever sounds kind of nice when you ask me like that."

Sam stifles out a laugh, his brown eyes glossy like syrup. He looks like a man in love, and he is in love. As he traces hearts on the side of my face, he murmurs out, "I wanna take you somewhere tomorrow."

"Where?" I ask, tilting my head in question.

His lips curl into a sideways smirk, and he whispers in answer. "It's a surprise."

"You're always surprising me. Can't you just tell me?"

He shakes his head and smiles. "Not this time."

Narrowing my eyes, I huff and breathe out a laugh. "Fine."

"Trust me, you're going to like this one," he promises.

I lace my fingers through his sandy locks and say, "I always like your surprises."

With one more glimmer in his eye, he steers me forward until his lips are back on mine, and then the night fades away while we fall into each other, making this moment ours. Sam Brooks may very well be my undoing, but I'll gladly fall into the night with him. He always seems to catch me.

"Where are we going?" I giggle, my eyes peeled shut from the velvet blindfold wrapped around my eyes.

"I told you, it's a surprise," he chuckles over the roar of his truck's engine.

"Well, how much longer?" I pout, folding my arms across my chest.

"Just five more minutes, pretty girl," he says with amusement dripping off his tone. His hand lands on the top of my thigh, and he keeps it there as he drives along, rubbing small circles with the pad of his thumb.

"Alright," I murmur through a smile, content in the moment.

I'm in a light blue floral maxi dress, my beachy waves soft against my shoulders, red lipstick coated across my lips, comfortable sandals like he said to wear. I'm not sure where we're going, but he said I might want to wear a dress, but no heels. I've tossed ideas back and forth, thought maybe we'd be going on a boat or maybe a poolside dinner somewhere fancy, but he won't tell me a single thing, so I'm just left bouncing ideas over and over inside my mind.

When the next song stops spinning on the static of the radio, Sam's truck comes to a halt, and my heart starts thundering at the possibilities. He definitely hasn't given anything away, but he's been acting strange the past week. Whispering to his brother across the room, slipping Kayla something small into her hand, private conversations on the back patio through his phone. Something is *definitely* up, I just don't know what.

"Alright, angel," Sam says as he opens my door and unclicks my seatbelt, "I'm gonna lift you up. Just put your arms around me and hold on."

When he lifts me up and holds me close to his chest, I wrap my arms around the back of his neck and press my lips to his ear. "Promise not to drop me?" I ask, just like the night he tugged me into his arms in the middle of the dance floor.

I feel the curl of his lips against my cheek as he replies, "What makes you think I'd ever let go?" The exact words he said to me that night when he was holding me up by a thin thread, promising never to let go. And look at us now. He never let me go.

As I hold onto him, I smell the scent of salt in the air and the crisp summer breeze through my hair. I hear the lap of waves against the shoreline and light footsteps across what sounds like smooth rocks and sand. And as I nuzzle into the side of his neck, I hear the blood in his veins galloping, like his heart's thundering just as loud as mine is.

Something tugs inside my chest, pulling till I'm almost overwhelmed with emotions that want to break free. I'm not positive what this is or what he's doing, but somehow I know it's something extraordinary. Something I'll remember for the rest of my life.

Am I yours, Sam? Am I your forever?

Sam sets me on my feet carefully, and I'm automatically met with the feel of smooth sand against my sandals, so I kick them off and let my feet bury into the soft texture. I hear him step back as he clears his throat over the sounds of splashing waves. "Okay, sweetheart. You can take your blindfold off and open your eyes."

One, two, three.

Tugging the blindfold off, I let it fall free to my feet. My heart's beating a million miles an hour as I stare at Sam, my mouth dropped in astonishment. He's down on one knee, all dressed in black and white. Black slacks, white button-up shirt, black tie flying in the wind, hair all tousled just like I like it. A big, nervous smile is curled over his plush mouth. And his eyes—big brown orbs made of molasses and honey, all soft and starry as he stares up at me. And there's red rose petals all around us, along with flickering white candles placed in lanterns. It looks like one big romantic daydream.

Is he... proposing? The glowing onyx in his eyes tells me yes.

"Sam..." I breathe as tears gather in the back of my eyes.

"Violet Skye Emery, love of my life," he starts, taking my hand in his.

"Yes?" I smile, nearly choking back a happy sob.

Using his other hand, he drags his fingers through his tousled locks and sighs as he smiles up at me. "You have flipped my world upside down in the best way possible. From the club, to showing me how to open myself back up to love, to being there for my girls through all their ups and downs the past few months. You were always what was missing. That little puzzle piece that completed me."

I brush a falling tear from my cheek and hope my mascara isn't smudged. But that doesn't matter. The only thing that matters is the man I love who's kneeling on one knee in front of me.

He continues, his brown eyes twinkling like starlight. "My girls love you, I love you, and I'm completely crazy about you. I can't imagine another day without you. You're it for me, Violet," he smiles lovingly. "This is the spot I chose you. Right here, the first time I took you here. I made a decision, and it was you. It was *always* you."

"You chose me here?" I whisper, letting my words get swallowed by a breaking wave in the distance.

"I did." He nods, never taking his eyes off me. "And I'll continue choosing you over and over again, for the rest of my life. So, without further adieu." Sam digs inside the pocket of his slacks and pulls out a shiny ring. One that's encrusted in sapphire and light pink diamonds, all twisted to perfection like vines around the silver ring. It's breathtaking. This is *all* so breathtaking, and I can't help the giant gasp that falls from my mouth. He takes my hand again and holds the ring up, where I can see it sparkle under the shades of purple and pink hues of the dying sunset. "Violet Skye Emery, would you please do me the honor of making me the happiest man in the world and marrying me? I think Violet Brooks has a nice ring to it, don't you?"

There's no hiding the happy tears that leak from my eyes like a running faucet, or the wide grin that's stuck like glue across my mouth.

"Yes, yes! A million times yes!" I shout into the salty sea air. When he stands up, I jump into his arms and kiss him like I've never kissed anyone else in my life. Slow, languid, drinking him down like he's the oxygen that keeps me breathing. And when I taste him, I taste forever.

When we pull apart, he takes my left hand in his and slips the shiny engagement ring onto my ring finger. "Let's see how this fits you, angel."

After it's in place, I admire the swirl of colors and what they might mean. "The perfect fit," I say in awe, still stunned by how beautiful it is. "Sam, it's breathtaking…"

He traces every inch of the ring, from the band to every single flashy diamond, like he's enamored by it, too. "The pink is for the way you lit up my club in shades of bright pink. The blue represents the oceans I'd cross just to see those shimmering blue eyes of yours, just like our love—unbreakable, all-consuming, and the most beautiful adventure I ever had the pleasure of setting out on with you. And the swirls of colors in the middle represent us—how we're infinite like the stars in the night sky."

I swallow, clear my eyes of the mist, and blink up at him, utterly speechless. "That's so beautiful…"

"You're beautiful," he says with the flash of a sideways smile.

Clasping my arms around his neck, I graze my lips over his and whisper, "I love you."

"And I love you," he says back in a dreamy, lovesick daze, "my beautiful angel."

Before I let him kiss me again, I pull back and knit my brows together. "But wait, when did you ask my dad?"

He chuckles and tilts his head as a mischievous smirk curls across his lips. "Last month when we went up to go visit your parents. I pulled your father aside when you weren't looking."

"Of course you did." I giggle, shaking my head. "You mean when you two went for a walk through the vineyard?"

"Mhm," he hums with that same devilish smirk I fell for under the glowing red lights of his club.

"I should've known."

He folds an arm across my lower back and curls a flyaway strand of hair behind my ear. "Been planning this for months. I didn't know when, but I knew where I wanted to ask you."

I let my eyes linger to the red petals and flicker of candles surrounding us. "You set up all the roses and candles yourself?"

He shakes his head and lets a smile tug at the corner of his mouth. "Bryson might've helped out. And the girls, they helped me light the candles before."

"But wait, does that mean…"

He tilts my chin up past his shoulder, where a group of rocks sit sprawled across the beach and a little hill sits not far from us. "Up there. They filmed it and everything."

"You mean we'll have pictures of this?"

He bites his bottom lip and nods. "Framed and mounted on the wall."

As I look up, I see Kayla and Kelsey holding a *Welcome to the family, Violet!* sign up, and Bryson's got an expensive camera in his hand, smirking like he caught every single word we said.

I turn to face Sam, my eyes big and dreamy as I melt into him. "You're really going to be my forever?"

He grazes his knuckles across the side of my cheek. "I meant it when I said it last night, angel. You're the only forever I ever want to choose again."

"Forever is an awfully long time." I sigh, seeing if he'll flinch, but he doesn't. Not even a little bit.

"Mhm. But you're *my* forever, Future Mrs. Violet Skye Brooks." He leans his forehead against mine and brushes the side of his thumb across my bottom lip.

I take my left hand and run it through his hair, leaning in just enough to whisper across his lips. "And you're my forever, Sam Alexander Brooks."

And then we're one in the same, two waves that collide into each other, melding into one till we're lost in each other. We were always meant to be this way, Sam and I. We just had to find each other through the dark shades of life. It wasn't easy, but this was more than worth it. *He's* worth it all.

I finally found where I belong. It's with Sam, sharing his club, making new memories, building a life with him, Kelsey, and Kayla. This is our time, and I won't waste another second of it.

As I look out toward the fading sunset slipping behind the low tide, I see forever promised in shades of shimmery blue waves. There's me and Sam, and the forever we've always longed for.

I finally found where I belong. I'm home.

Acknowledgements

There are so many people I want to shout out. Writing a book was a lot more work than I thought it'd be, but I'm so glad I did it! Violet and Sam came to me like a hurricane. I did not see them coming, but I just knew I had to write about them right away. Their story came to me in a matter of days, and I just love them so, so much. I have found out that when a story hits you, you just need to write it. Someone out there is waiting to find your story!

First and foremost, I would not be here without the support my mom has given me over the years. She has been my rock and has always supported my dreams. Thank you for always being there for me. No words can express how much I appreciate you!

To my friends who kept me going and told me not to give up on writing this book, thank you! You know who you are, and I am forever grateful to have you in my life.

Thank you to my beta readers and my editor Hannah. You helped make this story better all around. And to my cover artist, Sam, for bringing the vision of Violet and Sam to life. Writing this story was one thing, but putting everything else together was not a piece of cake.

I hope all my readers enjoy this healing ride that Violet and Sam take you on. Till next time!